Mind Your
Own Business

Also by Lutishia Lovely

Sex in the Sanctuary
Love Like Hallelujah
A Preacher's Passion
Heaven Right Here
Reverend Feelgood
Heaven Forbid
All Up In My Business
Crush

Mind Your Own Business

LUTISHIA LOVELY

Kensington Publishing Corp.

DAFINA BOOKS are published by

Kensington Publishing Corp.
119 West 40th Street
New York, NY 10018

Dafina and the Dafina logo Reg. U.S. Pat. & TM Off.

ISBN-13: 978-1-61793-036-2

Printed in the United States of America

For my sister, Dee, who has put her foot in countless soul food dinners and made you want to slap somebody! But the tastiest ingredient she adds is love. . . .

ACKNOWLEDGMENTS

Writing acknowledgments is always a challenge, but today, I truly don't know where to begin. It seems as if every person I now know or have ever met in some way contributed to this moment—being able to release yet another story and to finish another book. Because this series deals with a subject close to my heart, food, the matter is further complicated. How do I say thank you to all of the wonderful cooks who are responsible for my love affair with food, and with the fact that I am a chef in my own mind? Surely I'll miss somebody, but here goes....

Big hug and lots of love to the first cook in my life and at whose elbow I first tested the waters...my mama! She is still one of the best cooks I know. Her sister, my Aunt Ernie, makes me happy every time I come to New York. And their mother, my late grandmother Amanda Jane Harding...oh my goodness. I'd get out of bed at the crack of dawn for her down-home country breakfast, and there was nothing like being sent on our road trip back to Kansas with a batch of her fried pies. My brother, Johnny, is a barbeque maestro, and even though I no longer eat meat, my mouth still waters at the memories of his skill with a grill. He is part of the reason why I barbeque everything from lentil burgers to portobello mushrooms. I'm still trying to come close to those ribs! A huge thank-you to all of those "church mothers" who made Sunday afternoons special with their soulful spreads. And to friends like Eden and Kai, whose meals I've enjoyed on occasions too numerous to count, thanks for all of the love you've shown me at your dining-room tables.

I have to thank the Food Network and people like the Neelys, Paula Deen, Aaron "Big Daddy" McCargo, Jr., Sunny Anderson, and Bobby Flay. I've gotten so much joy from watching these people live their passions. There are other chef favorites on this network, but these mentioned particularly inspired me as I focused on soul food for this book.

As always, it is with fondness and immense gratitude that I thank my editor, Selena James, and my agent, Natasha Kern. These ladies are amazing and are not only part of my "team" but are dear friends as well. Selena, your editing of this work was simply exquisite. You are the best in the biz, girl, period, end of story! Kensington is a top-shelf publishing company and I also send big hugs to—and here's where I start getting into trouble by naming names—Adeola, Mercedes, Alex, Lesleigh, Robin, Paula, Hillary, the marketing and sales staff, art department, and every single person who has anything to do with this book getting into the readers' hands... I bow.

To book clubs everywhere... y'all are my favorites, and I can't thank you enough for your continued support. Some readers aren't part of a club but are some of my biggest fans. I'd like to virtually hug a few: my big brother, Johnny; Kenny and Nicole Royal, Yolanda Latoya Gore, Orsayer Simmons, Denise Mitchell, Charles Henry Hall, Tasha Dillard, Trina McCall, Lisa Banks, Bre Foreman, Genetta Smith, Jamaal Russell (who gave me the biggest compliment—reading AUIMB while watching March Madness!), Sharmon Lynette, Quierra Johnson, Utonda Johnson, Veronica Johnson, James Morgan, Katrina Jones, Kristy Subber, Anaya Harris, Marsha Williams, Allyson Deese—oh my goodness—I could go on and on and on! Rhea Alexis Banks, Dera Jones Williams, Carmen Blalock Johnson and Olivia Davis Stith are just four of the dozens of reviewers who take time out of their busy schedules to peruse my pages. Thank you. To Ella Curry, Rachel Berry, Tamika Newhouse, Rob Batista, Nikkea Murray, Written Magazine's Michele Gipson and all the other BlogTalkRadio show hosts. Thanks for helping us spread the word on literature in general and my novels in particular! And speaking of radio, a big hug to ReShonda Tate Billingsley who graciously allowed me to fill her From Cover To Cover shoes (KPFT 90.1 FM, Houston, TX) while she went on the *Marriage Material* tour. Co-hosting with Pat Tucker was absolutely fabulous, made me want to dust off my broadcasting shoes and put 'em back on! Thanks, ladies. To all of the fans and supporters I meet on the road, with a special shout out to Bernard Henderson at Alexander Books in San Francisco, Cherysse Calhoun at Marcus Books in Oakland, and Dera Jones Williams, whose blog superbly captured that evening, Renee at Zahara's in Inglewood, Ellen Sudderth, her hubby, "Big Daddy" Frank, E.S.P Productions, and all the folks in Newport News who showed me a great time including Wendy, Shelia, Charlene, Carlene, Deborah, Marsha, April, Renee, Patricia, Robin, Candace, Tanya, Katherine, Terry, Roland and Denise. Much love to my NN beauty and barber shops—Robin at Red-Headed Stepchild, and Arty and the fellas at Tomorrow's Image. To Alice and her gang at Raytheon who work while my audio books play in the background. Big hug!!! To soul food restaurants around the country, including Tiffany and the gang at Marina Del Rey's Aunt Kizzy's Back Porch, and Nedira and the crew at Richmond's Tropical Soul. To Nikkea Smithers and RWA. To Tawana Dorsey-Smith at the Main Street Library, and to librarians everywhere. Muah!

To all of the chains, but especially to the small mom-and-pop independent book stores who include me in your orders... I am deeply grateful. To my author friends whom I cherish... you know who you are and I hope you know how much I love and appreciate you! Last but certainly not least, to you, the one now holding my baby in your hands. Your support is immeasurable and the gratitude I feel toward you goes beyond words. If I'm ever in your city, "hollah at me!" Next to writing, meeting readers is one of my favorite things to do!

1

"Why can't a woman be on top?" Bianca Livingston demanded, tossing shoulder-length, straightened hair over her shoulder. She stood over her older brother as if ready to strike, looking totally capable of kicking butts and taking names. Her quick smile, short stature, and girly frame had caused many men to underestimate her—to their peril. But anyone seeing her now—shoulders back, hands on hips, her perfectly tailored black suit and four-inch heels adding to her aura of power— would believe her capable of running almost anything. "I'm as qualified to run the West Coast division as you are, even more so, matter of fact."

"You're qualified to run the kitchen, *maybe*," her older brother retorted. Jefferson suppressed a smile. He'd taunted his sister from birth, and he did so now. Her fiery personality was the perfect foil for his laid-back teasing. But even with his ongoing provocations, this time Jefferson's antics masked the seriousness of his quest. He had every intention of being the Livingston who moved to LA to establish the Taste of Soul restaurants both there and in Nevada. But unlike most Livingstons, he didn't like confrontation or competition. He'd quietly made his bid to step away from his cushy position in the finance department to run the West the same way he cooked his ribs: low and slow. "Isn't that why you spent the last nine months in Paris?" he queried to underscore his point. "Learning the fine art of cooking so that you could give our soul food some class?"

Actually, Bianca had fled to Paris to get away from the chain around her neck otherwise known as fiancé Cooper Riley, Jr. But only one other person knew this truth—her cousin, Toussaint Livingston. Initially, forestalling the marriage everyone else believed was a *fait accompli* was also why she'd expressed interest in running the West Coast locations. But now, after months of talking with Toussaint, who, besides being her confidant and a Food Network star, was also the ambitious brainchild behind their company expanding out West, Bianca wanted to relocate to put her mark on the Livingston dynasty and make the West Coast Taste of Soul restaurants shine.

Bianca replied, "Need I remind you that I have not only a culinary certificate from Le Cordon Bleu, but also an undergrad and a graduate degree in business administration?"

"No, little sis, you don't need to remind me." Jefferson's smirk highlighted the dimple on his casually handsome face, his sienna skin further darkened by the November sun. His deep-set brown eyes twinkled with merriment. "But do I have to remind you that I have double masters in business administration and finance?" Jefferson had been the first Livingston in two decades to follow up his stint at Morehouse with two years at Wharton's School of Business.

Bianca, knowing that she couldn't go toe to toe when it came to her brother's education, tried a different route. She walked away from Jefferson and sat in one of the tan leather chairs in the artistically appointed office. Reaching for a ballpoint pen that lay on his large and messy mahogany desk, she adopted a calmer tone, yet couldn't totally lose the petulance in her voice. "Jefferson, the only reason Dad is promoting the idea of your heading up the location is because you're the oldest."

"And the son, don't forget about that. You know Dad doesn't want to see his baby girl fly too far from the nest."

"Okay, probably that, too," Bianca conceded. It was no secret that when it came to her father, Abram "Ace" Livingston, she was the apple of his all-seeing eye.

"Besides, how are you even considering relocation when you've got a fiancé champing at the bit to get married? Cooper has been more than patient with you, Bianca. Not many men would let the woman they love move to the other side of the world, even if it was, as you successfully argued, for the union's greater good. What did you call it? Increasing your company value and the marriage's bottom line? As if being a Livingston isn't value enough? No, Bianca, Cooper allowed the wedding to be pushed back once already. He's not going to delay it a second time. And you know he isn't moving to LA."

Tears unexpectedly came to Bianca's eyes. She abruptly rose from the chair where she'd been sitting and walked to the window. The glory of the day, boasting colorful autumn leaves framed by a sunny blue sky, was lost on her. "You're probably right," she said, quickly wiping her eyes. "If everyone has their way, in six months I'll be married and in nine have a baby on the way." *But how can I marry Cooper after what happened in Paris?*

"Hey, sister, are you all right?"

Bianca jumped. She hadn't heard Jefferson rise, hadn't been aware that he'd walked from his desk and joined her at the window. "Actually, no, if you want to know the truth. Jeff, I—"

"Hey man, oh, Bianca, I'm glad you're both here." Toussaint Livingston burst into Jefferson's office, and now rushed toward his cousins on the other side of the room. The seriousness of his countenance took nothing away from a face that models would envy, along with six feet, two inches and almost two hundred pounds of delectable dark chocolate. "We need to roll to y'all parents' house right now. Emergency family meeting."

Their conversation forgotten, both Jefferson and Bianca turned at once, talking simultaneously.

"What's the matter?"

"What's going on?"

Bianca's heart raced with concern. "Why are we meeting at Mom and Dad's house, Toussaint, and not in the conference room?"

Toussaint turned and headed for the door. "That's what we're getting ready to find out. I'll meet y'all there."

Fifteen minutes later Toussaint, Jefferson, and Bianca joined their family members in the living room of Ace and Diane's sprawling Cascade residence. Toussaint's parents, Adam and Candace, and his brother, Malcolm, were already there. The trio from the office was the last to arrive and as soon as they sat down, Ace began speaking.

"We've got a situation," he said without preamble. "Somebody's stealing company funds."

Reactions were mixed, with bewilderment and anger vying for equal time.

"Who is it?" Bianca demanded, ready for battle though the culprit remained unnamed.

"We don't know," Ace replied. "But it's definitely an inside job."

The family members looked from one to the other, a myriad of thoughts in each mind. *Who could it be? How did this happen? Is the guilty party somehow connected to someone in the room?* One family member even pondered the impossible: *Is the thief one of us?*

"What kind of money are we talking about?" Toussaint asked. "Hundreds, thousands . . . more?"

"A couple hundred thousand," Ace replied, his tone somber and curt.

Again, responses were symphonic.

"What the hell?"

"Who could do such a thing?"

"Oh, hell to the *N-O*. We're not going to take this lying down."

"You're absolutely right, baby girl," Ace said to Bianca. "We're not going to stand for this, not at all. Nobody steals from our company without feeling the wrath of a Livingston payback."

2

Three hours later and Bianca was still reeling. *Whose hand is in the cookie jar... and how did they grab all of that money without anyone's knowledge?* The Livingstons had bandied about a variety of scenarios and made a chart of potential employees, past and present, who they felt best poised for betrayal. Bianca's eyes narrowed as she remembered one name that had come up, a woman who'd had an affair with her cousin and who'd worked for the Livingston Corporation until her relationship with Toussaint abruptly ended. This ex-marketing director had disappeared into thin air and, as far as anyone knew, was no longer in Atlanta. But with the Internet making the world smaller, click by worldwide click, Bianca didn't count out the woman she'd never trusted. Whoever was stealing from what had been a relatively dormant bank account could be anywhere.

A knock at her door startled Bianca from her musings. Belatedly, she remembered Cooper's phone call and subsequent promise to drop by. She took a breath and steeled herself for the encounter. "Hey, Coop," she said, standing back from the door to let him in.

"Hello, dear," Cooper replied, the kiss on her forehead as sexy as that which an uncle or grandfather would bestow. "You look troubled. Come here and tell Papa all about it."

Bianca fought the urge to roll her eyes and, going against every fiber of her being, dutifully followed Cooper into the living room of her designer-decorated townhome. She loved her split-level, three-bedroom spread: the hardwood floors and gourmet kitchen; bright yellows and oranges tempered by ebony wood; windows everywhere, letting in the bright autumn sunshine. The cheery surroundings were in stark contrast to her ever darkening mood.

Cooper sat down and tried to pull Bianca into his arms.

"Please, Cooper," Bianca said, placing more distance between them. "I'm . . . not in the mood."

"Some women would welcome the touch of their fiancés at a time like this."

"I'm sorry."

Sorry for what, Bianca? Stringing out our engagement for two years? Becoming more and more engrossed with your work? Or our not having made love in almost a month? Instead of voicing these questions, Cooper refocused on Bianca's bad mood. "What's going on, dear? Something at work?"

Bianca nodded.

Cooper leaned back, waiting.

Bianca hesitated for only a moment before answering. For obvious reasons this matter was confidential, known only to the Livingston clan, the private investigator Ace had immediately hired—and the thief. But not only was Cooper almost a family member, but his analytical, lawyer mind might see clues or connections where Bianca would not.

She turned to face Cooper. "Somebody's stealing company funds."

His only reaction was a slight narrowing of the eyes. "From one of the restaurants?"

"No, from corporate."

Cooper sat up, rubbing his chin in thought. "Corporate, huh? That's interesting."

"Very."

"Any ideas as to whom it might be?"

"A few." Bianca stood and began to pace. "But the most obvious one right now is our ex-marketing director, Shyla Martin. I think you met her two years ago, at the company Christmas party."

Cooper pondered this statement, even as he remembered why last year's Christmas party had been subdued and low-key. "What does she look like?"

"Tall, attractive. She was Toussaint's date."

"Oh, *her*," Cooper replied, nodding. "Sure, I remember Shyla. I remember thinking that she was funny and intelligent, and that she and Toussaint made a good couple."

"Yeah, well, she thought they made a great couple, too. And she wanted to make their union permanent." *Oh, shoot. The last thing I want to do is put marriage on Cooper's mind.*

But she'd already done so, as Cooper's next words verified. "So there are women out there who want to get married."

"Coop..."

"Okay, I won't press right now. But we've got to make plans for the future, Bianca. Neither of us is getting any younger. It's time to get married and start a family...soon."

Bianca returned to the couch and sat down. Her brow was furrowed in thought—about the theft, Cooper's words, and other things.

"What happened?"

Bianca's eyes widened at Cooper's question. *Am I that transparent? Are the memories so poignant, so strong, that they're written all over my face?* "What do you mean, what happened?" she asked breathlessly.

Again, Cooper's eyes narrowed, as they often did when his sharp mind whirled. "Between Toussaint and Shyla...what happened?"

"Oh, right, between Toussaint and Shyla. You know what happened to them, Cooper. Alexis St. Clair happened."

"Of course I know about Toussaint's wife, Bianca." *And the baby they're expecting.* "But I didn't know that Alexis caused the breakup between him and Shyla, nor would I imagine Shyla as the type of person who would go to these extremes as a result."

"It wasn't just about their breakup." Bianca sighed, remembering that she'd never shared with Cooper the extent of what went down between the Livingstons and their former employee. She gave the short version: how Shyla Martin's attempt to come between Toussaint and the love of his life had cost Shyla her job.

"Oh, I see. Shyla not only lost love, but she lost money, too." Cooper nodded his head. "That makes your assumption that it is her imminently more plausible." Cooper eyed Bianca, noting her stiff countenance and rigid neck. "Come here, dear," he quietly commanded, even as he reached for her arm. "Don't you worry your pretty little head about a thing. We'll get to the bottom of this."

This time, Bianca did not resist as Cooper pulled her into him. Talking this situation out reminded her of the things she loved about him, and one of those things was that he made her feel safe. In many ways this fair-skinned, freckle-faced man was like her dad, Ace Livingston, and Bianca would never deny that Cooper was a good man who came from an upstanding family. But that was the problem. She respected him, admired him, even loved him—as one would a good friend. But Bianca wasn't *in* love with him, the way she wanted to be with a man when she walked down the aisle. The way she'd fallen for a Frenchman in Paris, after only two months of dating. Cooper might be able to help her solve the mystery of who stole the company money. But as Bianca laid her head on his shoulder, she wondered who would help her solve the mystery of how to get over the man who'd stolen her heart.

3

On the other side of town, in the comfortable surroundings of the same den where the news had broken, stealing was also the topic of conversation. After work, the Livingston men had returned to Ace's house for further discussion on the day's news. They were joined by Sterling Ross, the tall, dark, debonair family friend who was also one of the country's most preeminent detectives. Jefferson watched Toussaint prowl the room, while his dad, Ace; his uncle, Adam; and his cousin Malcolm refreshed their drinks. Sterling flipped a page on his pad and continued writing notes.

"I think the money trail will lead to Shyla," Toussaint said, a slight scowl marring his otherwise perfectly chiseled face. Like a fine wine, thirty-three-year-old Toussaint Levon Livingston only got better with age, and like everything else, marriage and impending fatherhood agreed with him. "She went away a little too quietly, no fuss at all. I know Shyla, and trust me, that's not like her."

Ace returned to his seat and passed a hand over his smooth, bald head. "You paid her two hundred thousand dollars, son. I'd say that's a fuss. Granted, she wasn't happy about leaving the company—"

"She wasn't happy about leaving Toussaint," Jefferson interjected.

Ace grunted. "But I don't think she'd stoop to stealing. Shyla is classier than that."

"Besides," Adam continued, "the choice is almost too obvious. It's been a year since she left the company. All of her company credit cards were cancelled immediately. How would she have accessed the account? Why would she risk her reputation, not to mention her freedom, by stealing from us?"

"Because she's being influenced by the man who shot you, that's why!"

Toussaint's observation quieted the room. Sterling stopped writing. The name of the man who'd left Adam Livingston clinging to life on the Livingston Corporation's parking lot pavement hadn't come up in the earlier meeting. At that time, the focus had been solely on past and present Livingston employees. But now everyone's mind was on the man who'd eluded capture for almost a year: Quintin Bright.

Adam responded. "We know that for a while they were in the same place at the same time. But we don't know if they met—"

Toussaint snorted his disbelief.

"And if they did meet," Adam continued, "we have no idea what they talked about. And even if our name did come up, would a man like that admit to a crime, and would a woman like Shyla keep quiet about it?"

"For a brothah like Q?" Toussaint offered. "She'd keep quiet *and* she'd stay in touch. Shyla might be classy, Uncle, as you say, but she's got a messy side."

"Wait," Sterling said, holding up his hand. "You guys are getting ahead of me. Adam, you know the identity of the person who tried to rob you?"

"Robbing was the last thing on that asshole's mind." When Sterling's brow rose, Toussaint realized that he had said too much. Robbery was the motive police assumed had led

Quintin Bright to shoot Adam, the motive quoted in newspaper articles and television reports. The Livingstons had done nothing to dispel this assumption.

Sterling looked, waited.

This was a trusted friend, Adam deduced, one who needed to know about Quintin in order to do a thorough investigation. Adam knew this even as he hoped that outside of the family the whole story of the Bright/Livingston feud would never be told, a feud that began when Adam's wife, Candace, had asked Quintin to be her personal trainer. They'd gotten personal all right, and it had almost cost Candace her marriage. Adam took a deep breath and continued. "His name is Quintin Bright."

"How do you spell that?" When Adam answered, Sterling scribbled the name on his pad. "Motive?"

Adam hesitated and Ace spoke up. These twins didn't look alike, but their minds were always in sync. "There's some bad blood between us and Quintin."

"Us? As in the entire Livingston family?"

"When you mess with one of us, you mess with all of us," Malcolm stated matter of factly, looking like a younger version of his dad: stocky build, soft cognac-induced pouch, and close-cropped black hair showing hints of gray.

"How are you so sure it's this guy"—Sterling looked down at his pad—"Quintin Bright."

"He said something just before he shot me," Adam replied. "And he admitted to one of our employees that he shot me."

"Then why isn't this guy behind bars?"

"Fled the country," Toussaint answered.

"Not enough solid evidence to have him arrested and extradited," Jefferson added.

Sterling scribbled furiously. "Any idea where he is?"

Now it was Adam's turn to pace. "We know he stayed in Jamaica for a month or so."

"With Shyla Martin?" Sterling asked, connecting the dots from the earlier conversation.

"We know that they were there at the same time. We don't know if she stayed with him, or for how long."

Sterling nodded as he wrote, and then continued listening to Adam.

"Around six months ago, he was in St. Croix."

"And now?"

"We don't know." Ace told Sterling about an employee, Chardonnay Johnson, the woman to whom Quintin had confided about the shooting and whose friendship with Quintin had helped the family keep tabs on him. "When he told her he was in St. Croix, Chardonnay suggested meeting him there." Ace thought about telling Sterling why, but refrained. That the Livingston men wanted to deliver their own brand of justice before turning Quintin over to authorities was a desire best kept among the Livingston men. "Even though she told him she'd only been joking, he became very suspicious, and to our knowledge, hasn't called again."

Sterling nodded, rubbing his jaw. "Hum." He tapped his pen against the pad's edge. "Chardonnay Johnson? You say she's an employee?"

"Yes," Toussaint answered. "She started out as a waitress at one of our restaurants and is now the assistant manager."

"And she's satisfied with her job? No doubts as to where her loyalties lie?"

The Livingston men looked from one to the other. They all knew what Chardonnay was loyal to: that which started with an *M* and ended with a *Y.* They also knew that thanks to them, the money they'd paid her to keep the lines of communication open between her and Quintin, and the hardworking father of her youngest child with whom she was now living, Chardonnay was living better than she'd ever dreamed she could.

Would she do something to mess that up? Adam wondered.

Did she somehow stumble onto an even bigger cash cow than that of a new condo and a job promotion? Ace asked himself.

Malcolm, Jefferson, and Toussaint had musings along the same lines but said nothing.

"When it comes to this investigation," Malcolm finally offered, "I think we should view anyone and everyone guilty until proven innocent."

Sterling nodded. "I think you're right." He turned to Ace. "I'll stop by your office tomorrow, get a list of all of your employees, and get copies of all of the bank statements and transactions relative to this account. We've already moved the bulk of the money, so hopefully the bait that we've left in there will be enough to trap our prey. Until then, gentlemen, let us professionals handle it. I know that you Livingstons are a strong, determined group, but this time, I don't want y'all taking this matter into your own hands."

The men mumbled their agreement, even as they relished the thought of getting Quintin alone on a deserted island beach and having him become intimately acquainted with a slew of Livingston fists. The only thing stopping them from what otherwise would be a mandatory beat down was the multi-million dollar lawsuit that would surely result from such actions. Following Sterling's exit, Toussaint looked at his watch and stood. "It's getting late," he said. "I probably should head home."

Adam smiled. "And it's only eight thirty? That Alexis Livingston is something else. I never thought I'd live to see my youngest son domesticated, but boy, she has done the job."

Toussaint said his good-byes and was soon walking briskly toward his Mercedes. His dad was right. Alexis St. Clair Livingston had turned him into a willing homebody and soon, he'd be pulling into the parking structure of their downtown penthouse. Before that, however, there was a matter of business for Toussaint to attend to, another stop that he needed to make. He figured there was no time to lose.

4

Chardonnay Johnson placed her six-month-old baby on the couch beside her and stretched. Sometimes, she still felt the need to pinch herself and ensure that she wasn't dreaming. It wasn't the Huxtables', but Chardonnay's life looked unlike any she would have ever imagined. A year ago she was the single mother of two living in the projects. Tonight, she lay on the couch in her three-bedroom condo, smelling the dinner that the father of her youngest child was preparing. He wasn't the finest man walking the planet, but her coworker Bobby Wilson had a tantalizing tongue and a magic dick, and knew his way around a kitchen better than anybody.

"Bobby! Make some gravy to go with those mashed potatoes!"

No answer.

"Bobby!"

Bobby rounded the corner and leaned against the doorjamb, wiping his hands on a towel as he eyed Chardonnay. Even with twenty pounds of post-baby weight on her, she still looked good. He could get hard just thinking about her. "Girl, when are you going to stop yelling at me? I told you, I'm not one of your kids."

"Please, you might as well be. You know you're going to do what I ask you. I don't even know why you're tripping."

"Because somebody needs to teach you some manners, and I'm the one to do it. If you want some gravy, ask me nicely. And then I'll *think* about making some."

"Whatever, Bobby. I'm not begging you for shit."

"Oh, no? Not even this?" Bobby cupped his ample manhood and wriggled his eyes. "Cool. I'll just sleep on the couch tonight." He turned and walked back into the kitchen.

Chardonnay was not only strictly dickly, but she was addicted to sex. It was a rare night that went by without Bobby laying the pipe, and working on the second glass of her namesake had already made her horny. And she'd known this man long enough to know that he could be as stubborn as she was. "Bobby, will you please make some gravy to go with the mashed potatoes...please?"

"Of course I will, baby." Bobby grinned as he sprinkled flour into the steak drippings and began to stir in broth. He loved Chardonnay and didn't care who knew it. This love is why he'd stopped screwing Congressman Jon Abernathy, this and the fact that Jon was too damned possessive. It was also why he was dodging the blatant comings on from another brother, even though these money-laden invitations were getting harder and harder to ignore—not to mention making him hard at the mere thought of such a meeting. Bobby forced his thoughts away from this temptation. He didn't have time to think about that right now. His focus was on making smooth and creamy gravy that he would soon sop up with the fluffy, homemade biscuits baking in the oven. Then later, he would sop up Chardonnay's sweetness... just like that. "Call the kids in, 'Nay. Dinner is done."

Chardonnay bit back a sarcastic comment and rose from the couch. She was trying to take her best friend Zoe's advice and change her brash ways. Old habits died hard, but she was trying. Zoe had been right all along. Bobby was a good man, and now that she knew what one felt like, she wanted to keep him around. She walked to the door, opened it, and stepped back in surprise.

"Toussaint, what are you doing here?"

Toussaint looked beyond Chardonnay and saw Bobby coming out of the kitchen. At the same time, two rambunctious children, a boy and a girl, pushed past him.

"Is the food ready? I'm hungry," the boy announced.

"Smells good, Bobby. I'm eating a lot!" the girl added.

Toussaint watched the children run toward Bobby and thought of his own seed on the way. Thoughts of what—or more important who—was waiting for him at home spurred him to action.

"Hey, Chardonnay. Sorry to come by without calling, but I wanted to talk to you directly, not over the phone."

Bobby told Tangeray and Cognac to go wash their hands and then came to stand behind Chardonnay. "Hey, Toussaint." His tone was casual, but his face was questioning.

"Hello, Bobby." Toussaint shot a quick glance at Bobby before refocusing on Chardonnay. "Can you step outside?" he asked her.

Bobby moved from behind Chardonnay and stood beside her, protectiveness in his stance. "What is this about, Toussaint?" And then, remembering that this was his boss, he added, "If you don't mind me asking."

"I do mind," Toussaint shot back.

"It's cool, Bobby." Chardonnay spoke quickly, stepping out the door at the same time. "Go ahead and fix the kids' plates. I'll only be a minute."

Toussaint placed a gentle hand on Chardonnay's arm. "Let's talk in my car." Once he'd unlocked the car doors and they were both inside, he turned and spoke immediately. "Have you seen Quintin?"

Chardonnay frowned at the question. "Seen him? Hell no, I ain't seen Quintin. Is he back here?"

Toussaint ignored Chardonnay's question and asked another of his own. "Have you heard from him?"

"No!"

"Not one phone call, an e-mail, nothing? You haven't heard from Quintin in six months?"

The fact that Toussaint was her superior didn't keep Chardonnay from copping an attitude. She crossed her arms defiantly. "Did you think my answer was going to change because you're in my face instead of on the phone? I've been telling you for the past two months that I haven't heard from Quintin. No calls, texts, e-mails, or letters."

"When was the last time you spoke to him?"

"Damn, Toussaint, what is this about?"

"Chardonnay..." Toussaint's tone showed that patience was wearing thin.

"Okay, Toussaint, I'm sorry. It's just that I'm as frustrated as you are. I got paid every time Q called me. I *want* him to call me." *That fool is messing with my paper!*

Toussaint nodded, understanding Chardonnay's frustration. The family had promised her a hundred thousand dollars if she could discover Quintin's whereabouts and lead the authorities there.

"Quintin never called me as much as he did that first month after Mr. Livingston got shot." Chardonnay sighed, uncrossed her arms, and looked at the darkening sky. "Y'all have heard every tape from every conversation. Which is why you shouldn't be surprised that I haven't heard from him. You heard how suspicious he sounded the last time we talked."

Toussaint tapped the steering wheel with long, strong fingers. His family and the police had heard every conversation and taped every call. But Quintin had not only called from various locations, he'd also used calling cards or prepaid cell phones every time. And most important, he'd never again admitted to shooting Adam, had even denied it when Chardonnay mentioned it point blank. Toussaint gave the wanted man credit: Quintin Bright wasn't as stupid as he looked.

"Yes, I remember how he questioned you. I'm still wondering about that." Just like he was wondering about Shyla

Martin, and was planning to find his ex-lover to pay her a visit. But Toussaint didn't share these thoughts.

"What's there to wonder about? The man shot somebody. He's paranoid."

"I guess you're right." Toussaint started his car. "Sorry to have interrupted your dinner, Chardonnay. If Quintin calls again, remember to contact me the second after you hang up from him."

"Will do, Toussaint." Chardonnay stepped out of the car and walked away without looking back.

Bobby assailed her as soon as she stepped through the door. "What in the hell was that about?"

"What was what about?"

"Toussaint Livingston coming over here, that's what."

Having sworn to keep her involvement regarding Quintin a secret, Chardonnay shrugged and walked into the kitchen to fix her plate. But as she dished up steak, mashed potatoes and gravy, and fresh green beans, she was asking the same question: what was that about? Toussaint was obviously aggravated, much more so than a year-old crime should warrant. *What's going down now in Livingston-town?* That was the question. Chardonnay was nothing if not nosy. She knew that finding out the answer was just a matter of time.

In another car, in another place, someone else was wondering what was going on.

"I just checked the balance," a harsh voice whispered. "Somebody made a huge withdrawal. I thought you said nobody touched this money, that it was basically a dormant account!"

"I don't know what happened," a quiet voice replied.

A nervous finger tapped cold, hard steel, fingering the trigger. "Well... you'd best be finding out."

5

Even in the swirl of drama, the show must go on. That is why the day after Ace's announcement about a thief in the midst, it was business as usual at the Livingston Corporation. Adam pored over reports from the sales and marketing team, Ace conducted a Skype conference call with his restaurant managers, and in Jefferson's office, the focus was on the company's imminent expansion to the West Coast.

"You know, Bianca paid me a visit," Toussaint said casually, eyeing his cousin for reaction.

"I had a feeling she might. 'Persistent' is Bianca's middle name. Everybody knows she wants to move to La-La land. And maybe she should." Jefferson leaned forward, the Livingston intensity that ran in his blood seeping through his laid-back personality. "But that doesn't mean she should do so as manager of the West Coast location. I'm the man for that job, cuz. That fact shouldn't even be up for discussion."

"If it were anybody but Bianca, it wouldn't be," Toussaint countered. "Plus, I still can't get over the fact that you want to parcel out your responsibilities as Director of Finance and jump back into the day-to-day grind of running a restaurant."

"I have my reasons," Jefferson responded.

"So you've said. Wanting to get back into the thick of things."

Jefferson had known from the beginning that his surprise bid to run the West Coast restaurants would raise eyebrows. Probably the most introverted of the third-generation Livingstons, Jefferson had been content to dominate behind the scenes, ensuring the company's solvency and expanding its bottom line. He'd told his father and uncle that the bid was being made because he'd grown too far away from the heartbeat of the company—the restaurants—and that this would be the only time he could take a year or so away from his duties in finance and revitalize his food management chops. He'd be chained to the desk once he became CFO.

"I'm not worried about Bianca," Jefferson continued. "Daddy will never cast a vote for Bianca moving out west."

Toussaint reached into the crystal bowl on Jefferson's desk and helped himself to a handful of gourmet mixed nuts. "You're probably right. Besides, Bianca might get to Hollywood and lose all focus. You'll go out there and get the job done, no doubt." When it came to the Taste of Soul restaurant opening in Los Angeles the following year, Toussaint would personally see to it that the job got done. Corporate responsibilities precluded him from doing what he wanted, going out to manage the establishment himself. Bianca was well qualified, but she had a mind of her own. Jefferson was more "go with the flow." Toussaint wanted someone malleable in sunny LA, someone who would do what he wanted, the way he wanted it done. "Listen, I'm planning a trip out west next week. The renovation is almost complete and I need to meet with the designers. It's time to start lining up personnel. You want to roll with me?"

"Sure." Jefferson started to continue, but the ringing office phone interrupted him. One look at the caller ID told him that he definitely wanted to take the call, and he wanted to be alone for the conversation. "Hold one moment," Jefferson said after he'd answered his direct line. He placed the call on hold. "Listen, cuz, I need to take this. But let's talk later. Shoot over the schedule and I'll have Yolanda book my flight."

"You might want to book her on that flight as well," Toussaint joked. He'd suggested more than once that his cousin increase his attractive assistant's duties to some that went beyond the office and into the bedroom. "Mix a little pleasure with your work."

"That's your script, dog, not mine. Just forward your flight and hotel info to her so she can make my reservations. And close the door on your way out." Jefferson ignored Toussaint's questioning look and waited until the door was securely fastened. Then he took the call off hold. "Hello, beautiful."

"Oh, you think so? I can't tell."

Jefferson laughed, visualizing the caller's pretty, pouty face. The sun hadn't stopped shining since he'd met Keisha Miller some months ago, and his life had not been the same. "Sorry about last night, baby, family meeting. But don't worry. I'm getting ready to make it up to you."

Happiness flowed through the phone like a breeze. "Really? How?"

"I'm coming to LA next week."

Keisha squealed, lying back on the couch. The café au lait beauty eyed her freshly manicured nails as Jefferson continued to talk, and she was already planning a shopping trip. If her man was coming to visit, she needed new clothes! "When are you coming, baby? How long are you going to stay? Will we be able to hang out together? Ooh, Jeff, I bet you'll be working the whole time!"

Jefferson's rumble of laughter began in his stomach and spilled out all over his life. He'd never been this happy. "Whoa, baby, one question at a time."

"Are you coming for work, or for me? Please say me, Jeff, I miss you."

Jefferson answered honestly. "Both."

Keisha turned from her back to her side, tossing her long, curly hair away from her face. "With all your family around, when am I going to get a chance to lick that chocolate lollipop?"

Jefferson shifted, said lollipop immediately expanding. Like most Livingston men, Jefferson was packing major arsenal in his sexual weaponry. "My stick is ready and waiting, baby."

"Hang on, baby, I need to get this real quick." Keisha's quiet, flirty demeanor changed in an instant as she clicked over to the other caller and fairly growled into the phone. "What in the hell do you want?"

Jefferson hit the speaker button and placed the phone on the receiver. He spread out the floor plans Toussaint had given him, the layout for what symbolized the company's next frontier. But as he waited for Keisha to come back on the line, he wasn't really seeing the kitchen and dining room layouts. His mind's eye was fixed on the day the woman of his dreams came into his life.

"Jeff, you made it!" A willowy, bohemian-dressed woman glided to Jefferson with arms outstretched. She was a vision in loveliness, with almond-shaped hazel eyes framed by long lashes, a full pouty mouth, a graceful neck and surgically enhanced breasts. Her thick, bone-straight hair was loosely piled on top of her head and secured with jeweled chopsticks. "Thanks for coming to my show!"

"I wouldn't have missed it," Jefferson replied, kissing the Atlanta-based painter known simply as Divine. "But I only have a few moments. I'm seeing you on my dinner break before heading back to the office."

Both art enthusiasts who'd met at an exhibition several years ago, Divine and Jefferson were good friends from the start. He'd been involved at the time they met, and she'd been seeing someone once his relationship ended. Now they were both available, but the friendship remained platonic.

"You know, all work and no play makes Jeff a dull boy!"

"Sometimes true, but fortunately, I love my job." Aside from the "rite of passage" years that Jefferson had spent working at Taste of Soul's Auburn location, years that spanned high school through college, he'd worked in the Livingston Corporation's accounting department, and within two years would be the company's CFO. Additionally, he worked very closely with the brokers who managed the Livingston Corp's portfolio, and was reasonably versed in stocks, bonds, hedge accounts, and day trading. Jefferson not only enjoyed work because of his love for numbers, but because it kept him from focusing on his loneliness.

Divine linked her arm in Jefferson's and led him down the hallway. She noted his strong arm, nice scent, and hoped that she could continue to hide the truth—that she'd been in love with Jefferson since day one, but afraid of losing his friendship if he ever found out. "I understand, Jeff." She couldn't resist giving his arm a squeeze. "I love my work, too."

"Well, let's see it!"

The two walked down a long, artwork-lined hallway that opened into a large, airy, rectangular room. To the left was a champagne fountain and next to it, a table of hors d'oeuvres. Vibrantly painted drawings lined the walls and occupied easels. Divine's collection was at once abstract and whimsical: a flowering trumpet, a woman's loc-stream waterfall, budding baby faces filling a vase. The paintings were beautiful, but Jefferson didn't see them—because they paled in comparison to the work of art standing before him, hands on hips, head cocked, studying a painting.

"Who's that?"

Divine, who'd been rambling on about her piece titled *Rambunctious*, stopped mid-sentence. "Jeff! You haven't been listening to a word I've said. This is the piece that I thought would fit perfectly in your home office. It's...oh, never mind. Come on, I'll introduce you, though I just met her myself."

Divine squelched the jealousy that rose up unbidden. Head held high, she walked over to the patron who'd pulled Jefferson's attention away from her show. "Hey there, Keisha. Seeing anything that you like?"

"Divine, I really love this one! I'd never put all of these reds together but...wow...this would look nice in my place."

"Simon is handling the sales. Just give him the number and he'll handle the transaction, which includes shipping and delivery directly to your house."

"Girl, please, I'm just dreaming. I can't afford a painting like this."

"I'll buy it for you."

Keisha turned wide, hazel eyes on the stranger standing next to the artist her brother had told her about. She'd been so excited about the painting that she hadn't even noticed him, but now that she had...*hum, he's kinda cute.* She performed a quick, surreptitious once-over, noting what looked like designer shoes and a Rolex watch peeking out from a starched, beige sleeve. Keisha normally went for pretty boys, but there was something about this stranger—besides the directive she'd been given to get close to him—that intrigued her. Perhaps it was his laid-back confidence, or the way he wore wealth like a natty old sweater. Then again, it could be his teddy bear vibe, the one that suggested she'd find comfort and security in his arms. Keisha smiled. *This is going to be a better night than I'd hoped. I won't mind getting to know you at all.*

"Keisha, meet Jefferson Livingston. Jeff, Keisha."

Keisha's smile was as bright as her eyes. "Nice to meet you, Jeff."

Jefferson shook the hand that Keisha held out. "The pleasure is mine." At this moment Jefferson thought of Toussaint, wishing that he had some of his cousin's swagger. In the office, around facts and figures, Jefferson was confident, fully in control. But around women, it was another story. Jefferson was shy. His last girlfriend, a loud, overpowering Gemini who'd dumped him after he refused to buy her a house, had done nothing for his trust in women or his romance skills. For entertainment, Jefferson often hung out with college frat brothers, but more and more he desired to hang out at home with a woman . . . his woman.

"You like the painting?" he asked, nodding toward the vibrant work. "I'll get it for you."

Keisha coyly looked down. "Oh, no, I couldn't let you do that. It's too much."

"It's by a fantastic artist, well worth the price."

"Ha! Now that's the truth!" Divine looked over toward the door just as a new group of patrons entered, and was thankful for a reason to run from the look of attraction she saw in Jefferson's eyes—an attraction for someone other than her. "Excuse me, y'all, more guests to greet!"

Both Jefferson and Keisha watched Divine leave, then turned back to each other. For a moment neither spoke, and for Jefferson, it was as if the air had left the room. There was something childlike about this woman who stood before him, something that immediately brought out his protective, chivalrous, and generous sides. *This is crazy, man. You don't even know her.* But Jefferson knew one thing—he wanted to.

All thoughts of work aside, Jefferson asked Keisha out to dinner. After purchasing three paintings, including the painting Keisha had admired, Jefferson had taken Keisha to an out-of-the-way Italian restaurant. Over four delicious courses and a bottle of wine, Keisha proved to be everything Jefferson's ex was not: attentive, engaging, totally absorbed in his dreams to become CFO of the company and eventually, if possible, its COO. They left the restaurant and ended up at Jefferson's place. Keisha sexed him good, and he returned the favor. By the time Keisha revealed that not only did she not live in Atlanta, but that she was a single mother raising two children, it didn't matter. Jefferson had already fallen in love.

"Sorry about that, Pookie." Keisha's voice lacked the happy effervescence of a few moments ago.

Jefferson's heart warmed at Keisha's pet name for him, even as he immediately noticed her change in mood. "Everything okay?"

"Just my family, getting on my nerves."

"Your kids?"

"No, I love my children. It's the rest of them I could live without."

Jefferson laughed. "Come on, now. It can't be that bad." Having been raised in a hardworking close-knit family, any of whom would give his life for the other, Jefferson couldn't imagine that Keisha was serious.

"They're all right, I guess. But I don't want to talk about them. I want to talk about us, and your trip. When are you coming and how long can you stay?"

"Sometime next week. I'll try and plan it for the latter part and stay over the weekend." Not only did Jefferson want to check out the restaurant location, he wanted to meet with a home realtor.

"Can't wait to see you," Keisha whispered, her voice sultry, hot, mirroring the nana she idly fingered.

"Me either, baby. Three weeks is too long."

"I wish we could be together for real."

Jefferson stifled a sigh. The longer he was with Keisha, the more he wanted the same. But bringing a ready-made family into the Livingston clan would be tricky at best. His father's approval could probably be easily won, but his mother, Diane Livingston? A harder sell for sure. Not to mention Bianca, Toussaint, Malcolm, Adam, and Aunt Candace. Those were different scenarios altogether.

6

"How're my two favorite women?" Toussaint came up behind his wife and gently patted her stomach.

Toussaint's wife, of almost six months, Alexis St. Clair Livingston, continued stirring the homemade tomato vegetable soup she'd just prepared, even as she leaned back into the comfort of her man's arms. "How are you so sure this is a girl?"

Toussaint wrapped his arms around his wife and buried his nose in the crook of her neck. How he'd lived all those years as a carefree single man and thought it was the good life, was now beyond him. Where before he would have spent the evening at FGO—For Gentlemen Only, the local gentlemen's club—or squiring his newest beauty around town, now he looked forward to nothing more than coming home at night to a home-cooked meal and a night of loving. He raised his head and flicked his tongue against Alexis's ear. "How was your day, baby?"

"Lovely," Alexis replied, turning around to face him. She placed her arms around his waist. "But better now." She rested her head against Toussaint's strong chest before lifting her head to welcome his kiss. Thick, soft lips brushed against each other before mouths opened and tongues twirled.

"Umm," Toussaint murmured, deepening the kiss. He

nudged them both a foot or so away from the stove, then lifted Alexis up on to the counter. "I've been thinking of this moment all day long," he whispered, sliding a hand under Alexis's baby-doll top and tweaking a bare nipple, already standing at attention. He'd always admired his wife's full, weighty globes, but with the pregnancy, they seemed to grow bigger every day. He broke the kiss, only to reach for the cotton fabric covering his treasure and lifting it over Alexis's head. Before she could react or respond, he'd sucked a hardened nipple into his mouth, swirling his tongue around the areola, and searching for the hem of her short, denim skirt.

"Toussaint, the soup," Alexis whispered, even as her legs spread of their own accord. Toussaint found his target and began lightly flicking the nub between her already-wet folds. He pulled her closer to him and sank his middle finger deep inside her. Alexis moaned and began grinding her hips, reaching for the clasp of her husband's belt buckle. Toussaint's sexual appetite was voracious. He'd never thought one woman would be enough to satisfy him. But he'd been wrong. Alexis was always willing to match him stroke for powerful stroke. Toussaint swatted away her hand, pulling her even closer to the edge of the counter and spreading wide her legs. Alexis leaned back against the cabinets, feeling exposed, vulnerable, and absolutely on fire. "Turn off the burner," she managed to whisper, between notes of the symphony Toussaint played on her punani with his fingers. Chagrined at the diversion, Toussaint quickly turned off the burner before kissing Alexis's inner thighs and then placing his tongue where his fingers had been. Alexis gasped as Toussaint's tongue hit its target, strong and powerful, lapping her nether nectar as if it were ambrosia. Her fingernails dug into his shoulders as she held on for the ride. Toussaint alternated between licks and strokes, nips and kisses. He shifted, nine inches of powerful manhood straining against his slacks.

"Come here," he commanded, though there was no need

since he had already lifted Alexis from the counter and was carrying her over to the breakfast nook. He hurriedly shed his slacks and boxers and then made fast work of pushing the denim mini past her round hips and to the floor. Toussaint sat on the edge of the booth, positioned Alexis over his massive erection, and then moaned as she sank down on his hardened shaft. For a moment they just sat there, content and fully connected. Toussaint placed soft, whispery kisses at each side of her mouth before thrusting inside it. Alexis covered the big, strong hands that clasped her breasts, as she slowly rose up and sank back down again. And again. She threw her head back, ran her hands through waist-length locs and increased the pace. Her muscles clenched, holding Toussaint's dick captive inside her walls. The hiss of breath from Toussaint made her smile. *Yeah, baby, I know what you like, too!* This pace continued for a few moments—up, down, in, out, rocking side to side. Toussaint ran his hands over Alexis's baby-soft skin, creating goose bumps along the way. Alexis leaned forward, creating a delicious friction that spurred her husband on to go farther, deeper. With a growl, Toussaint lifted Alexis off of his lap, stood, and turned her toward the booth seat. Alexis balanced herself on one knee, offering Toussaint a panoramic view of bootylicious. He immediately took advantage, grasping her hips and sinking in deep—over and again. Moans and groans filled the room, mixed with love . . . and gratitude. As Toussaint placed Alexis against the wall, tears came to her eyes. It had been almost a year since their intimate Cabo San Lucas nuptials and still Alexis wondered how she got so lucky. How she could be blessed to feel so much love when at one time, she felt that she would never love again.

"Baby, are you ready?" Toussaint's thrusts became faster, deeper.

"Yes," Alexis replied. "Ooh, baby, yes!"

"Come to me, sweetheart."

The request was simple, plaintive, punctuated by loving

thrusts. A swirling sensation began at Alexis's core and vibrated out with an intensity that caused her legs to tremble. She exploded in ecstasy. "Toussaint!"

Toussaint's grunts quickened and soon he followed his wife over the edge. They cuddled in the breakfast nook.

"I love you," Toussaint whispered.

Alexis nodded. "Me, too."

Two hours later, Toussaint and Alexis relaxed in their master suite. Alexis sat perched against a mass of pillows on their king-size bed thumbing through a design magazine, while Toussaint scrolled through his text messages beside her.

"I watched your show today," Alexis said. "It was good."

Toussaint smiled, eyeing his wife. "You liked it?" For the past several months, Toussaint had been the new darling on the Food Network. On his show, appropriately called *Taste of Soul*, he and Chef, the man behind the restaurant chain's delicious cuisine, went to the homes of unsuspecting housewives and helped them prepare an evening meal. Needless to say, these often-harried mothers were always grateful and, after rubbing shoulders with the handsome Livingston, a little smitten as well.

"Yes, but not as much as that woman liked you. 'Just a little more salt, darling,'" she continued, mimicking Toussaint. "'Yum, that tastes good.'"

Toussaint laughed. "I know you're not sitting there being jealous of a gray-haired old lady."

"Old ladies need love, too. You'd better watch yourself before you end up with a stalker."

Toussaint didn't respond. He'd become engrossed in sending a text.

"Thought we weren't going to bring work into the bedroom anymore."

"We aren't," Toussaint replied. "Jeff sent me the confirmation on his travel arrangements for next week. I was just letting him know that I got it."

"Travel arrangements dealing with the new Taste of Soul location, correct?"

"Ha!"

"Uh huh."

"Don't give me that 'uh huh,' Ms. Interior-Designer-Reading-*Architectural Digest*. What client's project are *you* working on?"

"The most important one I've ever worked on." Alexis put down the magazine and looked at Toussaint. "Your child."

"Aw, baby." Toussaint leaned over and kissed Alexis lightly on the lips.

"We have to hurry and get the nursery ready. The time is flying."

"It sure is. Your stomach is still flat. But pretty soon this"— Toussaint placed a hand on Alexis's stomach—"is going to get in the way of our groove."

"It's your *child*, Toussaint! I'd say this constitutes a necessary interruption."

"Baby!"

"Oh, calm down, Toussaint Levon. I've already looked into that. We can keep doing the do as long as it's comfortable, baby."

Toussaint placed his phone on the nightstand. "That's good to know." He got ready to cuddle, but before he could reposition himself, his phone rang. "Hey, Bianca."

"Hey, Cuz."

"What's up?"

"I have an idea I want to run past you."

"Make it quick. I'm getting ready for bed."

"No worries. What are you and Alexis doing this Saturday night?"

"Not sure, why?"

"I want to invite y'all over for dinner?"

"For what? A dinner party or something?"

"No, just y'all."

"Okay. Let me run it by Lexy and call you tomorrow."

"Okay, cool. Tell her I said hi and we'll talk tomorrow."

Toussaint hung up the phone and turned off the ringer. He turned off the lamp on his nightstand. Alexis did the same and moved closer to Toussaint to cuddle.

"Bianca invited us over for dinner."

Alexis turned her back toward Toussaint so they could spoon. "Oh, yeah? Just for dinner, or do you think there's more?"

Toussaint nestled Alexis closer to him and kissed her bare shoulder. "You never can tell with Bianca. But if I know Coop, it will be to announce their wedding date."

7

The Riley house was quiet. It was always quiet. As Cooper closed the door to the sprawling estate, after using his key to gain entry, he pondered on the fact that he'd never heard a loud sound emitted from this home in his life. He'd always been amazed at the lively exchanges that happened in the homes of his friends: raucous laughter, booming music, everyone talking at once around the dinner table. In Evelyn Maureen Riley's home, these luxuries were not allowed. Cooper's mother always prided herself on running an immaculate home—in both style and behavior. His father's stern countenance and firm hand left no room for argument. The honorable judge, Cooper Riley, Sr., ran a home as tight as his courtroom. The strict upbringing had produced two near-perfect children with four-point grade averages, faultless manners, and spotless records. It was a pristine lifestyle that Cooper respected, even though it sometimes drove him crazy. So crazy that people would wonder why, as a grown-ass man, he was still living in his parents' home.

"Junior, is that you?"

"Yes, Mother." Cooper removed his shoes and stepped into the sitting room just off the foyer. Each room in the Riley home was named for a color. The White Room, with a mahogany hardwood floor covered by a white mink rug, was furnished with matching loveseats in stark white brocade, a white leather recliner, and a bone-colored hutch. A subtle splash of earth tones was provided by throw pillows and pricey, framed art.

"Did you have a good day in court today, son?" Evelyn wore heels and a silk wrap dress and sipped sparkling water from a Waterford goblet.

"It was fine, Mother." Cooper walked over to the hutch, poured himself a glass of water, and sat on the loveseat opposite Evelyn. He wasn't in the mood for talking, wanting nothing more than to go to his room and brood. But that would only make his mother suspicious, so to circumvent a line of questioning, he endured the small talk.

"This client, do you truly believe he is innocent?"

Cooper stifled a sigh at the question. It was similar to those that had frequently arisen following his decision to become a defense attorney instead of a prosecuting one. His goal had been to help the downtrodden, those often wrongly or unjustly accused of crimes. His parents had thought his focus noble, yet edgy and potentially controversial. It was of utmost importance to both Evelyn and the judge that Cooper defend only those citizens deemed worthy. For this reason, Cooper had played it safe, chosen his clients carefully, and experienced a near 75 percent win rate in his short yet illustrious career.

The truth of the matter was this: Cooper didn't know whether the man who'd been accused of robbing a downtown bank was innocent. But for the first time in his life Cooper had gone with his heart instead of his head. He'd decided to represent this particular teen—who was being tried as an adult because of extensive prior arrests—simply because he felt it was the right thing to do.

"Cooper? Son, you're a million miles away. What's the matter?"

"Sorry, Mother, guess I'm just a bit fatigued. What were you saying?"

"I was saying that we're having a dinner party this Saturday and would like for you to invite Bianca. Your sister and Charles are coming; her in-laws are watching the grandchildren."

Cooper nodded.

"Speaking of grandchildren," Evelyn continued as she wiped a nonexistent piece of lint from her wrinkle-free dress, "perhaps I should plan another dinner soon, one attended by Bianca and her parents. Your father and I are trying to be patient, Cooper, and allow Bianca and the Livingstons to take the lead. It is their daughter getting married after all. But son, it's been almost two years. Everyone is expecting you two to marry. If this engagement stretches on much longer, people will begin to talk."

"And we can't have that, can we, Mother," Cooper quietly responded, suddenly wishing that he was drinking something stronger than sparkling water. "Heaven forbid that there is ever talk about the Rileys."

Evelyn raised a hand to her throat, her brows raised as well. "Cooper!" she exclaimed in a hushed whisper. "Heaven forbid, indeed, that there is ever an errant word spoken about us!" Evelyn eyed her son critically. "Everything is fine between you and Bianca, isn't it? There is nothing happening, or not happening, that you need to share?"

Cooper finished his drink and rose quickly. "Everything is fine, Mother. I'll go and place a call to Bianca now. As always, I'm sure she'll look forward to seeing all of us again."

Later that night, Cooper tossed and turned, unable to go to sleep. His phone call to Bianca had gone unreturned, adding to the uneasiness that had been growing ever since her return from Paris. Cooper had known Bianca since they were children; their parents had been friends for decades. He'd been in love with her almost equally as long. But this near-genius mind could not ignore the facts: the love of his life was slipping farther and farther away from him. Cooper had always viewed

Bianca as his ticket out of ho-humness, his pass into a world of glamour and glee. Bianca was everything he was not: beautiful, outgoing, and effervescent. He adored her. In the light of this truth, Cooper came to another conclusion. Bianca Dionne Livingston had to become his wife. If she didn't...he didn't know what he'd do.

In another room, in another place, someone else thought of Bianca. As if conjuring her up, his phone rang. "Yes?"

"I think we've located her."

"Bianca?"

"Yes."

For the first time in months, the Frenchman smiled.

8

Chardonnay checked her appearance in the mirror located near the pass-through. Since becoming assistant manager of the Buckhead location Taste of Soul she'd become more conscious of properly representing the establishment and the excellence it stood for. At one time, the only aspiration Chardonnay had was to find a man rich enough to take care of her and her kids. Bobby wasn't rich, but the brothah sure knew how to take care of home. Chardonnay would be the first to admit that having him around had definitely changed her, somewhat softened her sharp edges. And having others look up to her, asking for advice or depending on her to make decisions, had given Chardonnay something else she'd never known: pride. All of these other positive changes notwithstanding, it didn't hurt that she was getting ready to serve the owners' wives.

Chardonnay placed two glasses of lemon water on the table and reached for her pad. "Hello, Miss Candace, Miss Diane. How are you ladies doing today?"

"We're good, Chardonnay," Diane answered. "And yourself?"

"Can't complain. Well, I could, but it wouldn't do any good anyway. Life goes on regardless."

Candace eyed Chardonnay critically. "You're right about that." Even though Chardonnay had been credited for saving her husband's life, Candace still disliked her. She'd be the first to admit that had Chardonnay not come to the Livingston Corporation parking lot and found Adam lying on the pavement the night he was shot, her husband may have died. Still, Candace couldn't stand the fact that they'd both slept with Quintin. It's one of the reasons Candace knew she'd never totally trust her, would always question her truthfulness and loyalty, even though Chardonnay had sworn to Candace's son, Toussaint, that she'd stopped hearing from Quintin. But now wasn't the time to think of such things. Candace shifted her focus, took a quick look around the room. The place was packed and bustling, something that Taste of Soul execs would no less expect during the noon rush. "Looks great in here," she said, forcing a smile on her face as she looked at Chardonnay. "You're doing a good job."

Unaccustomed to praise or flattery, instead of responding Chardonnay quickly changed the subject. "Can I start you two off with an appetizer, the Ojay's Onion Bunion or some Ruffin Rib Tips?"

Diane looked at the menu. "That battered and fried Vidalia onion does sound delicious."

"It's better than crack," Chardonnay replied. "And it comes with either ranch or spicy barbeque dipping sauce."

"That sounds good," Candace responded. "But I'm trying to keep my weight down." The previous year, Quintin, as her personal trainer, had helped Candace lose twenty-five pounds. Unfortunately, he'd almost helped her lose her marriage as well. Following the discovery of their affair and its subsequent ending, Adam had bought her an in-home gym. Now, she had to depend on good old discipline, making sure that one of her regular exercises was pushing herself away from the dinner table before she pigged out. "I think I'll go right for the entrée, Diane. What about you?"

Diane nodded. "That sounds good. What are today's specials, Chardonnay?"

"Today we have the Pendergrass Pork Chop, smothered in onion gravy; the Marvin Gaye Meatloaf; and Aretha Franklin's Fried Catfish—all served with either two or three sides. Chef also just created a plate called 'Etta's Good Eating.' It comes with two pork ribs; a chicken wing, leg, or thigh; a hot link sausage; and either two or three sides. I'd personally go for this sampler: you get the best of everything."

After a short deliberation, Diane opted for the sampler plate, while Candace passed on the specials and settled for the Spinner's Salad: a combination of dark leafy greens, red onions, cherry tomatoes, fresh sweet corn, and black-eyed peas, tossed in a savory vinaigrette. Unable to resist a little taste of cue, Candace also ordered the rib tip appetizer. After Chardonnay returned with their sweet teas and left the table, Candace and Diane settled into some much-needed sistah-girl time.

"You know, you're slipping," Diane teased. "This is the first time we've gotten together in two weeks."

"Girl, I know. And I've missed our tête-à-têtes. It's just that lately I've been feeling blah, not motivated to do much of anything. I think I'm going through the change."

"Well, Candace, you are entering that time of life. I went through it early, at fifty-three. You're going on fifty-five, so I wouldn't be surprised. Have you talked to James?" James Bronson had been the family physician for more than twenty years.

Candace fiddled with her straw. "I need to make an appointment."

Diane sat back, eyeing her sister-in-law and best friend with concern. "Is that all that's going on?"

Candace shrugged, took a sip of tea.

"Can, girl, talk to me."

One second passed. Ten. Fifteen. When she spoke, Diane had to strain to hear her. "I still miss him."

Diane thought—no, *knew*—that she'd heard incorrectly. "What?"

Candace looked Diane straight in the eye. "My former personal trainer, ex-lover, the man who almost ruined my marriage and my life. I know I shouldn't. I know it's wrong. But I think about him, almost every day."

Even though they were in one of two semiprivate booths, separated from the general dining room by a glass partition, Diane still spoke barely above a whisper, and through gritted teeth. "You're damn right you shouldn't. And you're damn right it's wrong. Q is not only all of those things you mentioned, Candace, he's the man who shot your husband!"

Candace looked at Diane with large, sad eyes. "Yes, that, too."

Diane eyed Chardonnay, who was at a nearby table. After Diane got her attention, Chardonnay rushed over. "We need two glasses of wine, Chardonnay."

"Red or white? We have—"

"Just bring us a bottle of Merlot, Chardonnay," Diane replied, a bit more harshly than she'd intended. "Whatever you have that's top shelf."

"Right away, Mrs. Livingston," Chardonnay replied, intrigued beyond belief at what topic of conversation had the Livingston wives imbibing like winos at one o'clock in the afternoon. *Hum. What is going on behind closed doors at y'all's house?* Chardonnay wondered if it had something to do with Candace's husband, Adam, and their marriage; wondered if that was why Toussaint had stopped by her house for an update. She'd often wondered if Quintin really had shot Adam Livingston as he'd initially told her, and if so, why. In the days following the tragedy, Chardonnay had come to her own salacious, if unsubstantiated, conclusions. *So is it about Adam? Or that fine glass of wine in your bed, Miss Diane?* At twenty-eight years of age, Chardonnay normally focused on the tenderonis.

Ace was old enough to be her daddy, but he had a swagger that exuded power and charm. She'd do him in a minute if somebody named Diane and another somebody named Bobby weren't standing in the way.

Back at the table, Candace's discomfort grew. "Really, Diane, a bottle of wine in the middle of the day? From Chardonnay? You know that nosy heifah will take that info and run with it."

"Run where? To her man, who's the sous chef? Or one of the other workers? Chadonnay is too smart to risk her job, and she knows that if any gossip got back to us, that's exactly what would happen. Besides, having someone talk about us drinking wine is the least of our worries, chickie. I want you to talk to me about this...obvious *obsession* you have with Quintin Bright! No, better yet, let's not talk about this here, right now. We're going to get these orders to go, and then, my dear sister, you've got some explaining to do."

A half hour later, with soul food sans wine, the ladies arrived at Diane's house. They settled into the kitchen where Diane heated up the food just for something to do. Neither woman had an appetite. Little was said as Diane removed the food from the microwave and plated their meal. When she put the plates on the table, neither woman reached for a fork.

Finally, Diane reached over and squeezed Candace's hand. "Talk to me, Can."

Candace sighed, looked beyond Diane to the cloudy November day evident beyond Diane's dining room window. "I'm so ashamed."

And you should be, is what Diane thought. "Tell me about it," is what she said.

After a pause, Candace spoke. "After the shooting, at first, I hated Q. You know that. When Adam was in the hospital, and during the month after, when he was recovering at home, all I could think about was how much I wanted Q arrested, or worse. I wanted him to pay for what he'd done to my husband, to my family."

"I know, Can. I was there." Diane stopped, wanting to say more. But she didn't. Now, she deduced, was the time to listen, not accuse.

"A few months ago, I had a dream about him . . . about Q. It was so real, Diane. In it, he was coming toward me, crying. He kept shouting, 'I'm sorry, I'm sorry!' I woke up and felt like he'd been in the room . . . as if he'd actually invaded the sanctuary Adam and I share.

"I felt so guilty after having the dream, because when I awoke, I didn't feel angry at him, I felt sorry for him. I wanted to comfort him."

"Candace, you were intimate with the man. It makes sense that your feelings would be mixed."

"They shouldn't be! He tried to kill my husband, Diane! He tried to take Adam's life. And here I am, remembering things I shouldn't. About how he made me look . . . made me feel . . ."

"What did Adam say when you told him about the dream?"

"Are you kidding, Diane? Do you think I'd ever bring up Quintin with him?"

Diane hesitated, but not for long. "I think you should, Candace," she said softly, as if she were walking on eggshells. "We all know what can happen when we keep secrets between spouses."

"Yes, I know, especially when it involves the only act of unfaithfulness among the Livingston clan in fifty years."

"I'm not judging you, Candace. And Adam has forgiven you. But it's obvious that you're still beating up yourself." Diane saw tears forming in Candace's eyes. She reached over and squeezed her friend's hand. "The best thing you can do for your family, and your marriage, is to not keep anything from your husband, Candace. That's what brought the drama on in the first place."

Candace picked up a napkin and wiped her eyes. "You really think I should talk this over with Adam? That he'd be happy to hear that I'm thinking about the man who fucked his wife and then shot him?"

"Well, damn, Can. Now that you put it that way..."

"Exactly. I can't tell him, Diane. The last person I want to bring up to Adam is Quintin. I just have to get over these crazy feelings I have about something that is over and done with."

A sudden thought caused Diane to sit straight up. "Candace."

"Huh?"

"Have you heard from Quintin?"

Justified or not, Candace immediately got an attitude. "No, Diane! Do you think I'd hear from the man who both our family and the police have been seeking for almost a year, and not tell anyone?"

Diane held her own. "You're having dreams about him and just told somebody."

Candace stood. "This was a bad idea. I never should have said anything."

"Don't second-guess your decision, Candace. I'm glad you did. And again, I'm not judging you. I can't. I've never been in your shoes. Ain't been nobody for me but Ace since he tapped me with the joystick. Sorry, Can, but that's real talk. Now maybe I got ahead of myself earlier. Maybe it's best that you keep these thoughts about Quintin between you and me. But don't shut me out, Can. And don't do anything foolish. If you hear from Quintin..."

"He wouldn't dare call me."

"You're probably right," Diane quickly agreed. "But if he does, go straight to Adam. And then call the police."

9

Later that night, Diane grappled with what she'd learned from Candace earlier in the day. Her husband of thirty years immediately noticed that something was wrong. After she and Ace had finished dinner and were relaxing in the den, he turned to her. "Well, are you going to tell me on your own or am I going to have to drag it out of you?"

"What?"

"C'mon now, woman, whatever's been bugging you all night. And don't tell me this is about the missing money. I saw that side of upset. This is something else."

Diane scooted over to Ace and put her back to him. He turned, reached for her neck, and began to knead it. "I want to tell you, Ace, but . . ."

Ace noted how tight Diane's muscles were. "Sit on the ottoman."

Diane complied. Ace stood behind her and continued his massage. "You want to tell me something but what?"

"But Candace told it to me in confidence and I can't break her trust."

"Uh oh." Ace straddled the ottoman and sat behind Diane. He rubbed her arms and shoulders, moved her hair, and kissed the nape of her neck. "What's going on now with Can?" He kneaded her shoulders a moment longer. "Does this involve my brother?"

Diane pulled away from Ace. "Maybe I should just mind my own business."

"If it involves Adam, it is my business." Ace cupped Diane's chin, turned her face toward him. "What is it, baby?"

"Okay, I'm going to tell you, but you have to promise that you'll let Candace tell Adam in her own time."

Ace's countenance turned stormy. "Is she having another affair? Because if she is—"

"No, Ace. Candace isn't seeing anyone else."

"She'd better not be. I mean it, Diane. I won't let that woman hurt my brother like that again."

"She won't. It's just that... she had a dream about Quintin some months ago and, well, he's been on her mind ever since."

"What in the hell does that mean? He's 'been on her mind.'" Ace made air quotes as he fixed his wife with a look.

"She feels guilty because she's been thinking about him, remembering..."

"Oh, I see. Remembering what it was like to screw a man who was not her husband." Ace stood and paced the room. "My sister-in-law is a real class act. Daydreaming about the man who shot her husband, my brother!"

Diane immediately regretted her decision to tell Ace. She should have known how angry he'd get. "Baby, don't get all riled up about it. It's just a passing phase, a hormonal thing." Diane told Ace about Candace going through menopause. "Remember how crazy I got during that time?" she finished. "My mood swings and crying spells?"

"Don't leave out hot flashes." A calmer Ace walked to the couch and sat down.

Diane left the ottoman and joined him there. "It's just a phase she's going through," she reaffirmed, rubbing Ace's smooth bald head as she nestled into him. "I'll help her through it."

"Somebody better help her. Because if she wrongs my twin again, God had better help us all."

Candace watched Adam get ready for bed. She found comfort in observing this evening ritual, one Adam had honed to perfection during the thirty-plus years they'd been together. First, he removed his jewelry in the same order he put it on—watch, Morehouse class ring, wedding band, gold chain—and meticulously placed it in the respective jewelry box compartments. He disappeared into their walk-in closet, where Candace knew he was taking off his shirt, then slacks, then undergarments—everything except his black socks. After putting on his robe, he walked from the closet to the bathroom where, again, Candace knew exactly what he was doing and the order in which he was doing them: pee, shower, rub on cocoa butter lotion, floss, brush teeth, eye himself in the mirror for a few seconds, pull in his gut and look a second or two more, pull on his robe, and exit.

As Adam walked toward her, Candace smiled. "What?"

Candace shrugged. "Just checking out how good you look and thinking about how much I love you."

Adam removed his robe and crawled into bed. "Oh, is that so?"

"Yes." Candace moved closer to him, began stroking his flaccid member. "It's so."

Adam gave Candace a quick kiss on the mouth. "I love you, too, baby." Then he rolled over, bringing Candace's arm around his waist. Soon, light snores filled the air.

Candace waited until she was sure Adam slept deeply, then removed her arm from Adam's midsection and rolled onto her back. Stifling a sigh, she stared into the darkness. *This is the part I didn't tell you, Diane. That Adam and I rarely make love these days.* In the months following her affair, Adam had been more attentive, and Candace had enjoyed his eight, thick inches, even though Adam had never learned how to swing the bat he'd been blessed with and wasn't open to being instructed. The lovemaking hadn't been magic, but it had been regular, two to three times a week. Slowly but surely, this had changed. Now it was maybe once a week, and a "wham-bam-thank-you-ma'am" at that. Which is why when Candace fell asleep, she didn't dream about her husband. She dreamed about the long, super-strong schlong of her ex-lover, Quintin Bright.

10

"Wow, something smells good." Toussaint moved past Bianca and entered her townhome.

Bianca hugged Alexis, and then followed them both into the living room. "I've fixed some tasty treats for you to enjoy."

"Treats? Girl, you said dinner. I'm starved!"

"And you will leave here fully satisfied, promise. Have a seat, guys. Toussaint, I want to fix you a drink I made up, called a *soultini*. Alexis, would you like sparkling cranberry, apple, or grape?"

"Oh, man. She's using us as guinea pigs, Lexy."

"Baby, I think we'll live." Alexis settled herself next to Toussaint. "Grape sounds good, Bianca, thanks." After Bianca left the room, Alexis called out, "Do you need any help in the kitchen?"

"No, I'm good. Just relax and enjoy."

"Where's Coop DeVille?" Toussaint walked over to the iPod docked in its station and, after flipping through the menu, changed Bianca's atmosphere from '60s soul to twenty-first-century neo-soul.

Bianca ignored Toussaint's question. "Stop messing with my music!" she instead admonished from the kitchen. "There's a reason Otis Redding and the like are on my stereo!"

"I see y'all are going to try and gang up on a brother until Cooper gets here. And why do I feel like I'm at Taste of Soul?"

"Because that's the way I want you to feel," Bianca replied, walking over to the iPod. She flicked the menu with her thumb and soon Marvin Gaye was hearing things through the grapevine. "I want the down-home vibe of soul music with the upscale flair of TOSTS."

"Toast?"

Bianca brought out their drinks. "To TOSTS and the West Coast!" she toasted, once they'd all received their glasses.

"What's toast?" Toussaint repeated.

"You'll see." Bianca walked out of the room and then returned shortly afterward carrying a tray of appetizers.

"We're not waiting for Cooper?" Toussaint's attention was quickly diverted when he looked at the tray Bianca set down. "Chinese food? Really, Bianca?" Toussaint asked, as he eyed the egg rolls decoratively arranged on pristine white saucers. "You think that Taste of Soul is going to morph into Taste of Chinese? I don't think so."

Bianca's eyes twinkled as she rose to her full five foot four. "Toussaint, Alexis, we're not going Taste of Chinese. We're going Taste of Soul Tapas Style!" She motioned for them to begin eating and then sat on the ottoman in front of them.

Toussaint's dubious expression showed that he was hardly convinced. "Girl"—he reached for his saucer of egg rolls— "what are you up to now?"

Bianca crossed her arms. "Taste and see."

Toussaint picked up the diagonally cut egg roll half and sniffed. His brows rose. "Greens instead of cabbage? Interesting." He took a bite and closed his eyes, chewing slowly.

Alexis had barely finished her first bite before commenting. "Bianca, this is delicious! It tastes like soul in a roll!"

"Exactly, Alexis!" Bianca exclaimed, clapping her hands together as she stood. "And that's what this appetizer is called:

a soul roll!" Her eyes twinkled with excitement as she looked at Toussaint.

Saying nothing, Toussaint quickly finished off the first egg roll half and picked up the second one. Bianca could hardly stand it, but she forced herself to wait until he spoke. "What all did you put in here?" he finally asked.

"The filling is a combination of turnip and mustard greens, red onions, carrots, garlic, all sautéed just this side of tender. I wanted to still capture the crunch of the egg roll, while embracing the well-developed flavors of soul food." Bianca stopped talking, held her breath, and waited.

"What meat did you season it with?"

"No meat. In a nod to the diverse clientele I see patronizing this establishment, I went vegetarian for this dish. The smoky flavor was developed with Braggs Amino Acid and the meaty texture is actually smoked tempeh."

Toussaint put down his saucer and fixed his cousin with a serious look. "That was absolutely delicious, Bianca. I'm getting the feeling that this isn't something for the Atlanta menu. Talk to me."

Bianca jumped right in. "It's for LA, Toussaint. Not the Taste of Soul already planned, but a second location there, on the west side, smaller and more upscale than the one currently planned. Offering high-end signature drinks, appetizers, and a swanky, luxurious meeting place for the elite." The more excited Bianca became, the more she talked with her hands. "A place to see and be seen, start your evening, or drop by for late-night cocktails after a concert, ball game, or successful date that the couple doesn't want to end.

"While living in Europe, one of the trends I saw and fell in love with was the tapas bar, which, as you know, is now gaining popularity in the states. A menu filled with small-plate appetizers, which the patron can mix and match to create either an appetizer or a full meal. I can see it, Toussaint, in an area of

LA filled with high-end real estate and high-end restaurants, where people with money or those who wish they had money go to feel good."

"Why do I get the feeling you already have a place in mind?"

"Because, dear cousin, you know I learned from the best!"

Bianca walked over to a side table and returned with a single sheet of paper. "I know you guys are leaning toward Jefferson for the management position, but cousin, I can feel it. I'm the one for this job! Take a look at this overview while I finish the spread in the dining room."

Ten minutes later, Toussaint, Alexis, and Bianca sat around a table laden with tasty tapas-style treats: cornbread crostini topped with either a pinto bean or black-eyed pea tapenade, rib tip sliders, mini smothered steak tips resting on pureed grits, crusted macaroni and cheese balls, crispy chicken nuggets set on toasted bread circles, "frenched" dunking drumettes, more soul rolls paired with barbeque and au jus dipping sauces, and thirteen other dishes.

"For those wanting a more substantial meal, I propose these side dishes. It departs a bit from the typical tapas menu, but at the same time ties in with the traditional Taste selections." Bianca completed the spread with sides of mashed potatoes and gravy, cabbage soup, oven-fried green tomatoes, truffle-oil-infused navy beans, kitchen sink salad, and the item Bianca felt would become a fan favorite: sweet sticks. "I was thinking about shoestring potatoes when I cut them," Bianca answered, when Toussaint asked about the sweet potato fries preparation. "I wanted them thin, but not too thin, and they absolutely had to be crispy on the outside but tender on the inside."

"Girl, you did your thing on these fries." Toussaint noticed she'd brought out two different bowls. "These are both the same, right?"

Bianca shook her head. "One batch brings the heat. Customers will be able to order them either 'safe' or 'spicy.'"

"Bianca," Alexis began, after polishing off her fifth dunking drumette and reaching for her napkin. "This idea is a hit, not only for a store in Los Angeles, but I can see these dishes added to all of the existing locations as well."

"Maybe later," Bianca quickly countered. "But for the first few years, I want them exclusive to TOSTS. If people want soul rolls, beanie crustini or sweet sticks, they've got to come to my place in LA."

"Your place, huh? Are you forgetting that both Ace and Malcolm have all but cast their vote for your brother? And I don't think Dad is too far behind them."

Bianca thought as she nibbled on a sweet stick. "I know the odds are against me, that the family wants me to marry Cooper and settle down. But I want something else, Toussaint... success. Malcolm has his world-famous Soul Smoker, you're the new Food Network star." She fixed serious eyes on Toussaint. "I want TOSTS on the West Coast." Bianca wanted something else, Xavier, but that was a desire that she couldn't voice right now.

The evening was a smashing success. Toussaint was Bianca's favorite cousin, Bianca was the kid sister he never had, and whenever they got together the teasing was endless. After continued probing, Bianca admitted to Toussaint that Cooper hadn't been invited to this dinner and that she hadn't yet told Cooper about her plans to relocate and establish one of the finest upscale eateries the country had ever seen. Alexis couldn't say enough about her delicious, tapas-style soul food, and Toussaint admitted that her spin-off idea had just leveled the playing field between her and her brother.

As soon as he'd settled Alexis into her seat and started the car, Toussaint dialed up Jefferson.

"Hey, Cuz. I was just online checking out the Laker schedule. Thought we might try and catch a game while in LA."

"That sounds great, Jeff. Give us gents something to do while the ladies go shopping."

"Alexis is coming?"

"Yes."

"Who else?"

"Your sister."

"Bianca? Dang! That girl gets on my nerves. How did she wrangle an invitation?"

"By bringing an idea to the table that cannot be ignored. Bianca ain't playing when it comes to snagging this management position. You'd better up your game, son. Real talk."

11

Anyone who watched Adam and Ace Livingston stroll into downtown Atlanta's Bank of America office building would know that important people were now on the scene. Their panache was effortless; confidence and success oozed from their pores. The twins were in their mid-fifties and while Adam's paunch and love of cognac contributed to him looking more his age, health-conscious, jogger Ace could pass for ten years younger. But both men were handsome in that distinguished kind of way, with nice thick lips and deep-set brown eyes set in an undeniable air of sophistication. The hand of a skillful, artistic barber was evident in Adam's close-cropped black hair lightly sprinkled with gray. His tailored black suit fit perfectly, emphasizing broad shoulders and somewhat hiding the paunch. The stark white shirt that contrasted with the light wool jacket was spotless, as were the shining designer loafers encasing pedicured feet. The subtle scent of Hugo Boss clung to him as tightly as did his prestige. Ace wore black as well, his double-breasted suit tailored to show off broad shoulders, a flat stomach, and strong buttocks. His smooth bald head begged to be rubbed, and many women who watched him pass wanted to oblige. When a female looked at Ace Livingston she knew two things: one, he was packing and two, he knew how to

work what he was working with. His walk was just that powerful, and that promising.

The two men stepped off the elevator and walked to a
nondescript door at the end of the hallway that bore no signage. To the right of it was a simple, silver plaque bearing one
name: STERLING. Beneath the plaque was a larger, silver rectan-
gle housing a doorbell with intercom. Ace pushed the doorbell
and after announcing them, heard the quiet buzz of an un-
locking door that bid them enter.

The inner offices of Sterling Ross Investigations were as
opulent as the outside was ordinary and the single, side door
belied the square footage commanded by this investigative
firm. Polished cherrywood furniture gleamed against the ivory,
silk-covered walls as did the shiny, silver accessories including
handles and doorknobs. The deep-ply carpeting was a burnished
tan, and pricey, original artwork of various Atlanta landmarks
added both style and color to the meticulously appointed
space.

The men spoke to the pretty assistant who had buzzed
them in, and then followed Sterling down a short hall and into
his massive, corner office. After both men declined an offer of
something to drink, Ace got right down to business. "Thanks
for agreeing to see us on such short notice."

Sterling leaned back in his black, executive chair, his countenance one of calm authority. "Sure, gentlemen. What can I
do for you?"

Ace looked over at Adam before speaking. "My brother
and I had a conversation this weekend about something we
think you should know about."

After an extended pause, Sterling responded, "I'm listening."

One second passed. Two. Five.

Adam twisted his Morehouse ring. Ace massaged his newly
grown goatee. Sterling waited.

"This is a rather difficult and sensitive subject," Adam

began, still not looking at Sterling. "It is something that is only known within our family. After this meeting, I want it to be something known only to my family"—Adam finally looked up, fixing Sterling with a penetrating stare—"and you."

Sterling's only reaction was a slight nod. "You have my word."

"My brother and I believe that you should put Quintin Bright at the top of your suspect list, concentrate on finding him and if for some reason he turns out not to be our man, move on to the other names listed."

"He's already on the list, gentlemen," Sterling said, "along with Shyla Martin and the other employee names you provided."

"Yes," Ace countered, "But for right now, we want his to be the *only* name on the list. We want your singular focus to be on catching this man."

Sterling slowly picked up a pen from his desk, twirled it between his thumbs and forefingers. "I see."

"You don't, but you will." Ace said.

Adam continued, "Quintin had a thing for my wife." *Actually, with my wife, but all right, Adam, close enough for jazz.* "He was her personal trainer and...I guess there was a little rhythm between them." Images of the kind of rhythm that probably transpired between them almost made Adam lose his train of thought. He closed his eyes against his thoughts, forced the mental pictures away, and continued. "I found out about his...interest...and put a stop to things. Not long after that, Quintin's fitness center got shut down by the city of Atlanta."

"Quintin blamed Adam," Ace said. "That's why he came after him that night in the parking lot."

"He thought I'd ruined his business," Adam concluded. "So he decided to try and take my life."

"Did you?" Sterling queried, still the epitome of patience and calm.

Adam eyed Sterling for a long moment. "Anything that happened to Quintin Bright was his own doing."

Sterling met Adam's stare. "I see." His astute, calculating mind was one of the reasons Sterling excelled as an investigator. Said astute, calculating mind now whirled with an assurance that the *rhythm* between Quintin and Adam's wife probably happened in places other than the gym. "So when you survived, you think that Quintin continued his retaliation by somehow tapping into this account."

Sterling looked from one brother to the other. Adam and Ace nodded.

"The question is, how did he do it?"

Again, a look passed between the twins. Ace looked at his watch and stood. "That's what we want you to find out."

As soon as the Livingston brothers left the office, Sterling turned to his computer. Since his meeting with the Livingston clan, he'd focused the first part of his investigation on the account itself, noting how the money had been withdrawn, and from where. The results had been interesting: there'd been mostly withdrawals of ten thousand dollars or less through checks written to food industry–type businesses. It was easy to see why the checks could fly under an accountant's radar without drawing suspicion. If the culprit hadn't gotten greedy, writing two checks back to back for over twenty thousand dollars, the theft may have gone unnoticed until the account was drained.

Sterling clicked a few more keys, then leaned back and waited for the pages to download. "Okay, Quintin Bright, let's see what you've been up to." *Because rest assured, once I know just who you are . . . I'll find out exactly where you are.*

Computer keys were click-clacking behind another nondescript door. Quintin Bright looked at the banking screen and frowned as he viewed the balance: $79,234.80. Two weeks ago, when he'd made the last withdrawal, there had been almost half a million dollars in this account, which had financed his constant travels of the past year. He knew it had been risky to up the withdrawal amounts, but the shady, backstabbing partners who'd helped him stay underground had left him no choice. He'd paid them their "keep quiet" money, and now his gravy train was running out of gravy.

"Damn!" *Somebody had to have peeped those checks going through and alerted somebody else. Probably that wimpy muthafucka Adam or his punkass chump brother, Ace.* Quintin's smile was predatory as he thought back on the past year: the beautiful Caribbean countries, nice hotels, and fine women he'd enjoyed at the Livingstons' expense. He'd felt a huge "eff you" every time he'd placed that roll of hundreds in his pocket, every week straight for almost a solid six months. "Damn!" Quintin repeated, getting up to walk around the small, cramped room. As soon as he'd noticed the drop in balance, he'd immediately adjusted his lifestyle. He still had fifty, sixty g's, but without more coming in, that amount wasn't going to last long. And with someone now obviously watching the cookie jar, Quintin was hesitant to draw out the rest. But Quintin knew how much he'd grown used to the relatively luxurious lifestyle he'd enjoyed while on the run. And he knew something else: he wasn't ready for it to end.

12

"What's in LA, Bianca, huh?" Cooper's righteous anger showed on his face and in his voice. "Or perhaps I should ask *who* is out there?"

Bianca walked around Cooper, went into her walk-in closet, and returned with more clothes. "I told you already," she said, folding the nonwrinkle fabrics and placing them into her suitcase before turning to face her accuser. "This is business."

"It's always business, Bianca. That's the problem. First, you come to me with some cockamamy reason why you can't attend my parents' dinner party, leading to an interrogation of the Evelyn kind, and now you're going to LA on business that you can't discuss? I'm your fiancé, Bianca, soon to be your husband. There should be no secrets between us." Cooper followed Bianca into the master bath, where she was retrieving toiletries for the trip. "Do you hear me, Bianca?" he said, his voice uncharacteristically loud. When she would have walked past him, he grabbed her arm. "Talk to me, dammit! I'm tired of feeling like an addendum to your life!"

"Okay, fine!" Bianca hissed, jerking her arm out of Cooper's grasp. "I'm going to Los Angeles with Toussaint and Jefferson to look at a property. The Taste of Soul chain is expanding out west, at least two locations. There. Satisfied? Now you're all up in my business."

"What's the big deal about that, Bianca? Why didn't you think you could tell me that your company is expanding to the west...unless...wait a minute, Bianca. You can't possibly be getting ready to tell me that this expansion is going to take you out west for extended periods of time." When she didn't answer, Cooper pressed. "Tell me, Bianca. Tell me that you're not going to leave again—run away from me, from *us.*"

This was not the conversation Bianca wanted to have with Cooper, not right now, even though with Xavier occupying more and more of her thoughts, she'd known she'd have to do it eventually. Still, she figured she had at least another month or so to come up with a way to let him down easy, this man who'd been her friend for most of her life. But maybe there was no easy way to call off a marriage. Maybe there was no easy way to break someone's heart.

Okay, Bianca. Let's bear the bad news one drop at a time. She placed the toiletry bag in her carry-on and plopped on the bed. "Cooper," she began with a sigh. "I didn't want to say anything until it was official, but...I'm being given serious consideration to head up the West Coast operations. If I get the job...I'll move to Los Angeles."

For Cooper, the air left the room.

"Los Angeles, huh? You haven't been home six months and now you're ready to go someplace else? For how long?"

Bianca took a deep breath. Cooper deserved to hear the truth. "I'd be relocating there, Cooper, indefinitely."

"Relo—what? That's absurd, Bianca, and absolutely unacceptable. My practice is here, our families are here...our lives are here! We can't—I can't—just pick up everything and move to Los Angeles. Nor would I want to. And I can't believe you'd do this either, not to me...to us." He backed up, leaned against the wall, crossed his arms. "Is there somebody else?"

"Coop, no . . ."

"I didn't want you to leave Atlanta and go to Paris. It was a bad idea all along, too long for us to be away from each other."

"It's what I needed to do, Coop, before getting married, having children, tying myself down."

"So that's how you describe a future with me: being tied down."

"Not with you, Cooper, with anybody. And I'm not saying those words like they're bad. It's just a figure of speech. There are certain freedoms one loses when they marry, that's just a fact."

"Being tied down, losing your freedom. Why did you accept my proposal, Bianca, if you had no intention of following through?"

"Cooper, let's not do this now. I'm tired—"

"Tired of me?"

"You're upset."

"I have every right to be!"

"Cooper, please . . ."

"I'm tired of being Mr. Nice Guy, Mr. Patient, waiting for you to get this drive and wanderlust out of your system. But the more time I give you, the longer you want. It's been almost two years, Bianca, and I'm tired of waiting."

With that, Cooper turned on his heel and walked out of the bedroom. He didn't stop walking until he was seated in his BMW. There, he gripped the steering wheel, willing his heartbeat to return to its regular pace. Cooper had asked a lot of questions this night, but now the main one swirled around in his head. *Do you really plan to marry me, Bianca?* Starting the car and driving away, Cooper knew very well why he hadn't asked that question: her answer might be one he wasn't ready to hear.

13

They'd been in the air just over an hour and now Toussaint, Alexis, Jefferson, and Bianca sat aboard the private jet enjoying a meal of swordfish, jasmine rice, and fresh green beans expertly cooked by the chef. Toussaint and Alexis had done most of the talking, with both Bianca and Jefferson quiet for different reasons. After they'd finished a decadent dessert of chocolate lava cake, Alexis asked Bianca to join her in the sitting area at the back of the plane.

"Whew, it feels good to put my feet up," Alexis said as she stretched out on the couch. "If this baby is taking so much out of me now, I can't imagine what nine months will feel like."

"But you're what, four months already? And barely showing? You look good, girl."

"Thanks, Bianca. I appreciate that. Toussaint tells me the same thing. And when I look in the mirror I agree. I don't look big, but I *feel* big! Just wait until it's your turn. You'll see."

A dark shadow passed over Bianca's face, one that she quickly tried to cover with a smile. But even if Alexis hadn't seen it, which she had, she still would have known that all was not well with Bianca.

"You want to talk about it? You've been rather quiet all day."

Bianca sighed, looked out the window, and beheld a cloud-filled sky that could only look so beautiful at thirty-five-thousand feet. "It's me and Cooper," she said at last.

"Problems?"

"Hmph. To put it mildly." Bianca paused. Alexis waited. When Bianca spoke again, it was in an even quieter voice than before. "I don't want to marry him, Alexis."

Alexis sat up. *Did I just hear what I thought I heard?* "What?"

Bianca turned to look at Alexis. "I know it's what everybody else wants, what my parents and his parents want. But it's not what *I* want. I love him, but I'm not *in* love with him. And I don't want to get married." Bianca breathed a huge sigh of relief. It was the first time she'd said these words out loud, and even though she knew there were rocky days ahead, she felt better already.

"Have you told Cooper how you feel?"

"Not in those words. I've told him that I'm not ready to get married, but what I haven't said is that I'm not ready to get married to *him*." Bianca reached for her water bottle, took a long sip. "I don't know how to do it, Alexis. He's going to be so disappointed. Everyone will."

"Better disappointed now than devastated later. You don't want to enter a marriage reluctantly, filled with uncertainty and doubt. I mean a little uncertainty is normal; marriage is a big step. But when it's the right man, Bianca, any doubt you feel will pale in comparison to the love and the joy in your heart at saying 'I do' to the man you absolutely love with all your heart."

"The way you felt when you married my cousin."

"The day I married Toussaint was the best day of my life. The second best day was finding out that I was pregnant with our child." Alexis unconsciously placed a hand on her stomach, her face a study in contentment.

Bianca eyed this newest member of the Livingston family. Though her aunt Candace had had her doubts, she herself had

liked Alexis from the beginning. There was no doubt in anyone's mind how much Alexis loved Toussaint and how happy
she'd made him. More important, there was no doubt how
happy Toussaint made her. For a long time, Bianca had known
that Cooper couldn't bring her the kind of happiness necessary to sustain a lifelong commitment. There hadn't been a divorce in the Livingston family for decades, but Bianca knew
that if she continued down this trail, hers would be the first.

Alexis reclined back on the couch. "How long have you
known?"

"Known what?"

"That you weren't going to marry Cooper?"

Since my first orgasm with Xavier Marquis, is what Bianca
thought. "Since living in Paris," is what she said.

"Is there someone in Paris?" Alexis softly inquired. "Someone you left behind?"

No one knew about Bianca's cataclysmic, whirlwind affair
with the Frenchman who had Bianca's heart. She'd never
thought to tell anyone because she'd always considered theirs a
temporary dalliance, a "when in Paris do what the Parisians
do" sort of thing. Bianca hadn't even realized that Xavier had
stolen her heart until she returned to the states, and more
specifically, to Cooper, with no heart left to give him.

"His name is Xavier," Bianca said. "We were together the
whole time that I was in Paris, temporary, no strings attached,
the way both of us wanted."

"Why?"

Bianca shrugged. "Obvious reasons. His family line dates
back to some monarchy, and their marriages are arranged. He's
slated to marry some third or fourth cousin before he turns
thirty-five."

"What?"

"Girl, it's no biggie. That's how they roll in royalty. And,
trust and believe, the opposition would be just as fierce from
my family."

"How can you be so sure?"

"Turning down the son—no, let me rephrase—turning down the successful, affluent, *African American* son of not only one of the city's most respected judges but also the son of a close family friend for a Frenchman whose family would disdain me at best? And at worse, disinherit him from his millions? It sounds crazy even to me when I say it out loud. But from the time Xavier and I met, we clicked, connected in a deeper way than I've ever felt before. A week into the affair we were finishing each other's sentences, knew what the other was thinking without voicing it out loud. It was like we'd known each other forever, Alexis, like we'd always been in each other's lives. I've never felt the way I did in the arms of Xavier. Never felt so loved, cherished, content."

"So . . . why don't you go for what you want?"

Bianca shook her head. "Even if I wanted to, it's too late now."

"Why?"

"The night Xavier and I got together, we both thought it was a one-night stand. I know, I know," Bianca said hurriedly, holding up her hand to stop Alexis's comments. "Out of character for me, to be sure. But I'd attended a party with a friend of mine, probably drank too much wine, had been flirting with him all evening, and when he asked me to join him on his estate . . . I said yes."

"And then . . ."

"And then one night turned into two, and then three, and then a week. I knew what I was doing was crazy, but he made me feel so happy and the loving was so good. . . . Anyway . . . he knew that I was there attending cooking school. But I told him my name was Bianca Knowles.

"Knowles?"

"Like Beyoncé. Forget it," Bianca said, waving her hand dismissively. Once our thing turned into . . . something deeper, I almost told him the truth. But by then, we'd both already decided that ours could only be a passing phase, something temporary. I told myself it was for the best, that it would be easier to leave him if I knew there was no way we'd ever see each other again."

"He doesn't know your last name, but do you know his?"

"Yes."

"And you have his number?"

"I have *a* number. He probably has several."

"Then call him, Bianca."

"And say what? He's already slated to marry someone else. So why does he need to know that he has a colored girl in America turned out behind his fine ass? I have too much pride for that, Alexis. Especially when I know there's no future for us."

"I guess you've got a point." Alexis stood and stretched. "But no matter how hard it is, Bianca, you're doing the right thing by not marrying Cooper. Going into a marriage unhappy doesn't bode a good ending. And can I give you a piece of unsolicited advice?"

Bianca nodded.

"When we get back to Atlanta, have the talk with Cooper, break things off. There's never going to be a right or easy time. But the sooner you do it, the sooner both of you will be able to go on with your lives."

"You're right. I need to let him know." Bianca stood and gave Alexis a hug. "Thanks."

At the front of the plane, the men were also discussing relationships.

"I never thought I'd say this, but marriage agrees with you, man."

Toussaint nodded. "That it does. That girl back there is my heart. What about you? It's been a while since you've mentioned anyone special, and I don't think I've seen you with a date since Divine came to the Christmas party last year. Y'all hanging out or what?"

Jefferson understood why the family kept mentioning Divine. She was the one who accompanied him to most social events, and with whom he was mostly seen. Add the fact that she was very attractive and they'd been friends for a while and the assumption was obvious. If Keisha hadn't come along, who knew what might have happened between them. But she had come along and because of that, Jefferson didn't see a romantic liaison with Divine in his future. Keisha was the woman for him and before long, Jefferson deduced, this was a fact that every Livingston would have to understand.

14

"I absolutely love what they're doing with the interior. And the location is fabulous!"

All remnants of Bianca's heavy heart as it related to her situation with Cooper had been replaced by a heady euphoria at seeing the future Taste of Soul location.

"Yes, we really lucked out on this spot," Toussaint agreed. "Culver City is central to a lot of other cities, close enough to the hood to be convenient to our target market, yet innocuous enough to pull in everybody who likes good food."

"I like that the building is close to the freeway," Bianca added.

"And the mall," Alexis said.

"The mall's a block away," Toussaint continued, "and all of Sepulveda is lined with businesses, not to mention that this is a major thoroughfare from the ocean to the valley."

"Business is going to boom, right from the beginning," Bianca gushed, her eyes sparkling. "I've just got a feeling."

"What about you, cousin?" Toussaint asked Jefferson. "You've been pretty quiet. Does this look like a place that you could see yourself running?"

"Man, you know that I can run anything, anywhere."

"True that."

Bianca turned to her brother. "But you've been Director of Finance for the last few years. It's been a while since you've done the day-to-day grind of a restaurant."

"No longer than it's been for you."

"Yes, but I spent seven months cooking almost every day. Cooking school put me back in a similar environment."

The four got into their rented luxury car. Toussaint programmed the GPS and soon they were headed to Marina del Rey and their rooms at the Ritz. Conversation flowed, with Jefferson adding the least to the conversation. Once they'd gotten to the hotel and entered the lobby, Toussaint turned to Jefferson. "Okay, Jeff, it's the Lakers at eight!"

"Uh, no, man. Plans have changed."

"You're kidding me, right?"

"I forgot to tell you, brothah. Something came up."

A knowing smile appeared on Toussaint's face. "Oh, it's like that? All right then, cool. I'd take a woman over Kobe any day of the week." He watched Jefferson walk to the elevator and then turned to the ladies. "I guess that leaves me to fend for myself with you two. What do y'all want to get into?"

Alexis spoke up right away. "I want to get into a shower, into a restaurant, and then into bed."

Bianca made a face. "Stop talking like a married, pregnant woman."

"I *am* a married, pregnant woman!"

"Ha! Touché. Then let's say we do dinner together and then, Toussaint, maybe we can find something to get into."

Toussaint looked at Alexis. "Baby?"

"Y'all feed me and then you can do what you want to do."

An hour later, Jefferson answered his phone. "You downstairs?"

"Yes, Pookie," Keisha purred.

"You wearing that Laker purple and gold?"

"Yeah, and I hope you like my outfit."

"I'm sure I'll like whatever you're wearing, Keisha, and I'll especially like taking it off of you later on."

Jefferson exited the elevator, quickly walked through the lobby, and within minutes was sitting in the front seat of the brand-new, roomy SUV that he'd leased for Keisha. "Dang, Keisha," he said. While getting in and fastening his seat belt, he noticed various fast-food wrappers, bags, and toys on the floor and seats. "Y'all live in here?"

"Good to see you, too, Jefferson." Keisha leaned over and laid a kiss on Jefferson that made him forget all about the trash.

Jefferson licked his lips and scanned Keisha's curvy body wrapped in a tight gold dress. "Um, I needed that, baby."

"Hard day?" Keisha pulled out of the hotel driveway and began navigating the dense LA traffic like a pro.

"Better now." Jefferson leaned back the seat and relaxed his six-foot frame. He placed a hand on Keisha's thigh, eyeing her again.

"Is everything on schedule? Will you still be moving here in a few months?"

"Good question," Jefferson replied. He'd watched Toussaint and Bianca interact during the walk-through and admitted that Bianca had been the more participatory team member. The questions she'd asked were relevant and astute. Her opinion sometimes conflicted with Toussaint's. Jefferson noticed that, too. But when it came to the interior design, she and Alexis chatted away as if she already had the job. It wasn't that Jefferson couldn't have asked those same questions, or shared ideas on wall and floor colors. But the truth of the matter was, he didn't care. He knew that Toussaint was leaning in his direction to be the one hired and he knew why. What was more, he was fine letting Toussaint handle all of the details, to basically be the purveyor of his cousin's dreams. Jefferson simply wanted to move to Los Angeles to be with Keisha. End of story.

15

The following Monday morning, Toussaint walked into his uncle's office. Adam, Ace, and Malcolm were also there. "Gentlemen...good morning!" Toussaint bypassed the table where the men sat and stopped at the back table, which held water, juice, coffee, and rolls.

"In a good mood, I see," Malcolm said. "Things in LA must be looking good."

Toussaint set his coffee and bagel on the table, removed his jacket, and sat down. "Things in LA are looking fantastic." He carefully separated the cinnamon raisin circles, slathered on a generous helping of cream cheese, and took a bite.

"Don't let our little meeting interrupt your breakfast," Ace said drily.

"I won't," Toussaint responded, around a bite of food.

"Where's Jefferson?" Ace asked.

Toussaint swallowed his food. "He isn't here?" Jefferson hadn't flown back on the private jet, but Toussaint assumed he'd finish getting his LA freak on in time for work on Monday.

"Yolanda said he isn't in and hasn't called."

Toussaint shrugged, took a sip of coffee. "He may be running late, too. Which, gentlemen, may be just as well. I'd been looking at Jeff for this assignment, but Bianca might be the one for the job."

Three voices responded simultaneously. "Bianca?"

"I know she's giving Jeff a run for his money," Ace said. "But she's getting ready to get married, and I'll tell you right now that it will be a cold day in you know where before you see a Riley leave Georgia for anything other than a vacation."

"That's for sure," Malcolm agreed. "I ran into the judge at FGO and he was fairly beaming at the thought of Bianca becoming his daughter-in-law."

"Victoria finally let you out of the house long enough to go to the club?"

"Yeah, whatever, man," Malcolm responded. But there was a smile on his face. They'd had their problems in the past, but in the last year Malcolm and his wife's marriage had gotten stronger than ever. Before, he'd spent at least two or three nights a week at For Gentlemen Only, an upscale club for the city's elite. But since their marriage in general and sex life in particular had gotten back on track, Malcolm could more often than not be found at home in his top-of-the-line man cave or in the master suite.

The telephone rang. Ace pushed the interoffice line. "Yes."

"Ace, sorry to disturb you, but this is Yolanda. You'd asked earlier about Jefferson?"

"You heard from him?"

"Yes, just now. He's still in Los Angeles and will be back late tonight. He can be reached by cell if anyone needs him."

"Okay, thanks, Yolanda." Ace ended the call.

"Jeff is still in Los Angeles?" Adam said with a chuckle. "Son, it looks like Jeff might have a thing or two to say about Bianca running that restaurant."

"Whoever runs it will have a job on their hands. This will be our largest location to date, with double the staff that's at our other locations. Additionally, we plan to expand the weekend hours. The first six months, year even, will be pretty brutal. Whoever does it is basically going to be married to their job."

"And again I say, Bianca's out." Ace frowned as he looked at Toussaint. "She'll be married to Cooper Riley, Jr., not the West Coast Taste of Soul."

Inside, Toussaint grimaced. On the flight back from Los Angeles, Bianca had told him what she'd earlier shared with Alexis: She was breaking the engagement with Cooper.

"I know she's got her life here and all," Toussaint finally responded, "but Bianca fits Los Angeles like a hand fits a glove."

Ace reached for his copy of the LA trip summary that Toussaint had e-mailed all of the players the previous night. He put on his glasses and began to scan it as he talked. "Unless that glove can work from Atlanta and include Cooper Riley, I suggest you try a different fit. Bianca has done wonderful work for the company and will continue to do so. But she'll soon be thirty years old. It's time for her to settle down."

Evelyn Maureen Riley was thinking the exact same thing. Which is why she sat dressed to the nines in a classic Chanel suit with pearls and heels. She'd been bothered since two Saturdays ago, when Bianca had missed the family dinner. When she'd asked Cooper about her whereabouts, he had been evasive. It wasn't so much that Cooper didn't want to share the information with her, but Evelyn believed that he didn't know. *And what on earth happened last Wednesday?* Evelyn was absolutely certain that something had indeed occurred. Since then, Cooper had been moody, quiet, and extremely withdrawn. Usually a homebody with predictable behavioral habits, he'd been a no-show at most of the breakfast and dinner tables. The final straw had come the previous weekend, when Cooper had taken an unexpected overnight trip to Birmingham, Alabama. At least that's what Cooper had told his parents. But something told Evelyn that he'd been right there in Atlanta, escaping her questions and relentless pressure to "get that girl down the aisle, Cooper Riley. Or get someone else."

Evelyn sat perfectly poised and perfectly still as she waited for the call to go through. When it did, she smiled. "Hello, Diane. This is Evelyn." Pause. "I'm very well, thank you. Busy as always, not enough hours in the day."

A robe-clad Diane sat at a bar chair in her kitchen, sipping coffee. "Life does get busy sometimes."

"Which is why I won't prolong this conversation. Diane, I'm wondering if we can meet for lunch today, say, one o'clock?"

Diane had come downstairs from her bedroom relishing the fact that her calendar was open, that for the day she was footloose and fancy free. But she had an idea why Evelyn wanted to meet, and quite frankly, Diane had questions, too. "Sure, Evelyn. One o'clock is fine."

They settled on a location. "Wonderful, darling. I'll see you then."

Evelyn replaced the receiver and finished her tea. She was very much looking forward to meeting with Diane. They'd been friends for a long time. Evelyn hoped that Diane would be able to provide insight on the delay in their children's wedding. Because if she couldn't, Evelyn had one more person with whom she was going to request a meeting. *You're a nice enough woman, Miss Bianca Livingston. But if you don't want to marry my son, there are plenty of other women who will.*

16

Bianca and Jefferson pulled up to their parents' place at the same time, thinking the same thing. It was time for a grilling, and not the kind that happened with fire and meat.

Bianca stopped at Jefferson's car just as he exited. "What did she say to you?"

"That she'd made a pot of stew, too much for her and Dad to eat alone. Then she played the cake card by letting me know she'd just finished icing a German chocolate baked from scratch."

"Ha! Mom is something else."

"What about you?"

Bianca sighed. "A little more straightforward, and I don't know whether that's good or bad. She wants to talk about the wedding."

Bianca and Jefferson walked through the unlocked front door. "Hey, Mama!" he called out.

"Where's everybody at?" Bianca said, walking past the empty living room to the den at the back of the house.

Diane rose to greet her children. "Y'all know where to find us," she said, giving a hug and a kiss to first Bianca and then Jefferson. "Can I get you something to drink?"

"I'll take a shot of what the old man is imbibing," Jefferson replied. He wasn't much for hard liquor, more of a beer man, but tonight he felt that fortification might be in order. Between thoughts of the West Coast restaurant, moving to LA, and missing Keisha, his tumultuous mind was in need of a chill.

"One shot coming up," Ace said, getting off the couch and coming toward his children. This close-knit clan had always been affectionate, "touchy feely," their grandmother Marietta called it. He hugged them both before walking to the bar.

Bianca took the glass of sparkling white wine that her mother offered. "That stew smells good, Mom."

"Girl, it's delicious, I can't even lie. And your father already messed up my cake by taking a big chunk out of it. I'd barely slathered on the icing before his saucer hit the counter."

"You know it's my favorite," Ace said.

"Whoa, what's the deal on that, Mom?" Jeff asked. "I thought you said you made that cake for me?"

Candace rolled her eyes. "Oh, Lord, a whole cake in there and y'all going to fight over who had the first piece."

Everyone laughed. "Jeff, if it will make you feel better, I'll make another one tomorrow . . . just for you."

"Yes, it will make me feel better," Jefferson said. He walked over and kissed his mother on the forehead. "Thanks, Mom."

"Thirty plus and still being spoiled," Ace mumbled. "Boy, you better hope you get a woman that will treat you half as good as your Mama does."

Bianca snorted. "Nobody will spoil Jeff that badly."

"And you should talk," Jefferson retorted. "You've got Daddy wrapped around your finger. Girl, you get anything you want."

Three pairs of eyes looked at Bianca. She shrugged. "That's true."

Everyone laughed again.

After chatting casually while finishing their drinks, the crew moved to the dining room. Soon, piping hot bowls of thick, beef stew were being ladled from a flower-printed tureen that had been in the family for generations. Generous slices of still-warm cornbread slathered with honey butter were served on the side. For several moments, the only sounds were grunts, slurps, and silver spoons hitting ceramic bowls.

After it became clear that neither of her children was going to be forthcoming with information, Diane adopted a casual tone and began. "Okay, guys... what's going on with you two?"

Jefferson and Bianca looked at each other and then at Diane. "What?"

Ace immediately jumped in. "Jeff, you missed work yesterday, and Bianca, you went to Los Angeles last week and conveniently forgot to tell us about it."

"I had lunch with Evelyn yesterday," Diane continued.

"And I had a chat with Toussaint," Ace said, knowing eyes fixed on Bianca.

Bianca couldn't help but smile. This was her parents at their finest: working as a team. It had been this way as far back as she could remember, her parents presenting a united front when it came to their children. A spoiled Bianca had tried more than once to gain Ace's sympathy after being denied by Diane. She'd run into her father's study with tears in her eyes. He'd pick her up, kiss her cheek, and utter before she opened her mouth, "Whatever your Mama said."

After taking another couple bites of soup, Bianca put down her spoon and wiped her mouth. "So... how was lunch with Miss Evelyn?"

"Interesting. I went there expecting to discuss the wedding, but instead we talked more about her concern that the wedding might not happen. She also said you missed a dinner engagement at their house on Saturday night."

"Cooper didn't tell me about that until the last minute, by which time I'd already made other plans."

Diane decided to not ask what plans were more important than time with one's fiancé and his family, or what plans her daughter had made that didn't include Cooper. A mother had to probe gently in order to keep the info flowing. "I told her how busy you'd been with work, but assured her that you'd call her this week."

"Mom!"

"You need to talk with her, Bianca, and that's after you talk to Cooper."

"Why, was Cooper there as well?" Bianca had vowed to remain calm during this visit and in doing so not raise her parents' suspicions. But it looked as if it was too late for that; Evelyn already had.

Diane eyed her daughter over the rim of her water glass, took a drink, and set it down. "Evelyn said that Cooper's demeanor has changed in the last few months, that he is not at all happy that you two haven't set a firm date." Bianca remained quiet. "It has been a long engagement," Diane continued, her tone soft and without judgment. "Cooper is a wonderful man, honey, and a family friend. He has been very patient, all the while you were in Paris and in the months since you've been back."

"The brothah has been patient," Jeff added.

"I don't see what the problem is, girl," Ace said, around a mouth of cornbread. "You two pull out your appointment calendars, find a free weekend, and set the date. Simple as that."

Bianca scooped out the last spoonful of her soup and took her time eating it with the last of her cornbread. The reality of what she was about to do made it hard for her to swallow the delicious bite. Since the LA trip and her conversation with Alexis, she'd been mulling over the best way to break the news. *And should I tell my family before I tell Coop?* Bianca knew that she wouldn't get out of the house tonight without saying something. At the end of the day, there was very little that happened among the Livingstons that all of them didn't know about. She put down her spoon, wiped her mouth with a napkin. "I'm having second thoughts."

The cacophony was instantaneous.

"Second thoughts?"

"Girl, what's there to think about?"

"You're not going to marry Coop?"

Bianca held her hands out in defense. "I know it doesn't make sense to y'all. But it's how I feel."

"How long have you felt this way, Bianca?" Diane asked. "Just two weeks ago I mentioned the Four Seasons as a possible wedding location, and you nodded and talked as if everything were fine."

"I was still grappling with it then, Mom. Still am."

Ace rocked back in his chair and crossed his arms. "Honey, have you told Cooper about these reservations?"

Bianca shook her head. "I know I should, but..." Not one to cry often, Bianca felt herself tearing up.

"Baby, you haven't seen upset until you call off this engagement." Ace pushed back from the table, not wanting to hear any more from Bianca and hoping that his wife could talk some sense into her head. "Son, want to join me in the study? I want to run something past you."

"Okay."

The two men excused themselves from the room.

Diane rose and began clearing the table. "You know your father hates to see you upset." Bianca got up and began helping her mother. The conversation continued from the dining room to the kitchen. "The Rileys are good friends of the family," Diane said. "I don't have to tell you how uncomfortable a breakup will be."

"Believe me, Mom, I've thought of all of that."

"I must say I'm surprised that you're having second thoughts. Our families have known each other practically since you were a kid. You've always gotten along well with Cooper, even before you started dating. I thought you were really in love with him."

"At one time, I thought so, too."

Diane stopped putting dishes in the dishwasher, then slowly turned and faced her daughter. "And now you know you're not?"

Bianca fixed her mother with a solemn look. "Now I know that there are levels of love, and Mama...I don't think that Cooper can give me the kind of love I want."

17

Jefferson quietly sipped his drink as he watched Ace perform a near-nightly ritual: the lighting of the cigar. First, his father had rolled the cigar in his fingers as he'd talked, taking a second here and there to sniff the fragrant tobacco. Now, he reached over for a pair of scissors made especially to snip the end of his Don Pepin cigar. After carefully snipping the end, Ace reached for a box of matches—he refused to use a butane lighter so as not to compromise the cigar's taste—and after lighting the match, puffed his cigar to life.

"This is the best one yet," Ace said, after taking a few puffs.

"Oh, yeah?" Aside from a turkey or a brisket, Jefferson had never smoked a thing in his life and therefore couldn't relate to his father's fascination.

Ace nodded. "Just came out last year; you get a little taste of chocolate, molasses, a hint of cinnamon." Ace puffed again. "Yes, son, this is the way to end the evening after a long day." The two men sipped their drinks a moment in companionable silence. Ace eyed his son, placed his cigar in the crystal ashtray. "How was Los Angeles?"

Jefferson shrugged. "Big, crowded, lots of traffic."

Ace raised a brow. "Is that why you stayed through Monday?"

"Decided to stay the weekend, check out the city, relax a little," Jefferson replied, as an image of Keisha's face in the throes of lovemaking wafted into his mind. The weekend had been just that: lots of sex followed by lots of sleep. There'd been only one minor spot on his otherwise perfect extended weekend—an offhanded comment that Keisha had made regarding his family. He'd revisited that part of their conversation off and on since returning to Atlanta, and still didn't know why what she said bothered him so, especially since it was true.

"I want my family to meet you," Jeff murmured, after Keisha had sexed him so good that he almost proposed marriage right there on the spot. If he didn't know better, instead of her mouth, he'd have sworn that a vacuum sucked him dry.

"I don't think they're ready to meet me," she responded, caressing his deflated sac. "And I know I'm not ready to meet them."

"Why not?" Jefferson had his own reasons for employing caution when it came to telling the Livingstons about Keisha. He never would have thought that she, too, had reservations.

"They'll judge me," she finally answered.

"Let me handle that," was all he'd said in reply. With two children by two different men, Keisha was right. Some members of the family would judge her. But Jefferson hoped that when they got to know her, they'd fall in love with her...just as he had.

"How's the progress coming on the building?"

Jefferson welcomed Ace's diversion from his uncomfortable thoughts. "So far, the contractors are on schedule. This location is definitely taking Taste of Soul to the next level."

"And you think there's enough traffic potential to justify the large space?"

"I think the dining room will stay full and that the

bar/lounge area will become a hot spot." Jefferson continued, telling Ace of his ideas about incorporating Taste of Soul into community events and, in time, opening up a catering arm as well."

"It all sounds good, son. But we've got to be patient. It may take a couple years for this location to turn a profit."

"I don't think so, Ace. I think that—"

"Hey, Dad, I'm leaving," Bianca announced as she sailed into the room. Ace rose to his feet to hug his daughter. "Sorry to interrupt, brother," she continued over Ace's shoulder.

"Excuse me a moment," Ace said to Jefferson as he walked Bianca to the front door. They paused just on the other side of it. "Now listen, baby girl. We all love Cooper and the Rileys are good friends of ours. But you forget about what I said earlier. Take your time with this marriage thing."

"I know you want me to get married."

"Yes, baby. I think it's time. But I want you to be happy, too."

"Thanks, Daddy." Bianca hugged her father, hoping that he would still feel this way after hearing her future plans. "Oh, and Ace," she said, reverting to the name she called her father when business was being discussed. "Will you be coming in early tomorrow? I'd like a meeting with you and Uncle Adam."

"I'll be there at nine. What's the meeting about?"

"Taste of Soul, of course," Bianca answered, purposely being vague. When her father frowned, she kissed him on the cheek and headed down the steps. "Don't worry, it's all good. See you in the morning."

Inside the study, Jefferson finished his cognac and placed his snifter on the table. His father was taking longer than necessary to return to the den. He didn't doubt why: Bianca was preparing to make her case for why she should manage the West Coast Taste location. *That is, if you haven't already.* When it came to business, Jefferson knew that his sister was tenacious. He also knew that, truth be told, she could run any business as well as or perhaps even better than he could. When it came to the West Coast move, it wasn't about business. This time, for Jefferson, it was personal.

18

The next day, Bianca walked into the smaller Livingston Corporation conference room filled with poise and confidence. She'd stayed up until two a.m. the previous night, perfecting her PowerPoint presentation. She'd even designed the accompanying handouts herself. Bianca had a trusty assistant in Crystal, but today, she wanted everything to be perfect.

Adam and Ace strolled into the room. "Good morning, Ace, good morning, Uncle Adam," she said, giving each man a quick kiss on the cheek. "Thanks so much for meeting with me. This won't take long. I'm just waiting for one more person to join us and we can get started."

Before Ace could ask, his question was answered. Toussaint strode into the room, talking on his cell phone. He ended the call, greeted those around the table, and took a seat. A quick look passed between the twins. Bianca took a sip of her coffee and then clicked on the first slide. It was colorful and intriguing, filled the screen. *TOSTS: Taste of Soul Tapas Style.*

"Gentlemen," Bianca began. "As you know, I am very excited about our expansion to the West Coast. I've also made it known that I would like to head up that operation. I know that Jefferson has also expressed an interest in managing the

West Coast. But where he has an interest in running a restaurant, I have an interest in not only managing a successful eatery, but also in raising our profile and brand and expanding our reach into the food industry. This"—she pointed to the screen and then passed out the folders in front of her—"is Taste of Soul at the next level."

Down the hall, Taste of Soul was the last thing on Jefferson's mind. With Keisha's sizable assets all over his Skype screen, he was thinking of a totally different kind of meal.

"Damn, girl," he said, spreading his legs to accommodate his rapidly expanding hardness. "You know I'm trying to work." Even so, when she turned over and spread her legs wide to reveal the paradise he'd recently inhabited, his dick hardened even more. "Stop it, Keisha."

Keisha talked dirty as she pleasured herself. In spite of his protestations, Jefferson began to stroke himself. He was just about to pull out his piece when the door opened.

"Hey, man," Malcolm began before stopping short.

Jefferson hurriedly clicked off Skype and rolled his chair up until his stomach almost touched the desk. *Damn! What am I thinking? About to jack off in the corporate offices like some kind of pervert . . . without even locking the door!*

"Uh, hey man," Jefferson finally replied, staring at his computer as if he were working on something hard. In actuality, he was working on losing his hard on.

Malcolm remained by the door, his brows creased. *What the hell? If I didn't know better, I'd swear Jeff was . . . no . . . couldn't be.* Malcolm shook off the feeling of discomfort and crossed the room. "How was Los Angeles?"

"It was cool," Jefferson said, just as his cell phone rang. He looked at the ID. "Call you back," he said brusquely and hung up.

The act didn't go unnoticed by his astute cousin. "Pesky female?"

Jefferson smiled. "Determined one."

"Ha! I see." Malcolm sat on one of two plush, leather chairs facing Jefferson's desk. "So how was LA?"

"It was cool. It's going to be a bit of an adjustment, but..."

"Anything for the family, right?"

"Right." Finally back to normal, Jefferson casually leaned back in his chair. "How's the Soul Smoker business?" The device that Malcolm had invented last year, a sleek metal cylinder in which even the cooking novice could make tender, succulent barbeque every time, had taken off like a rocket since launching on QVC. It was now sold in many of the chain stores, and continued to do well online. "Must be good since we rarely see you around these days."

"I'm still handling my business, make no mistake about that. It's just that now, I usually get here about seven and leave at one or two. Then I put in three to four hours managing my other business before wrapping up any Livingston Corporation loose ends when I get home."

"Victoria okay with this workaholic schedule?"

"You take care of home and tap a sistah right...and they're okay with almost anything."

"Man, I'm glad to see you and Vicki back on track. From what I hear, y'all were cutting it close for a while. Heard you were hanging with Joyce Witherspoon for a minute."

"That's old news." Malcolm rocked back in his chair, remembering how close he'd come to breaking the Livingston legacy with the event planner who once upon a time had brought big business to the company's catering arm. All of that ended when Victoria found out about their business relationship and nipped it in the bud before it became an intimate one as well. "No affairs, no divorces, the Livingston legacy still stands." *At least for us men.* Malcolm's eyes narrowed as he remembered not being the only one in the family tempted by outside forces last year. His mother had also battled temptation...and lost. "Hey, I ran into Coop last night at the club.

What's this about Bianca planning a move to LA and delaying their wedding again?"

Jefferson filled Malcolm in on the latest: Bianca's second thoughts where marriage was concerned as well as her desire to head west. "But I have a plan," Jefferson concluded. "I plan to mount a vigorous campaign to make Taste of Soul a buzz phrase in the catering world. And I hope that you don't mind that I consulted with Joyce Witherspoon about it."

"As long as she stays away from me and my family, I don't care what she does. Still, I'm not so sure what kind of help she can give you, being that she's based in Atlanta."

"It was a chance meeting at a jazz concert a couple of weeks ago. We chatted a bit, I told her about the expansion, and she gave me the name of an event planner in LA, someone with connections to celebrity and sports events, which is exactly what I'm looking for."

"Sounds good, Jeff. Looks like in a couple of months you'll be packing your bags. What does Divine think about that?"

Instead of answering that question, Jefferson asked one of his own. "Y'all really like her, huh?"

Malcolm shrugged. "Don't know her well since you don't bring her around the family much. But she's fine. I know that."

"Divine is cool but we're just friends."

"How are you going to be just friends with somebody who looks like that?"

"Timing, I guess. I was with the gold digger when we met and it's only been a few months since she ended her last relationship. We'll see what happens. You never can predict how life will turn out."

Jefferson was sorely tempted to tell Malcolm about Keisha, but Malcolm's phone rang. As his cousin left the office and headed to his own, Jefferson knew that it was time to bring Keisha out of hiding and place her by his side.

Down the hall, Bianca closed her office door and squelched a squeal. Both Ace and her uncle had been blown away by the TOSTS idea. They'd been even more impressed that she'd already researched locations, crunched the numbers, and secured two major investors. The Livingston Corporation's financial outlay would be minimal, and yet they'd still be majority owners. These silent partners were simply interested in flipping their money: as soon as they'd made back double their investment, they'd be gone.

Bianca had also made a very strong case for why she'd be the better manager for the West Coast location, using her recently amplified skills in the kitchen and personal research in healthy eating as huge bargaining tools. All of this had been outlined in her PowerPoint presentation, and underscored when Crystal brought in what Bianca had earlier prepared— several samples from her proposed tapas-style menu. Her father had loved the sliders while Ace's favorite had been the macaroni and cheese balls. Bianca had believed her presentation stellar, and after what her uncle had said, she was sure of it.

"Bianca," Adam had said as the meeting concluded, "up until an hour or so ago, I was convinced that Jefferson was the person for this job. But after what you've showed us, I must admit it: you just might get my vote."

19

Jefferson stepped from the jetway into the Los Angeles International Airport and wondered if he'd ever get used to the hustle and bustle of such a big city. Truth be told, Jefferson was more country than city. He loved spending time on his grandparents' sprawling, farmlike estate just inside the city limits of Lithonia, a small community about twenty miles east of Atlanta. Jefferson could see living similarly and being as happy as a clam. Would Keisha enjoy the simple life, he wondered? And would his family enjoy Keisha?

Jefferson thought of his family's inquiries into his love life lately, and how they'd all assumed who was the woman in his life. Divine would be an easy addition to the Livingston family. She was beautiful, smart and a successful artist. But it was Keisha who'd won his heart, and it was his love for her that made him put aside his personal preferences and move to La-La land. *Otherwise,* Jefferson concluded as he navigated his way through the crowd and headed curbside, *I could stay back East for the rest of my life.*

Jefferson's phone vibrated. "Hey, baby."

"You here, Pookie?" Keisha asked, her voice soft and breathy.

Jefferson's entire body relaxed. There was something about

Keisha that made him feel pampered and protective at the same time. "On my way to curbside, you out there?"

"I had to circle around, but I should be there in less than five minutes."

"Can't wait to see you, baby."

Keisha laughed. "Me either."

Moments later, Jefferson put his luggage in the backseat of Keisha's SUV and climbed inside the vehicle. He leaned over and kissed her, running a hand under her minidress to caress a soft thigh. When his hand continued to travel without meeting any fabric underneath he whispered, "What do you have on under here?"

"Nothing."

Jefferson groaned. Keisha laughed, put on her blinker, and eased into the busy airport traffic.

"Where are the kids?" Jefferson asked, shifting his hardening body while also trying to shift his mind away from the delicacy that was awaiting him between Keisha's thighs.

"Mama's watching them for a couple hours."

"Your mother?" Jefferson tried without success to keep the surprise out of his voice. Keisha didn't talk much about her family, but the little that she had shared about her mother and their relationship had not been positive. "I thought you said she was a bad influence."

Keisha shrugged. "She is, but she's still their grandmother. Plus"—she cast a sultry eye in Jefferson's direction—"I couldn't wait to have a couple of long, uninterrupted hours with you all to myself." She pulled into the valet area of Embassy Suites, where Jefferson usually stayed during his visits. Within ten minutes they were inside the suite, and within ten more minutes, Jefferson was eight and a half inches deep inside Keisha.

Twenty minutes later the lovers lay in each other's arms, having enjoyed a down and dirty quickie. Jefferson pulled the sheet over them both and held Keisha tighter in his arms. "Um, I'm hungry, baby."

"Already?" Keisha mumbled into his chest.

"Ha! No, I can wait a few minutes for round two. I was thinking about room service."

Keisha laughed, and Jefferson's heart flip-flopped. "Oh," she said, snuggling into Jefferson's warm body. "Yeah, I guess I could eat something."

Jefferson reached for the menu that lay on the nightstand. After they ordered, he rested on one elbow, and with the other hand, brushed strands of hair from Keisha's face. "I miss you when I'm in Atlanta," he said softly.

"I miss you, too, Pookie. When are you moving here?"

Jefferson flopped onto his back, once again pulling Keisha to his side. He thought back to Malcolm's recent comment. *Looks like in a couple months you'll be packing your bags.* "In a couple months. The restaurant is scheduled to open in March. I've chosen a realtor and will meet with him soon." He turned and looked at her. "Where would you like to live?"

"Anywhere you are."

"That's why you're my baby," Jefferson said, kissing Keisha's temple. They lay in companionable silence for a moment. "Keisha."

"Hum."

"Does your family get together for Thanksgiving?"

Keisha thought back to their last family get-together, on the Fourth of July, when her cousin ChiChi had found out that her recently paroled boyfriend, Crunk, had been two-timing her with JaNiqua, ChiChi's best friend. Unfortunately, neither Crunk nor JaNiqua knew their news had been put on blast—until they'd had the nerve to arrive at the cookout... together. ChiChi attacked JaNiqua, Crunk hit ChiChi, and one of Keisha's brothers gave Crunk and his friend Willie, who'd tried to intervene, a beat down. Throughout the entire incident Keisha's mother—who was two sheets, three blankets, and four comforters in the wind—kept blasting Teena Marie and singing an out-of-tune "Square Biz." Later, Crunk showed up at ChiChi's with a gun and shot up her house *and* her car, which inspired NayNay's father, Keisha's Uncle Looney, to hunt down Crunk and beat him *again*. To say her family was dysfunctional was putting it mildly. Keisha loved her family; she just didn't *like* them all of the time.

Taking the clue that she didn't want to talk about her family, Jefferson decided on another route. "Baby?"

"Huh?"

"What are you doing for Thanksgiving?"

"I don't know. Maybe just chilling at the house, me and the kids."

"Who's cooking?" Jefferson knew from past conversations that most of Keisha's children's meals came courtesy of a box, a microwave, or paper bags stamped with a golden arch.

"I can make a spaghetti casserole."

Spaghetti, for Thanksgiving? is what Jefferson thought. "Oh really?" is what he said.

"Yes." Keisha rolled over and stared at the ceiling. "My favorite uncle taught me. Uncle Bernard." Keisha closed her mind against the parade of "uncles" her mother had brought home during those early years, and focused on the man who came the closest to "father" that she ever knew. "We ate good when he was around," she continued. "Steaks, sloppy joes, fried chicken, pork chops. Mama was still working back then. One night, her birthday, Uncle Bernard wanted to do something special, and he wanted us to help. My brothers didn't want nothing to do with the kitchen, but I was so excited to do this for my mom. I helped him make a spaghetti casserole. He even put vegetables in it, which I hated, but it was still good! And we baked her a cake, with the frosting and everything. It was so much fun. . . ." Keisha became quiet, remembering.

"I bet your mom was so proud of you."

Keisha sat up, shook her head.

"No?"

"No," she whispered, as a lone tear slid down her cheek.

"Me and my uncle had just finished frosting the cake. We didn't have candles so I thought to grab the box of matches and stick those in instead. 'That's genius, baby,' Uncle Bernard told me." A wispy smile flitted across Keisha's face. Another tear fell. "He picked me up and hugged me, told me I was a smart girl, and thanked me for helping him. When Mama walked in, I was in his arms.

"She went ballistic, called me a 'triflin' bitch,' and accused me of trying to take her man. Uncle Bernard tried to calm her down, told her what had happened and why he hugged me. But she was too drunk to listen to reason. She ended up throwing the cake across the room and putting Uncle Bernard out of the house. After that, she sent me to live with my grandmother. I was twelve years old."

Keisha shook her head slightly, as if coming out of a trance. "Me and Mama's relationship was never the same after that. And I never saw Uncle Bernard again either. But I'll always remember that casserole, made with hamburger, cream of mushroom soup, veggies, cheese. It was so good," she finished in a whisper.

Jefferson sat up and pulled Keisha into his arms. He remembered the first meal he had prepared for his family: baked chicken, green beans and mashed potatoes. His parents had oohed and aahed at the finished product, with Ace making a big deal when asking for seconds. Or being at Malcolm's house the month prior, when Malcolm's son, Justin, had prepared a chicken in the Soul Smoker. Malcolm had praised the kid as if he'd just won *The Next Iron Chef.* Cooking was something that had lovingly been passed down from one Livingston to another. They could all, as folks said, "throw down." He couldn't imagine life without supportive parents, wouldn't have been the man he was without Ace in his life. This made him think about Keisha's two sons, whom he had yet to meet because Keisha didn't want them to have a lot of uncles, as she had. Who were their influences? Was it her brothers? Were their fathers in their lives? It suddenly occurred to Jefferson that although he'd been seeing Keisha off and on for six months, he really didn't know a lot about her. But he wanted to.

"Tell me some more about your childhood," Jefferson gently coaxed.

Keisha was grateful for the timely knock that announced that room service had arrived. Later, after a longer, more thorough round of lovemaking, Jefferson shared memories from his childhood. He also opened up to Keisha about his deepening feelings for her, how he wanted to meet her children and make them a more permanent part of his life.

Keisha was quiet, overwhelmed with emotion. When she'd met Jefferson her goal had been simple: get the man and get his money. She'd never dreamed he'd fall in love and want to spend the rest of his life with her. When it came to the future, Keisha had never imagined it could be happy, like this. But it could. She knew that now. A husband, a baby daddy, was within her reach. There was only one problem: another man whom she also loved was standing in the way.

20

The Livingstons had a lot to be thankful for: Toussaint's Food Network show continued to garner high ratings; Malcolm's Soul Smoker sales were through the roof; and the Taste of Soul empire, having survived the most recent economic downturn, was poised to make a tidy profit for the year. On the home front, blessings continued. No one had died, marriages were sound, folks were healthy, and the newest family member was poised to make his or her entrance in less than six months. Marcus and Marietta stood side by side, surveying the sea of smiling faces gathered around them. Marcus's hand squeeze was almost imperceptible, but Marietta felt it and understood its message: *Etta, we done good.*

This year, almost thirty people gathered at Marcus and Marietta Livingston's estate, situated just outside Lithonia, Georgia. The weather had cooperated with Candace and Diane's plan to host this year's dinner outdoors. It was sunny and sixty-eight degrees and inside the tent that had been erected for the occasion, people were comfortable in dresses and shirtsleeves. Kids ran around outside, a mean game of bid whist was happening on one side of the room, miniature golf was being played just beyond the tent's opening, and lively gossip abounded as the women covered the buffet with the best soul food spread east of LA.

"I don't care what people say about her," Alexis said, placing a large tin of candied yams in the three-part warming tray, next to the macaroni and cheese and sausage cornbread dressing. "I like OWN. An African American woman running her own network? Not television show, mind you: *network*! I'm going to support it no matter what shows are in the lineup."

Diane moved over a tray of greens, green beans, and a tomato/corn/okra medley to place down a piping hot platter of fresh-baked rolls. "I believe in support and all, but I think it would be nice to have more blacks on there."

"Oprah Winfrey owns it, that's black enough for me!" Mama Marietta opened up a Soul Smoker and took out a succulently prepared slab of ribs. "Ooh, I can't get over this boy's creation. The meat cooks perfectly every time!"

Ten minutes later a hungry group of people stood in a circle, hands clasped, waiting to give thanks. Each person was asked to say one thing for which they were grateful. The blessings ranged from the serious ("Lord, thank you that our circle remains unbroken, that all my children have once again gathered at my table," delivered by Mama Marietta) to the silly ("God, thank you for letting me beat my brother on Wii," honestly stated by Malcolm's seven-year-old daughter, Brittany.) Candace's voice shook as she thanked God for her family, especially her husband; Diane thanked God for her children's success; and everyone—but especially Bianca—understood the message delivered in Cooper's prayer: "Thank you, Father, that by this time next year, one of these Livingstons will be a Riley."

Plates laden with mounds of food soon sat on the three circular tables of ten. Conversation abounded, amid the constant clacking of silverware hitting plates. The family patriarch, Marcus, regaled the group with tales of a young Adam and Abram, and how they were sometimes able to fool their mother into believing each wasn't the twin who was supposed to be punished. Cousins who'd missed the past few Thanksgivings shared tales of what was happening in their world. And through it all, wine, water, and sweet tea flowed freely.

"You all right?" Alexis asked Bianca when they'd gotten up at the same time to refresh their plates.

"Not really," Bianca replied. "We're leaving in a bit to have dessert with his family. I don't want to go."

Alexis looked at Bianca with concern. "You've got to."

"I know."

"What are you going to do, Bianca?"

Bianca shrugged, suddenly losing her appetite for the black-eyed pea salad she'd put on her plate. She put hers down and refilled Cooper's plate with a generous helping of fried turkey and a barbequed hot sausage link. "I don't know what I'm going to do, Alexis. But whatever it is, I've got to do it soon."

Back at their table, Jefferson noticed how Cooper's eyes never left Bianca. One thing he'd never have to wonder is how much Cooper loved his sister. Which is why he wished his sister felt the same. Just last night he'd asked her how things were going with her and Cooper. "They're not," she'd replied. Jefferson speared a chunk of scalloped potatoes, chewing thoughtfully. How was it, he wondered, that his sister could be here with someone she didn't want, when he was afraid to introduce the woman he loved to his family?

On the other side of the country, the woman Jefferson loved sat at the table enjoying dinner with her sons.

"This is good, Mama," Antwan said, plunging another forkful of spaghetti casserole into his mouth. "Can I have another piece of garbage bread?"

"Ha! It's *garlic* bread, baby," Keisha told her four-year-old. "Eat some of that salad and then you can have another slice.

She looked over at the seven-year-old man of the house. "You want some more, Dorian?"

Dorian rested his jaw on a balled-up fist and frowned. "I want to go over to Granny's."

Keisha sighed, even as she noted how with his scrunched-up face, Dorian looked more and more like his uncle. Not wanting to focus on her family, she closed her eyes and instead thought about Jefferson. She'd replayed their conversation over and over in her mind, how fun and special the holidays with his family had sounded. Keisha loved her family, but hardly a gathering went by without someone getting beat up or cursed out, with most of them drinking until they were "tore up from the floor up." Keisha wished that she and her boys could have been with Jefferson, but since that wasn't possible, she'd gone out and purchased a nontraditional Thanksgiving feast, one that she could prepare herself. She was even proud of the pumpkin pie that sat on the counter, though it came courtesy of Marie Callender. She'd invited her best friend, Shaunzie, and Shaunzie's girls, but they'd gone over to Shaunzie's new man's family's house. So Keisha determined to have a happy, thankful day . . . with just her and the boys. *Maybe it's time I met them,* Jefferson had suggested on his way back to the airport. Keisha would like nothing more—not only for Jefferson to meet her sons, but for him to become the father they never had.

A knock on the door interrupted her musings. Dorian dashed to the front door. "Mom! Guess who!" he exclaimed.

"Who?" Keisha asked. *Maybe Shaunzie decided to join us after all.* Keisha walked into the living room, saw her brother, and stopped short.

"Why the frown, sis? Happy Thanksgiving!"

"You know you didn't stop just to share holiday cheer," Keisha stopped in front of the older brother she'd loved since birth. "Q, what do you want?"

21

Q sniffed around the room. "Is that food I smell, as in food you cooked? Naw, couldn't be. Because that food smells good."

"Yeah, whatever, nucka," Keisha retorted, even as she blushed at the praise. "You want some?"

Quintin shadowboxed with Dorian, swung an excited Antwan onto his shoulders. "Should I chance eating some of your mama's cooking, boy?" he asked him.

"It's good, Uncle Quintin," Antwan responded.

"And there's pie!" Dorian chimed in.

"You must be expecting company," Quintin said, following Keisha into the kitchen. "If it's who I think it is, a brothah would need to make a fast exit. Don't want to mess up my money train, if you know what I mean. But wait a minute. Of course you do. Ha!"

"Stop it, Q, that's not funny. And don't talk so loud. You don't want the boys to hear you talking like that."

"Quit being paranoid, little sis. They don't know what's up."

"Kids these days know more than we realize. Keep your convo on the down low." She dished up a plate of spaghetti casserole and placed it in the microwave. "You want some salad?"

"Naw, I'll pass on the rabbit food. Why aren't you over at Mama's?"

"Didn't feel like dealing with a bunch of drama today. Why aren't you there?"

Q looked inside Keisha's cabinets, pulled out a bag of chips, and munched. "Had some business to tend to first," he said, eyeing Keisha pointedly.

"Don't even start." The microwave dinged and Keisha reached for the plate at the same time someone knocked on the door.

A few seconds later, her son called out. "Mama! Can we go outside?"

"Stay in front," Keisha responded. "Don't let me catch you out of the yard.

"I mean it," Keisha continued, setting Q's plate in front of him and then picking up her children's leftovers. "I don't want to do any more, Q."

"I told you that this will be the last time, girl. It's one last withdrawal and it's his savings account, which a baller like him probably rarely checks."

"But a hundred g's? That's going to get noticed. I told you from the beginning that you should have been saving that money, instead of trying to live large. If you had, you wouldn't be sitting here now, with your hand out."

"And you wouldn't be sitting over there with a pipe dream, a fairy tale, thinking you might have a future with somebody like him. Trust me," Q said, around a bite of spaghetti. "When it comes to people like the Livingstons, people like you and me are good enough to fuck, but not good enough to marry."

Keisha fiddled with the uneaten salad still on her plate. Her brother was probably right. He'd told her about the affair with Jefferson's aunt, and how when it was over Candace had kicked him to the curb without a backward glance. She hadn't even come to his rescue after her husband somehow managed to get Q's business closed down. Keisha had agreed with her brother that shutting down his livelihood was scandalous, but she'd also pointed out that two wrongs, especially a wrong that almost took a man's life, didn't make a right.

"He told me he loved me," Keisha said softly.

"He loves what's between your legs, little sis," Q replied.

"He wants to meet the boys."

Q snorted. "And when is he taking you to meet his bougie-ass family? Did he tell you that?"

Keisha shook her head.

"Exactly. Sure, he's thrown a little money at you these past six months, set you up in this place, bought you a car. But, Key, he could do those things without even blinking. That shit was probably in his petty cash. What I'm saying is, it didn't really mean anything. Now I, on the other hand, have been taking care of you from the beginning, right?" Q paused. "Right?"

"Right," Keisha whispered. It was true. Keisha had two brothers, but Q was the one with whom she was close. Having different fathers never mattered. From the time he'd punched out Cordell for spraying water into her freshly pressed hair, Q had been Keisha's protector. When their mother was too drunk to buy food, Q would go and steal dinner. He'd been her provider. And after the relationships with her children's fathers had ended in disaster, Q had been her comforter. He'd always had her back and now, as much as it pained her, she had his. "This is the last time, Q. I mean it."

Q smiled. "That's right, the last time. I'ma grab this money and then me and baby girl are going back down to Jamaica. With that plus the little I have left, I can open up my jerk shack and live like a king . . . for a long time."

On the East Coast somebody else was planning her escape, from a would-be in-law's dinner table.

"The flan was excellent, Mrs. Riley," Bianca said, wiping her mouth on an embossed napkin of stark white linen.

"Thank you, Bianca, dear. And really, don't you think it's about time you started calling me Mom?"

Bianca smiled but said nothing, as she imagined herself fleeing the room, screaming at the top of her lungs.

The overanalytical mind of Cooper Riley, Jr., however, missed nothing. "What do you say, Bianca? Mom Riley, or Mama?"

"Cooper! You know I've never liked that word. It sounds so...well...mammyish. No offense, dear," Evelyn added, clasping Bianca's hand. "Cooper calls me Mother, and I adore that. Perhaps you can call me that as well."

"Yes, he's always called you Mother," was Bianca's non-committal answer.

"And he's always called me when he needed money," Cooper, Sr., said with a twinkle in his eye. The elder Cooper was no-nonsense on the bench but exercised his dry sense of humor in private circles.

"That was supposed to be a joke," Cooper, Jr., explained. "Ha ha, Dad."

"Bianca, don't let them hurry you into this. I called my mother-in-law by her surname for years."

"But not after we married, Judge."

Judge Cooper reached for a toothpick and reared back in his chair. "Well, let them get married first, dear."

Evelyn let out an exasperated breath, then, to cover the real reason, addressed her husband. "Really, Judge, at the table? In front of guests?"

"Bianca isn't a guest, Evelyn. She's family." Still, Cooper, Sr., put down the toothpick and picked up his tumbler of Scotch.

Calm veneer back in place, Evelyn smiled. "Would you care for a bit more sherry, Bianca?"

"No, thank you. I don't think I could eat or drink another thing."

"Well, it sounds like you had quite the spread at your grandparents'. I'm afraid ours pales in comparison, though I must say the roasted duck and *boulangere* potatoes that Kathy prepared were divine."

"I'm sorry I missed them," Bianca said in reference to Cooper's older sister. "How are the children?"

"Oh, please, don't ask," Cooper replied. "Get Mother talking about her beloved grands, and we'll be here all evening."

The four continued sharing small talk through dessert. Bianca offered to help Evelyn clear the table, but Cooper had other plans. "Mother, you'll get that, won't you? I have someplace to take Bianca."

Evelyn looked at her son with affection. "By all means, you two go on out and enjoy yourselves. Annie will clean up later."

As soon as they'd entered Cooper's brand-new BMW sedan, he leaned over for a kiss. Bianca's response was less than enthusiastic.

"What is it, Bianca?" Cooper asked, with restrained patience. "There's been something going on with you all day."

"I'm sorry, Coop," Bianca said. And she was. Sorry about a lot of things. But mostly sorry for Cooper that after tonight, she'd no longer be wearing his ring.

22

"I did it." This was Bianca's three-word greeting once Alexis answered the door.

Toussaint came up behind his wife. "Did what?"

The two moved aside so that Bianca could enter their home. She'd intended to confide only in Alexis but then asked herself, what was the point? Evelyn would be on the phone to Diane as soon as Cooper broke the news. Within twenty-four hours, everyone would know. "I broke up with Cooper."

"You did what?" Toussaint asked.

"You heard me." Bianca walked over to the eight-foot custom-made couch and plopped down.

"Say it isn't so!"

"Oh no, Bianca." Alexis walked over and sat next to her in-law and close friend. "Are you okay?"

"You guys got any wine?"

"Sure you don't want something stronger?" Toussaint asked as he moved to the bar.

Alexis rolled her eyes in the direction of her husband. "What happened?"

Bianca gave the short version of what happened when, after Cooper asked to make love at her place, she suggested that they stop first and have a drink.

"He knew something was up," Bianca said, taking the glass of pinot noir that Toussaint offered. She took a sip, and then another. "The end of our relationship was written all over my face."

"Wow, Cuz. I know that for Cooper this was quite a blow. He must have been livid."

"I think I could have handled angry, but the hurt, haunted expression on his face when I delivered the news nearly tore me apart. I truly care about Cooper, you guys," Bianca said, tears forming in her eyes. "But I couldn't see spending my life with someone whom I was simply fond of. I want more than that, like what you guys have." She looked from Alexis to Toussaint. "Is that wrong?"

Toussaint leaned against the wall. "It's not wrong to want what you want, Cuz. And nobody can decide that but you. Sure, we all grew up with Coop, are good friends with the Rileys...but at the end of the day, marriage is a big step. You can't choose someone based on familial relations or their pedigree. Many people marry for things other than love, but that's not how we roll. I'm sorry to see you hurting, Bianca, but better now than later."

Alexis looked adoringly at her husband and then at Bianca. "I agree."

Toussaint looked at his watch. "Baby, I'm going to meet Jeff at the club, knock back a couple. I'll leave you ladies to chit chat." He leaned down and kissed his wife.

"Okay, baby."

Toussaint walked over to Bianca and gave her a hug. "It'll be all right, Bianca."

Bianca hugged her cousin. "I hope so."

Alexis waited until Toussaint had left. Then she turned to look Bianca squarely in the eye. "So?"

"So, what?"

"So since you're throwing caution to the wind, are you

now going to go after what you truly want: the man you left in Paris, the one who has your heart?"

It wasn't often that Xavier stood up to his father, but now was one of those times. "I can't tell you how long I'll be gone, because I don't know!"

"And the business is supposed to look after itself while you're gone."

Xavier took a deep breath to try and control his escalating temper. "Pierre has agreed to handle everything until I get back."

"It is not Pierre's responsibility, but yours!" Xavier's father bellowed. Edouard Marquis did nothing to hide his ire from his son.

Xavier realized that seeking understanding was a waste of time. He'd gone round and round pleading his case for the past three weeks. "Father, it is done. I am going. I'll be back as soon as I can."

"What is so important over in America?" Edouard scowled as he watched his son's retreating back. "Or should I say who?" Xavier kept walking. "Fine, go ahead and sow more wild oats. But remember, your wife has already been chosen."

Xavier whirled around. "I did not choose her."

"But you will marry her...or else."

"Or else what?"

"Or else say good-bye to the fortune that awaits you."

Blazing blue eyes stared into determined brown ones. It was one of the few physical attributes father and son did not share. But the rest—tall, dark, handsome, strong-willed—had all been passed down in the genes.

Xavier straightened broad shoulders, the cleft clearly evident in his defiantly raised chin. "So be it then," he said at last. "Good-bye, Father."

23

Since the breakup, Bianca had buried herself in work. But since the phone call, she'd been unable to focus. The call had come from her dad. A meeting had been called for ten o'clock. When she'd asked what it was pertaining to, he'd simply said, "LA." *Has a decision been made? Is this why Jefferson was so happy when I saw him in the break room this morning? But no, Ace loved the tapas concept, and so did Toussaint. That West Coast job is mine! Isn't it?*

Bianca pushed back from her desk and walked to the window. The day was crisp, the sun high and bright. She took in the beauty of the skyline and the cumulous clouds above the tall buildings. As often happened when her mind wandered away from work for even a moment, thoughts of Cooper filled her mind. *I'm so sorry that I hurt you, Cooper. Are you okay?* There'd been complete silence from Cooper since Bianca had lowered the boom on their relationship Thanksgiving night—exactly one week ago, when she'd gotten up from the barstool, hailed a taxi, and ridden out of his life.

The ringing office phone shook Bianca from her reverie. It was the distinctive ring announcing an outside call. *Cooper perhaps?* Bianca checked her watch: 9:40. She looked at the caller ID and breathed a sigh of relief. "Hey, Lex."

"Hey, girl. You got a minute?"

"Yes, but not much more than that. We have a meeting at ten."

"No worries. I just thought about you and wanted to see how you were. I wanted to give you some space, but since I hadn't heard from you, just thought I'd check in."

"I appreciate it."

"So . . . how are you, Bianca?"

"Okay, I guess. Work keeps me busy."

"Have you heard from him?"

"No. But that doesn't mean he isn't talking about it. His mom called mine and is none too pleased at the retracting she'll have to do regarding the engagement. Mom offered to help, and I told Mom that whatever story they wanted to offer was fine, including saying that he was the one to end the engagement, not me. But they're upset, and I understand. So now, not only me and Cooper but our families are estranged." Both women were silent for a moment, thinking of the drama often surrounding family dynamics. "I plan to call Miss Evelyn at some point," Bianca continued, "and personally apologize for any embarrassment I've caused the family. There's just too much on my plate to deal with her right now. But soon . . ." Bianca checked the time on her computer screen. "Listen, Lex, I should go."

"I understand, but listen. Why don't you join Toussaint and me for dinner tonight. We're meeting at Aria's, seven o'clock."

"Thanks, Alexis. I just might do that."

Bianca gathered the papers on her desk and did one more check of her appearance. Today she wore a tailored, cream-colored suit with a rust-colored cashmere shell, a drop-pearl necklace, and matching earrings. A rather understated ensemble except for her shoes—cream and gold Jimmy Choo ankle boots—a nod to Bianca's adventurous side. Her hair was pulled back in a simple ponytail and secured with a bone-and-gold clasp. Makeup was minimal, highlighting her naturally smooth, caramel skin and defined bone structure. Bianca dabbed gloss on her lips, reached for her folder, strode confidently down the hall, and entered the conference room.

"Hey, y'all," Bianca greeted Toussaint and Jefferson, who appeared deep in conversation as she entered the room.

"Hey, sis."

Bianca walked to the side table, poured herself a glass of lemon water, and joined them at the conference table.

"What's crack-a-lackin', Cousin?"

Bianca took a sip of water. "You tell me."

"Looking forward to the weekend. Lexy and I are turning the third bedroom into a nursery."

"I thought y'all were looking for a house."

"That, too." Actually, Toussaint and Alexis were looking for properties in Atlanta and Los Angeles. If things went as Toussaint planned, he'd be spending quite a bit of time out West during the next five years.

Jefferson shifted in his seat, reaching for the vibrating phone in his pocket. He had a text message, and punched the envelope icon to open the screen.

Beautiful home just came on the market. In your desired area. Priced to sell. Call soonest, Vince.

Jefferson smiled. As soon as the decision for him to manage Taste of Soul West became official, he'd call back Vince and also have his assistant schedule a trip to Los Angeles. The schedule called for TOS West to open in March. He had staff to hire, menus to tweak, marketing and PR to coordinate, and a family to house. Jefferson planned to move as soon as possible. The end of the month would not be too soon.

Malcolm entered the room talking on his cell phone. He nodded to those at the table, then finished his conversation in a low tone. "Sure, baby. Tell her we'll be there." He silenced his ringer and joined the group. "How's everybody doing?"

"I'm good," Jefferson replied.

Toussaint nodded. "Hey, bro."

Malcolm eyed Bianca. "What about you, Bianca? Everything all right?"

"I'm okay, Malcolm, thanks." Of course he'd know about the breakup. Bianca imagined that Diane had called Candace shortly after hanging up with her daughter, and again after Evelyn called. From there it would have travelled down to the sons and over to the grandparents, cousins, and in-laws. It had been a week. Bianca was sure that everyone knew by now.

Malcolm turned to Toussaint. "Your wife wants Vickie and me to join y'all for dinner tonight. She said it's on you."

Toussaint raised his brow. "Did she now?" he asked, smiling.

"She invited me, too," Bianca replied. "And since it looks like I might work through lunch, I'm going to be hungry enough to order everything on the menu!"

Toussaint's retort was cut short by Adam and Ace entering the room, closing the door behind them.

"Good morning, everyone," Adam said.

"Morning," Ace added.

After a brief round of pleasantries, Adam got right down to business. "As y'all may have guessed, this meeting is about Taste of Soul West."

Ace continued. "Over the past few weeks, we've spoken to all of you individually, and, Jefferson and Bianca, we've pored over the proposals you provided. As a businessman, I'd be blessed to have either of you on my team, and as a father, well"—he paused, unexpectedly choking up—"I'm extremely proud."

Adam opened his leather portfolio and took out two sheets. "Jefferson, your idea to expand market awareness through event catering is solid. It's helped us expand our brand here in Atlanta and"—Adam looked down at Jefferson's outline—"especially with the focus on high-end events, Hollywood and the like, it could be economically beneficial as well." Adam picked up the second sheet and looked at Bianca. "Bianca, you have come up with an idea that is as intriguing as it is appealing. But it's quite a stretch from what people have come to know as the Taste of Soul brand. I admit that I wasn't previously familiar with this tapas concept and, while they were delicious, I'm not sure these bite-size appetizers and high-end drinks will be enough to sustain a business."

"It's sustaining businesses all over Europe," Bianca quickly countered.

"I didn't say it wasn't a good idea. I'm just saying I don't know if it is a good idea for us, for our brand, and our customers. However, I do believe your ideas of offering healthier versions of our traditional soul food dishes is spot on."

Jefferson adjusted himself in his seat. He'd toyed with the idea of lightening up the lard-rich menu, but in the end had decided to stay with tradition. His ideas of exchanging turkey for pork and olive oil for bacon fat never made it into his proposal.

Discussion continued, with everyone chiming in. Malcolm pointed out that Bianca's idea would appeal to clientele who wouldn't necessarily travel to a traditional Taste of Soul restaurant while Toussaint underscored the tried-and-true success of Jefferson's catering plan to heighten the restaurant's marketing profile. It was no secret to either Jefferson or Bianca that Toussaint liked the tapas idea. But he liked the idea of controlling what happened in Los Angeles even more and knew that he could better do that with Jefferson than he could with Bianca. That's what made his decision so hard.

After another twenty minutes of discussion, Ace called the vote. "I believe we've all put considerable thought into this matter, and whoever ends up managing the West Coast chains will work closely with Toussaint, who will work closely with us to make sure that the brand remains constant, even as we tweak certain aspects to appeal to that region's clientele. So with that said . . ." Adam took out six sheets of blank white paper and passed them around the room. "Everybody cast your vote."

Two minutes later, the pieces of paper were handed to Ace. They were his children, which was why Adam said he should be the one to make the announcement. Ace had agreed, even as he'd remained conflicted. Jefferson was his first-born, the likely choice for such expansion. Bianca was his baby girl, whom he wanted to protect forever. He knew how badly she wanted this position, to prove herself and, probably, to put some distance between her and her ex-fiancé as well. At the end of the day, this was about business and Ace had voted for the child he felt ready to deal with the business and with LA.

After opening up the last of the folded pieces of paper, Ace gathered them up and put the pile into his leather-bound notebook. He looked from Jefferson to Bianca, and around the room. "It is my pleasure to now announce the manager of Taste of Soul West. Congratulations goes to"—Ace nodded to the winner and gave a slight smile—"Bianca."

Bianca clasped her hands with glee and then, glancing at her brother, immediately curtailed her celebration. Having always viewed him as more of a country bumpkin than a city slicker, she'd been surprised at how much Jefferson wanted the job. She hoped that in time he would come to agree that the right choice had been made.

"Sorry, Jeff," she said, squeezing his forearm.

"It's all good," he said, without looking up.

After congratulations, the meeting was adjourned. Toussaint immediately requested a meeting with Bianca for the following Monday. Adam spoke to Jefferson about a new project in which he wanted his nephew's leadership and expertise. The project involved Taste of Soul's catering arm, incorporating some of the ideas from Jefferson's L.A. proposal and also moving up the timeline of his promotion to CFO. In the end, that is why Adam had cast his vote for Bianca. Jefferson's continued presence in Atlanta was critical to the company's bottom line. The group left the conference room, and Bianca immediately returned to her office, closed the door, and danced a jig across the room. *I did it! I got the job! I'm moving to the West Coast.* Without thinking, she raced across the room and reached for the phone. "Just wait until Coop—" Bianca caught herself and placed the phone back on the receiver. She was probably the last person Cooper wanted to talk to. Bianca had been so caught up in avoiding marriage that she'd forgotten that, along with being lovers, she and Cooper used to be great friends. He was a good sounding board, a great listener, and always provided sound advice. Bianca was surprised to realize that she missed him. *Did I make a mistake? Was I so busy looking at the trees that I missed the forest?* Maybe she'd been wrong. Maybe marriage wasn't all about that "swing from the chandeliers" kind of love. Maybe it was about having someone to call and share good news. Perhaps it was even about not having to move cross country alone, but with someone you'd known since childhood, someone you trusted, by your side. Last week Bianca had been certain of what she wanted. Right now, words from her grandmother Marietta wafted into her thoughts: *Be careful what you pray for . . . you just might get it.*

Jefferson walked into his office and gently closed the door. He sighed, took off his suit jacket, and flung it on the loveseat. Loosening his tie, he walked to the window, stared without seeing the beautiful December day. This morning his life was all planned out. One meeting and six votes had thrown all of his puzzle pieces up in the air.

Jefferson's outside line rang. His look was resigned as he answered the call. "Yeah, baby."

"Oh, no. You don't sound happy."

"Bianca got the job."

Silence.

"I know, baby, I'm sad, too."

"Does that mean we won't be together?"

Jefferson's heart clenched at the tears he heard in Keisha's voice. His fist clenched, too. When it came to the business, there was very little that Jefferson had requested. For the most part, he was satisfied letting the more competitive Livingstons grab at the brass rings. He'd carved his niche in finance, laid low, played it cool. Managing the West Coast business was all he'd ever asked for. *And I didn't get it. But I'll be damned if I lose twice.* He began flipping through his electronic rolodex.

"Pookie, you there?"

"Yes, baby."

"Did you hear what I asked you?"

"Yes, I heard, and yes, we are going to be together."

There was a pause, and Keisha's voice dropped even lower. "But . . . how?"

"Let me worry about that. You just start packing."

"Are we going on vacation?"

"No," Jefferson said. "You and your boys are coming to me. You're moving to Atlanta."

Silence.

"Baby, did you hear me?"

"Uh, yeah, I heard."

"And you're not happy because . . ."

"I'm happy, but . . ."

Jefferson sat up. "But what?"

"It's . . . nothing." Keisha painted a smile on her voice. "You just shocked me, that's all. And then there's your family . . ."

"Let me handle my family."

Jefferson was contemplative as he hung up the phone. He hoped that his family would accept Keisha but no matter their reaction, his decision was made. Keisha was getting ready to be a part of the Livingston life. The chips would have to fall where they might. Jefferson felt better already.

24

"We made the right choice, Twin," Adam said, placing two cubes of ice into a tumbler and adding a splash of cognac.

"It doesn't stop the fact that I hate to see baby girl move so far away. Paris was bad enough, but I knew that was temporary. I was really hoping she and Coop could make a go of things... that she'd settle down right here." Ace reached for his own glass, draining his soda in one long gulp.

Adam returned to the chair in his home study, slapping his twin's shoulder as he passed him. "It'll be all right," he reassured.

"That's what Diane keeps saying," Ace replied. "Of course, she's trying to convince herself of that fact."

"Ha! She's trying to drown her sorrows in shopping, too. Candace has been bringing in shopping bags all week and hiding them in the guest room that became a closet. Like I don't look at the charge card bills."

Ace shook his head. "Women."

The doorbell chimed. Adam looked at his watch. "That Sterling is as prompt as they come."

"Consummate professional for sure."

Moments later, Sterling joined Adam and Ace in the study.

The small talk was short and sweet. Sterling got right to the point. "I have a few interesting developments for you."

"So that fool had the nerve to take more money from the account?"

"No, we actually shut that down by taking most of the money out. Scared him away. It's okay though. I was able to track down those two larger withdrawals from two months ago. One went through a company called Wholesale Foods in North Carolina, another was made out to a place called Organic Meat & Poultry in New Orleans."

"Did you visit those establishments?" Ace asked.

Sterling nodded. "Bogus, as I figured. The addresses were mailbox businesses. Whoever is stealing the money obviously has somebody who can launder these checks through their legitimate business, probably pocket a percentage for their troubles, and give the rest to . . . whoever's behind this."

Adam and Ace looked at each other. The more they'd discussed it, the more they were convinced that Quintin Bright was the man behind the mischief. Both men were champing at the bit to nab his ass. And since Quintin shot his brother, Ace wouldn't mind a little bonding time with the brothah before he went behind bars: his fists bonding with a few choice body parts.

"Does any of this tie in with Quintin?" Adam asked.

Again, Sterling nodded. "Quintin was born in North Carolina, but spent part of his childhood being raised by a grandmother in New Orleans. A couple people ID'd him as having been there recently, but clammed up when I started digging too deep. My guess is he's been throwing a little money around, buying silence."

Ace snorted. "Will throwing some more money around buy information?"

Sterling smiled, his teeth straight, white, perfect for a toothpaste or whitening commercial. "Patience, gentlemen. We've got our fish. We're going to reel him in nice and slow like. He's gotten away once. I don't intend for it to happen again."

Getting away is exactly what was on Quintin's mind, and Keisha's sudden development of a conscience wasn't sitting too well with him. "Look, Keisha, you're in this just as deep as I am. You busted into his computer, stole the info, gave it to me, and spent some of the money. That makes you an accessory to this shit. So don't sit there telling me what you won't do, and how all of a sudden you're so in love with him instead of his money."

Keisha fought back tears as she tried to make her brother hear reason. "That's just it, Q. I did get into this for the money. But things have changed."

"Please, I don't even want to hear it. Wasn't for me, you wouldn't even have met his ass. I'm the one who scoped out his habits, bought the ticket for you to fly to Atlanta, set you up to be at the gallery where I knew he'd come and hang out with that dyke-looking friend of his . . . all of that." Q scowled, remembering the blunt rejection he'd received when trying to push up on the statuesque artiste. Few women turned down Q's nine inches, so her being a lesbian was the only logical conclusion he could draw.

Keisha cried openly now. "Q, I'm in love with Jefferson. And he loves me!" She'd meant to keep her move to Atlanta a secret from her brother, but now she used it as a means to hopefully make him see reason. She walked over and sat next to him on the couch, placed a hand on his arm, and looked at him with pleading eyes. "Q, Jeff is moving me and the boys to Atlanta. He's giving us a whole new life, giving me a chance I never ever thought I'd get. I helped you get a lot of money, Q."

"You got your share."

"And now," Keisha continued, ignoring his last comment, "please, let me have this chance at a new life."

Q leaned back on the couch, crossed his arms, and looked at his sister. "You really love him, huh?"

Keisha nodded.

"You're really going to get all the way in bed with those traitorous, treacherous Livingston muthafuckas . . . even though they've got a bounty on my head, even though one wrong move and my ass gets sent to jail for a long time, maybe even for life."

"That's because you shot somebody, Quintin! That shit ain't my fault . . . it's yours!"

"Still, you're betraying your blood to sleep with the enemy."

"And you're threatening to betray me for money. What's the difference?"

"The difference"—Q's voice was low and menacing, his look matching—"is that I am not to be fucked with, sister. I shot one Livingston, I'll shoot another."

Keisha's eyes widened.

"That's right. If you want to have that 'happily ever after' with your boy, you'll make this last withdrawal." It was so quiet, you could hear a pin drop. "Do you hear me, Keisha?"

Keisha nodded.

"And you'll do it, right?"

She nodded once, and then again, as a lone tear rolled down her cheek.

25

Candace and Diane sat in Diane's living room, their eyes glued to the TV screen. "Girl, is that my son?" Candace asked, her eyes shining with admiration.

"You have to admit it, the cameras love Toussaint."

"And according to his fan mail, so do the ladies."

"That's probably why the producers decided to make Alexis a part of the Christmas show, so the viewers can see that not only is Toussaint married, but that he has a baby on the way."

The ladies continued to watch as Toussaint and Chef, the main culinary expert for the Taste of Soul chain, delighted a thrilled viewer by preparing oven-fried chicken, barbequed beans, and crispy, Cajun cole slaw in her home kitchen. Toussaint's show hadn't been on a year, yet his ratings often compared to those of the Neelys, Guy Fieri, and Bobby Flay. The men bantered back and forth while making sure that the viewer fully participated in the meal's preparation. As the segment wrapped, the blue eyes of the mother of two from Cleveland, Ohio, sparkled. "These are the best beans I've ever eaten," she exclaimed.

"And you could be next," Toussaint said into the camera, with a wink. "Keep those cards coming, because you never know when we'll be in your neighborhood, delivering a little ... taste of soul."

The two women continued to watch as the network went to commercial. "Watching them prepare that food has gotten me hungry. What you got in there, Di?"

"I wish I had some of that chicken, to tell you the truth! But you'll have to settle for turkey salad. I made it yesterday."

"Don't tell me this is leftover from Thanksgiving."

"Technically, yes. I'd purchased some legs to add to the dressing, but we ended up using the bird that Mama bought. They were in the freezer, and I decided to use them before they got too old."

"Sounds good."

Candace followed Diane into the kitchen. Diane reached into the refrigerator and pulled out the container of turkey and another of dirty rice. "You want a bottle of sparkling water?" she asked Candace.

"Sure."

Diane reached for a bag of whole grain rolls, eyeing her sister-in-law as she did so. "You're looking good, Can ... a little glow to your face and pep in your step. Have you started working out again?"

"I thought I told you about the in-home gym Adam and I ordered. We've started working out in the evenings ... together."

Both women were silent a moment, Candace remembering what had happened the last time she started working out and Diane understanding why Adam had purchased an in-home gym.

"So ... how are things?"

Candace took a swallow of water. "Better. I've forced myself to stop thinking about Q. And I got a little help ... from Adam."

"You told him?" Diane had suggested this very thing, but later had questioned whether that had been good advice.

Candace shook her head. "I couldn't, Diane. Adam is very sensitive when it comes to Q, and understandably so. And I should kick my own ass for daring to fantasize about the man who shot my husband!"

Diane set a plate of a turkey sandwich, heated dirty rice, and chips in front of Candace and took a seat at the island across from her. "That is pretty crazy, Can." The women paused, took a few bites of food. "So how did Adam help?"

Candace smiled, and Diane could have sworn a bit of red began creeping up her neck. "We were watching cable one night and saw an infomercial."

"About..."

"Sex toys."

Diane stopped in mid-chew. "What?"

Candace giggled. "Yes, girl. We ordered almost everything we saw and got the shipment two weeks ago."

"I can't believe your conservative husband went along with this."

"Not without a little prodding, no pun intended."

"So the toys have added some sparks to the bedroom?"

Candace nodded. "That and a little pill called Testora. And before you ask, yes, it is a sexual stimulant, a male enhancer. Well, it's enhancing all right. Adam is making it do what it do like never before."

"I'm happy for you, Candace."

"Yeah, me, too. I love Adam very much and can't see living my life without him. I think both of us are trying very hard, determined to make our marriage work. What about you and Ace? Amazing as always?"

"We're lucky women, Candace. Men like Ace and Adam don't come along every day."

"I admit that Adam is amazing. But it seems that bedroom skills is the one thing that these twins don't have in common. I remember you telling me years ago about Ace's prowess, and his size."

Diane shrugged. "You got me there, sistah. Maybe Ace took after Daddy Marcus while that part of Adam came from the Cole gene pool." Diane was referring to Marietta, who was a Cole before she became a Livingston.

"It don't matter. Because like you said, men like our husbands don't come along every day. That's why for the rest of my life, I'll be making it up to Adam for acting like a damn fool and being unfaithful."

26

Diane shifted her pelvis, allowing her legs to spread further, accommodating Ace's thick girth. No words were spoken as Ace lifted off her slightly and then slowly sank down into the comfort he'd felt for more than three decades. Slow. Steady. Breathing deeply. Hearts beating as one. Ace searched for Diane's mouth, scorching it with his tongue, mimicking the motion of his hips, pouring love in like water, and appreciation like a winter's breeze. Diane squeezed buttocks, their firm roundness belying the fifty-five years they'd been around. He plunged deeper, and a hand went to his smooth, bald head, her mouth slack with pleasure, his eyes scrunched from the concentrated effort that went into pleasing his woman, pleasing himself. Her moans started from way down deep, eased up to the back of her throat, and burst forth with the power of her climax. Ace's pace increased, as did his panting, until he, too, fell over into orgasmic ecstasy.

Ace rolled off of Diane, yet held her close. For a while, their faint yet labored breathing was the only sound heard in the room. Finally Ace leaned over and kissed Diane's cheek. "Was that good for you, baby?" he whispered.

Diane chuckled softly, sounding more like the seventeen-year-old she'd been when Ace first had her than the woman with two of his grown children, who'd been married since Parliament Funkadelic put one nation under a groove. She snuggled next to Ace, running her fingers over the familiar ridges of a chest lightly sprinkled with springy, graying hair. "Always." *And it's still good.* "You've been holding it down for almost thirty-five years."

"Damn! Has it been that long?"

"Longer. We've just been doing it legally for thirty-five, but you've been hitting it longer than that."

"Where'd the time go, baby?"

Diane shrugged. "It's flying."

"Jeff will be thirty-three this year, Bianca turns thirty. . . ."

"By the time we were their age we had a house, family, the business. . . ."

"Did Bianca surprise you, breaking up with Cooper?"

"Yes and no. Something has been going on with that girl since she went to Paris."

"You don't think she got sprung by some *voulez-vous coucher avec moi . . .*"

"*Ce soir,*" they ended together, laughing. Diane continued, singing, "Either that or some *gitchi gitchi ya ya da da.* Ha!"

"And what's up with Jefferson? When is the last time he brought a girl around?"

"It's been a minute," Diane responded. "Although he and Divine are close."

"You think they're close close?"

"Hard to tell. You know she was engaged for a while to that pro basketball player, and then rumors started flying that she was gay."

"As I recall, the rumor was that they both were."

"But then she attended last year's Black-and-White ball with Jon Abernathy—"

"A ho if there ever was one."

"Ace!"

"Just calling it like I see it, baby...." Ace suddenly sat straight up.

"What is it, baby?" Diane asked.

"You don't think my son is gay, do you?"

Diane laughed out loud. "The operative words in that sentence are 'your son.' No, Ace, Jefferson is not gay."

Ace relaxed against the headboard as he repositioned the sheet around him. "I don't think so either, but you start to wonder why a healthy, thirty-something male isn't spending more time with the ladies."

"Maybe he's just being discreet about where he's spending his time. We are his parents, Ace. It's not like he'd tell us everything."

"Or anything."

"Exactly. And remember a month or so ago, when he spent that weekend in Los Angeles. I don't think he was up there alone, do you?"

Ace relaxed more. "I guess you're right."

"Of course I'm right. I'm always right."

"On that note, it's time for me to go take a shower. Because you're getting ready to talk some sho-nuff shit right now." He flung off the sheet, purposely directing it over Diane's head.

"Forget you, man," Diane laughed, throwing off the sheet and coming up to grab Ace from behind. They danced into the shower singing their own, off-key rendition of Lady Marmalade.

27

Chardonnay looked up, surprised, as Bobby walked through the door. "What are you doing here?"

"Woman, I live here," Bobby answered, lugging two bags of groceries into the kitchen.

"Yeah, but it's New Year's Eve. Who'd you bribe to get the night off?"

Bobby came from the kitchen bearing a single rose. "Would you believe luck shines in my favor every once in a while."

Chardonnay took the rose, sniffed it. "What's this for?"

"Damn, woman, you ask too many questions. Why can't you just say 'thank you,' and tell me how much you appreciate my thinking about you?"

Chardonnay stood and wrapped her arms around Bobby's neck. She used to not be able to stand the sight of him, but she'd be a fool not to admit that Bobby Roosevelt Wilson was growing on her. "Thanks for the rose, baby."

Bobby grinned, squeezing her juicy behind. "You're welcome."

Bobby walked back into the kitchen. Chardonnay followed. "Dang, Bobby. I wish I'd known you were going to get off. I could have gotten somebody to watch the kids, and we could have gone to a party or something."

"I'm way ahead of you, Nay." He stopped putting away groceries and turned to hug his woman. "My sister is going to keep the kids."

"Your sister? The Bible-thumping holy roller who told me I was going to hell?"

"She didn't say that."

"She might as well have, turning her nose up at Cognac's tattoo and asking me if Tangeray had a dress to wear to church. The only one she halfway likes is Bicardi, and that's because he's yours."

"His name is Bobby. I told you not to be calling my son an alcoholic beverage," Bobby said.

"You didn't have a problem calling out this alcoholic drink when I was turning you out last night."

Bobby smirked. "True dat."

"His name is Bobby Bicardi, and I can call my son what I damn well please!"

"Whatever, white wine."

"I don't want my kids around somebody like her, thinking she's better than everybody. Who knows what she'll tell my kids."

"Sharon is good people, baby . . . she means well. They have a big celebration at their church, with fun activities for the kids. She said that they can spend the night. Come on," Bobby continued when Chardonnay remained silent. "It'll be our first time out since the baby . . . come on."

"Okay. They can go, but I'm telling Cognac to report back everything she says, so if sistah-girl knows what's good for her, she better not say a damn thing about my kids!"

Two hours later, a dressed-up Bobby Wilson and Chardonnay Johnson sat looking a bit out of place but relatively happy at an upscale Italian restaurant, where Bobby brought Chardonnay because he wanted to take her "someplace different." The waiter brought the menus. After scanning them for several moments, Bobby spoke up. "I'm ordering for us."

This brought an immediate scowl to Chardonnay's face. "Why?"

"Because you'll order either spaghetti or lasagna, and I want us to try different things."

"How do you know what I'll order?"

"Okay, Nay, what were you going to order."

Chardonnay started laughing. "The spaghetti."

"See what I mean, fool?" Bobby was thoroughly enjoying himself. "I got this." When the waiter came, Bobby was in his culinary element, ordering things that he himself had never tried but with which he was familiar from his time spent with Chef. He started them out with antipastos of roasted veal loin with celery salad and air-dried beef with arugula and black olive vinaigrette. To appease Chardonnay's desire for something familiar, Bobby ordered Caesar salads, then penne with Italian sausage and a gorgonzola cream sauce, and grilled lamb chops served with a fresh mint pesto as their main courses.

The sommelier came with his wine suggestions, and after pouring their first glass, Bobby made a toast. "To a night of doing things differently."

"I don't know about all that," Chardonnay said as she clinked glasses. The truth was, she was beginning to relax and enjoy herself, something that she'd rarely allowed herself in the twenty-eight years she'd been on the planet. Life for her hadn't been easy, and a caustic, tough exterior had been her means of preservation. Her best friend, Zoe, had always told her that Bobby was a good man. She was right. Bobby was a very good man, worker, and father. *Girl, for tonight, you've got no kids and no worries. So just relax and let this man wine and dine you.* Chardonnay took another deep sip of the wine, sat back and decided to enjoy herself.

She and Bobby enjoyed small talk, feasting on their appetizers, laughing and basking in the joy of simply being together. And then she saw him, walking across the room, heading in her direction. A short, attractive woman was by his side. "Oh, hell."

Bobby followed Chardonnay's eyes to the handsome, sharply dressed man heading their way. *Damn. I knew I shouldn't have told him my plans for tonight.* While Bobby had stopped being intimate with Jon, the congressman was still a regular at Taste of Soul, and Bobby had tried to remain friendly.

"Hello, Bobby, Chardonnay. Fancy meeting you two here." Jon Abernathy shook Bobby's hand, then took Chardonnay's and brought it to his lips. She tried hard not to roll her eyes and regurgitate her valtellinese.

"Hi," Chardonnay said, not trying to hide her chagrin. She knew good and well that it was not a coincidence that the good congressman was bringing his new year in at this restaurant. For some reason, she'd never liked this man, always traded stations when he came into the restaurant. He was a handsome man, nice enough . . . but there was just something about him.

"Hey, Jon," Bobby said, choosing to remain cordial. "Happy New Year, man."

"Happy New Year to you, too. Bobby, Chardonnay, this is my friend Dawn. Dawn, this is the chef I told you about, the one we're trying to lure away from Taste of Soul." After introductory pleasantries, Jon continued. "Would you two care to join us? I have two bottles of premier bubbly on ice, enough to share." A look passed between Jon and Bobby. Dawn missed it. Chardonnay didn't.

"No, thanks, man. This is a special evening for me and my woman." Bobby looked lovingly and proudly at Chardonnay. "Tonight is for just the two of us."

"You sure? We can get a corner—"

"Honey," Dawn interrupted. "I think these two lovebirds want to be alone."

A frown flitted across Jon's face before he pasted on a Colgate smile. "By all means, then," he said, kissing Chardonnay's hand and giving Bobby a soul brother's handshake. "Enjoy your evening."

"Fancy meeting you two here," Chardonnay mimicked as soon as Jon and his date were out of earshot. "Why did you tell him we'd be here?"

"Baby, it just slipped out in conversation when he ate at the restaurant earlier this week. How'd I know he'd show up?"

"He's chasing you like a bitch in heat." Chardonnay's eyes narrowed. "If I didn't know better I'd . . ."

Bobby's eyes narrowed as well. "You'd what?"

"I'd say there's a little down-low action going on."

"With who?" Bobby demanded. He'd worked hard to keep his financially profitable liaison with Jon Abernathy under wraps, and planned for what they'd shared to stay that way. Even now, as he entertained the idea of sexing yet another brother, he intended for this lifestyle to continue as it had always had . . . down low.

Chardonnay knew Bobby's bark was worse than his bite, so that's not why she backed down. She did so because it was New Year's Eve, she was loving the food, feeling the wine, and not wanting Jon Abernathy's gay-looking ass to mess up her evening. So she put on a smile, rubbed Bobby's leg with her stocking-clad foot, and changed the subject. But inside, the issue was far from over. *Mama's gonna find out what needs to be found out . . . trust and believe.*

By the time dessert arrived, Jon's interruption had been all but forgotten. Chardonnay's eyes lit up at the chocolate confection placed before her: a chocolate lava cake topped with freshly made chocolate chip gelato. "Damn, this almost tastes better than sex," Chardonnay said, after experiencing a mouthful of the gooey delight, the heat from the melted chocolate lava blending deliciously with the cool Italian ice cream.

"Umm, that's a thought," Bobby said, enjoying his white chocolate tiramisu laced with a nutty liqueur. "Maybe we can order one of those to go . . . for later." The look Bobby gave

Chardonnay left no doubt as to what he'd do with the chocolate once he got home.

"Oh, hell." The clank of Chardonnay's fork as it hit the plate shattered the romantic ambiance.

"What?" Bobby asked.

"There's something in my dessert. It's probably a roach. Where's the waiter?" Chardonnay demanded, her voice gaining volume with each word. "I'm getting ready to own this mutha—"

"Baby!" Bobby reached over and grabbed Chardonnay's hand. "Baby," he repeated, a little softer this time. "Just calm down."

"But Bobby, there's something in my food! Something hard and . . . crunchy."

"How do you know it's crunchy?"

"It feels crunchy, dammit! It ain't no cake my fork just touched, and it damn sure ain't no ice cream. Waiter!"

You can take a sistah out of the ghetto, but . . . "Chardonnay, shut the hell up," Bobby hissed. "You got everybody in this place looking at us."

Chardonnay looked around and indeed about fifty pairs of eyes were beamed in their direction. Never having been one to shy away from an audience, a feeling-no-pain Chardonnay stood and made an announcement: "You might want to double-check what you put in your mouth . . . 'cause I just found something in my food! I mean, what you put in your mouth is your business, but . . ." Chardonnay felt woozy and sat down. "I'm just sayin' . . ."

"Sir, madam, what is going on?" The manager rushed over to the table, followed by the chef.

"Something's in my food!" Chardonnay cried. "And I'm going straight to the Internet with this story if y'all don't show me the money!"

The manager turned to the crowd. "Please, we apologize for the disturbance. Please continue your meals." He sent the chef back to the kitchen and then turned back to Chardonnay. "What did you find in your dessert, madam?"

Chardonnay gestured toward the plate. "I don't even want to know what it is. But it's right there," she said, pointing to the middle of the plate. "Something hard and crunchy. I think it's a roach."

The manager reached for Chardonnay's fork. "May I?"

"Hell, yeah. I'm not eating any more. In fact, I'm feeling pretty sick right now."

Bobby shook his head but said nothing as both he and Chardonnay watched the manager carefully pick a hard, round object from the middle of her dessert. "Ah, I think I've found the foreign object," he said, his voice subdued. He reached inside his suit coat, pulled out a handkerchief, and, after wiping off the object, placed it on the table. "Madam . . . your roach."

Chardonnay gasped. In front of her sat a one-carat, marquise-cut diamond ring. She cast wide eyes on Bobby, but before she could speak he rose from the table, reached for the ring, and got down on one knee in front of her.

"Baby, you know I love your crazy ass. So much so, that I want you to keep me laughing for the rest of my life. Marry me, Chardonnay, and make me the happiest man in Atlanta." Bobby took a shocked Chardonnay's hand and gently placed the ring on her finger.

"It's not a roach," she whispered.

"No, it's not." Bobby replied. "So . . . you gonna leave me hanging or what?"

"What? Oh, yeah. Yes! Yes, of course I'll marry you, fool!" Chardonnay jumped up from the table and pulled Bobby into her arms. "It wasn't a roach, y'all," she yelled to the onlookers. "It was a ring! I'm getting married!"

The rest of the diners joined in the celebration, cheering on the moment when Chardonnay became engaged. All, that is . . . except one.

28

In the private dining room of the Livingston Corporation, Toussaint, Alexis, Malcolm, and his wife, Victoria, enjoyed a scrumptious, seven-course meal prepared by Chef. Having both endured brutally busy schedules all year with little time to socialize, these two brothers were enjoying the laid-back evening, and Alexis relished better getting to know her sister-in-law.

"I'd love to know how you do it," Alexis said, taking a break from her expertly prepared rack of lamb to enjoy a sip of sparkling grape juice. "Balancing home and family. You have five children, and I'm doubting whether I can handle one!"

"It gets easier with practice," Victoria responded. "And the family is a lot of help. Do you plan on hiring a nanny?"

Alexis glanced at Toussaint before responding, and was glad to see he was deep in conversation with Malcolm. "Toussaint wants me to, but I kinda want to handle things on my own. At least for the first few months."

Victoria looked at Toussaint and then at Alexis. "Are you getting ready to have two babies on your hands?"

Alexis smiled. "Maybe."

"I caught that look," Toussaint said, reaching over and

clasping Alexis's hand. "What y'all over there saying about me?"

"We were just discussing what a wonderful father you'd be, and how excited we are to bring our little boy into the world."

"You mean daughter."

Malcolm looked up. "Y'all don't know what you're having yet?"

Alexis shook her head. "We want it to be a surprise."

Malcolm shook his head. "Bro, your life is getting ready to be one big surprise after another." The table quieted momentarily, each remembering Malcolm's surprise number five from one year ago—a daughter named Victory. Said surprise now had her father wrapped around her finger, and while Malcolm had been dead set against any more children, he now could not imagine life without her. "But it's all good, man," he continued, thoughts of Victory and his other children bringing light to his eyes. "Children are a blessing."

He leaned over and kissed Victoria, who then responded, "Hard work, but blessings nonetheless."

Chef came to remove their dinner plates. The rack of lamb set atop a carrot and cauliflower puree had been fall-off-the-bone tender, and the wine he'd paired with the meat perfection. The two couples offered praises, and Chef, in his characteristic, humble personality, simply smiled and said thanks. After taking their dessert choices—deep-dish peach cobbler for the ladies and Grand Marnier–glazed pound cake for the men—Toussaint reached for his glass. "That brothah is earning his tip tonight!"

"You can say that again," Victoria said. "You'd think that one couldn't improve upon something as classic as lamb, but the way he marinated it, and then basted it in a butter gravy? Goodness, gracious of life!"

"Jeff is going to be mad he missed out on this," Toussaint said.

"Where'd you say Jeff was again? Bianca hanging out with

the folks makes sense. She's leaving town next week. But I was sure Cuz would fall in here with something hot to trot, impressing and everything. When it comes to his love life, that boy's too quiet. Who's he digging, Toussaint? Do you know?"

Toussaint shook his head. "I thought that maybe he and Divine were taking things to another level. You know they've been friends for years."

"Well, wherever he is," Victoria said, "I hope he's having as good a time as we are. This was a great idea, Malcolm, us bringing in the new year together."

"Yeah, it's nothing like the throw-down celebrations we used to do, that took us two days to recover from, but this nice, quiet night feels right, marks the beginning of a new era in our lives." Toussaint winked at Alexis.

Alexis picked up her sparkling drink. "To a new year, and a new lifestyle."

The others raised their glasses. "Cheers."

Another toast was happening on the other side of town. "I still can't believe it, Pookie. All of this for me?" Keisha asked, as she accepted the crystal flute filled with premium champagne.

Jefferson brushed Keisha's lips with his own. "All for you."

Keisha dared not pinch herself. If this was a dream, she didn't want it to end. She looked at her knight in shining armor standing across from her, looking ruggedly handsome in his signature pullover and casual slacks. The man who'd swooped in and rescued her and her boys from the hood, from staples of canned tuna and ramen noodles. And now here she stood in a gorgeous, three-bedroom townhome with fireplaces and vaulted ceilings, a two-car garage, and fenced-in backyard. With the type of man she'd dared not even dream about just six short months ago.

Keisha finished scanning the classily furnished abode, her eyes coming to rest on Jefferson. He was staring at her, his expression unreadable even as it seemed to smolder from within.

She suddenly felt shy and hoped her sparkly black mini and jeweled Manolo Blahniks were deserving of Jefferson's steady gaze. "What?" she murmured.

"What?" Jefferson's mouth was the only part of him that moved.

"The way you're looking at me. What's wrong?"

A smile, slow and lazy. "Nothing, baby. Everything is right. You came to me and made my world right again."

"Oh, Pookie." Keisha's eyes shone with unshed tears. "So . . . what should we toast to?"

"To you, what else?"

"No, baby. To us."

"Yes . . . to us.

Upstairs in the master suite, Keisha's phone, which she'd silenced, rang for the umpteenth time. This time, the caller left a message: *Don't worry about returning my calls. I know your ass is down there. Which means that I should be seeing some money in my account within forty-eight hours. If I don't . . . your boy is getting ready to find out all about the woman he's moved into his house. You know I can blow up your world with a phone call, girl. Don't mess with me, Keisha. I'ma text you the account number to make the drop. Forty-eight hours. That's how much time you got. Oh, and happy mutha-fuckin' new year.*

29

"I wasn't trying to front you, Q. This is the first chance I've had to call." Keisha had been rudely awakened from both her sleep and her dreamlike lifestyle with a phone call from her brother. It was the second of January, just after nine a.m., and Keisha had just returned to bed after eating a hearty breakfast that Jefferson had prepared, and seeing her boys off to school. Keisha wasn't used to having a man around, had forgotten how much work they could be. She loved her new life, but she'd also looked forward to a couple hours of uninterrupted sleep. And now this. "Q, please, just give me a little more time. I just got here!"

"Time is what I ain't got, little sis. I've been feeling funny ever since they tapped that account and took out almost all the money. It's just a matter of time before somebody starts adding. I want my stuff on lock, just in case they put one and one together . . . and get two."

"But how obvious is that going to look?" Keisha countered, her voice rising in agitation. "I move in, money goes missing. You think he's not going to add that up?"

"Not if you're creative. Tell him you need the money for something, to fix the house or buy a car. Man like that has so much money that it shouldn't be nothing to cop a couple hundred thou if you working it right."

"Maybe later, but not right now, Q! He spent a lot of money bringing us down here, not to mention buying the house, clothes for the boys, everything. We haven't been here a week. Let me get situated first and—"

"Oh, so that's how it is. It's all about you now."

"Q, you know that's not true."

"Oh, ain't it? Because that's all I hear you talking about. What that fool has done for you, how you need to get situated, and how you just need a little more time. What about when I needed stuff and let it go so I could take care of you. Huh, little sis? Are we having selective memory now?"

Keisha took a breath deep enough to hopefully calm them both. "Q," she said, her voice lowered. "I can never repay you for what you did for me as a child. How you protected me, provided for me, for all of us. I'll never forget that...."

"Of course you won't. And I bet you won't forget your family either."

"No," Keisha whispered, as she took a seat on the plush, velvet chaise in her master suite. "You know I won't."

"So why do I have to beg, Keisha? Why do I have to beg you to help me save my life?" Q's voice was soft, whiny, the way he used to sound when he was ten years old and Keisha was seven.

"Hey, Q, remember that time when we went to the beach with Uncle James? Had that picnic with Mama and Dee and the neighbor kids?"

Q chuckled. "I'll never forget that shit. Dude went to KFCs, brought hella fried chicken and cole slaw—"

"And beans..."

"First time to the ocean. I never saw something so beautiful."

"I was scared."

"You were at first. Until I helped you into the water..."

"Forced me in!"

"Ha! End justified the means, didn't it?"

The siblings retreated into themselves, remembering happier times.

"I wonder whatever happened to James?" Keisha said, after a pause.

"Heard he died, car accident."

"That's too bad. He was a good man."

"They all were; Mama ran them away."

Keisha sighed. "I worry about her, Q. She's trifling and scandalous and a straight-up alcoholic . . . but she's my mama."

"Don't worry about that. I've been handling her business ever since I got the hookup: rent, utilities, and what not."

This statement gave Keisha pause. In this moment she realized that Juanita Mason's welfare had never been much of Keisha's concern. All this time she thought her mother had survived the way she always had: by relying on the men she could lure into her home and bed. But it had been Q doing what he always did—take care of everybody. As great as Jefferson was to her, Keisha had no idea where she'd be without her big brother.

"I'll do it tomorrow."

"Huh?" Q was still checking out the better days on memory lane and barely heard his sister.

"Jefferson will be gone all day tomorrow, and he's having dinner with his parents."

"Ooh, and little sis ain't invited?"

"Don't, Q. Jeff loves me. We have every intention of going public when the time is right."

"Don't mind me, sis. Their uppity asses is playing in my favor right now. But don't get too comfortable, Keisha. Look out for number one. They play with our kind for a little while, but not for keeps. I'm speaking from experience."

"Jefferson loves me, Q. We might even get married."

"He said that?" Keisha didn't answer. "Don't get caught up in a pipe dream."

"Q, I've got to go. Jefferson's calling."

"That's cool, but Keisha?"

"Huh?"

"Do it tonight."

Keisha was nervous for the rest of the day, while she picked up the children and then picked up dinner at a local Thai restaurant. Even though they were on the other side of town, and even though she didn't know what they looked like and they didn't know her, Keisha still had this inexplicable fear that somehow she'd be found out by the Livingstons. It's the reason she hadn't yet tasted Taste of Soul, figuring that somehow someone would know that the food being ordered was for the woman Jeff was hiding.

When they arrived home, Keisha let the boys play in the backyard for a couple hours. Then she fed them, bathed them, and prepared them for bed. It was early, but if things were going to be easy tonight, the atmosphere would have to be just right. She'd spoken again with Jefferson and expected him home around seven. Looking at her watch, she saw that it was six-thirty. *I don't have much time.* Keisha showered quickly, put on a sexy, satin mini and matching heels. She brushed her hair until it was shining and then let it hang loose, the way Jefferson liked it. She put on the diamond teardrops he'd given her for Christmas, sprayed on his favorite perfume, and had just finished reheating the Thai food when he walked in the door.

That night Jefferson, in a highly uncharacteristic move and at Keisha's urging, had two shots of tequila and wine with dinner. She screwed him fast and furious. He came and passed out.

Keisha found the information she was looking for. The next day, Q got what he was looking for.

30

"Why did I ever say I wanted to move here? What was I thinking to say I wanted to head up the West Coast division?" Bianca chided herself as she exited from the 405 and eased onto the 90, heading to Taste of Soul, West Coast style. She and her assistant had been in town less than a week, and to say she was overwhelmed would be a gross understatement. There were plumbing problems in her "newly refurbished" condo, the "perfect" assistant manager she thought she'd found had lied on his application, the owner of the building that she wanted for TOSTS had raised his asking price by 25 percent, and premenstrual hormone fluctuations had Bianca horny as hell! "And I actually scratched, fought, and begged to get this position? I actually asked for this misery?" *I must have been out of my ever-loving mind!*

The cell phone wired through her radio rang. "Hey, Toussaint," she said after pushing the speaker button.

"Hi, Bianca. How's it going over there?"

"Out of control." A heavy sigh accompanied Bianca's truthful statement.

Toussaint chuckled. "I've been there. Opening a restaurant is one of the hardest jobs out there, and you're trying to do that *and* a tapas bar. That's insane, Bianca."

"It was much easier on paper," Bianca admitted. "But I'm now interviewing for a top-notch manager to handle the grind at TOSTS, once I get everything in place."

"Smart thinking. And remember, I'll fly out there as often as I can."

"With a baby on the way, that won't be much."

"I'm sure Malcolm will help pick up some slack, and Jefferson, too. We're all here for you, Bianca." Silence. "So talk to me, Cuz. What else is going on?"

Bianca was glad to share her concerns with Toussaint and to get his valuable advice. "I have three interviews this afternoon," she finished. "And I plan to meet with the realtor next week. I want that property on Sunset Boulevard, but only if I can get it at the price that was first quoted, or less."

"Hold your ground," Toussaint replied. "The economy has rebounded, but the real estate market in California is still struggling." Toussaint pulled up his electronic calendar. "I have a few free days next week. Would you like me to join you in that meeting?"

"I'd love to have you here, Toussaint. I think that after this month, things will calm down, but right now . . ."

"I know, it's a lot. You just have to remember to keep breathing and know that everything will work out exactly as it's supposed to."

"OMG, dude, that is definitely Alexis talking right there."

"Ha! I guess she is rubbing off on me, huh?"

"Y'all are rubbing off on each other."

"Okay, Cousin. I'll text my flight info once I get it."

"And I'll send you all of the info on the Sunset property."

"Okay, cool."

Bianca reached the restaurant and felt a surge of excitement as she pulled into the parking lot. Even with all the chaos and stress, Bianca's adrenaline flowed at the thought of what was to come, of how this and the other location would look in two short months. *You're right, Toussaint. I can do this!* Ten minutes later Bianca sat in her office, looking over résumés. She was cautiously optimistic about the application she was now holding—a chef who'd worked in various soul food restaurants for the past five years. What made this applicant stand out was that like her, he'd trained at Cordon Bleu. *Cordon Bleu. Paris.* Bianca sat back and allowed herself the rare luxury of not fighting the thoughts of Xavier that flooded her mind. *I miss you, Xavier.* It was the first time Bianca had admitted this truth, even in her own mind. One thought, and she was immediately transported back into strong arms, a hard body, a powerful tongue, and a long, thick. . . . Bianca forced away the thought that was causing pussy pulsations and refocused on the résumé. George Stevens. *Hum, wonder if he ate at many tapas bars, and how quickly he'll master those dishes. Or maybe he'll be a better assistant manager here, and then I can focus on TOSTS. Could that work?* "You'll get the questions answered soon enough," she muttered to herself and was soon buried in the next items on her agenda.

Two hours later, Bianca was finishing lunch in her office when her phone rang.

"Your one o'clock is here, Bianca," Crystal said brightly.

"Okay. Give me a few minutes."

After clearing the trash from her desk, Bianca walked into her private bathroom, where she brushed her teeth and quickly reapplied her lipstick. She was still getting used to the short haircut that she'd spontaneously decided to get following her breakup with Cooper. Given more time, she would have tried to tame some of the natural curls that, without the discipline of a hot iron or strong brush, had a mind of their own. But duty called, and she was preparing for an interview, not to walk the runway. Bianca reached her desk and called Crystal. "Send him in."

Reaching for his résumé, Bianca clicked on her computer and brought up the questions she'd prepared based on George Stevens's information. She looked to the right of her desk, ensuring that the folder on TOSTS was nearby. She planned to interview George generally on his cooking skills, but thought that if her hunch proved correct, he'd work out better at her baby: Taste of Soul Tapas Style.

"Hello," Bianca began, as George entered her office. "I'm Bianca Livingston."

"George Stevens," the man replied. He was short and robust, with a shock of blonde hair, twinkling blue eyes and a ready smile.

Bianca liked him right away. *But can he cook soul food?* "I see you've worked for several southern restaurants," she said, after a few more pleasantries had been exchanged. "How did this direction of your career come about?"

"My grandmother lives in Tennessee," he answered. "I grew up eating greens, neckbones, black-eyed peas and . . ." He stopped talking, as loud voices were heard just outside Bianca's office.

"I don't care who you are," Bianca heard Crystal yelling. "You can't go in there without an appointment!"

"Oh, really?" a male voice replied, his calm voice dropping even lower. Bianca couldn't hear the rest of his statement. What she had heard caused her stomach to flip-flop. An accent. An attitude. She could have sworn it sounded just like . . .

The office door swung open.

"Xavier!" Bianca cried.

"I already called security," Crystal panted, rushing into the room just seconds behind Xavier.

"Bianca." Xavier's eyes were filled with love as his quick, long strides ate up the distance between them. He pulled a shell-shocked Bianca from her chair. "Bianca." This whispered greeting was followed by Xavier crushing her to his chest and holding her tight. For a moment, Bianca was stunned into paralysis, her mind not keeping up with the rapidly unfolding events.

Two burly security guards rushing into her office snapped her out of her trance.

"Put your hands up and back away," the tall, African-American guard commanded.

"Do it now!" the slightly shorter, burly partner said.

"Wait," Bianca placed a hand on her chest, fighting for breath and clarity. *Is Xavier really here, in my office? How'd he find me?* Suddenly it was too much, and Bianca sank back into her chair. "Wait," she said again, lower this time. "Thanks, guys, but...I know this man. I can handle this."

The taller guard hesitated. "Are you sure you don't want us to stay around...make sure you're okay?"

"I'm fine," Bianca said, now looking from the guards to a perplexed Crystal. "Really, it's all right." Bianca turned to George. "George, please give us a moment. Have a seat outside. Crystal will be out there shortly." Bianca waited until George had left and the door was closed. "Crystal, this is Xavier Marquis, someone I met in Paris."

Crystal crossed her arms and scowled. "Well, he's someone I *just* met and he was rude, arrogant and totally disregarded the fact that this is a workplace!" Now that Crystal was calming down, she also realized he was quite attractive. But nobody pushed past her and interrupted her boss, no matter how fine he was. "I told him that you were conducting an interview and he couldn't come in here!"

"I'm sorry, Crystal," Xavier said sincerely before he turned back to Bianca. "I had to see you," he explained. "To wait another minute, another second, would have been too long."

Bianca took in Xavier's determined expression. "Crystal, please give my apologies to George and reschedule his interview for this time next week, if he's available. And...hold my calls." When her assistant seemed reluctant to leave her alone, Bianca added, "Thanks for looking out for me, girl but, I'll be fine."

Crystal took one last look at Bianca, and at Xavier, and then left the room.

Bianca waited until Crystal had closed the door. Then she

turned to Xavier feeling a rush of emotions as her heart pounded in her chest. Had he come because he loved her? Or was there another reason. She deduced that there was only one way to find out.

"Xavier," she said, barely above a whisper. "What are you doing here?"

31

"*Mon amour, mon chéri, comment je vous ai manqué!*" Xavier walked over to where Bianca sat at her desk. "I've missed you," he repeated, reverently cupping Bianca's face in his large, strong hands. "I've missed these...."

Later, Bianca would swear that a shock of electricity went through her when Xavier's lips touched hers. Suddenly, the four months that they'd been apart, and the years of unsatisfying sex she'd had before knowing what true love felt like, all melded together in the pit of her core. Desire poured forth like molten lava, hot, unpredictable, and totally unexpected. Before she knew what was happening, Xavier had scooped Bianca into his arms and sat them down in the chair Bianca had just vacated. He turned her body into his and deepened the kiss. His tongue stroked the inside of her mouth—determined, purposeful—even as his hands roamed her body, reacquainting themselves with every curve.

Bianca melted. An appropriate response since her body was on fire! She'd dreamed of his touch, relived this embrace a thousand times, and none of those imaginations came close to this: the real thing. Emotions roiled as she felt a hand on her knit top, and then under it, massaging the globes encased in a silk bra.

"*Je vous aimé, mon coeur, je vous aimé,*" Xavier whispered, once he broke the tongue dance and placed kisses over Bianca's face and neck. His fingers had found their goal and now rubbed a chocolate areola into hardness. His tongue longed to do the same, and his snake was fairly hissing to stroke the cat.

Xavier raised Bianca's top and sucked a pert nipple into his hot, wet mouth. "Xavier," Bianca moaned aloud. Thoughts swirled. *He loves me? He's here, in California, in my office, and he's saying . . .* wait! Through the haze of passion came the realization that Bianca was panting and nearly naked mere feet from her assistant at her place of business. She thought this and at the same time felt Xavier's hand reach past the hem of her skirt and start a purposeful journey up her thigh. It was time to either stop the madness or truly let it begin.

"Wait!" Bianca forced distance between their two blazing bodies and took deep breaths. "We can't do this here—"

"But we must do it now," Xavier interrupted, his hazel eyes now almost black, and boring into Bianca. "I've waited so long, *chérie*, my body is on my fire and yours is the only one who can put out my flame." He rose from the chair and gently placed Bianca on her feet. "Fix yourself and get your things. We leave now."

It wasn't quite a splash of cold water, but Xavier's authoritative, no-questions-asked tone brought Bianca back to reality. She took a step back, lifting a defiant chin. Their similar personalities—determined, stubborn, independent—contributed to the sparks that flew whenever they were together. It's what she loved about him. It's what she couldn't stand.

"That didn't sound like a question, Xavier."

"I didn't mean it to."

Oh, no, he has the audacity to look at his watch?

"If I have to pick you up and carry you out of here, I will. And as much as to do so would turn me on even further, it may prove a bit embarrassing in your workplace."

Arms slowly crossed was Bianca's response.

Now it was Xavier's turn to take a breath and rein in his

temper. "Bianca, I've waited a long time and come a long way to see you. Woman, do not tempt me much further with your impertinence!"

One second passed. Two. Ten. Xavier took two steps and prepared to lift Bianca into his arms.

"Okay, okay, wait, Xavier. In case you haven't noticed, I have a business to run. You can't just waltz in here and demand I..." *Damn, his lips look good and they felt even better....* "Give me a second and I'll be ready to go."

An hour and a half later, Xavier and Bianca lay freshly showered and fully satiated on crisp one-thousand-count Egyptian cotton sheets. Bianca nibbled on the fruit tray from room service, while Xavier played in her damp curls.

"Why did you cut your hair?" he asked.

"I was ready for a change."

"I like it."

"Thank you." Bianca sat up and wrapped the sheet around her. "So, Mr. Marquis, when did you decide to cross the Atlantic to see me?"

Xavier rolled over onto his back. Bianca didn't miss the ripple of muscles that followed this move, or the soft black hair that was sprinkled across his chest forming into a line that spilled into thick groin hair. She continued to gaze at six-foot-two inches of white chocolate, perfectly formed and eternally tempting: broad chest, narrow waist, nice hips, tight butt, big thighs, big...everything. The only thing better than his massive licking stick was that he knew how to use it. Those books that said size didn't matter had obviously never heard of Xavier Marquis or talked to any of the women fortunate enough to have made his intimate acquaintance.

"Xavier," Bianca repeated, swatting him playfully. "Did you hear me?"

Xavier arched a perfectly shaped, thick black brow in reply.

"When did you plan this trip, and why didn't you call me?"

"You know exactly why I didn't call. You were a very bad

girl, Bianca, for which later on . . . I'm going to have to spank you."

The threat, delivered so lightly yet so deliciously with an accent that parted legs at will, had Bianca's still-quivering body wanting him yet again. She snuggled against his lean, taut body, content to simply be where he was.

"I went a little crazy when you left me," Xavier began after a pause. "Not at first. At first, it was as you Americans say: business as usual. I picked up a couple chicks—"

"Uh, do I really need to hear *that* part?"

"*Chérie*, you ruined me for them. They were nothing compared to you."

"Okay, I like *that* part."

"I wasn't even interested, physically, anything. So I had my people contact the school to get more information on you. And that is when I realized that you had been bad, that you hadn't told me your real last name."

Bianca giggled, remembering how she'd come up with the last name Knowles simply because at the time, Beyoncé had been playing in the background.

"Ah, yes, funny now. Then . . . not so much."

"I'm sorry, baby," Bianca said, kissing his cheek. *Why can't I keep my mouth off this man?* "You know how it was when we met. We both thought it was going to be one of those wild adventures, a spur-of-the-moment rendezvous. What happened in Paris was supposed to stay in Paris."

"My guys turned over the city. You were gone. I felt so helpless and believe me . . ."

There goes that sexy brow rise again . . .

"That is not a feeling with which I am familiar."

The thought of a man turning the city upside down made Bianca feel all warm and fuzzy. "So then what?"

"I managed to secure your files from the school."

"What?" Bianca sat up. "How? That's private information!"

"Baby, money makes everything available." This thought caused a frown to skitter across Xavier's face, but he quickly dismissed the family drama he'd left behind in Paris. "As soon as I knew where to find you, I began planning this trip."

But my files read Atlanta. There was nothing in them about LA.

I flew to Atlanta first. It only took a couple phone calls to find out that you were the new manager of operations for the West Coast.

Bianca lay contemplating what Xavier had told her and realizing how little she knew about him. Aside from the fact that he had some type of connection to the royal family and that his family was extremely wealthy, she didn't know much.

"What type of planning did you have to do? I can't imagine that you have the authority to leave work and take a few vacation days."

Xavier snorted. "Don't be ridiculous, *cherie*. When it comes to the one I love, I have the authority to do what I like. Even when others don't like it."

Bianca searched Xavier's face. Instead of shying away, he turned to face her.

"This is the second time you've used the *L*-word. Is that a Parisian thing, where saying 'I love you' is almost the same as 'Have a nice day'?"

"No," Xavier responded, his voice low, his breath moist against Bianca's cheek. "I say I love you because *vous êtes mon souffle*. Because you are my breath."

"Xavier, that's so sweet, really. But this is all so sudden, so surprising. I haven't had time to sort out my feelings for you."

"It doesn't matter. I've made the decision for both of us."

"Oh, really? How you figure?"

Xavier rolled over onto Bianca and pressed his rapidly hardening shaft into her equally burgeoning heat. "This is quite simple, *mon trésor*. I lost you. I found you. Now, I will never let you go."

32

Bianca returned to work at four p.m., almost three hours after rushing out of the office with a hastily uttered explanation to Crystal about taking Xavier to see the location on Sunset. Her suit was wrinkle free and makeup had been reapplied, but there was no getting around her freshly washed do.

Being the consummate professional that she was, Crystal watched her boss approach as if not a hair was out of place.

"Thanks for rescheduling the other applicants," Bianca said when she reached the desk. "Are these all of the messages?"

"I sent the others through to your Outlook." And then, because she couldn't resist: "So ... how did your Parisian boy like Sunset Boulevard?"

"What?"

"Uh, Sunset Boulevard, TOSTS. Where you said you were taking what's his name ... Savior?"

Bianca smiled, glad for the few extra seconds to form the answers to Crystal's questions. "Close. Xavier." She spelled out his name.

"So ... did you show Xavier the West side site? Or did you show him something else?"

"Crystal!" Bianca felt her face flush, and she couldn't contain her smile.

"Excuse me, boss, but I'm just sayin'. A sistah like me would have showed him what was under the big-girl drawers!"

Bianca warmed at Crystal's comments, having shown Xavier everything a *few* times in three hours. "Um, right; Xavier," she replied, flipping through the mail in an attempt to cover her discombobulated state. "I showed him a few places."

Crystal's eyes narrowed with the dawning of the potential reason behind her boss's new hairstyle. "Bianca!"

Bianca's eyes flew up. "What?"

"You...didn't. I mean, hey, it's really none of my business, but...did you?"

"Did I what?" Bianca repeated, more slowly this time.

"Did you find a new hair salon on the West side, close to the TOSTS location?"

The twinkle in Crystal's jokingly innocent eyes told Bianca that her astute assistant knew exactly what was up.

"Get in my office, heifah," she hissed. When Crystal complied, Bianca shut the door. "What I am about to share with you can go no further. The first day I hear any of this repeated will be your last day on the job, okay?"

"You know I don't talk out of school, Bianca. What's going on?"

"When I went to school in Paris, I met Xavier and fell in love." Crystal's expression turned thoughtful, and Bianca felt certain she was thinking about her recently cancelled engagement. "When I returned home, to Cooper, I knew our situation wasn't the happily ever after that he wanted. It wasn't what I wanted either. I wanted what I'd found in Paris." Bianca's eyes began shining. "It seems as though Xavier feels the same way. He came here to tell me that he's never stopped thinking about me, and he's determined to continue the relationship."

"From the looks of things"—Crystal once again eyed Bianca's freshly washed hair—"that won't be too hard."

"Oh, forget you, Crystal," Bianca said, silently thankful for the honest exchange. It occurred to her in this moment that, aside from Alexis, she hadn't talked about Xavier with anyone. She also realized how much she wanted—no, needed—to talk this out. In one quick decision her loyal assistant of three years, who'd continued to work in public relations during Bianca's time abroad, made the transition from employee to confidante. "He loves me, Crystal," she continued with a frown, pacing the room. "And I think I love him."

"Then what's the problem?"

Bianca sighed. "His family would never accept me and my family would never accept him."

"Why not?"

"Isn't it obvious?"

"Why, because he's not black?"

"He's white, and even more specifically, he's not Cooper Riley."

"But you've ended the engagement."

"You're right, Crystal. I've let go. But I think my family is still holding on, still hoping we'll get back together."

"Will you?" Crystal asked, her eyes filled with concern.

Bianca took a deep breath and met Crystal's gaze. "No."

Cooper Riley sat in a corner booth of FGO staring into a tumbler of Scotch, looking for the answers to his life. The past six weeks had gone by in a fog and most times, he still hoped to wake from the nightmare that began with the words: *Cooper, this isn't going to work.*

"Dammit," he muttered, taking a drink from the glass and slamming it back down on the table. *Why did you do this to us, Bianca? Everything was set, our lives would be perfect. Why did you have to go and fuck it all up?* Cooper drained the rest of his drink and looked around for a waiter. He was normally a two-drink man, but lately, between Bianca's betrayal and his mother's nagging that had resulted in his buying a townhouse sight unseen, he'd taken to drowning his sorrows by hitting the proverbial sauce . . . and hitting it hard. "Harold, send her over," he said to the host, who nodded and walked to the bar on the other side of the room.

"It looks like you could use a double, and the drink's on me."

Cooper looked up and scowled. "Why? Who are you?"

"An angel sent to take your mind off your troubles. May I?" When he nodded, the stunning female sat on the other side of the booth. "Actually, I've had a stressful day myself. Came here to try and forget some unpleasant news."

"Then how are you going to cheer me up?"

"Haven't you heard that misery loves company?" The woman fixed him with a sexy smile and waited until the waiter had set down their drinks. "I say let's get to know each other. Maybe we'll find something to be happy about."

Cooper allowed his eyes to roam over the woman's long, straight hair, flawless tawny skin, kissable lips, and luscious round orbs hovering over a low-cut dress. His manhood twitched its approval. Obviously, he'd missed more than Bianca's conversation. A smile slowly crept across his face. "Okay, angel, I'm game to try your plan. Cooper Riley," he finished, with an outstretched hand.

"Shyla Martin," the woman responded, a bit chagrined that Cooper didn't remember her from the Livingston Corporation Christmas party. Smiling, Shyla decided to give him a break. It had been two years, and the fact that Cooper didn't remember her might work to her advantage. "It is a pleasure to meet you." The two clinked glasses. "Now, what has you drowning your troubles in drink?"

"A cancelled engagement."

What? You and Bianca Livingston are not getting married? "You?"

"A similar tale. But what woman would be crazy enough to let a man like you get away?"

"One who wanted to get away herself."

Shyla moved from her side of the booth, sat down next to Cooper, and placed a hand on his thigh. "I say that one woman's loss could be another one's gain. What do you think?"

Cooper looked into Shyla's bright eyes, then down to her partially open lips glistening with gloss and promises; at the orbs that rose and fell with each seductive breath. "I think"— he ran a finger along Shyla's cheek—"that you may be right."

33

Shyla tapped her finger on the steering wheel, contemplating whether or not to darken the doors of her old stomping ground: Taste of Soul, Buckhead. Her mind had been a whir of ideas ever since last night's romp with Mr. Big-Shot Attorney, Trust-Fund Riley. As she recalled the evening, a sly smile scampered across Shyla's face. The lovemaking had been average, but he was worth way more to her than the size of his jurisdiction. Afterwards, she'd poured more drinks and he'd poured out his heart: how he and Bianca had been friends since childhood, had dated for more than two years, and how she'd suddenly and unceremoniously dumped him during the holidays. Shyla had listened with compassion, agreeing that Cooper had been wronged and assuring him that Bianca wasn't worth his mourning. "Success is the best revenge," she'd reminded him, just as she'd reminded herself a year ago, when she, too, had been dumped from the Livingston camp. Last night, she'd barely slept, plotting and planning how she could take the two halves she was juggling and make them a winning whole. On one side was Cooper, more than ready to show everybody his worth, especially Bianca. On the other side was the man who just wouldn't go away no matter how hard she'd tried to make him. Shyla continued to watch the patrons coming and going from Taste of Soul as she remembered the conversation that had driven her to grab a drink at FGO.

"Q, I thought I told you not to call me again."

"Baby, is that any way to treat a partner in crime?"

"We are not partners, Q."

"Then friends?"

Shyla rolled her eyes. "Look, Q, I admit that we had a great time in Jamaica. We were good outlets for each other. It's what we both needed. But we're both back stateside, back to reality. You were a memorable part of my past, love, but you don't fit into my future. It's not personal, Q, it really isn't. I think you'll make a great husband to somebody . . . but not me."

"Look here, baby girl," Q continued, as if Shyla hadn't spoken, or he hadn't heard. "I'm getting ready to get set up real nice, go back to Jamaica and buy that spot I used to work at. Already bought a house down there, right on the water. It'll be paradise every day, baby. And I want you with me."

"Q . . ." Shyla responded.

"Baby . . ."

Memories of the things this ex-lover did with his long, stiff tongue and even longer, stiffer schlong made Shyla waver for a moment. But then she remembered that outside of the amazing sex, pristine beaches, good food, and gorgeous sunsets . . . Ocho Rios, Jamaica, was boring as hell for a moving, shaking, make-it-happen woman like her. "Q, I'm not coming to Jamaica with you. Final decision; I won't change my mind."

"Not even if a certain set of folks might learn how helpful you were to a brothah once we revealed our true identities?" Q's voice remained smooth and low, but still, the energy shifted.

"Is that a threat?" Shyla covered her sudden nervousness with bravado. She definitely planned to get back at Toussaint for what he'd done to her, but only if she could throw the rock and then hide her hand.

"I'm not one to be messed with, Shyla. You should know that by now."

"I don't want to mess with you, Q." Her voice turned flirty, as Shyla decided that honey worked better than vinegar sometimes. "Isn't that the problem? Q, you're the best sex I've ever had in my life, and if that was the only thing I wanted to live for, I'd hop on the next thing smoking and meet you on the island. But you know my story, you know who I am. I want more. I want..."

Shyla's focus shifted as she watched a young woman walk into the restaurant with two boys in tow. *Is it just my imagination because I'm thinking of him or does that child look like Quintin? Okay, girl, you're overreacting.* During their conversations, Quintin had proudly stated that he had no baby mama drama in his life, and that he intended to be the one to decide if and when he would start a family. *So no, that wasn't Q's son.* Still, as Shyla decided against going inside the establishment, started her car, and reached for her headset, she continued to watch the goings-on at the restaurant, her curiosity piqued about who the beautiful young woman was who'd entered Taste of Soul.

A few seconds later, her call went through. "Hello, Cooper. It's Shyla, how are you?" Pause. "Really, what's wrong?"

Cooper walked over to the bookcase that spanned his far wall and casually browsed its weighted shelves. "It's my mother. She's driving me crazy about the breakup."

"The solution to that is easy enough. Stop taking her calls."

"Then she'd only walk over to my wing and knock on my door."

Shyla's eyes widened. "You still live at home?"

Cooper shrugged. "Hey, it's the cheapest rent in town."

"Perhaps monetarily, but it sounds like it's costing you in other ways. Why don't we meet for dinner and discuss possible locations for your new digs?"

Cooper sighed. "I already own a place."

"You do?"

"Yes, but we still need to meet."

Shyla smiled. "Of course we do. I have some very naughty things I'd like to do to you."

A slight smile marred Cooper's otherwise stern expression. "I have a potentially nasty thing to run by you as well, Shyla Martin."

"Oh?" Shyla purred.

"Yes. It's the fact that I finally remembered why you look so familiar. You worked for the Livingston Corporation and we met at their party. I think it's pretty *nasty* that you didn't tell me that."

Inside Taste of Soul, Keisha quieted her boys while she browsed the menu. The waitress was right: everything sounded delicious. Keisha paused, took a drink of her cola, and looked around her. She was glad she'd taken Jefferson's advice and gotten out of the house, and she was glad she'd taken Q's advice and tried out the restaurant. Like Q had said, except for Divine, nobody in Atlanta knew who she was and the chances of running into Jefferson's friend in this area were remote. It had been three weeks since Keisha and her sons had moved to Atlanta and except for dinners on the outskirts of town and trips to pick up her sons from school, Keisha had rarely ventured out of the house, choosing instead to shop online, take an in-home cooking course, and try to navigate the process of running a home. When Jefferson had called and told her that a meeting was going to keep him at the office until seven p.m., Keisha knew that home cooking, fast food, and delivery were all unsatisfactory options.

There was another reason Keisha felt the need to get away from home. It had been two weeks since she'd stolen the money from Jefferson's bank account, and all was quiet on the eastern front. That was the problem. It was too quiet. She knew that Quintin had gotten the money and was planning to leave the country soon. She also knew that February was coming, and with it, new bank statements for the month. Did Jefferson handle his own accounts? Did his accountant, and would the accountant watch savings accounts as closely as checking? How did people who didn't live from paycheck to paycheck roll? How often did they check their balances? Ever since watching the fact-based Lifetime movie about a woman who'd stolen another woman's identity, Keisha had been on edge. She'd needed a change of scenery and conversation. Between Harold Melvin & the Bluenotes telling everybody to wake up and the friendly, chatty waitress, she was getting both.

"Those your boys?" the waitress asked as she approached the table to take their order. Keisha nodded. "Girl, they are both so handsome. Your oldest is going to be a heartbreaker, I can see it now."

Keisha smiled. "I don't know about all that, with his bad behind. But, thank you."

"You can't see it? Look at those eyes! I'm jealous of those long, curly lashes." The waitress noted his dark skin color, which was different from his mother's lighter hue. "They must take after their dad." The waitress had almost said "dads," plural, based on her own situation. Thankfully, she rephrased even as the word was coming out of her mouth.

"That one"—Keisha pointed to her youngest—"has my eyes and mouth. Everything else is his daddy's. And interestingly enough that one"—she pointed to her other son—"is almost the spitting image of his uncle, who is also his hero."

"Now isn't that something?" the waitress said.

"Isn't it? I told my brother it's because he was living with me during my pregnancy, getting on my nerves the whole time." Keisha smiled at the memories.

"I look just like Uncle Quintin, Mama?" the young boy asked, beaming.

"Why are you asking that silly question? You know you look like Q."

Chardonnay almost choked on "What the hell?!" and ground her teeth together to keep from crying out. She gripped the order pad to keep her composure and tried to remain casual as she carefully eyed the woman's oldest son. *He's got his eyes, his nose, his skin coloring . . . oh my God, this has got to be the sister that Q talked about! What in the hell is she doing here, in Atlanta? Does that mean her brother has come back, too?* Just last week, Toussaint had come in asking if she had any new information for him. She couldn't wait to take her break and make a call. *Who knew that instead of searching for it, answers would find her. And who knew that lady luck liked barbeque?*

Keisha turned back to the menu's first page. "Wow, there are too many good choices here. What would you recommend?"

"Oh, girl, it's all good," Chardonnay answered "It all depends on what you like. My favorites are the James Brown Babyback Rib Snack, Redding's Ribeye Steak and Aretha Franklin's Catfish. Those all come with two or three sides, depending on whether you get the regular or large. From the kids' menu, my hardheads always go for the riblets. But the chicken or fish nuggets are popular and delicious, made from scratch instead of frozen, and the Kool corn dog is made with a sausage link instead of a hot dog with either a barbeque or sweet mustard sauce for dipping."

Keisha placed her order: the James Brown Baby Back Rib Snack for her and the chicken nuggets and corn dog for her sons. Not being able to decide, she ordered a slew of sides figuring she could take home any leftovers: greens, barbequed beans, macaroni and cheese, potato salad, dirty rice, and French fries. Chardonnay winked at the boys, smiled at Keisha, and told her the order would be up in about fifteen minutes.

As soon as she'd placed the order, Chardonnay told the other waitress she'd be back in five minutes, reached for her cell phone, and walked out the back door. She was still pondering her luck as she punched in Toussaint's number while walking farther away from the building. Since being promoted to assistant manager, Chardonnay rarely waited tables and was doing so today only because an employee called in sick. And if that wasn't enough coinkydink, the fact that Keisha was sitting in her section was the *how 'bout dat now* on top of the *girl, you lyin'*.

"I can't believe this," she whispered, as Toussaint's line rang.

"Hello, this is Toussaint."

"Toussaint, this is Chardonnay."

"Yes, Chardonnay, what can I do for you?"

"What *I* can do for *you* is the reason I'm calling. I think y'all better start writing out that check for a cool hundred Gs."

Toussaint, who was in one of the break rooms at the Livingston Corporation, walked over and closed the door. "Talk to me."

"You're not going to believe this, but Quintin's sister is here in Buckhead, sitting in the restaurant right now!"

"How do you know it's his sister?"

Chardonnay told him what she'd just experienced. "I'm going to be my friendly self and get more information, but as of right now I'm 99.99 percent sure that I've just met the woman who is going to help me get paid."

34

Sterling, Adam, and Ace sat in Sterling's small but well-appointed conference room at the end of what had been a busy yet productive week. As always, Sterling was the epitome of elegance and style. Today he wore a charcoal gray, light wool suit paired with a lighter gray, silk shirt, a multitoned gray tie, and platinum accessories. His texturized hair shone with health and shea butter, and the small mustache he'd decided to grow was a nice touch. In a nod to casual Fridays, both Adam and Ace wore polo shirts and khakis.

"You were right, gentlemen. I've found the trail, and it leads to Quintin Bright." Sterling's satisfied expression was the only private nod to a job well done.

"That son of a bitch," Adam growled.

Ace nodded in agreement. "How'd you do it?"

"Grease enough palms and lips get loose. One of the joints through which he laundered money was more loyal to Mr. Green than they were to Mr. Bright."

Adam's jaw twitched in anger. He no longer saw images of Candace in Q's arms, but his knuckles still ached to connect with flesh every time he thought of the man who'd shot him twice—in his back with a gun and in the heart through his wife's betrayal. "What next?"

Sterling leaned forward, twisting a pure gold pen between manicured fingers. "The latest movement from him came out of Los Angeles. I've got a contact out there trying to track him down. When that happens, I'll plan a trip out West and go from there."

"But we have enough to nab him, to prove that he stole the funds?" Quintin Bright had eluded police for almost a year. Ace wanted to make sure that once captured, the thief wouldn't slide through their fingers on a technicality.

"That's why we're moving forward cautiously, to make sure every angle is covered, legally and ethically. Don't worry, Ace. By the time we cuff him, our case will be airtight."

Later that evening, Ace breezed into his home with a smile on his face. He was happy to hear the sound of the Staple Singers wafting through the house and surprised but pleased to smell dinner cooking.

"'Cause if you don't respect yourself," Ace sang, coming into the kichen and hugging Diane from behind.

"Ain' nobody gonna give a good cahoot," they finished together.

Diane turned around in his arms. "Hey, handsome," she said, with a quick peck on the lips.

"Hey, baby," Ace responded, grabbing a handful of booty. "Why are you cooking? You know I like to take my baby out on Friday nights."

"I know, sweetie, but your baby been running herself ragged all week. She just wanted to chill with her man tonight."

"Speaking of chill," Ace sniffed the air—"is that chili I'm smelling?"

"Close, succotash." Diane released herself from Ace's embrace and turned around to stir the dish that she prepared as if it were chili's cousin: beef, beans, onions, garlic, and tomatoes, with the added ingredients of green beans and corn.

"Smells good, baby!" Ace walked over and opened the oven.

"Man, if that cake falls, that's your ass. If you don't get out my stove!"

"Just want to see what you've got burnin' on the griddle, baby." Ace came behind her and pulled her into his arms again.

"Hum, somebody is frisky this evening. What did they put in your Kool-Aid at work?"

Ace nuzzled Diane's neck. "We're getting ready to catch him, baby."

Diane stopped stirring, turned, and asked, "Who, Quintin?" Ace nodded.

"Baby, go wash up and I'll fix plates. You can fill me in while we're eating dinner. You know I want to hear the whole story. I don't want you to leave out a thing!"

Across town, Adam and Candace sat at one of their favorite restaurants, enjoying the floor-to-ceiling windows that offered a spectacular city view. Adam had just told Candace about the meeting with Sterling and the near-positive identity of the alleged thief.

"How do you feel, baby?" Candace asked, reaching across the table to grab the hand wrapped around a tumbler of cognac.

"Better," Adam responded, raising his eyes to meet his wife's. "But I won't be totally satisfied until that man is behind bars and begins to reap the consequences of his actions."

Candace smiled, silently thanking Diane once again for demanding that she force thoughts of Quintin out of her mind and concentrate on her husband. Talking honestly to Adam about their sex life, her desires, and even about the affair had worked wonders. An initially hesitant Adam now enjoyed trying out Candace's new toys. And who knew such enthusiasm and stamina could come courtesy of a little blue pill?

"If I say 'I'm sorry' a thousand times, a million times, it will never be enough."

Adam leaned back against the booth's plush, dark leather.

"Baby, don't worry about that. It's enough to hear you say you love me."

"Adam Livingston, you are the very beat of my heart. You are the only man I've ever loved, and the only one I ever will love. I love you, baby. I love you! And if I say that a thousand times, or a million, it won't be enough either."

"Remember that a little later when I've got you in the bedroom."

"Baby, it's what you do to me in the bedroom that I'll never forget."

Adam smiled confidently and lifted his glass in a toast to his wife. *How did I think I could ever live without this woman? And how did I ever think a muthafuckin' kid's shit could compare to some Livingston love?*

35

"Find out anything?" Alexis asked Toussaint. It had been twenty-four hours since Toussaint had found out that Keisha was the name of the woman at the restaurant. Chardonnay had also discovered that the woman had just moved to Atlanta, knew few people, and seemed a bit lonely. Chardonnay had given Keisha her number, told her she'd be glad to take her around to the best clubs. Now, everyone could only hope Keisha would take the bait and call. Well, almost everyone. Toussaint had put Keisha into every search engine on the Internet, along with various combinations of Keisha/Quintin, Keisha Bright, Keisha/Atlanta and Keisha/LA.

"Nothing," Toussaint said, shaking his head and leaning back to stretch a body that had been hunched over a computer for two hours.

"Maybe it's time to give it a rest for a while. See what happens in the next week or so."

"Yeah, baby, I guess you're right."

"Of course I am."

"Ha! Well, why don't you slide that correct lusciousness over here and help me forget all about it?"

Alexis slid onto her husband's lap with ease. Soon their

tongues were swirling in a familiar dance and bodies were tingling in all the right places.

"Ow," Alexis exclaimed, when Toussaint tweaked her nipple. "Baby, I told you. They're sore."

"Sorry, baby."

They continued kissing. Toussaint reached for the elastic waistband on Alexis's maternity pants and, after rubbing her round stomach, moved his hands farther down.

They enjoyed each other for a few moments longer before Alexis broke the kiss. "Baby, I'm sorry. But I don't feel like having sex right now."

"No problem, baby. Let's make love instead."

Alexis gave Toussaint a look.

"Okay, okay. Then can we at least f—"

"Toussaint!"

Toussaint laughed, "Just for a few minutes?" Alexis's expression read *brothah, please.* "Can I just put it in a little bit? Just the head, baby, just the head." From Alexis? More silence. Toussaint turned into Mars Blackmon from the Spike Lee joint. "Please, baby, baby, please!"

"Ha! Toussaint, you are crazy! That's what the boys used to say in high school to try and get us out of our panties."

"Didn't work then either, huh?" Toussaint shifted in the chair and willed down his erection.

"Absolutely not!"

Toussaint lifted Alexis's top and bent his head down toward her stomach. "Baby girl, Daddy loves you, but you're messing with my groove right now!"

"How are you so sure that it's a girl?" Alexis asked yet again. He'd addressed the baby as "she" from the moment they'd learned of her pregnancy. "If I push out a Toussaint, Jr., I hope you're not disappointed."

Toussaint kissed her temple. "Alexis, you and the baby healthy, that's all I want."

They enjoyed a companionable silence for a few moments, the sounds of a smooth jazz radio station providing ambiance. Alexis stirred in Toussaint's arms. "You heard from Bianca lately?"

"Matter of fact, I haven't."

"Hum, me either. I left her a message yesterday and she texted back that we'd talk soon. I suppose she's pretty busy. . . ."

"Yeah, I guess. I sent an e-mail yesterday, told her I was flying in next week."

"Uh, hello, when were you going to tell me?"

"I thought I told you!"

"Uh, that would be an 'I don't think so.'"

"I'm sorry, baby. I thought I did. It's been so crazy at the office, and then with the info on Keisha and the update on Q . . ."

"It's okay, sweetness. How long will you be gone?"

"Probably just a day, two at the most. Bianca's narrowed the potential assistant managers down to five people. She's choosing two from this group—one for each LA location. She wants me to come in for the final interviews."

"I wouldn't mind living there, you know."

"Los Angeles?"

Alexis nodded.

"Me either, though I can't see Atlanta not being my base. I think at the very least we should buy a condo out there, and as soon as you're back from the pregnancy, we should start looking for a house."

Alexis squealed. "Are you sure, Toussaint? I know how much you love this penthouse."

Toussaint shrugged. "It was just all right until a certain world-renowned interior designer came and laid it the bump out! But now, I've got a family. It's time for me to ditch the bachelor pad and move into a real home."

Alexis pushed away from Toussaint's chest, and stood. "I'm going to take a nap. Want to join me?"

"I don't think so. It'll leave me even more frustrated."

"Or satisfied. You never know when my hormones will shift and put me in the mood."

Toussaint eyed the love of his life as he slowly rose. "Since you put it that way . . . a brothah's got to take his chances."

As he followed Alexis up the stairs a thought flitted across Toussaint's mind—another time and another woman who'd wanted nothing more than to be his wife, have his child, and move to Los Angeles. *Funny thing about life,* he thought as he quickly shed his clothes, eased between cool sheets, and spooned his wife. With Shyla, he'd not for one moment thought she was his partner for life. Yet he'd known Alexis would be a part of his future from the time she'd blessed out a traffic cop who'd dared to ticket his car, and then refused to tell Toussaint her name or give him her number. *Good thing I'm persistent,* Toussaint thought, as he felt Alexis's booty slowly grind back against him. He'd chased and chased her until she caught him. Until now, Toussaint had never known that being trapped could feel so good.

36

"Do you like it?" Cooper asked as he walked through a brand-new townhome on Atlanta's west side.

"It's not about what I like, honey. You're the one who's going to be living here."

Cooper leaned over and touched his lips to Shyla's temple. "This is true, my darling, but hopefully not alone."

Shyla smiled, squeezed his forearm, and followed him into the guest room that would make a nice home office/study. She was so glad she'd survived Cooper's ire over her Livingston connection. That she'd been fired from the company helped convince Cooper that there was no love lost between her and his almost in-laws and to that end, gave them even more in common.

Cooper walked to the middle of the room and looked around. "I do think I could be comfortable here," he said, responding to a comment Shyla had made earlier. "I could have a bookcase built along that wall, an entertainment center over there."

"Yes, and this room comes with a private bath, so if you entertained clients it would be totally self contained."

Cooper nodded, even as his expression changed.

Shyla noticed immediately. "Thinking about your parents again?"

"Mother, mostly. She will be furious."

"I know, honey, but you said that you thought your father would understand."

"That doesn't mean he'll disagree with my mother. The judge hears enough arguing on the bench. He abhors conflict or disruptions in his personal life."

Shyla walked over to Cooper. In her heels, she could look him squarely in the eye. "Cooper, you're not a kid anymore, you're almost thirty-five years old. And as much as you respect your parents, moving in to this place is about you. It's your decision, not theirs." *How many times do I have to convince you of that? Geez!* Shyla tried not to do what she'd done since she and Toussaint had parted: compare every man to him. In this moment, however, it was difficult, and Shyla allowed herself the luxury of remembering lustful, torrid nights spent in Toussaint's penthouse, where they'd make love from the living room to the kitchen and from the patio to the den. "This place has good bones and plenty of room. It's also move-in ready. Add the touches of the right interior designer, and I think you could truly be happy here."

"And the right woman."

"What do you mean?"

"I've never lived alone, and I'm not sure I want to start now. When I move into this place, will you join me?"

Hum, can you do it, Shyla? Can you give up inches for dollars and trade searching for security? Then she thought of the bigger picture, how Cooper's disdain for the Livingstons matched her own, and how she felt that somehow her retribution for being rejected by Toussaint could be tied in with Bianca's salty dismissal. "I can't commit right at this moment," she finally answered, while giving Cooper a reassuring smile. "We don't want to move too quickly. Let's just take it one step at a time."

And maybe I won't have to give up anything. Maybe I can have my cake and eat it, too.

Shyla linked her arm through Cooper's and they walked out of the town house, again noting how much they liked the landscaping and the fact that the corner unit was framed by a dense group of trees. Cooper had been told that his neighbor in this gated community was a single businessman who was often out of town for months at a time. Once Cooper moved into the town house, his relative privacy was assured.

Shyla smiled as Cooper locked the front door and pocketed the key. "So, Mr. Riley, what do you think?

Cooper gave Shyla a peck on the mouth. "I think I'll move in this weekend."

37

Bianca and Xavier held hands as the bronze-colored stretch limo approached. As soon as it pulled up, a uniformed driver jumped out, opened the passenger door, and ushered them inside.

"I can't believe you talked me out of the office," Bianca chided, even as she fell back into soft, leather-cushioned seats.

"*Chérie,* it's Valentine's Day, one of America's most popular holidays."

"One of the most commercial, that's for sure."

"Ooh, listen to my economy-conscious entrepreneur. Where is your sense of romance?" he murmured, scooting over to nibble her ear. "Where is that heart overflowing with love?"

"Probably somewhere in my in-box that's overflowing with work!"

Xavier reached for the champagne that was chilling in a silver ice bucket. "Shh. Let's speak no more of work this weekend. Here in Las Vegas, let's only speak of us."

After a deep, wet kiss to punctuate his statement, Xavier popped the cork and poured the pricey bubbly into crystal flutes. It had been almost a month since he'd walked into her office and back into her life, and Bianca's heart still melted at the sight of him. They'd spent their first full night together in his hotel suite. The next day, he'd moved into her condo. They'd talked nonstop, catching up on each other's lives, sharing thoughts for the future, goals, and dreams. Xavier had told Bianca about his father's threat to cut him out of the family fortune, even as he assured her that by most people's standards he'd still be a fairly rich man. She'd assured him that his diminished royal standing didn't matter and that they could build a dynasty together.

Xavier's business acumen had been one of Bianca's biggest surprises. She'd never considered how growing up in a family that owned several businesses would make him so knowledgeable in this field. But he was, so much so that she'd acquiesced when he'd taken the lead with her baby, TOSTS. Having grown up in Europe, frequenting tapas-style restaurants and similar cafes for most of his life, his suggestions had been impressive, his insight refreshing and sensible. He'd reminded her that when it came to celebrity clientele, he could bring in the bling. His cousins partied with many of the country's A-list actors, especially those foreign born who'd found success on American soil. And after he'd dressed in a suit for a night of fine dining, Bianca had known that Xavier would be the host of TOSTS. What Bianca didn't yet know was that, if Xavier had his way, she and he as a couple would be the bling of Hollywood, the toast of Tinseltown.

The limousine pulled into Aria, one of Sin City's plush hotels. They were greeted by their own, personal concierge, who secured their luggage and then walked them to their private elevator.

"I like your style," Bianca said to Xavier, as the elevator whisked them to the property's top floor.

Xavier's eyes traveled the length of Bianca's body. "And I like yours, *mon chocolat doux*."

"Umm, you make 'sweet chocolate' sound so sexy!"

They reached the penthouse floor and seconds later, the concierge opened the door into paradise. After showing them the suite and its amenities, and while Bianca and Xavier enjoyed another glass of champagne in the living room, the hotel employee emptied their luggage, put away their things, and then discreetly disappeared.

"Baby, I love it!" Bianca had been to Vegas many times, but she'd never treated herself to such luxury. The floor-to-ceiling windows offered panoramic views and the lights from the Strip in the twinkling of dusk were breathtaking. She turned to Xavier, and as absolutely stunning as the outside view was, the interior sights were equally amazing, especially the white chocolate Parisian whose darkened eyes peered at her unabashedly with desire.

"Come here," he commanded.

Bianca floated into his arms. Soon, his scorching kisses had Bianca burning up. *What is it about this man that turns me into a nympho?* She didn't know, nor did she care; she only wanted to get them both out of their clothes and to make love on the massive bed that boasted custom mattresses and Egyptian cotton sheets.

"Baby, let's do it," she panted. "Let me get some of that good, hard loving." Bianca stepped back and began unbuttoning Xavier's shirt. "I want you to give it to me good, just the way I like it."

Xavier stayed her hand, his eyes twinkling. "Perhaps we should take a shower first."

Bianca pulled her knitted top up over her head and unclasped her bra. "We can take one afterward." She reached for Xavier's belt, unbuckled it, then reached for the button on his slacks.

"Let's at least check out the shower." Xavier grabbed Bianca's wrist and then gently yet firmly led them toward the master suite.

Bianca didn't protest. To get to the bathroom they had to pass the bed. Bianca didn't plan to go any farther than that. She took one step into the room and gasped. "Where did this come from?" she asked, her hands rising to her mouth in total surprise.

"My kisses are nothing if not distracting," Xavier said, beaming. "It looks as though I owe the concierge a little something extra for his services."

Bianca was shocked into silence as she continued to look around the room. Lit white candles of various sizes and shapes were on every available surface. Orchid petals covered every surface as well. *Where did the concierge store all of this?* And how had she not smelled the flowers that were now intoxicating her with their scent?

Bianca walked over to Xavier with tears glistening in her eyes. "Baby, this is incredible. Thank you so much."

Xavier lifted her hand to his mouth and kissed it. "This is nothing. For you, I will give the world."

Bianca looked around the room again and for the first time noticed a small box on the window's ledge. She turned to Xavier. "What's that?"

Xavier shrugged.

Bianca rushed over to find out. The only thing better than buying herself presents was somebody else buying them! "Oh my goodness, baby, it's beautiful!" She lifted the diamond bracelet from its velvet interior and noticed a note underneath. "What's this note say?" she asked, once again directing the question to Xavier.

Xavier chuckled. Bianca's happiness was his total joy. "Read it and find out, *mon coeur.* . . ."

Bianca unfolded the white, linen paper: *This is part of something else. Check under the pillow.* Bianca did, and squealed again at the ten-carat, teardrop diamond necklace resting against another folded piece of paper on top of the sheet. "Xavier, you shouldn't have done this!"

"Oh, but I did."

"All this for me?"

"All this and more."

Bianca's heart raced as she unfolded the note: *You probably should put this away, in the dresser perhaps.* She opened her mouth to speak, but quickly closed it after remembering Xavier's past two responses. Still, she continued to glance at him as she crossed over to the dresser. She opened the first drawer and saw various types of lingerie: bras, panties, and thongs, and underneath them... another note: *Don't stop yet.* In the next drawer were several nighties with matching robes. Bianca laughed, doubting with Xavier's voracious appetite that her skin would feel any of them for more than a second. She admired the beautiful design of the long, silk number with a slit to the waist and then tossed it aside to open three more drawers containing perfume in one, three pairs of earrings in another, and in the last one, three pairs of the most amazing shoes that Bianca had ever seen. She picked up a shoe of the most unusual pair, which was also her favorite. Done in pearl white, the back and heel were a soft, leather fabric while the softest fur she ever felt covered the ankle boot's front. Stones sparkled from the bands criss-crossing the front. It was clear that whoever had designed this shoe had lost his or her mind in the best way possible.

"Who on earth is this?" Bianca asked, her voice breathless with excitement and awe.

"Christian Louboutin is a friend of the family," Xavier casually offered. "I called him after I'd found you and then sent him one of your shoes."

Bianca gasped, even as Xavier had already answered what would have been her next question: how had he perfectly nailed her size? "You're why I can't find my..." She was too flabbergasted to finish the sentence.

Xavier looked at her sheepishly and held up his hands in surrender. "I told him to send it back." He nodded to the shoe still in her hand. "Forgive me?"

Bianca smiled. "A thousand times." She continued to examine the shoe. "Is this real fur?"

"Forgive my political incorrectness, but yes, darling, Russian sable."

Bianca fingered the straps and realized the stones sparkling from the band resembled those of her earlier gifts. Reality dawned. She looked at Xavier with disbelief. "Don't tell me these are—"

"Diamonds? Top of the line, with perfect cut, clarity, and color? Okay, I won't admit that, but I will tell you this: if Cinderella loses her shoe at the ball, a very lofty reward will be required for its return."

"These are *ridiculously gorgeous*," Bianca cried. She spun around and clasped the shoe to her chest. "I've got to try these on." She reached into the drawer for the boot's mate . . . and saw yet another note.

"Not more! Xavier, I can't take it. I'm about to pass out."

"I'll catch you," he answered without pause. "And then I'll take full advantage of your unconscious state."

"Ha! And you would, too." Bianca placed the boots on top of the dresser, reached for the note, and wondered if one's face could get paralyzed into a permanent smile. *The shoes will go nicely with what's in the closet.* This time, even though she'd asked twice already without getting an answer, she couldn't resist asking yet again. "What's in the closet?"

Xavier just smiled.

Bianca walked slowly to the closet, her heart beating faster with every step. She opened it and her legs almost buckled beneath it. "Xavier! What is this?"

Xavier's chuckle was deep and rich. "What does it look like?"

Bianca turned to face him, her eyes wide. "What. Is. This?"

Xavier, who'd been watching the beautiful drama unfold while he leaned against the doorjamb, pushed off of it, entered the room, and came to stand beside her. "Let's see," he said in mock seriousness, examining the hanging garment. "We would call it a robe, but in America you say . . . dress?"

"Xavier, these are fricking wedding gowns!"

"Ah, yes, that is exactly how they are described."

"Xavier, why are wedding dresses hanging in my closet?"

"Because, *mon chérie*," Xavier calmly replied, "I thought while getting married you'd prefer them to jeans."

38

"If there's one thing I can't stand, it's some noisy-ass kids. I didn't leave my bad seeds back home to come and have to beat somebody else's kids' asses." Chardonnay huffed, puffed, and weaved her way through Imperial Palace's crowded lobby area on the way to the bank of elevators. A quiet Bobby, determined to keep the peace at all costs, was hot on her heels. They joined a few other couples and one large family—complete with Chardonnay's "noisy-ass kids"—and entered a soon-crowded elevator.

Bobby took advantage of the opportunity to press up against Chardonnay. This was getting ready to be the best weekend of his life, and nothing would spoil it. "It's been a long time since I've been here," he said. "I'm feeling lucky tonight."

"I know them slots better be hot," Chardonnay retorted. "Last time I was here, I lost my money faster than an addict buys crack. What the hell you looking at?"

The blond-haired, blue-eyed child, who'd probably never seen a black woman before—at least probably not one wearing a skintight, leopard mini, thigh-high boots, and hoop earrings appearing big enough to be worn around small waistlines—sought shelter behind his mother's leg. Her eyes, and those of her husband and three other children, remained glued to the neon numbers announcing each floor. When the bell dinged and the doors opened, they almost tripped over each other rushing out of the elevator.

"She was just curious," Bobby offered, in a low voice meant for Chardonnay's ears alone.

"So!" Chardonnay spoke loud enough that even those waiting for the elevators in the lobby could hear. "Parents like that should take their kids out more! Take 'em to the hood, watch BET, do something so that their brats ain't looking at me like I'm some damn freak. This is Imperial Palace, not Circus Circus!"

The bell dinged again and an older couple moved forward to exit. The man's Hawaiian shirt competed with Chardonnay's dress for attention while his wife's blue hair proved that old biddies were rocking the look long before punkers thought it the style. "I trained my children not to stare at people," she offered, with a nod and smile. She looked Chardonnay up and down, like someone of an age where they felt they had the right. "I'd never have the nerve to wear it, but... I like your dress."

"Thank you," Chardonnay said graciously, obviously pleased that someone in this packed hotel had manners.

"That's why the little girl was staring," Bobby added. "She probably liked it, too."

A little over twenty-four hours later, in a small wedding chapel just off Las Vegas Boulevard, witnessed by her best friend, Zoe Williams, and Zoe's boyfriend, Drake, Chardonnay Johnson became Chardonnay Wilson. The ceremony was short, barely five minutes, but it was heartfelt. Her brash, hard-nosed friend would have denied it, but Zoe could have sworn she saw tears in Chardonnay's eyes.

Afterward the four enjoyed a complimentary lunch for newlyweds, Drake and Bobby hit the blackjack tables while Zoe and Chardonnay hit the mall.

"Girl, I don't even know why you're trippin'," Chardonnay said, as Zoe headed toward Crystals, a luxury shopping mall.

"What?" Zoe asked, her eyes shining as she looked at the sleek steel and glass structure beckoning them in.

"Hmph. It don't look like I can afford to even walk into this joker, let alone buy anything."

"That's part of the fun," Zoe responded. "Can't afford it, can't be tempted."

"Yeah, whatever, Zoe. . . . Whoa, look at these sculptures."

The two women oohed and aahed over clothes, shoes, bags, and jewelry as they flitted in and out of stores. In this time, Chardonnay realized just how much she'd missed Zoe. After a misunderstanding a year ago, their friendship had waned. The two had had a heart-to-heart and gotten back on track, but then Zoe's relationship with Drake deepened and Chardonnay moved in with Bobby, again bringing distance as each woman navigated her new situation. But all of that was forgotten now as they window-shopped and people-watched. Chardonnay provided running commentary on the folks passing by. Zoe couldn't remember when she'd laughed so hard.

"Look at that skinny heifah," Chardonnay said, as a tall, attractive brunette walked into Paul Smith. "She looks like a cross between 'oh no you didn't' and 'dammit I'll bite cha.' "

"Ha! Girl, stop!" Zoe almost spewed out the smoothie she was drinking.

"She used to be a stripper, got plucked from the pole by either a baller or a man in his eighties, and is now maxing out the fool's credit card on some ugly-ass clothes."

"How do you know they're ugly?"

"Did you see the outfit she was wearing?" Chardonnay raised her brows. "I rest my case."

"Looks like a men's store she went into," Zoe said. "Let's go check it out. Maybe they'll have something in there we can buy our guys."

"Yeah, maybe we can split a pair of socks. I'll give Bobby

one and you can give Drake the other! Or maybe we can—"
Chardonnay stopped mid-sentence and yanked Zoe behind
the escalator. "Oh. My. God."

"Chardonnay, what is wrong with you?"

"Girl, look!"

Zoe followed Chardonnay's pointed finger. "That's Bianca!"

"Uh huh." Two pairs of widened eyes watched Bianca
browse past the row of shops on the other side of the aisle.
Their mouths dropped open when a drop-dead-gorgeous
stranger joined her, wrapping a possessive arm around her
shoulder before dropping it down for a clear, firm pat of her
ass. In that moment, any doubt as to the nature of their relationship was resolved.

"Who the hell is that?" Zoe whispered.

"I know who it ain't: Cooper Riley. No wonder his ass got
kicked to the curb. That white boy is fine as hell!" The two
women continued to watch. "I wonder what they're doing
here." Chardonnay's mind swirled with a world of possibili-
ties.

"Taking a break from work, obviously." Zoe turned to
Chardonnay. "Maybe that's it. Maybe he's one of the new west-
side employees."

"A sistah sure knows how to mix business with pleasure if
that's the case." They watched the scene unfolding across the
way as if it were a movie, held their breath as the handsome
man kissed Bianca's hand, then straightened the ring on her—
"Is that a wedding band?" Chardonnay's loud whisper attracted the attention of two women passing by.

"Girl, be quiet!"

"I think I saw a ring, Zoe." Chardonnay's eyes sparkled
with excitement. "Girl, some kind of mess is going on, and I'm
not going to rest until I find out just what." Chardonnay took
a step toward the couple.

"No, Char, we can't go over there!"

"Why not?"

"Because . . . she just broke up with Cooper and I've never seen this man before. Trust me, I'd remember. So what if this is some kind of clandestine affair that she doesn't want anybody to know about?"

"News flash, Sally," Chardonnay pointed to herself. "Somebody knows."

Zoe continued to eye the smooching couple. "I think we ought to just mind our own business."

"And if I don't get all up in her business, I'm going to lose my mind. Hey, Bianca!" Chardonnay yelled, sashaying from behind the escalator and heading in her employer's direction.

Zoe reluctantly followed behind, sure that this would not end well.

Bianca's heart stopped as she heard her name called. Recovering quickly, she turned around, clasping her hands behind her. "Chardonnay? Zoe? What are y'all doing here?"

"Just came down here to take care of a little sumpin', sumpin'," Chardonnay said, sticking the third finger of her left hand in Bianca's face. "Me and Bobby came down here to do the do. I'se married now!"

Bianca brought her right hand around and examined the ring. "It's lovely, Chardonnay. Congratulations."

"Thank you, Bianca. What are you doing here?" The question was directed at Bianca, but Chardonnay's eyes were fixed on the gorgeous stranger beside her.

"We're here on business," Bianca said, quickly thinking on her feet. "With how well the business is thriving, expansion is always on our minds."

"Is this one of your new employees?"

Oh my goodness, this child has too much nerve and no brought-upsy. Zoe fought not to roll her eyes.

"This is Xavier Marquis, a consultant."

After introductions and a few more pleasantries, the foursome went their separate ways.

"Wow, he was even finer up close," Zoe said, after they were a safe distance away. No comment from her normally talkative friend. "Bianca certainly looked happy, there was a glow on her face." Chardonnay snorted, but otherwise remained silent. "I'm glad we went over there and found out exactly what was going on. They're here on business, and he's a consultant."

"And I'll tell you where he's consulting," Chardonnay said out of the side of her mouth. "Right between sistah-girl's thighs."

"See, Chardonnay, that's how lies get started."

"If a lie got started, she did it." Chardonnay stopped and turned to Zoe. "Did you forget how brothah-man tapped her ass before we walked over there, how they were looking at each other goo-goo-eyed before we stepped up? And why did Bianca keep her left hand behind her back the whole time? I'll tell you why. Because Mr. Man-With-The-Accent put a ring on it, that's why! My bet is Bianca got married, and my other bet is Mama and Daddy don't know nothing about it. My name is Chardonnay, not Sade, but I can spot a smooth operator. And I'd leave my marriage bed to get some of that—"

"Okay, Char..."

"I'm just saying—"

"And maybe you're right. But let's let Bianca handle her business while we handle ours." Zoe looked at her watch. "It's been two hours. The men should have had enough blackjack by now. Let's head back."

The two walked out into the crisp, winter air and headed back toward the hotel that now felt a world away. They didn't mention her anymore, but both of the women's minds were on Bianca. While Zoe had advised Chardonnay otherwise, she, too, wondered about the sexy stranger and just what his relationship was with her boss's daughter. She wondered why they were here, where they were staying, and what all Xavier bought her after they'd left. The man reeked of money, and Zoe imagined Bianca laden down with bags before they returned to their paradisaical dwelling.

Though the focus was different, Chardonnay's mind was also on Bianca. She wondered just who Xavier Marquis was, when Bianca got married, and how much this Livingston sibling was willing to pay Chardonnay to keep her marriage a secret.

39

"Man, this place is crowded," Malcolm said as he looked around. "It's been a while since I've been here."

"It's been a minute for me as well."

Malcolm and Toussaint nodded at various employees as they made their way to a corner booth at the Taste of Soul located less than ten minutes from the Livingston Corporation's executive offices. Founders Marcus and Marietta Livingston had made it a rule that every Livingston dine at Taste at least twice a month, and fifty years later, that rule was still in effect. Fortunately, Chef's great cooking made this not a problem but a pleasure. Ace's idea of jukeboxes filled with soul tunes in every establishment only added to the fun. Heads bobbed as people laughed and ate. A lone diner snapped his fingers as he heard all about love land from Charles Wright and the Watts 103rd Street Rhythm Band and afterward, another table crooned openly as the Five Stairsteps assured the patrons that things were going to get easier. The brothers' chests swelled with pride. Running a business that made people happy had always been their destiny and was now their legacy.

"So talk to me, brother," Malcolm said, once they'd placed their orders. "How's it going on the home front?"

Toussaint sighed as he leaned back into the booth. "You've been there five times, man. You know *exactly* how it's going."

Malcolm chuckled. "Alexis getting a little stingy with the loving?"

"It's driving me up a wall, man. I don't know if I can take it!"

"Oh, you'll take it," Malcolm said casually. "There's no other choice. You're a Livingston, and that's what we do."

"Yeah, I know. The Livingston legacy." Toussaint's eyes traveled to the large, framed pictures on the room's back wall. One was of his grandmother, Marietta, and the other of Marcus, the patriarch. "No affairs, no divorce." Toussaint shook his head. "Man must have been crazy to make that promise."

"His grandfather was." The two men became silent, both thinking about the story that had been passed down for generations: how after losing the one he loved when his master sold him, a slave vowed that his seed would never know such heartache. He eventually jumped the broom with another and had a son, Marcus's grandfather, and drummed the virtues of loyalty into the young boy's heart. No affairs, no divorce. And the legacy began. "Hey, what's up with your boy Jefferson?"

"Man, I don't know, but something is going on. The only time I can catch him is at the office and the former homebody is now rarely at his space. Bianca is acting funny, too."

Malcolm took a drink of his sweet tea and dipped a homemade potato chip into Maceo's mustard green and artichoke dip. "How do you mean?"

"I can't quite put my finger on it, but just like Jefferson, she's acting...different. When it comes to Taste West or TOSTS, you can't shut her up. But on the phone yesterday, her mind wasn't in it. I think they're both hiding something. I just don't know what."

"Do you think Ace and Aunt Diane know?"

"If they do, then Mama and Daddy know, too." Toussaint

finished off a black-eyed pea fritter, then pushed the appetizer plate toward Malcolm. "Those are good, man."

"I don't think so," Malcolm concluded, thoughtfully chewing the delectable morsel made of peas, green onions, and various spices. "I know how Mama confides in you, Toussaint. If Candace knew anything, then you would, too."

Toussaint looked up as the waitress approached with their platters. But his attention wasn't on the smothered pork chops or the chicken-fried steak. His eyes were glued to who'd just walked into the building. "Man, just my luck."

"What?"

"You're not going to believe who just walked in here."

One look at his brother and Malcolm needed only one guess. "Shyla."

Toussaint nodded.

"So Shyla Martin is back in town."

"She's got a lot of nerve." Toussaint looked down at the delicious fare that surrounded his smothered chops: mashed potatoes, greens, and fresh, skillet-fried corn, and tried to rekindle his appetite.

Malcolm was having no such problem. He cut off a sizable piece of steak, dipped it into the mashed potatoes and gravy on his plate, then followed it with generous scoops of cabbage and okra. "Wonder what she's up to," he said after a few more bites.

"Whatever it is"—Toussaint finally picked up his fork—"can't be good."

On the other side of the room, Shyla's inner turmoil was masked by an outward calm. She'd seen Toussaint's Mercedes parked in front and therefore wasn't surprised by his presence. And determination had outweighed her fear. To help Cooper in his goal of destruction, Shyla needed information on Bianca. All of the Livingston Corporation's employees had been warned against Shyla months ago, following her termination. She'd believed any ins to this dynasty's goings-on had been effectively blocked. And then she'd remembered Bobby.

Shyla strolled into the take-out area of the restaurant and picked up a menu. Just before leaving her home, she'd shed jeans and a sweater for a sweater dress and boots. The soft, tan material hugged her body in all the right places, evident by the appreciative glances the male patrons offered. *This could have been yours,* she silently told Toussaint. *Read it and weep.*

Within moments, what Shyla had hoped to have happen indeed occurred. "Hey, gorgeous," Bobby said, wiping his hands on a stark white apron streaked with barbeque sauce. "Aren't you a sight for sore eyes."

"Hello, Bobby."

"How are you doing, Shyla? Girl, I haven't seen you in ages."

"I've been busy, and I'm doing fantastic."

"You're looking fantastic."

"Thank you. You're looking fine, as well. Is life treating you all right?"

Bobby smiled broadly. "I couldn't be better. Me and Chardonnay got married last week."

A two-time baby mama beat me to the altar? Shyla's indignation was tempered by remembering who'd met Chardonnay at that altar. Shyla would die a spinster before marrying a man like Bobby. "Congratulations," Shyla said, and she was sincere.

"Yeah, me and my girl flew to Vegas and tied the knot. Heard Bianca was there, too."

Shyla was immediately all ears, but looked sufficiently bored. "Oh, really," she said, while gazing at the menu.

"Yeah, Chardonnay ran into her at a mall. Said she was with some white guy."

Oh, really? is what Shyla thought. "Hum," is all she said.

Bobby reached for his vibrating cell phone and read a text message. "Look, Shyla. I gotta go. It's been nice talking to you."

He nodded his head in the patron's direction and headed through the kitchen to the restaurant's back entrance.

Five minutes later, Bobby's head moved up and down on his lover's shaft and five minutes after that, a low growl signaled this lover's release. Bobby reached for the towel he'd retrieved from the kitchen and cleaned them both before tossing the now useless rag on the floor. He sat low in the seat, and looked around the area. They were parked in an overflow lot off the back alley, two businesses down from Taste of Soul. His lover had further shielded them by parking next to a dumpster. That he didn't see anyone, and didn't think anyone could see them, made him no less uncomfortable.

"I can't believe you risked everything to come here!"

The man's large hand covered Bobby's. "I had to take my chances."

Bobby snatched away his hand and glanced around again. "Don't do that shit, man. I'm not your dude or nothing. I told you. This is just sex." He reached for a cigarette but it remained unlit. "What if someone saw you? Saw us?"

"Thank you for not smoking around me. It's really a nasty habit, you know, not to mention unhealthy." Judge Cooper Riley, Sr., calmly zipped up his pants, redid his belt buckle and checked his appearance in the rearview mirror. Satisfied that he looked the part of what he was, a well-respected conservative court judge, he turned to Bobby and simply said, "I couldn't wait."

40

"Something's up with Bobby." Chardonnay sat at Zoe's kitchen table for the first time in months, smoking a Newport and sipping on her namesake.

"Why do you say that?"

" 'Cause he's been real quiet lately. And he told me that he had to close up the restaurant last night when I know for a fact that Chef stayed late."

"Girl, don't let that overactive imagination get you into trouble."

Chardonnay took another long puff of her cigarette. "I don't care who he's screwing," she finally said. "Long as he keeps pleasuring the puddin' and bringing the paycheck home."

Zoe plopped down in a seat at the table and reached for the pack. She'd given up smoking but when troubled or excited, occasionally indulged. "Please don't tell me that you think Bobby is seeing a woman."

"Naw, girl. I'll tell you something much more scandalous. I think he's seeing a man. See, John Abernathy . . ."

More than two thousand miles away, Toussaint was dealing with a mystery of his own. What was a wedding ring doing in his cousin's top drawer? He'd flown into town a day earlier, helping prepare for the West Coast opening less than two weeks away. She'd tried to act normal, but Toussaint felt that Bianca seemed skittish and distant. Even Crystal seemed on edge. Yesterday, he'd thought that something was going on. Today, he was sure of it. He rose, stepped away from Bianca's desk, and was looking at a grouping of pictures when she returned. Yet all he saw was the ring.

"Sorry about that," Bianca said, walking quickly to her desk. She scanned it surreptitiously, all appeared to be in place. She hadn't wanted to leave the office, hadn't wanted to give Toussaint a moment alone. But he seemed the same as when she'd left. "Now, where were we?"

"Where were we?" Toussaint drawled as he slowly turned around. "I'm not sure, Bianca, but I think you were just about to tell me your husband's name."

For a second, Bianca's world tilted on its axis. But she quickly regrouped. She was a Livingston, not a money-hungry skeezer. Somebody had just put in their last day on the job. "Don't tell me you'd believe somebody like Chardonnay."

"Chardonnay? What the hell does she have to do with anything."

Bianca eyed her cousin. *He seems genuinely surprised. But how else could he know about Xavier except that I refused to pay the skank her fifty-thousand-dollar shut-up money? Chardonnay carried out her threat to spill the beans!* Obviously not wanting to put all of her eggs in Q's basket, Chardonnay had widened her net by blackmailing Bianca as well.

"I saw the wedding ring."

"What wedding ring?" Bianca countered, looking at her hands. It was a feeble attempt, but she tried anyway.

"The one in your desk drawer."

Damn, damn, damn! Bianca had hurriedly removed the ring and tossed it in her drawer when Toussaint showed up at the restaurant instead of going to his hotel first, as she'd assumed he would. She'd forgotten to tell Crystal to get the ring and take it home with her. Time for damage control. "What the hell are you doing snooping in my stuff?" *That's it, Bianca. Anger, turn the tables, shift the focus, just forget about the ring!*

"C'mon now, Cousin. You know me better than that. I saw a string on my shirt and went searching for a pair of scissors. Looks like I found a secret instead."

Bianca walked to her desk, formulating Plan B. "So you found out I'm seeing somebody," she said in what she hoped was a casual manner. "So what."

Toussaint had known this girl from birth, had sneaked around and plotted with her too many times. He didn't for a second buy her cool, calm, and collected act. Walking over to her desk, he sat and looked her dead in the eye. "Seeing somebody, huh?"

"Yes." Bianca's voice faltered, even as she lifted her chin in defiance.

Toussaint stared at Bianca. Bianca stared back. Several seconds passed before Bianca looked away. "I love you like a sister, Cuz. Why are you lying?"

Bianca took a deep breath. "You can't tell Mama and Daddy," she finally said.

"But you have to . . . and soon."

Back in Georgia, an excited Chardonnay sat gripping the phone. For the thousandth time, she thanked God for whoever invented search engines and the Internet. Anyone with a less curious nature may have forgotten. But a man named Xavier, who looked as lavish as caviar, didn't come along every day. The Marquis part had been tricky, especially since she'd entered "marquee" into the engine when she searched the first time. She'd called Zoe and was less than thrilled when her cautious friend hadn't shared Chardonnay's excitement. "Leave it alone," Zoe had warned. "It ain't your business."

"Sorry for the interruption," said the caller into Chardonnay's ear. "Thanks for waiting. Like I said earlier, we received your tip and found it very interesting. The facts have been verified."

"I told you it was true!" Chardonnay didn't try to hide her indignation.

"Yes, you did, but we are journalists. Everything has to be verified."

"Girl, please. I read these papers all the time. If Beyoncé was pregnant every time y'all printed it, she'd have ten kids by now."

"Mrs. Wilson, I'll have you know that we here at the *Atlanta Enquirer* pride ourselves on accurate reporting. Which is why we verified your story and will publish our findings."

"That's all well and cool, but it had better not be until y'all send me my check. Or else you'll have another story to write... about the time y'all asses got sued."

There was a long pause on the other end.

Oh, hell, maybe I said too much. "Hello?" There was actually timidity in Chardonnay's voice—a first. "Girl, I was just playing with you. I'm not going to sue anybody."

"You won't have to," the woman replied, a slight chill in her voice. "I've just e-mailed a form for you to sign and mail. As soon as it's received and processed, your check will be in the mail."

Chardonnay hung up the phone and sat back in her seat. It wasn't the hundred grand she'd hoped for, but ten thousand wasn't bad for half a day's work. Chardonnay yawned, stretched, and headed for the shower. For a brief moment, she contemplated calling in sick. *Hell, I've made my money for the day.* But then she decided it wouldn't be prudent; best not to do anything outside the norm until the story broke. Once the story went national, she'd be home free. After all, she was likely not the only person who knew about this secret marriage. Bianca's assistant was bound to know something and Chardonnay knew for a fact that most men couldn't keep their mouths shut about whom they were screwing. Wasn't no telling who Xavier had told.

Soon Chardonnay was on her way to the restaurant, still reeling over how easy making that money had been. *Yeah, Zoe keeps telling me to stop sticking my nose where it doesn't belong.* And now Chardonnay was getting ready to stick ten Gs exactly where it was supposed to be: in a new, private bank account bearing only her name.

41

Jefferson had been staring at the same screen for fifteen minutes. He'd even walked away, refreshed his drink, and come back. Nothing had changed. The balance of his savings account was still short almost two hundred thousand dollars. Jefferson sat back and stared into the distance, looking for his money. With each passing minute, the gnawing in his stomach deepened and his fear increased.

He thought back to the day he'd set up the account, shortly after his thirtieth birthday. Following a recent Livingston tradition, his parents had gifted him with a million dollars. His first impulse had been to go on a spending spree. He even made a list: Maserati, Jacob the Jeweler pendant, sailboat anchored off the Florida Keys. The voice of reason's source had been unlikely. But Toussaint had been right. *Throw it in the bank for a minute, let the newness wear off. Then decide how you want to roll. That paper won't spoil, Cuz. You've got all the time in the world.* Divine had also encouraged him to save his money . . . unless he wanted to invest it in a certain art gallery. Jefferson had invested in the gallery, along with several other entities his financial consultant had suggested to round out his portfolio. He'd recouped his initial outlay of half a million dollars in less than two years and vowed to use the money solely for future milestones: marriage, kids, a doctorate degree. If it weren't for the fact that Jefferson had decided to bring Keisha out of hiding, introduce her to the family, and make her his wife, who knows when he would have discovered the discrepancy. Jefferson passed a weary hand over his face. He needed a second opinion from someone he could trust. Reaching for the phone, he dialed the number of the first name that came to mind.

"Divine, it's me. Are you at the gallery?"

"Yes."

"Stay there. I'm coming over."

Jefferson grabbed his jacket and headed out of the office. As he neared the door, the home phone rang. He checked the ID. *Keisha.* A squiggle of discomfort hit his stomach, but he quickly dismissed it. It wasn't as easy to dismiss the thoughts that came to his mind as he started the car, like why he'd called Divine and not the woman he planned to marry, and why two months after arriving in town Keisha was still hidden from his family. " 'Cause you're a punk," he mumbled as he turned the corner and merged onto the highway ramp leading to Little Five Points. The more Jefferson got to know Keisha, the more he loved her, yet the more he realized how different she was from members of his family, and how hard it might be for her to feel as though she fit in. And then there were her sons, Antwan and Dorian. He was surprised at how quickly they'd adapted to Atlanta, and how easily they'd become a part of his life. He was spending more and more weekdays at Keisha's house, and every weekend. *But your woman is still a mystery. You got to do something about that, man.* Because he knew one thing for sure: the dual life was driving him crazy.

Jefferson exited the highway and punched the speakerphone button. "Yeah, baby."

"Hey, Pookie, where are you?"

"Headed to the gallery. What's up?"

Keisha was immediately suspicious. "Why are you going over there?" She'd only hung out with Divine once since moving here and had gotten the distinct impression that Divine was less than thrilled about Jefferson's new love. When Keisha shared this with Jefferson, he'd said she was overreacting. Maybe so, but it had given her reason enough to back out of future engagements, and to try to limit Jefferson's involvement with his supposed best friend. "*I'm* supposed to be your best friend," she'd told him. Keisha felt it was time that she told him again. "Did she ask you to come over?" Keisha demanded.

"I won't be long. Have y'all eaten?"

"You didn't answer my question, Jefferson."

"That was the point." Most of the time, Keisha handled herself rather maturely for a woman who was only twenty-six. However, at times like these, the seven-year age difference between them became glaringly obvious.

"What's that supposed to mean. Are you fucking her?"

Jefferson's hands clenched the wheel. "Keisha, I don't have time for this right now."

"But you've got time for her? What is going on, Jefferson?"

"Are you really trying to do this right now, Keisha? Really?"

"I'm not trying to make you mad, baby. But you're all I've got. I don't know anybody here, and you're hanging out with her!"

"Maybe that's the problem, that you don't know nobody. I told you to get out, join a gym, get a job, do something besides sit in the house all day." Jefferson became silent, trying to stem his anger. This was his baby, the woman he planned to marry. And she was right. She didn't know anybody, and because of his own fears regarding his family finding out, he'd done little to acclimate her. "Look, baby, I'm sorry you're angry, and I'm sorry how you're feeling about my friendship with Divine. I really don't understand it, Keisha. You know she and I are just good friends. She introduced us, for God's sake."

"Yeah, but she was just being nice. She didn't really know

me. If she'd known you were going to start seeing me, she probably wouldn't have said a thing."

Jefferson pulled up in front of the gallery. "Maybe you're right, baby, but that's neither here nor there right now. It's not me and Divine, it's me and you. Okay?"

Keisha nodded, which, of course, Jefferson couldn't see.

"Okay?"

"Okay," Keisha whispered.

"Have y'all eaten?"

"No."

"Then I'll bring something over."

"That's okay, Jefferson. You're right, I need to get out."

"Okay, baby, but we'll talk later."

"Bye."

Divine met Jefferson in the gallery's foyer. "What's going on, darlin'," she said, hugging Jefferson warmly. "You sounded upset over the phone."

"Yeah, well, I'm even more so now."

"Come on back to the kitchen. I put on some tea."

Within ten minutes, Jefferson had spilled his heart out to his longtime friend—not only about the missing money but also about his plans regarding Keisha and the fears and frustrations that came with his desire to make her his wife.

"Wow, Jeff, that's a lot," Divine said, after listening intently. "What are you going to do?"

"That's the problem. I don't know."

"Want some advice?"

Jefferson smiled faintly. "I guess I wouldn't have come here if I didn't."

"Yeah, whatever, okay?" She punched him playfully. "First of all, you have to report the missing money."

Jefferson shook his head.

"You've got to, Jefferson. That's a crime, a felony! And whoever has tapped into your account may have the numbers to others in your family. The sooner you get someone on this, the better your chances of catching the culprit and recovering your cash.

"Two, you've got to tell your family about Keisha. And maybe you should ask yourself why it's taken this long. I'm your friend, so you know I'll support any decision you make... even if I don't necessarily agree."

"What, you don't like Keisha?"

"I don't know Keisha. And neither do you; at least, that's what it feels like when I talk to you. Sure, she's attractive and attentive and makes you feel good. That's all well and good, but if you're going to bring her into the Livingston clan, you need to do more. Where's the rest of her family and who are they?"

"I told you about her mother. If I had an alcoholic for a parent, it would embarrass me, too."

"Then what about her siblings, uncles, cousins, somebody. There's nobody in the family sane enough for you to meet? You need to do a background check, Jeff."

Jefferson's expression showed otherwise.

"Look," Divine continued, realizing that suggesting a background check wasn't the best of ideas. *If someone decided to check on me...* "It's your life, friend. You can do what you want to do. But I didn't call you, you called me, and I believe this was the reason: because I'd give it to you straight. You've known this woman less than a year, most of that time being from a distance. She's got two young sons by two different men whom you also know nothing about. You've never met anyone else in her life: no family, friends, coworkers, or neighbors. You may say otherwise, but I say that's strange."

Jefferson nodded his head slowly, letting Divine's words penetrate. "You're absolutely right, Divine. But to be fair, she hasn't met my family either."

"But yours is a public family. She knows their names, and can look them up online." *What am I, stupid? There I go again!* Divine's heartbeat increased as she thought of the skeletons in her own closet, damning secrets if revealed. Jefferson pushed back the barely touched tea and stood. "Thanks for being here," he said.

Divine stood as well. "Anytime," she said. "You know I love you."

"I love you, too."

Divine noted Jefferson's slumped shoulders as he walked down the hall. Her eyes were filled with concern. "Take care of yourself and keep me posted."

Jefferson lifted his hand and waved without looking back.

On the other side of town, Keisha sat in the Taste of Soul parking lot with her two sons. She'd gone there hoping that the friendly waitress would be working, but had been told it was Chardonnay's day off. She looked in the rearview mirror, and couldn't help but smile as she watched her sons devouring their kiddie meals. *At least somebody's happy.* Keisha wasn't hungry, but rummaged in her purse for a piece of gum, while she tried to decide on what to do. *Maybe I'll take them to a movie,* she thought. She was just about to ask her sons if they'd like to go when her hand hit a card at the bottom of her purse. She pulled it out and began to smile as she read the print: CHARDONNAY JOHNSON, ASSISTANT MANAGER, TASTE OF SOUL RESTAURANT. Keisha reached for her phone and dialed the number Chardonnay had handwritten on the back of the card. *Please be home.* Suddenly it became very important that, instead of waiting for Jefferson to show up anytime he wanted to, Keisha have someplace to go.

"Chardonnay? This is Keisha." Pause. "Keisha, the woman with the two handsome sons that you met in the restaurant."

Chardonnay, who'd been lying on the couch watching *The Real Housewives of Atlanta* reruns, sat straight up. "Keisha," she said, trying not to act excited. "What's up, girl?"

"Nothing much. That's the problem. I'm bored to death and was wondering if one, you wanted to maybe hit a club, and two, if you knew a babysitter."

"Yes," Chardonnay answered, as her mind raced. "Where do you want to meet? Or better yet, just come to my house. My husband ain't doing nothing. He can watch the kids for a couple hours 'cause I sure could use a drink. Let me give you my address."

Three hours and several Long Island Teas later, Chardonnay and Keisha returned to Chardonnay's house. Keisha picked up her sleeping sons, thanked Chardonnay for the good time, and left. Chardonnay watched the taillights from Keisha's SUV until they reached the end of the street and turned the corner. Only then did she reach for her cell phone and dial Toussaint's number.

"Toussaint, this is Chardonnay. Call me as soon as you get this message. I don't care what time it is, even if it's in the middle of the night. Call me."

42

Ace walked briskly down the quiet halls of the Livingston Corporation. It was a little after eight in the morning, one of Ace's favorite times to be at the office. Whereas his twin brother, Adam, preferred the tranquility of late night—often getting to work at ten or eleven and then staying well into the evening—Ace liked the morning time: calm, peaceful, just like this.

He reached his office door, shifted the mug of coffee that was in his right hand, and unlocked his door. The neat, well-appointed office welcomed him, with its dark, mahogany furniture and cocoa brown fabrics. Splashes of color, by way of artwork and pillows, reminded Ace of Diane, who'd put them there. His gaze passed over the diplomas and certificates of achievement that hung on the wall behind his desk, and when he sat, he allowed his eyes to rest on the small grouping of pictures on the left side of his desk: one of Diane; a family portrait when the kids were teens; one of his parents, Marcus and Marietta, in front of the very first Taste of Soul establishment; and another of him and Adam at a black tie event.

Ace leaned back in his chair, enjoying his morning java and going over the day's planned events in his head. There was a conference call with the TOS restaurant managers at ten thirty and a luncheon meeting with the department heads at one o'clock. Preparing an organizational report for the board of directors that was due next week would take up his afternoon. And tonight, he had a date with his wife. Ace smiled at the thought.

The blinking of the telephone stirred him from his relaxed state. He glanced at the clock: 8:10. That the call was inter-office caused his brows to crease. *Who else is at their desk at this time of morning?* "Ace Livingston."

"Good morning, Ace."

"Son! Well, this is a surprise. You starting to burn the early morning oil like your old man?"

"I'm not planning to make this a habit, Dad, but I was hoping to catch you before the day got underway. Do you have a few minutes?"

"Of course."

"Good, I'm on my way."

As soon as Jefferson stepped inside his office, Ace knew something was wrong. Unlike Bianca, who held her cards to her chest and had perfected the poker face, Jefferson wore his heart on his sleeve and his feelings were normally written all over his face.

Ace motioned Jefferson to join him over at the sitting area. As soon as they sat, Ace started in. "What's wrong, son?"

Jefferson took a deep breath, dreading the fact that he had to share this news. But there was no way around it. Somebody had stolen money from him and there was a very good possibility that this person was linked to the person who'd been stealing from the other coffers. Jefferson already had one secret: Keisha. He couldn't afford another.

He looked his father in the eye. "One of my accounts has money missing."

This revelation caused Ace to sit straight up. "Stolen?"

Jefferson nodded.

Ace's gut clenched. He carefully set his coffee mug on the

table before him and tried to still his suddenly shaky hand. "Are you sure?"

Jefferson nodded and relayed what had happened the previous day. "I have a meeting at the bank later this morning," he concluded. "And they'll begin an investigation right away. For now, the rest of the funds are frozen. So whoever the asshole is won't get any more of my money."

"Dammit!" Ace hissed. He was silent a moment, pondering his next question. He almost didn't want to know the answer, but he had to ask. "How much did they get, Son?"

"Almost two hundred grand." Jefferson's voice was barely above a whisper.

"Damn!" Unable to sit a moment longer, Ace began to pace. After another few seconds, he strode to the phone.

Jefferson watched his father stride purposefully across the room. "Who are you calling?"

"Adam and Sterling. Whoever broke into your account may be the same one who was stealing from the other. I don't plan on waiting for your bank's investigation. We need to move now and get to the bottom of this. That nervy son of a bitch has stolen from us for the last time."

Later that afternoon, Ace and Jefferson walked into Sterling's office and into the conference room where Sterling and Adam were already seated.

"What happened?" Adam asked, even before Jefferson's butt hit the soft, plush leather of the conference room chairs.

"Somebody hacked into one of my accounts, a savings account that I rarely use, that I'd set aside for specific purposes and haven't touched for over a year."

"What did they say at the bank?"

"That the transfer was made via computer to a bank in Kansas City. The funds were then withdrawn the very next day and the account closed down."

Ace looked at Sterling. "Then this is an easy case, right?

Whoever opened the account and took out the funds had to show ID. They probably have surveillance, too. So we just need to match a name with a face and catch this guy."

Sterling was his usual cool, calm, collected, and methodical self. "Things are rarely as easy as they appear," he responded. "We're obviously dealing with a professional here, someone who probably has several aliases, fake IDs, maybe even disguises to mask his true appearance."

Adam's frown deepened. "Are you saying there's a chance we may not catch him?"

Sterling shook his head. "I'm not saying that at all. It doesn't matter where this man runs or where he hides." He looked around at the Livingston men, his face a study in confidence. "We'll get him."

As soon as Adam, Ace, and Jefferson left Sterling's office, he reached for his phone. "Sterling," he said as soon as the call was picked up on the other end. "You still got Quintin Bright in your crosshairs?" There was a deep sigh at the other end, causing Sterling's hair to stand on end.

"I was just getting ready to call you," said a gruff, worn voice. "We've lost him."

43

"Lord have mercy, something smells good in here." Candace stepped into Diane's living room and gave her sister-in-law a big hug. "What's cooking?"

"Rump roast," Diane responded, before reaching for Adam to give him a hug. "Hey, in-law."

"Hello, Diane," Adam responded. He then greeted Ace with a soul brother's handshake. "Twin."

"What's up, bro? Come on back here and get you a drink."

"Did you talk to Malcolm?" Diane asked, as she and Candace walked into the kitchen.

"Yes, he and Victoria are coming. Toussaint might make it, but Alexis isn't feeling well."

"Oh, no. That's too bad. How far along is she?"

"Right at seven months."

"Hmph, I sure don't miss those days."

"Tell me about it. I never knew being a grandmother could feel so good; love 'em, spoil 'em, then send them back home for their parents to worry about!"

Diane sighed. "I wouldn't know." She walked over to the refrigerator. "What do you want to drink?"

"I'll take some sparkling water if you have it. What can I do to help?"

"Girl, this is an easy meal. The vegetables are cooking alongside the roast, except for the corn on the cob, which Ace is going to put on the grill. I baked a loaf of fresh bread and two pecan pies this morning." Diane looked at her watch. "Bianca's plane should have landed by now, so we can be eating within the hour."

"Oh, so she did make it home."

"Yeah, almost had to threaten her to get her to come back here."

"Sounds like LA is agreeing with her."

"My guess is somebody in LA is agreeing with her."

"You think she's dating? If so, that was fast. She just got out there."

"Call it a mother's hunch, but something is definitely going on with my daughter."

"What about Jefferson?"

Diane's voice dropped an octave. "Girl, that's what I wanted to talk to you about. He's bringing someone to dinner, somebody he wants the family to meet."

"What? Who is she?"

The doorbell rang.

Diane wiped her hands and headed toward the doorway. "I guess that's what we're getting ready to find out."

An hour later, Ace and Diane's dining room was abuzz with conversation, punctuated with the clink of silverware on china and the soft sounds of straight-ahead jazz playing in the background. The family hadn't done a large get-together since New Year's, and these Sunday gatherings were largely a thing of the past. That they were enjoying each other was clearly evident.

"I'm still trying to get used to Miss Bianca," Malcolm said, as he helped himself to another heaping serving of smothered cabbage, veggies, and roast. "You've gone all Halle Berry on us, cut off all your hair."

"I like it," Diane said. "Once I got over the shock. That girl used to cry if she saw five hairs in the brush; this child loved her long hair."

"Why did you cut it?" Candace asked.

Bianca shrugged. "Wanted a change."

"I think it looks good," Victoria said, even as she tossed her shoulder-length tresses over her shoulder. "Brings out your high cheeks and strong bone structure."

"I liked it better long," Ace said.

The conversation shifted from Bianca's life in LA to politics and from sports to African American society. All the while, Diane's surreptitious focus was on the young woman at Jefferson's side: young, attractive, and totally inappropriate. Not one to rush to judgment, Diane had felt discomfort from the moment the girl walked through the door. She looked the part of someone solidly middle class: navy pantsuit, soft pastel shell, even a string of pearls. But it would take more than a conservative outfit to get past Diane Livingston's inspection. Diane had looked into the child's eyes and seen a lifetime of living. She was convinced that whatever tale she'd woven for her son's benefit didn't begin to tell the whole story. Before it was all over, however, Diane fully intended to find it out.

Her opportunity came later, when the men had retired to the library/study for cigars and cognac, and Candace, Victoria, and Bianca cleaned the kitchen. Diane and an obviously uncomfortable Keisha sat in the family room, sipping white Russians.

"So," Diane began in a casual tone. "How did you and Jefferson meet?"

"At the Divine gallery," Keisha said in a low, soft voice.

"Oh, a lover of art. Well, that is something you definitely have in common with my son. At one time, I thought he was going to follow that path as a career. Have you ever seen any of his work?"

"Yes," Keisha answered. "There's a piece in our living room."

"Our? You two are living together?"

"Uh, no, ma'am. I mean *my* living room. Me and my..."
Keisha's voice faded, realizing her error. She and Jefferson had
decided it best not to mention Keisha's sons during this first
visit. But it was hard to keep them out of conversation; they
were such a part of her life.

"Your..." Diane prodded, waiting for Keisha to continue.

Keisha sighed and decided to be truthful. She loved her
boys and wasn't ashamed of any part of her life: drunken
mother, crazy family and stolen money notwithstanding. Besides, she didn't like perpetrating falsehoods with these snooty
people, felt that they weren't any better than her. So what if
their home was the most beautiful that she'd ever entered, if
their glasses sounded like chimes when you clinked them, or
that the chandeliers glistened with a thousand crystals. Whether
they liked it or not, Keisha Miller was getting ready to be a
part of their lives. The sooner they knew who she really was,
the sooner they'd know exactly what they had to deal with.
Because Keisha Miller, who felt like she'd hit the baby daddy
jackpot, wasn't going anywhere!

"My sons," she finally answered, straightening her back and
looking Diane in the eye. "I have two sons, seven and four. Jefferson is a great father figure, and my boys adore him. We're
hoping to add a daughter to the mix very soon." Keisha fortified her courage by draining her glass. "This is delicious,
Diane. May I have another?"

44

Diane wasn't the only one observing their guest. Toussaint had almost choked on his beer when Jefferson had introduced them. Since then, he'd been in emotional turmoil. What were the chances that his cousin's girlfriend shared the same name as Quintin's sister? And hadn't Jefferson said she was originally from LA? Toussaint observed Keisha carefully. Granted, she looked nothing like Quintin Bright, but with today's blended this, step that, and half the other, that didn't necessarily mean anything. Still, Toussaint had a sneaking suspicion that the woman who sat at their table was the very one Chardonnay had told him about three days ago. He couldn't leave without talking to his cousin, so when he heard Jefferson turn down his father's invitation to hit the greens with the rest of the men, he, too, declined.

"It's been a minute since you've brought a girl home to meet the family," Toussaint said, once Adam, Ace, and Malcolm had left the study. "Is it that serious?"

Jefferson nodded. "Very." He looked at his cousin and decided to share more. "I'm thinking about asking her to marry me."

"Marriage? Already?" Toussaint didn't try to mask his surprise. "How long have you known her?"

"How long did you know Alexis? When it's right, it's right, dog. Doesn't matter how long it's been."

Toussaint knew he had to tread carefully. The last thing he wanted was to get Jefferson on the defensive. Like most Livingstons, Jefferson could be very determined when he wanted to, and very loyal—even when that loyalty was misplaced.

"I agree with you, man," he said in a casual tone. He rose from the couch and walked over to the minibar. He raised his beer bottle. "You want another one?"

Jefferson shook his head. "No, I'm good."

Instead of returning to the couch, Toussaint walked over to the pool table. "How about a game of eight ball?"

"All right, then."

Toussaint began racking the balls. "Yeah, man, I think when I met Alexis it was love at first sight. I didn't know it, though."

Jefferson pushed the last couple of balls over to Toussaint. "Did she?"

"Ha! Are you kidding? Woman couldn't stand me when we first met. Thought I was bougie."

"You?"

"Can you believe it?" Toussaint shared the story about how Alexis had come to his car's defense when a parking cop was about to issue a ticket, and how after finding out whose car it was the officer, who'd gone to school with Toussaint, apologized to Toussaint and offered advice on getting the ticket nullified. "She went from being mad I was being ticketed to livid that I might *not* get one," Toussaint concluded, laughing as he remembered the story and the look on her face.

"That is crazy, man. All this time I thought Malcolm introduced y'all."

"No, her redecorating my brother's den was pure fate."

"And the rest is history."

The two men played in silence for a couple moments,

Toussaint's mind plotting the whole time. "Yeah, me and Alexis have a lot in common. She couldn't be more different than the rest of her family, though."

"How do you mean?"

"You see Alexis, classy, successful, motivated to do her best. Her mother, Jean, is nice enough, but married to a drunk. Her brothers are worthless." Toussaint shook his head. "Hard to believe they share the same blood."

Jefferson's ears perked up at the news he'd never known about his cousin's wife. Alexis and Keisha had something in common. Maybe it wasn't such a long shot for Keisha to be included in the fact after all.

"I think Keisha probably feels the same way about some of her family."

Toussaint sank the nine ball into a hole. "Oh, yeah?"

"Yeah. She doesn't talk about her family much, but her mother has been on drugs and alcohol most of Keisha's life, and the rest of her family seems to have a ghetto mentality as well."

"Have you met them?"

"No, not yet. Two ball, corner pocket." The ball nicked the perimeter of the pocket but spun out. "Damn!"

Toussaint chalked his cue. "Twelve," he said, pointing to the side pocket. "She have brothers or sisters?"

"She has a brother," Jefferson replied. "At least that I know of. She doesn't like to talk about her family. I think she's embarrassed."

"I don't know why. Every family has at least one relative who's embarrassing." Both men laughed, thinking of Diane's brother, their Uncle Woody, who made any gathering he attended a Comedy Central event. "I'm sure that when you meet them, you'll find out they're not so bad. I mean, Alexis's brothers seem like good enough people, just lazy as hell. My . . . let's say . . . interesting in-laws might meet yours one day since you're getting ready to pop the question and all."

"Yes," Jefferson said, nodding his head. This conversation made him remember Divine's words. She, also, had encouraged him to find out more about the woman in his home. They were both right. He loved Keisha. Nothing he found out about her or her family would change that. In that moment he decided that when he and Keisha got home that night...it was time for a conversation.

Later that night, Diane climbed into bed next to Ace, who was reading the sports section from the Sunday paper. She sat against the headboard, arms folded, staring straight ahead. She reached over for a magazine, thumbed through it without seeing anything, slammed it down on the nightstand, huffed, and folded her arms again.

"Okay, Diane," Ace said in resignation. "What's wrong?"

"Keisha Miller, that's what."

Ace eyed the woman whom he'd trust with his life. Diane had never been one to put on airs or think herself above others. So if she'd picked up on something, then something was there to be picked up on. He placed down the newspaper and turned toward his wife. "What'd she say, baby?"

Diane turned toward her husband, glad to discuss what had been bothering her all afternoon. She'd known that Ace and Candace were taking in a movie after they left, and Bianca had taken a red-eye back to LA. She'd hoped to bend Toussaint's ear, but Alexis had called and Toussaint had rushed out, leaving Diane no choice but to stew alone...until now. "You know what, Ace? It's not so much what she said that is bothering me, though there were some things I'll share...but it's what she didn't say. That is what's putting a hitch in her giddyap where I'm concerned."

"Let's start with what she told you."

"Okay. For starters, she has two kids. Did Jefferson mention them?"

Ace shook his head. "No, he sure didn't."

"I don't think Keisha had planned to mention them either.

I think it just slipped out. Then there was the fact that she moved here in January."

"What? She's not from here?"

"No, she's from LA. I'd bet any amount of money that Jefferson moved her; that child doesn't strike me as having money of her own."

Ace froze as a thought ran across his mind. "Diane, do you think this girl could have something to do with the missing money, the money that got stolen from Jefferson's account and maybe even the company one as well?"

Diane thought for a moment, and then began slowly shaking her head. "I don't see how that's likely. The money started missing from the corporate account months ago."

"Yeah, but Jeff said the withdrawal was made from his account two months ago."

Diane looked at Ace. "Right about the time that girl moved down here."

Ace rubbed his goatee, deep in thought. "Are you thinking what I think you're thinking?"

"Uh-huh."

Ace reached for the phone, which rang in his hand. He looked at Diane. "Toussaint." He pushed the talk button. "Hey, nephew."

"Hey, Ace. Listen, I need to stop back through there."

"Well, it's kinda late, Toussaint. Diane and I are already in bed."

"Sorry about that, but this can't wait. It's about Jefferson and the woman he's with."

Ace put the call on speaker phone. "This is about Keisha Miller?"

"Yes."

Ace and Diane's eyes met. "What about her?" Ace asked.

"I'm turning the corner to your house now. And uncle?"

"Yes?"

"You might want to pour yourself a drink."

45

"Good morning, Can."

"Hey, Diane," Candace replied breathlessly, without breaking her treadmill stride. "You're up early."

"I barely slept last night."

Candace turned off the exercise machine. "Why? What's wrong?"

"Girl, you're not going to believe it. Can you come over?"

"Absolutely. Have you eaten breakfast?"

"I don't have much of an appetite."

"No worries. Give me a half hour. I'm on my way."

Candace took a quick shower, donned a light warm-up outfit, and was out the door in record time. All the while she thought of Diane and wondered just what could be going on with her. Her guess was that it involved Keisha, the woman Jefferson had sprung on the family out of the blue. Candace would have been surprised if the child was over twenty-five years old, and would have bet her savings that the titties on that sistah had come courtesy of a surgeon's skilled hand. *A hot little gold digger*, Candace thought as she glanced at a neighborhood market and decided to stop in for their fresh-baked Danishes, figuring good food and gossip always went hand in hand.

"Good morning, Tina!" Candace sang as she walked into the market. She'd been coming here for years, and the little Vietnamese lady who ran the place was like a favored auntie, especially after explaining that she'd adopted the American name "Tina" because of her respect for Tina Turner, who'd given this woman the confidence to leave behind an abusive husband and start a new life in a new land.

"Miss Candace! What can I get for you today?"

"What do you have fresh?"

"I make fresh cinnamon roll, ready in five minute. Very delicious, can you wait?"

Tina's pastries were some of the best she'd ever tasted. "Of course I can."

"Be right back. You like coffee to wait?"

"No, thank you."

Tina disappeared behind a flimsy curtain, and Candace walked over to the magazine rack. She'd never be caught dead buying a trash magazine, but often browsed them while at the hair salon. She scanned the top shelf and then spied an *In Touch* cover resting atop a stack of *Atlanta Inquirer* magazines. She picked up the magazine and was just getting ready to open it when she noticed a woman of color on the other magazine's cover page. *Is that Halle?* she thought, as she reached down to get it. Seconds later, her gasp was audible. "Oh my God!" she screamed, so loudly that Tina came running from the back room.

"Miss Candace, you all right?"

"Oh my God," Candace repeated, reading the glaring headline in disbelief and running out of the store with paper in hand. She'd thought she knew why Diane was calling her. But now she realized that a girl named Keisha was the least of her sister-in-law's worries.

Candace arrived at Diane's home and hurried up the walkway. She rang the doorbell and tried the door at the same time.

Finding it unlocked, she opened it quickly. "Diane, it's me! Where are you?"

"In here, Can!"

Candace rushed into the kitchen and over to her friend. "I'm so sorry," she said, giving Diane a comforting hug. When she pulled back, there were tears in her eyes. "Girl, you must be beside yourself. What was Bianca thinking?"

Diane frowned. "Bianca?"

"Candace paused. "Yes, Bianca. Girl, I know that's why you called me over. No wonder you didn't sleep last night."

Diane looked at Candace with a confused expression, backing up a little as she did so. "Can, my restlessness was due to what I learned about Keisha. What are you talking about?"

Candace's hand flew to her mouth. "You mean you don't know?"

"Know what?"

"You haven't seen the paper? *The Atlanta Inquirer?*"

"No, I haven't seen the *Atlanta Inquirer.* You know I don't read that mess."

"Well, you're going to want to read this issue." Candace pulled the magazine from her purse and laid it on the island. The headline screamed into the silence:

SOUL FOOD HEIRESS MARRIES PRINCE!

If not for the barstool beside her, Diane would have crumpled to the floor. As it were, she slid onto the seat like jelly, her mouth slack, her eyes wide. She slowly reached for the paper. "What the hell is this?"

"Hopefully a big mistake," Candace responded.

"Where did you get this?" The question was asked more harshly than Diane intended.

"At Tina's Market. I stopped there to get some pastries, and she was baking some fresh. I went to browse the magazines while I waited and, oh hell, I didn't even pay for this magazine. Girl, when I saw Bianca on the cover I just freaked out and ran out of there like something was chasing me. I was sure that this was what you wanted to talk to me about."

Diane turned to the page for the cover story and began to read: "Bianca Livingston, daughter of Abram and Diane Livingston and heiress to the Taste of Soul restaurant fortune, recently dumped her attorney boyfriend of several years to marry the man of her dreams!" Diane looked at Candace as if dumbfounded, her voice sounding more incredulous with every word. "Sources say it was love at first sight for this Georgia socialite and her suitor, Xavier Marquis, whose father is closely tied to France's royal throne. When her parents refused their blessing on the union, Bianca fled to Los Angeles, risking career and family for true, lasting love." Diane threw down the magazine. "This is bullshit!"

"Of course it is," Candace quickly agreed.

"Somebody is getting ready to get the pants sued off of them," Diane fumed, reaching for her cell phone. "I'm going to own the *Atlanta Inquirer* when I get through." Diane paced the kitchen, waiting for Bianca to answer. It didn't occur to her in the least that in Los Angeles, it was only 6:05. When Bianca's cell phone went to voice mail, Diane dialed her daughter's home number. When it, too, went to voice mail, Diane hung up and immediately dialed again.

Finally, after Diane had hung up and redialed a third time, a groggy voice answered the phone. "Hello?"

Diane looked at the receiver, wondering if she'd dialed the wrong number. "Hello, who is this?"

"Who is this?" an indignant voice replied.

"This is Diane Livingston, Bianca's mother? Now who in the hell is this? Hello? Hello?" Diane set down the phone and put her head in her hands.

"What is it, Diane? Who answered the phone?"

Slowly, Diane lifted her head. "A man," she said, her voice monotone. "With an accent," she added.

It was Candace's turn to sink onto a chair. *Oh. My. God.*

46

Malcolm sat huddled with his engineer, Luis, excited about developing the next line of Soul Smokers. The success of the initial launch had been incredible, more than Malcolm had ever imagined. He and Luis now had their heads together to try and come up with a smaller, battery-run model that could be used on picnics, camping trips, and other venues where electricity wasn't readily available. Livingston Corporation business had kept him swamped the past month, but today there were no meetings, no conferences calls, and no luncheons. He'd even told Victoria to fix dinner just for the kids and to not wait up. He planned to put in a ten-, twelve-hour day, solely focused on the baby he'd birthed, the dream that had been his and his alone. He whistled as he walked toward the conference table at the back of the warehouse where Luis had spread out the diagrams. *Soul Smoker To Go!* Malcolm couldn't wait.

When his phone rang ten minutes later and he saw the number, he almost let it go to voice mail. But it was rare that his mother called in the middle of the day. "Hey, Mama, what's up?"

"We need you to come over to your aunt and uncle's house, son, right away."

"Why?"

"Family meeting, Malcolm, it's important."

Malcolm's sigh was audible. *Please, not today!* "Mom, look, this is really a bad time. I'm down at the warehouse with my engineer and—"

"This can't wait, son," Candace interrupted. And then the line went dead.

"I've got an emergency, Luis," Malcolm said to his engineer. "I'll be back as soon as I can." He walked across the warehouse toward his office, dialing his cell phone as he did so. "Toussaint."

"Yeah."

"Mama call you?"

"Yeah."

"Did she tell you what the meeting is about?"

"She didn't have to."

"So what's going on, bro? This is my first day at the warehouse in a month, and I'm really not too thrilled about being yanked away, especially if it's something that I can hear over the phone or later this evening."

"Trust me when I tell you, brother. This can't wait." Toussaint ended the call just as he reached Jefferson's office door. He hesitated before knocking, trying to formulate his thoughts. He'd asked Ace and Diane to give him a couple days to make absolutely certain that Jefferson's Keisha was Q's sister. But here it was barely twelve hours later and they'd called a meeting. Obviously, they'd felt that there was no time to lose.

The door opened, startling both Jefferson who'd opened it and Toussaint who stood just on the other side. "Dang, man!"

"Sorry, Jeff. I was just coming to see you."

"Meeting, you heard?"

"Yes," Toussaint said, falling into step with Jefferson's long strides. "Mind if I ride with you?"

Jefferson popped the lock on his BMW and soon he and Toussaint were rolling out of the parking lot.

"Look, Jeff," Toussaint began. "I need to warn you about something, man."

Jefferson glanced at Toussaint. "Warn me? About what?"

"About why your parents called this meeting."

"Oh, so you already know what this is about?"

Toussaint nodded, and took a deep breath. "It's about Keisha."

"Keisha? Why the hell are we having a meeting about her, and what the hell do you have to do with it?"

"Look, man, I wasn't even going to say anything until I knew for sure. . . ."

"Knew for sure about what?" The normally placid Jefferson had almost bellowed, and he was now doing sixty in a forty-five-mile-an-hour zone.

"Jeff. . . just stay calm, all right?" Toussaint adjusted his seat belt. "Slow it down, man."

Jeff looked down at the speedometer, only then realizing that he'd increased his speed and that he gripped the wheel as if it were a lifeline. He took a deep breath and tried to calm down. "Look, man, just tell me what's going down."

"There's a very good chance that Keisha Miller is Quintin Bright's sister." Five seconds of silence went by. Fifteen. Thirty. "Did you hear me, Cuz?"

The rumble started deep within Jefferson's chest but soon, loud guffaws reverberated off of the sleek, tan interior. "Keisha is Q's sister? Ha! That's what y'all think? That's what this meeting is about?" Jefferson started laughing all over again.

"Jefferson," Toussaint said somberly. He rarely called his cousin by his full first name. "This is serious."

"No, man. This is ridiculous." He reached a stop light and looked at Toussaint. "You actually believe that my girl is related to Q?"

"That's the story."

"And if you believe that then you probably believe what? That she's the one who stole my money?"

Toussaint relayed the information that he'd gotten from Chardonnay. "I don't want to believe it," he concluded. "I'm hoping it's a big mistake, that there are two Keishas and this is a big coincidence. But those are some pretty long odds."

The two men remained quiet the short distance to Ace and Diane's house. As Jefferson parked, he noted that Adam, Candace, and Malcolm were already there. Jefferson entered the house first. As soon as he turned the corner, he saw all eyes turn in his direction.

"Toussaint already told me," he began without preamble. "And I'm telling you, you're wrong."

"Sit down, Son, Toussaint," Ace commanded. "We'll get to Keisha later."

"No!" Jefferson said defiantly, his arms crossed and legs apart—a warrior ready for battle. "You brought me here to accuse my girl. I want to talk about it now!"

Diane got up and walked over to where Jefferson stood. "Here," she said wearily, handing him the *Atlanta Inquirer.* "*This* is what we have to talk about right now."

Jefferson looked down at the magazine cover. "Bianca married? What the hell?"

"What?" Toussaint snatched the paper from Jefferson, noted the page of the cover story, hurriedly turned to that page, and began to read.

You could have heard a Georgia mosquito flap its wings.

"Is this true?" Jefferson asked.

"I think so," Diane responded. "I called Bianca's house and a man answered. A man with an accent."

"That doesn't necessarily prove anything," Malcolm offered.

"I've also left messages, telling her to call immediately. Called her office line as well, and it just rings and rings."

Jefferson looked at his watch. "It's not even eight o'clock there yet, Mama. So of course she wouldn't be at the job."

"Which is why I know she's at home!" Diane said, her voice raised. "With *Xavier!*" she snarled.

Ace stood and began to pace. "I won't believe it until she tells me," he said almost to himself. "Bianca wouldn't do something like this to me, she wouldn't do this to the family."

"I want to believe you, Ace," Candace said. "Because this is some mess right here."

Adam looked up suddenly as a thought crossed his mind. "Anybody call Mama?"

"Oh, goodness," Diane said, rising to grab her cell phone. Unlike her and Candace, her mother-in-law, Marietta, read trash mags like Bibles. She even had subscriptions to a few. Right now, Diane hoped that one wasn't with the *Atlanta Inquirer*. She left the room to privately handle the call.

Jefferson, who'd sat down next to his father, turned and looked at him. "So this meeting was about Bianca, not Keisha. Sorry about yelling at you, Dad."

Ace answered, staring straight ahead. "This meeting is about Bianca *and* Keisha," he said.

Jefferson's shoulders slumped. "So you believe it, too." He looked around the room. "Y'all all believe what Toussaint said about my girl."

Malcolm looked at Toussaint. "What did you say about Keisha?"

The doorbell rang, interrupting Toussaint's answer.

Ace rose to his feet. "That's Sterling."

"Sterling?" *They've had my baby investigated?* Jefferson became angry all over again. His hands clenched as he watched Sterling, the ace private eye, stroll into the room. Just as Jeff got ready to speak, or more accurately, curse Sterling out, Divine's voice floated into his head. *You need to do a background check, Jeff.* Jefferson's face was a stone mask as he watched Sterling walk over and take a seat in one of the wing-back chairs. *You've never met anyone else in her life.* Jefferson jumped up from the couch, walked over to the buffet, and poured himself a glass of water. He was so wound up that he wanted to hurl the glass through the window. *There's no way this can be true. Keisha wouldn't do this!*

Diane walked back into the room, nodded at Sterling, and sat down next to Ace.

Ace reached for her hand. "Mama okay?"

"As well as can be expected, considering the bomb I just dropped."

"They coming over?" Adam asked.

"Of course," Diane said. "So we'd better talk fast."

Everyone knew what Diane meant. The family had made a unanimous decision not to inform Marcus or Marietta about the stolen company money or about the search for Quintin Bright.

Ace looked at Sterling, as did the rest of the group. "What 'cha got, doc?"

"They're related," Sterling answered without hesitation. "Keisha Miller is Quintin Bright's half sister."

47

It had been an hour since Sterling had dropped the bombshell: Keisha and Q were siblings. He'd also told them about the tail he'd had on Quintin and the rising mountain of evidence he had accumulated linking Quintin to the corporation thefts. Only days away from making a move to arrest him, Sterling had been beyond upset to learn that Quintin had once again slipped through their hands. It was why the family had no choice but to follow the instructions Sterling had left with them, the directive that had Jefferson nauseous and about to be sick.

"I'm so sorry, baby," Diane said. She was sitting on the arm of the couch next to Jefferson, rubbing his back. She couldn't remember the last time she'd seen her son cry. Her heart physically clenched with each tear he shed.

"I don't think I can do it," he said softly, his voice barely above a whisper.

"It's a lot to ask, Son," Ace admitted, his voice gruff with emotion.

Toussaint paced the floor, his emotions roiling between anger and sadness. Though only eleven months apart, Jefferson had always looked up to Toussaint more as an older brother than a cousin. Toussaint had schooled him about sports and girls, and more than once had protected him from a would-be thug. He'd take a bullet for the cousin now slumped in dismay, whereas if he ever saw Keisha again...it would be too soon. He stopped pacing abruptly. "Is there any other way we can do this?"

Ace slowly shook his head. "I don't see how. Quintin has eluded us for the second time now. His sister is the only connection we have, and if we lose her, we might not get another chance to snag this lowlife, and take him off the streets." Ace looked at his son, pain written all over his face. "But if you don't think you can do it, Son...we'll understand."

For a long moment, Jefferson didn't respond. Then slowly he looked up, his eyes fixed on Adam. "I'll do it for you, Uncle," he said, his voice full of emotion. "I'll do it for you."

Keisha stood back and looked in the mirror, almost not believing what she saw. She'd never been vain, particularly, but she knew that she was a beautiful woman. Everyone had told her so from the time she was born. Jealousy was one of the reasons for the contention with her mother, why they'd never particularly gotten along, and why she'd been sent to live with her grandmother when she was twelve years old. Juanita Mason couldn't have her boyfriends looking at her daughter harder than they looked at her.

Chardonnay's suggestion had been a good one, Keisha decided. The hair salon had done an excellent job of perming her naturally curly locks. Straightened, her hair hung down her back almost to her waist. The newly threaded eyebrows with the high arch emphasized the slant of her eyes, making her look almost Asian. An afternoon at the spa had left her skin baby soft and gleaming, like butterscotch about to melt. Keisha looked at the fresh bikini wax and almost giggled. Jefferson was an excellent lover, especially orally, and she knew from an offhanded comment he'd made that her hairless lips would turn him all the way on. Large, natural-looking breasts, a small waist, and flat stomach even after two boys made Keisha Miller a force to be reckoned with. *And now*, Keisha thought as she viewed her nakedness one last time before walking into the closet, *I'm getting ready to have it all*. Jefferson had called earlier, told her to get a sitter, and dress to impress. When she'd asked where they were going, Jefferson had been vague. "I just want to show you off," he'd said, in a low, quiet voice. But Keisha knew the truth. Jefferson was about to propose. And she wanted to look her very best.

48

For the first time since moving to Los Angeles, Bianca was thankful for the twelve- to fourteen-hour days her job required. The West Coast Taste of Soul opening was only two weeks away, and TOSTS was opening a month later. Bianca knew all about the family meeting; Toussaint had called her as soon as he'd left her parents' home. "I told you this would happen," he said by way of greeting. He'd been right, Bianca had admitted. She should have told them right after Toussaint found out. Instead, she'd begged him to keep it quiet, and that wasn't her only error. She'd also underestimated Chardonnay Wilson.

"Bianca," Crystal's voice came through the intercom. "It's him again."

"Dangit! If I'm not answering my cell phone, there's a reason! Sorry for yelling at you, Crystal."

"I know it's not personal."

"Good."

"You want the call?"

"Let him hold for a while; maybe he'll get the message."

Bianca glanced at the light flashing on her phone, showing the held call. She knew it was irrational, but she was still upset at Xavier for answering the phone that fateful morning.

Granted, the proverbial cat had not only been out of the bag at that point, as he'd calmly pointed out, but had been plastered all over the front page of Atlanta's premier gossip magazine, referred to by that town's locals as simply "A-I." But this fact meant little to Bianca that morning when her cover got blown. Chardonnay hadn't been there to lash out at, so Xavier had gotten the blame instead. When he'd further pointed out to her that he, too, had been on that cover, and that any day he'd more than likely be shunned by his immediate family and cut out of the will, Bianca had softened—a little. Two days after the incident, she let him back into the bedroom. One could only let anger interfere with the groove for so long. *So why are you still being so funky?* Bianca decided she'd have to ponder the answer to that question later. Right now, she had a business to run.

Scrolling through her to-do list, Bianca punched the intercom. "Crystal, did the graphic company call back with an estimated delivery date for the signage?"

"Not yet."

"Call them back and light a fire."

"Will do."

And so it went for the next two hours—Bianca barking out orders and Crystal executing them with precision and flair. All things considered, Bianca felt everything was coming together rather nicely. The interiors for both businesses were almost complete, the entire waitstaff had been hired, PR and marketing were right on schedule, and Bianca had made inroads with LA's social elite. A special coup had been snagging a meeting with Magic Johnson, a major force in LA's business world. Not only had he and Cookie already RSVP'd for the TOSTS opening night gala, but he'd also agreed to cohost the event.

"Bianca, I'm going to take a break, run and get a cappuccino. You want anything?"

"No, Crystal, I'm cool. Thanks anyway."

"No problem. Be back in about ten minutes."

"Don't forward the phone line. I'll grab 'em."

"Okay."

A few minutes later, Bianca pressed the intercom button. "Crystal, can you get the *L.A. Sentinel* on the line for me? I need to push that interview to next week." Bianca waited a moment. *Oh, shoot, Crystal's out.* Bianca laughed at herself for forgetting so fast. She scrolled through her contacts for the number and then realized that it must be in Crystal's rolodex file. Bianca started for the door, but then the phone rang. Instead of walking behind her desk to answer it, she simply reached over and picked it up, her back to the door.

"Good morning, Taste of Soul." Bianca listened as the caller went on about a charity event coming up in the area, something that could potentially be great PR for developing businesses. Bianca heard the outer door open. *Good, Crystal's back.* She placed the caller on hold and punched the intercom. "Crystal, can you pick up line one and take down some information?" Bianca waited a beat and then spoke a little louder. "Crystal?" Exasperated, Bianca placed the phone on the receiver, walked briskly to the door, and snatched it open.

"Mama! Daddy! What are y'all doing here?"

Diane reached into her purse and calmly pulled out the infamous *Atlanta Inquirer* copy with Bianca on the cover. Holding it out, her voice was deceptively calm. "I think we're the ones who should be asking the questions, Bianca. Don't you?"

Shyla watched Cooper read the *Inquirer* article before slowly crumpling it in his hand. If it were possible, she'd swear that steam was literally shooting out of his ears right now. As it was, they were tinged red with anger, and a slow blush was also creeping up his neck. To say Bianca's ex was livid would be putting it very mildly.

"I'm sorry," Shyla said softly, walking over to where Cooper sat at the kitchen counter. "But I had to show it to you. I didn't want you to get bum-rushed by a reporter or one of your colleagues. Plus, I thought of your father, and, well, I know how this type of news might affect your family."

"You did the right thing, Shyla." Cooper said, his jaw clenching with the will it was taking him not to go smooth off. It was the only part of his body that moved, that and his rapidly blinking eyes.

"You have every right to be upset."

Cooper snorted. "Oh, believe me. I'm beyond upset."

"Talk to me, baby. Tell me how you feel. I want to be here for you."

When Cooper looked up, his eyes glistened with unshed tears. "She played me."

"Yes, Cooper, she did."

Cooper's fist came crashing down on the counter, causing his mug of coffee to skitter and fall to the floor. Hot coffee and glass went everywhere. Shyla jumped, narrowly missing being scalded by the sweetened brew.

Cooper seemed not to notice. "My father, mother, everyone was fooled. We all thought that she loved me. *I* thought she loved me!"

Shyla gently touched his arm. "Maybe she did."

"How could she have loved me"—Cooper unfolded the crumpled paper—"when she was obviously sneaking behind my back with this jerk?"

"I don't know, Cooper," Shyla said. "But look at it this way. Better to have found out now, rather than after you were married. There's no telling what a woman who'd stoop this low is capable of. Now you can put this behind you and go on with your life."

"And let her get away with shaming my family and making me look like a fool? No, Shyla," Cooper said. He stood abruptly, crumpling the paper once again. "I'll never forget what Bianca did to me. Never!"

"Cooper, wait!" Shyla cried. She started to follow him, but

thought better of it. There was really no need. Cooper now hated Bianca and despised the Livingstons so much that he'd do anything to get back at them. Of this fact, Shyla was sure. So instead of chasing behind him, Shyla turned and slowly began picking up the shattered glass pieces. Yes, Cooper now wanted revenge as much as she did. For now, her job was done.

49

Ace pulled his rental car up to the hotel's valet. It had been a quiet ride from the restaurant, where he and Diane had met the infamous Xavier Marquis. Bianca had suggested that they meet in her office, but Ace knew that a public place would lessen the chances of his kicking the man's ass—something highly likely, given Ace's pissed-off state at that moment. Bianca was grown and wasn't legally bound to get her parents' permission for anything. She could do what she wanted. But the man, Xavier, the fool who'd dare wed his daughter without so much as a word between them...that was another matter altogether.

Even with diners all around, the first few moments with their new son-in-law had been quite tense.

"I owe you an apology," Xavier said, as soon as the four were seated.

"And I owe you an ass whoopin'," Ace immediately replied.

A slight narrowing of the eyes was Xavier's only outward reaction. "Fair enough. But for your daughter, Mr. Livingston, that is a whooping that I will gladly take."

★　★　★

Immediately upon entering the hotel suite, Diane walked over to and fell back on the bed. She felt tired, exhausted, more so than she'd ever been. The events of the past few days had drained her mentally, physically and emotionally. Her daughter's surprise marriage and the run through the gossip mill that was sure to follow, coupled with her son's sleeping with—no, living with—the sister of the enemy . . . it was all too much! How she wished that she could click her heels three times and be back in a life that was simple, predictable, with no hitches in the giddyap. In this moment, Diane realized that she'd not experienced that lifestyle in quite some time.

Diane heard the sound of running water and knew that Ace was in the shower. A part of her wanted to join him there, to stick her head under the running stream and let some of the heat from the water soothe her tightly wound muscles. But the other part of her couldn't move, other than to reach for a pillow to roll against her stomach and another one to put under her head. Over and over she relived the moment when Bianca had walked into the restaurant on Xavier's arm. It had been a strange moment for Diane, one in which her daughter's life seemed to pass before her in an instant: Bianca as a newborn, her first steps, kindergarten, dance classes, her foray into cooking with oven-fried chicken. A small smile scampered across Diane's face as she remembered Bianca's horror at starting her period just before gym class, and of threatening to not leave her room until the bleeding stopped. Her first boyfriend, *what was his name?* The debutante ball, and she and Cooper holed up in her room for hours listening to God-knew-who and talking about who-knew-what. *Cooper.* Diane rolled onto her back and brought the pillow with her. God knew that situation would now be even more of a mess. She'd checked the home messages and wasn't surprised to hear Evelyn's disappointment-filled voice. Diane wasn't sure Cooper's mom would believe that she was just as surprised about Bianca's marriage as Evelyn, and undoubtedly more upset. Diane could only imagine the talk that was burning the telephone lines in the state of Georgia and beyond. In this moment, Diane made the decision to not try to do any type of damage control, to not make a call or try to explain away the obvious: that her daughter had eloped. There would be no elaborate wedding planning, no silk dresses and dyed shoes to match purchases, no bridal shower or rehearsal dinners to plan. She and Evelyn would not get to coordinate mother-of-the-bride/groom dresses, and there'd be no need to buy Ace a new tux. A rite of passage had been stolen from her, a rite Diane hadn't even realized she'd wanted badly to experience until the chance had been taken away from her. So let the people talk, fill their minds with idle gossip. Diane had a family to keep together and a dynasty to support so when it came to OPP—other people's opinions— she just couldn't give a damn.

"Baby, you all right?" Ace gently sat on the bed, naked except for the towel wrapped around his waist.

Diane nodded.

Ace scooted up next to his wife, spoon-style, and took her into his arms. They lay quietly for several moments, comfort being found in the simplicity of touch. Finally, Ace stirred, a soft grind against his wife's backside. "He seems like a good man."

"Yes."

"Respectable."

"Handsome."

"Wealthy."

"Yes, there is that, isn't there?"

"That and the fact that he didn't back down from an ass whoopin'."

Diane's smile was genuine when she answered. "You've got to respect a brothah like that."

Another several moments passed. "Did you think it would ever happen to us, Diane?"

Diane turned to face her husband. "What, that one of our

children would marry royalty?" Both of them knew what Ace's question was really about. "How do you feel about it...a little milk in the Livingston coffeepot?"

It was so long in coming that Diane thought he wouldn't answer. But finally Ace hugged her, kissed her neck, and responded, "Time will tell."

Across town, Bianca lay in Xavier's arms, happier than she'd ever been in life. She'd come through her biggest fear—her parents meeting Xavier—and everyone had lived! Turning slightly, she gazed at the face of the man sleeping beside her, her heart bursting with love for him. How had he known exactly how to handle her parents? She'd been too shocked at their surprise visit to school him in how best to engage the formidable Abram "Ace" Livingston. Yet Xavier had dealt with the situation in the best possible fashion, by simply being who he was: the fearless man who apologized to her father while standing his ground and charmed her mother with genuine compliments and sex appeal. Now she breathed easier and actually looked forward to the restaurant's opening, when Xavier would get a true taste of the Livingston clan.

"How did you meet my daughter?" That's one of the first questions Ace had asked, after the waiter had placed down their drinks, along with a round of appetizers. Bianca smiled, remembering Xavier's colorful and slightly embellished tale of seeing her across a crowded room, and being drawn as if by magic to her side. "Her face glowed," he'd answered, "with a smile as impish yet mysterious as the Mona Lisa. Forgive me, sir," he'd continued. "But I knew at once that she would be mine." Bianca hadn't missed her mother's slightly raised eyebrow at this comment or the smirk that flitted across her father's face. *If only they knew how accurate were the words that Xavier had spoken.* Their first official date came just days later, a visit to the Louvre, where Xavier had possessed her totally and completely. There was a private chamber in that historical museum that would forever be marked with two lovers' unbridled passion. Bianca would never look at classic paintings the same.

She shifted, and Xavier wrapped a possessive arm around her. That's what she loved about him, she realized: that Xavier could be completely alpha male one moment and unabashedly sentimental the next. His love of art was what would form the foundation of friendship with Jefferson, she decided. Bianca frowned, thinking of her brother and more specifically about what her mother had said when she'd asked about him and Keisha. "He's doing what he has to do," was her enigmatic reply. *Doing what he has to do? What could she possibly have meant by that?*

50

Keisha looked across the table at Jefferson, who sat quietly, brooding. He'd been this way for over a week. When asked, he'd told her not to worry, that there were problems at work. But Keisha wasn't so sure. In her mind, his Jekyll-and-Hyde transformation had happened last Monday, when he'd left for work happy and smiling, gushing about the evening he'd planned, and then returned to take her to said dinner date quiet and withdrawn.

Their dinner date. Even though it had been the most romantic night in her life, Keisha's memory of the evening was bittersweet. The ride to the Sun Dial restaurant had been nice, but quiet. That's when Keisha's gut had first sounded a silent alarm. Jefferson had looked so serious, and slightly sad. Yet when she'd asked him about it, he'd blessed her with the lopsided smile that made her heart go pitter patter; had reached for her hand, kissed it, and told her again how beautiful she looked. They'd arrived at the oasis positioned more than seven hundred feet above the city just as the sun set, with tinges of pink and yellow painting the dusk, set against a cloudless sky showcasing Venus's early night twinkle. They'd sipped champagne in the lounge, serenaded by the sounds of a live jazz band, before being escorted to their table where, rotating a full three-hundred-and-sixty degrees, they took in some of Atlanta's well-known landmarks, including the Fox Theatre, the Georgia Dome, Stone Mountain Park, and the CNN center. Keisha had never eaten food that tasted so good: pan-seared duck and her first-ever fried oyster, beef tenderloin, and lamb cassoulet. By the time dessert arrived, in the form of a crème brûlée sampler, Keisha was delightfully giddy on bubbly and love, high on the altitude and the atmosphere. So much so that she missed the melancholy tremor in Jefferson's voice and the flash of anger that crossed his face when she mentioned her love for him. By the end of the evening, Keisha felt like Cinderella, Jefferson's BMW her pumpkin-clad coach. When the box carried by a white-gloved messenger arrived at their table, Keisha's heart had stopped, so sure was she of its contents. She gasped even before opening it, and then gasped again when she discovered that instead of the engagement ring she'd envisioned all evening, it was a less-meaningful yet equally beautiful diamond watch. It would be much later that Keisha would understand the significance of his present—that in that moment Jefferson really had known what time it was.

"Hurry up and finish your cereal, boys," she said as Jefferson pushed back from the table and brought her out of her reverie. "Time to go to school." She followed Jefferson over to the sink, where he stood rinsing out his bowl. "Hey, Pookie," she cooed, wrapping her arms around him from behind. Jefferson hadn't made love to her since their date night, and then it hadn't seemed as if he was really into it. Keisha, who'd had sex on the regular since turning fifteen, felt she was long overdue for some Livingston loving. "What do you say to me taking you to lunch, maybe getting a little... afternoon delight?"

"I have a meeting." Jefferson gently yet firmly removed Keisha's arms from around his waist. He found her touch repulsive and cursed his body for daring to react to her smell and softness; pictured her brother in his mind, the man who'd shot his uncle, and breathed a sigh of relief as hardness shifted from his dick to his heart. "And I'll probably be getting home late tonight. So don't wait up."

Keisha's hand went to her hip as she watched Jefferson stroll out of the kitchen. *What in the hell is wrong with him? And why am I walking on tiptoe like his mood is my problem?* As had often been the case since it happened, she thought about the money she'd stolen, and wondered if Jefferson had found out that it was missing. *No way,* Keisha decided. *If Jeff thought I'd taken all that money he'd be all over my ass!* Keisha placed her bowl in the sink with a bang and hollered at her boys to get their things. Whatever was going on with Jefferson was his problem, she decided. And she would not start feeling badly just because her man was in a funk. She'd drop Dorian off at school and Antwan at the upscale day care center she'd found, go shopping, and maybe even spend some time at the spa. She was living the life of her dreams, dammit, and she was going to be happy!

Yet for all of her bravado, Keisha returned home two hours later, not much happier than when she'd left. Shopping wasn't as much fun when always done alone, and her favorite masseuse at the spa was booked for the day. She'd called Chardonnay and gotten voice mail, then decided against dropping by to see her at the restaurant. In a rare moment, Keisha missed her family: her brothers, her cousin, even her messed-up mom. They might be a dysfunctional family, but they were all the family that Keisha had. Goodness knew she stood little chance to gain love from Jefferson's family. She knew Diane couldn't stand her, and she'd disliked his sister, Bianca, on sight. The only one she halfway liked was Jefferson's cousin, Toussaint. But the family would really be pissed if they knew her thoughts concerning that chocolate cutie: the fantasy where she enjoyed Jefferson and Toussaint at the same time.

"Fuck it," Keisha announced to the empty home's four walls. "I'm going where somebody appreciates me!" Keisha walked to her laptop and fired it up. She logged onto the Internet and began scrolling flights, looking for the earliest flights to LA. A trip was planned there anyway, she deduced; the entire Livingston family was planning to attend the West Coast restaurant opening. Surely Jefferson would understand her desire to go a week early, spend some time with her family. It would also give her time to school them. Jefferson had told her that he wanted to meet some of her family during this trip. She wanted to tell them what to say so their stories matched. After that, she reasoned, becoming Mrs. Keisha Livingston would be a done deal.

Keisha's cell phone rang, startling her. It rang so seldom these days that keeping it close was more habit than necessity. She looked at the screen and squealed. Right now, it was exactly who she needed. "Q! What's up, big brother?"

"What's up, sis?"

"I was just thinking about you!"

"Yeah, right."

"No, for real. I'm sitting here now booking a flight to Los Angeles. It's time to see everybody; I can't wait to see everybody, I even miss Rico's crazy ass."

Q laughed, thinking about their Mexican "cousin," whom the family had adopted after he and another Miller relative became good friends in jail.

"So what about you, Q? How are you? Where are you? Are you okay?" Keisha's eyes misted over, she was so happy to hear Q's voice. This was the man who had not only been a brother but a father figure, protector, confidant, and friend. She was glad she'd been able to help him escape, especially given how funky Jefferson had been lately. That thought spurred another—that it may be time to hit up his bank account again, for her this time. It was a startling realization that if Jefferson dumped her, she'd be back where she started: broke and alone. Keisha didn't like that thought. She didn't like that thought at all.

"Keisha!"

"I'm sorry, brother, what did you say?"

"I asked when you were going to LA."

"Hey, you know what? Maybe I'll come see you instead!"

"Girl, you really tripping now."

"No, I'm serious, Q. I need to get away for a minute. You were right; this family is a trip, a bunch of stuck-up bougies who think their shit don't stink. I can book a flight to see you and then meet them in LA for the opening."

"What about the boys?"

"They'll come with me. Dorian asks about you all the time. It will be good for you to see them."

It didn't take long for Q to agree to Keisha's suggestion. Truth of the matter, he missed family, too. Things were going well, his little restaurant/bar was thriving, and he'd even been kicking it fairly regularly with a cute little island girl named Constance. But Ochos Rios had been much more exciting when Shyla Martin had been there with him. Maybe Keisha could help him decide what should be his next move. In the meantime, he instructed his sister on *her* next move.

"Before you come over, I need for you to do something."

"What?"

Quintin was nothing if not convincing and by the time they ended the call, Keisha's next few hours had been all mapped out.

Thirty minutes later, Keisha closed up her laptop and reached for her keys. She and the boys were going to Jamaica! It was time to go shopping again.

Sterling took off his suit jacket, sinking into one of two recliners in his living room. If he was a drinking man, this would be the night for a good, stiff drink. Instead he popped the top on his ice-cold soda and rested his head against the chair back. *What a day.* It had been a rough one, having to tell a high-profile client, the well-known minister of a local megachurch, that his daughter was indeed stripping in a Tennessee club. He hadn't wanted to deliver the footage, taken with a camera hidden in a lapel pin. But the father had insisted, and Sterling had handed it over. It was the kind of moment that made Sterling thankful that he didn't have kids.

After drinking half of the soda, Sterling got up and walked into his office. He fired up his computer, and then turned to the desk behind him and hit the REWIND button of the large, black tape recorder partially hidden beneath a copy of the *Atlanta Journal-Constitution*. It had been a nightly ritual, listening to the voice-activated activities of Jefferson Livingston's household. So far, the rumblings had been boringly routine: television chatter, the animated voices of Keisha's sons, a couple of spirited calls between Keisha and that Wilson woman, and the muted conversations involving the man of the house.

Sterling fully expected to hear more of the same as he opened his e-mail account and began checking the day's inbox. The loud "Fuck it" from the recorder caused him to stop typing, and the next sentence caused him to turn, look at the recorder, and turn up the volume. By the time Sterling heard the slamming door that signaled Keisha's departure, he'd logged onto an airline Web site and booked his flight. Fatigue had left him, replaced by a surge of adrenaline and whirling of thoughts, plans being formulated as he typed. He left a message with the Atlanta police chief and called the security men who accompanied him on dangerous jaunts such as this. Jefferson had been reluctant to have his house bugged and phone tapped, his privacy stripped by his own form of betrayal. But if all went well, Sterling would be able to assuage Jefferson of some of his guilt, perhaps as early as the end of the week.

51

Keisha adjusted her bikini bottoms and settled back in the chaise. She hadn't known how much she'd needed to get away until her plane had taken off, didn't realize how much she'd missed her brother until he greeted her at the airport with a big, bear hug. She sipped her tropical drink and watched her boys frolic in the water with their uncle, laughing and playing without a care in the world. *This is how I'm supposed to feel, and this is how I'm supposed to live.* Not lonely and unhappy in a city where she knew no one, with a man who'd changed from a kind, attentive lover to a big old grouch. Jefferson had barely commented when she'd told him she was going to visit family in Florida, hadn't even questioned the suddenness of the trip. She was thankful that Q had called back while she was out shopping, suggesting that, instead of a direct flight to Jamaica, she go to Miami and then pay for her flights to the island with untraceable cash. Because of his foresight, she lay here footloose and fancy free, daydreaming of this as a lifestyle. Jefferson had whetted her appetite for the big life, but could she see herself with him for the long run? He wasn't bad looking, but he wasn't fine like his cousin Toussaint. He was nice enough, but not exciting like her old, thug-life boyfriends. If it wasn't for the fact that he was a freak between the sheets, with a long, thick bank account to match his long, thick bob and weave,

Keisha knew she would have lost interest in Jefferson a long time ago, if she would have even noticed him at all.

But even as she thought these things, a part of Keisha's conscience rebelled. It was the little things about Jefferson that made him special: his attention to detail and ability to give her what she needed even before she asked. How he'd buy little things for the boys, or agree to take them out just so she could have time for herself. She remembered how, after returning from a visit to Alexis and Toussaint's, Jefferson had waxed poetic about having a child of his own, and how if it were a girl, he'd want her to look just like Keisha. *So what happened? What made him change so in the last week, become withdrawn and moody and no fun at all?* Maybe this was the real Jefferson, Keisha decided. Maybe the man that she'd met had been the façade. She looked at her boys, so carefree in the water. The beach was one of the things they'd missed about California. Now, Keisha felt, she was missing more things about her old lifestyle. She began to think of a life without Jefferson, but with some of his money. *I'd better get to it quickly, get me some cash and bounce. That's what I'm going to do,* she decided. She was going to pull one last rip-off, get her a pile of cash from Jefferson's bank account, and then tell him and all of those other Livingstons to kiss her ass . . . just as soon as she got back home.

Keisha spread on more sunscreen, repositioned her glasses, and pulled her floppy hat down over her face. Had she not done this, perhaps she would have seen them: the four burly men walking purposefully toward the water's edge. Perhaps she would have seen Q's eyes go wide with knowledge, trying to run through the water and hit the sand. As it was, Keisha wasn't aware of anything until her boys started screaming, "Let go of my uncle! Mama! Let go!" Then and only then did Keisha sit up with a jerk, rip off her hat, and then fly off the chaise down to where they held Q with his hands behind his back.

As she reached her brother's side, a string of expletives was being unleashed. Between them, however, she heard six distinct words: "Quintin Bright, you are under arrest."

52

Adam and Ace sat in Adam's office, wrapping up the last few loose ends before they joined Candace, Diane, and the rest of the family, who'd already flown to LA. The CFO had just left them feeling light and happy, after he'd reported another healthy quarter for the Livingston Corporation.

"Hard to believe how hard we were struggling last year," Ace commented as he shook his head.

"Got to hand it to my boys, Twin. Toussaint's show on the Food Network and Malcolm's Soul Smoker helped to put Taste of Soul on the national map."

"The barbeque sauce is flying off the shelf, and I'm sure that's due in large part to Toussaint using it so much in his recipes and Malcolm's touting it every time he fires up a Soul Smoker."

"I think the commercial helped, too, with Mama and Daddy dressed to look like the classic painting of the farmer couple with a pitchfork."

"I'm still marveling that Daddy Marcus went along with that idea." Adam and Ace laughed at the commercial that had made their parents regional stars.

"When it comes to the greenbacks, Marcus Livingston will go along with a lot of things."

The sound of Adam's assistant's voice came through the intercom. "I know you asked not to be disturbed, Adam, but Sterling Ross is on the line. He says it's important."

"Thanks, Jolene. Put him through."

"Good afternoon, Sterling," Adam said once he'd picked up the phone. He listened intently, not saying a word. "Will do, man. Thank you. And thanks for the call."

Adam put down the receiver, and slowly reared back in his seat. His face was stoic, but his eyes were shining.

"Well?" Ace asked after several seconds went by.

A smile slowly crossed Adam's face as he answered. "We got him."

"Quintin?"

Adam nodded. "We got that son of a bitch."

Across town, Shyla stretched as she finished her latest report. For the past few weeks, she'd sent out fliers for freelance marketing consulting, and just yesterday had landed her first client. She'd been excited, still was. But after two hours on the computer and one page of notes, she realized just how lazy she'd gotten, and how rusty were her skills. She'd always viewed herself as a career woman, but maybe she'd take up Cooper's offer and let him take care of her after all.

Shyla walked into the kitchen, poured herself a glass of water, and then went into the den and turned on the television to CNN. The picture she saw almost made her drop the glass. A handcuffed Quintin Bright, looking hard and defiant, stared into the camera. Shyla scrambled for the remote and turned up the volume.

In addition to felony theft charges, Bright is being listed as a person of interest in last year's shooting of Atlanta businessman Adam Livingston. So far, no arrests have been made in that case. A spokesperson for the Livingstons said that the family intends to prosecute Bright to

*the full extent of the law. I'm Rachelle Ward reporting
for CNN News.*

Shyla muted the television and sat there in shock. *Felony
theft? Shooting Adam Livingston?* Shyla slowly realized that she'd
known very little about the man that she'd romped with in the
Caribbean sun. She'd known about his beef with the Livingstons, but he'd attributed that to his sleeping with Adam's
wife. According to Quintin, Candace had been madly in love
with him and had threatened to leave her husband. In a jealous
rage, Adam had pulled city strings and gotten Q's business shut
down. He said that had angered many people, especially the financial partners who'd invested in his gym. According to Q,
any number of people could have shot Adam Livingston, and
that only because of his relationship with Candace was the finger pointing squarely at him.

Shyla jumped up and ran to her phone, which was charg-
ing in the bedroom. She needed to talk to Cooper, and she
needed to do it now!

Chardonnay was back in the manager's office when her
cell phone rang. "Hey, Zoe, what's up?"

"Girl, they arrested Q."

"What?"

"I just saw it on CNN. It looked like some undercover
agents took him down in Jamaica."

"You saw this on TV?"

"Handcuffed and everything."

"What did the news say?" Zoe told her what she'd heard.
"I cannot believe that they arrested my boy!"

"Well, believe it. You can even Google it and read for
yourself. It's all over the Internet too."

"Damn."

"Wow, Chardonnay. You said that as if you're sad he got
caught. He shot Ace! I'm glad he's going to jail."

"I'll always dig Q. He may have done bad things but he's not a bad man. What happened to being innocent until proven guilty, Zoe?" *And what happened to the phone call about my money that I should have received by now?* "Look, girl. I gotta go."

As soon as Chardonnay got off the phone with Zoe, she placed two calls. The first one was to Keisha. She got voice mail, which wasn't totally surprising considering the circumstances: her brother getting locked up and all. Still, Chardonnay wondered how girlfriend was doing, how she was holding up under the pressure of keeping her identity a secret while being surrounded by the enemy. The Livingstons were no doubt gloating over their victory. How could Keisha watch this and not blow her cover? Chardonnay hadn't lied when she'd told Zoe of her feelings for Q. She'd always care for his well-hung behind. And while she'd only known Keisha briefly, she liked the young, nervy woman trying to come up any way she could. Which was why a part of Chardonnay felt remorseful at her two-faced position, and that the information she'd given Toussaint had ultimately helped have Q arrested. But as she made her second call Chardonnay kept her mind on the big picture: getting paid. When it came to Quintin Bright and Keisha Miller, nothing that had happened was personal. It was business.

"Toussaint," Chardonnay said when his voice mail came on as well. "This is Chardonnay. I just saw the news. Call me as soon as you get this message. We need to talk. You know about what."

53

Since her brother's arrest, Keisha had tried to stay calm. But the tranquil façade was getting harder to maintain with each passing moment. It had been almost forty-eight hours since the undercover agents had shown up on the beach, and Jefferson still hadn't returned her calls. When she'd seen them throw Quintin onto the ground, Keisha had almost passed out. If not for her boys and the fact that they were already freaking out, she would have lost it.

At first, Keisha had been sure that she, too, would get arrested. She'd grabbed her boys, pulled them to her side, and sworn that if the men took her, they'd have to carry her sons, too, because she was not going to let them go. But they barely even looked at her, just grabbed Q and hauled him off of the beach. Q had been furious, yelling at Keisha, asking her what was going on. *How in the fuck am I supposed to know?* Then, in a moment, his countenance changed. He became calm, stoic, probably because he saw that Dorian had started crying. "It's okay, little man," he'd managed, as the cops hauled him to his feet. "Be strong for your uncle, okay?" Then he'd looked at Keisha, said something that she was still trying to figure out, and yelled that he loved them. Then he was gone.

Keisha had stayed on the beach with the boys until almost

dark. She'd been scared to go back to Q's house, afraid that more agents were waiting to pounce. Since her brother had gone down, she'd felt certain that it was only a matter of time before they grabbed her, too. After all, even though there was no direct link between her and the earlier thefts, she'd initiated the last transfer with her own hands, from Jefferson's own computer with him sleeping just a few rooms away! Eventually, however, she'd returned to Q's modest yet well-equipped beach house and been relieved to see that it appeared unscathed, when she'd expected it to be turned upside down like the homes in the movies after drug busts. She'd gone through all of Q's things, had thankfully found some cash, and slowly, eventually, felt her heartbeat go back to normal.

So why isn't Jefferson calling me? Even with his sullen mood of late, this behavior was unlike him. Jefferson was the type of guy who'd call in the middle of the day for no reason other than to say that he loved you and was thinking about you. He'd call and ask her opinion, ask what she was doing, or just to take a break from his workload. She considered that perhaps since she'd left town, he'd decided to go to LA early. Maybe he was helping his sister get ready for their big event. But even if that was true, Keisha knew that they weren't working twenty-four seven. She couldn't figure out what was going on, and it was driving her crazy.

As was the fact that she hadn't heard from Q. She assumed that whoever had grabbed him was taking him back to Atlanta, but she couldn't be sure. She'd never known the details of his operation, but she did know that the money was laundered in several states before arriving at his bank accounts in God-knew-where. Belatedly, Keisha kicked herself for not putting aside her own nest egg, for not demanding more of the money she was getting for Q. But she'd been living with her ATM machine, her bank account, with no thought that the cash flow would hit a dry spot. And certainly no idea that the ending would be this abrupt.

"Mommy, I'm hungry," Antwan said.

"Me, too," Keisha's oldest son, Dorian, added.

Keisha looked at the clock and was surprised to see that it was two-thirty in the afternoon. Time had seemed to stand still since Q got arrested. Keisha couldn't even remember the last time she'd eaten, though a fifth of Patron Silver and cut lime slices were never far from her side. "Let me jump into the shower," she finally said to her sons. "Y'all put on your sandals. Then we'll go have tacos, okay?"

"Mommy, can we play outside?"

A vision of her sons disappearing with four burly men flashed into Keisha's mind. "No, stay in here and play video games. Y'all can play in the water after we eat."

Standing under the stream of a long, hot shower, Keisha's mind started to clear and with that came a renewed sense of power. Keisha had survived a lot of things in her life: the 'hood, sexual abuse, a druggie mother. There was no need to lie about it, Keisha concluded. The situation that she'd put herself in was beyond fucked up. Yet as she massaged the shampoo into her hair, she decided it was time for her to put on her big-girl panties and deal with it. *I'll take the boys to get some food and then we'll . . . oh shit! Q's restaurant!* It was the first time Keisha had thought about her brother's bustling business on the beach. Was it open? Had he called the manager to handle things while he was locked up? Keisha liked Constance, Q's girlfriend who also helped him run the restaurant. She was quiet, observant, and seemed to have a good head on her shoulders. *Maybe she knows some things that I don't know. Maybe she can help me!*

With a new, steely resolve, Keisha toweled off quickly, smoothed on a generous amount of sunscreen lotion, and decided to help herself feel better by donning one of the sexy minidress halters she'd bought in Atlanta. She decided against putting her hair back in a ponytail, opting instead to let it flow free. As she slipped into her sandals, her stomach growled. "Ha!

Boys, turn that game off, Mommy's hungry, too. Let's go get something to eat!"

They arrived at Q's restaurant moments later. Keisha was relieved to see it was business as usual, tables filled mostly with tropical-shirt-and-khaki-shorts-wearing tourists and a few locals sitting at the bar. Constance came over right away. The look in her eyes told Keisha that they needed to talk. Yet when she reached the table, she pasted on a big smile and talked to the boys.

"There's my handsome men-childs," she said in her lyrical accent. "I bet you want tacos and some colas, no?"

The boys nodded enthusiastically.

"What can I get you, Mama?" she asked Keisha.

"A taco salad," Keisha replied. "And a mojito...double shot."

"Coming right up."

Constance walked away and returned minutes later with the boy's tacos in bright red plastic bowls and their drinks in to-go cups. "You boys want to have like a picnic on the beach?"

They looked at Keisha and when she nodded, they told Constance that they did.

She looked at Keisha, her eyes speaking volumes. "I'll be right back."

Keisha watched the tall, dark, attractive woman chat with her sons as they walked several feet away from the concrete patio outfitted with two picnic tables and several smaller tables with either two- or four-person settings. So engrossed was she in taking in the deceptively tranquil scene around her that she almost didn't hear the beep signaling that an e-mail had come to her phone. Casually, she reached into her big, straw bag and pulled out her cell phone. Her heart skipped a beat. The e-mail was from Jefferson.

She punched the icon for Gmail, her heart pounding as the

page opened up. She didn't even look up when the waiter came over with her taco salad, yet as soon as he set down her drink, she grabbed it and drank half of it down with one, long gulp. Keisha had a feeling that no matter what Jefferson's message, she'd need to be fortified.

The page loaded. There was no subject line. Keisha opened the message. It was short, which Keisha figured could either be good or bad. *Only one way to find out.* She took a deep breath and began to read:

> Keisha, it's over. I know everything: that you are Quintin's sister and have been stealing from me. The only reason that you are not sitting next to him in jail is because of your sons. Even though you don't have a heart, I do. Use the tickets that you have to fly back to LA. There is nothing left for you in Atlanta. My attorney will contact you about your stuff. Let's hope our paths never cross again, Keisha. I really loved you. J.

Keisha's hands were shaking as she placed her phone down on the wooden table. *He knows? How does he know?* She put her head in her hands, racking her brain for answers. Somebody had to have told him about her...but who? When she'd met his family, she'd been very careful not to mention any names of her family members. She never talked to any of them when Jefferson was home. Hell, she didn't even know anybody in Atlanta. *I never talk to anybody! Except for...* Keisha's head shot up. *Chardonnay?* Keisha's mind whirled as she tried to remember their conversations. Had she ever mentioned Q's name? She didn't think so, but wasn't entirely sure. The couple of times she'd partied with Chardonnay had gone by in drunken blurs. Was it possible that she'd talked out of school while inebriated? And even if she had, even if she'd mentioned Q's name, would that have mattered? Chardonnay didn't know her brother, did she? Keisha finished the drink and ordered another. She stood and began to pace. Of course it was possible that Chardonnay knew Q. But even if she did, what did that matter? Keisha knew for a fact that she'd told no one about coming to the islands to see her brother, or that she was going from there to LA. So how did this happen? How did the police know where to find them? Had she somehow unknowingly led them to her brother's hiding place? If that was true, Keisha knew that she would never forgive herself.

54

Twenty-four hours ago they'd been in the midst of celebration, but anyone observing the room filled with Livingstons wouldn't have guessed it from their faces. It was the day after the opening, but Adam, Candace, Ace, Diane, Jefferson, Malcolm, and Toussaint hadn't gathered in Bianca's home to discuss the standing room only, star-studded crowds; the television, magazine, and radio coverage; or even the fact they'd literally run out of food. No, the family had gathered together with Sterling Ross to discuss how to proceed in the prosecution of Quintin Bright.

"So far we have two witnesses," Sterling was saying. "Two men who will testify that Quintin Bright laundered money through their businesses. We also have surveillance tape of Quintin making transactions at a bank in North Carolina." Sterling looked at Jefferson. "We also have the transfer that occurred from Jefferson's computer, the transfer that went to a bank in Kansas City before being withdrawn and placed into an off-shore account. However, we need to prosecute the person who made that transaction in order to add it to the evidence." The previous evening, Sterling had strongly suggested to Jefferson that he prosecute Keisha Miller, but so far, Jefferson had refused.

"Have we recovered all the money?" Adam asked.

Sterling shook his head. "We'll be lucky to get even half back of what was taken. But you don't have to worry about that. Your money was insured."

"That's not the point!"

"I understand, Adam," Sterling replied, his voice remaining calm, unruffled. "Remember that Quintin was on the run for almost a year. Chances are that a good deal of the money has been spent."

Toussaint's phone indicated a text message, one of half a dozen that had been sent in the past seventy-two hours. "We have another situation to deal with." Everyone looked at him. He held up his phone. "Chardonnay Wilson. She's been blowing me up since the arrest made news. We all know that she is calling about the reward money—"

Bianca exploded. "She will not get a dime!"

"Her information did help us find Quintin," Toussaint countered.

"Yes, and her information about my marriage caused scandal for this family. She's already gotten paid at the Livingstons' expense. Let whatever the *Inquirer* paid her be enough." She didn't have proof, but Bianca was sure that Chardonnay was behind the A.I. story.

Ace looked at Sterling. "What's our legal position?"

"It depends. Was this arrangement put in writing?"

"No," Toussaint answered. "Everything was verbal."

Sterling pondered what he'd heard. "In that case, the nature of how the reward is dispersed can be left to interpretation. All of the money can go to one party or the money can be divided among whatever entities contributed to the end result."

Malcolm cleared his throat. "Let's not forget that Chardonnay is not only pivotal to this case, but so far she's the only lead we have on the case that really matters: Dad's shooting."

The room quieted as the gravity of this reminder sank in.

"Damn!" Bianca hissed. "How'd that woman get all up in our business?"

"Because of Q," Toussaint simply replied.

"We need to huddle with the lawyers," Sterling said. "And I think they'll agree that we need to prosecute both charges simultaneously: felony theft and attempted murder. Which means that how we handle all of the potential witnesses will be important, including Chardonnay."

"I am diametrically opposed to that . . . woman . . . getting any of the reward money." Because of her parents' presence, Bianca reluctantly used a substitution for the b-word she really wanted to call Chardonnay.

"Technically it wasn't her," Jefferson offered. "Keisha is the one who led us to Quintin."

Silence. That Jefferson's ex would not be seeing any reward money did not need to be said.

Suddenly, Toussaint spoke into the silence. "Chardonnay doesn't deserve all of the reward money, and as much as her actions against Bianca upset me, she is still due something. We've given our word."

Candace had been quiet through this whole exchange. There was no love lost between her and Chardonnay. "Do you think it wise to keep somebody like this around—working for the restaurant I mean, involved in the day-to-day functions of the business?"

"I don't," Bianca interjected.

"Me either," Malcolm agreed.

"Let me handle Chardonnay," Toussaint said decisively. "We'll get her help in convicting Quintin. And then we'll get her out of our lives."

55

Quintin shifted on his cot and gazed through the bars of his prison cell. At least for right now, he was alone. Who knew what kind of asshole he'd have to fight if he got a cellmate? It seemed to always come to that in lockup: men flexing their muscles to call a piece of concrete their own, to have a little say-so in a world where they are no longer in control. Five years. That was the time on his last bid. And he'd sworn when he walked out, when he'd heard the clink of the heavy metal behind him, that that would be the last they'd see him inside. And now look. Here he was again.

He closed his eyes but was unable to sleep for the glare of the lights. Even after lights out, the world of a prisoner was never dark. At least not outside you. Large fluorescent bulbs intruded upon any semblance of true escape from the world around you, and as if that wasn't enough, the noise from other inmates interrupted attempts at peace. In Quintin's inner world, however, it was hard to find any light shining. That's if the interrogators were to be believed. According to them, they had evidence pointing to his stealing at least two hundred thousand dollars from the Livingston Corporation, and a witness linking him to attempted murder in the first degree. Of course, Quintin hadn't cracked. Hell, this wasn't his first time at the rodeo, and he'd watched enough of *The Wire* and *L.A. Law* to not say shit without an attorney present. He knew it would be hard to shake the money thing, but he'd be damned if he'd go out for an attempted 187. There were only three people who knew he'd pulled the trigger in the Livingston parking lot that night: him, Adam, and Chardonnay. It was Quintin's word against both of them, and after Quintin dropped some knowledge on Chardonnay's rogue ass, he no longer expected her to be talking.

And then there was the matter of how he got here in the first place. Somebody somewhere had put two and two together and come up with the fact that he and Keisha were related. But who? Keisha knew how important it was to keep their connection a secret, and being in love with Jefferson, had more to lose by being found out than he did. Quintin couldn't imagine her not being careful, knew for a fact that she handled her business well. So who'd slid between the cracks in their well-planned scheme, a setup that had worked flawlessly for over a year?

Quintin turned onto his stomach, tried to find a comfortable spot on the thin, worn mattress. His ass was in trouble, there was no doubt about it. But Quintin had a few cards up his sleeve. He didn't plan on going down without a fight.

The next morning, the sound of jingling officer keys alerted Quintin that something was up. "Bright," the guard said. "You have a visitor?"

Bright jumped down from the top bunk. "Who?"

The security guard shrugged.

"Female?"

"No."

Quintin's face remained passive as he was escorted down the hall, yet turned into a frown when he realized that, instead of to the bank of phones, he was being led to where criminals could speak privately with their attorneys. He'd fired the court-appointed asshole they'd given him on the first day.

Quintin had steeled himself to wait it out until Keisha called him, and then to get in touch with his boy in Long Beach—the Johnny Cochran-styled brothah who'd bailed him out of his last scrape and wasn't above taking a little under the table or beneath doing something unethical to gain a client's freedom. So who was waiting behind door number one was anyone's guess.

The security guard opened the door, and after Quintin had entered the room, closed and locked it behind him. Quintin sized up the man standing on the other side of the table, an average-looking brothah wearing glasses and an ill-fitting suit. *Who's this muthafucka?*

"Quintin Bright?" the gentleman asked, with his hand outstretched.

Quintin strolled over without smiling and instead of shaking the outstretched hand, put his hands on his hips. "Yeah, who are you?"

"I'm the attorney who's going to get you cleared of all of these charges."

"Oh, really?" Quintin asked. "How do you figure that?"

"Because I'm the best defense attorney this side of the Mississippi." Once again, the man held out his hand. "Cooper Riley, Jr., at your service. And when we get through with those asshole Livingstons, they'll be sorry that they messed with either of us."

56

Chardonnay sat across from Toussaint, trying really hard not to be pissed off. She had to keep reminding herself that she'd not been paid, and until she either got the reward money or hit the lottery, she needed the check from her restaurant job. But as soon as she got some long paper, she was going to tell these sons-of-bitches to kiss her ass!

"Sorry it's taken a while to get back with you," Toussaint said once the waiter had taken their orders and left the table. "But with the West Coast openings and everything else, it's been busy."

"I understand, and that's all well and good and all...but I just want my money. Mama needs a new pair of shoes, some clothes for my kids, a house, a car....Look, Toussaint, I know you're my employer family, but straight out...I just need my shit."

"That's what I needed to talk to you about, Chardonnay."

"Why? What is there to discuss?"

"The deal we made was reward money offered for the arrest and *conviction* of the person who shot Daddy. That's if we can even get the charge to stick."

"What about the felony theft? Q stole money from y'all, too."

"Yes, but that's a different matter altogether."

Chardonnay was rapidly losing the patience she was trying to hold on to. "How do you figure that? Whether it's for stealing or shooting, the bottom line is, y'all got your man and I'm the reason why!"

"First of all," Toussaint said, the epitome of swagger. "You need to calm down. Because your demanding attitude doesn't move or impress me, and your impatience isn't going to speed up the process at all. In fact, it may have the opposite effect." Chardonnay huffed but said nothing further. Toussaint went on. "The agreement with you, Chardonnay, was done with regard to my father's shooting, before Quintin stole money from the family. But your participation is no less important. We believe your testimony will be crucial to convicting Quintin for trying to kill my dad."

"Wait, brothah, slow your roll. I never said nothing about testifying against anybody. I ain't trying to be your witness. What I said is that I would help y'all find a muthafucka—I mean, excuse me, find Q. I never said I'd help y'all convict him. I've got too many family members doing time. I know what that's like. Unh unh... When it comes to locking a brothah up, y'all are on your own."

"I'm very sorry to hear that, Chardonnay," Toussaint replied, "because without your testimony, it will be difficult to convict Quintin on the shooting charges. Keep in mind, Chardonnay, this isn't an innocent bystander we're talking about; a brothah being railroaded by the system or framed for something he didn't do. This is the man who tried to kill my father. But if you don't want to help"—Toussaint raised his hands in surrender—"that's up to you. However, please keep in mind that that is a one-hundred-and-fifty-thousand-dollar decision."

Chardonnay left the restaurant without finishing her drink. Toussaint had given her a lot to think about, including a major curveball that she hadn't seen being thrown. It was one thing to tell the Livingstons where Q was, and technically, she hadn't even done that. It had made her breathe easier to lead them to Keisha, a woman she thought cool but with whom she had no emotional attachment. But Q had tapped her core, had sexed her in ways she'd never dreamed of and made her feel like a woman—physically, yes, but emotionally, too. She'd never been in love with Q, but she'd loved his dirty drawers.

Plus, she'd grown up in the hood, where one was more likely to have criminals as role models than doctors or lawyers. Snitching wasn't cool where she'd come from, which was why so many neighborhood crimes went unsolved. Those involved would rather deliver their own brand of street justice and one rarely trusted anyone on the other side of the law. Her contribution to date had been basically anonymous. Testifying while Q looked her in the face was another matter altogether.

Chardonnay reached her car and peeled out of the parking lot. Her phone rang, but when she saw that it was from an unknown caller, she let it go to voice mail. She never answered a number that wasn't recognized, and neither telemarketers nor bill collectors ever left a message. So a few minutes later she was surprised to hear the message indicator. She put on her headset and pressed her message icon: *You have one new message. To listen to your messages, press*—"Shut up, fool," Chardonnay said to the recording, hitting the star key to bypass it. "Just let me hear who called."

"Chardonnay, this is Keisha." Chardonnay's eyes widened. "You probably heard the news and know why I'm calling. There ain't no easy way to say this so I'm going to just be straight up. I know that you know my brother, and I have an idea you may have known that I was his sister, too. What I hope you don't know is how the law found us, because if you think the Livingstons carry some heat, you ain't seen nothing. The Millers and Brights are not to be messed with and should not be taken lightly. Atlanta ain't never seen nothing like how we do it in LA. So if you're choosing teams, Chardonnay, you better think long and hard about which side you're on. And if you're woman enough, this here's my new number... hollah at your girl."

Chardonnay played the recording twice more before she got to the restaurant. Even after chain-smoking Newports and hitting half a blunt in the parking lot, she was still no damn good. Between Toussaint and Keisha she was about to lose her mind. *I gotta have some help with this,* she determined as she sprayed on cologne, checked her eyes, and made her way to the employee entrance. *Because in order to play my cards right, Mama has to know what's in everybody's hand.*

57

Alexis came into the room and was surprised to see Toussaint sipping a drink as he looked out the window. "Hey, baby, I didn't hear you come home."

"I just got here."

She walked over and kissed him. He turned and gave as much of a hug as he could to someone almost eight months along. "How'd it go?"

Toussaint reached for her hand and walked them over to the couch. "I guess time will tell," he said as they sat down. "With someone like Chardonnay, you never know. The main thing to keep in mind is that her loyalty is to the dollar bill." Alexis laid her head on Toussaint's shoulder, rubbing her hand up and down his thigh. "Don't do that, baby."

"What? Since when does that bother you?"

Belatedly, Toussaint realized that his words came out more harshly than he'd intended. "Since my woman stopped making love with me," he said softly. "I haven't gone this long without sex since high school, maybe even junior high. I'm strong, baby, but I'm still flesh and blood."

"I'm sorry, baby, I wasn't even thinking. And you know I want to. It's just so uncomfortable, and your long dick would probably be banging our baby in the head!"

"Ha! No, it wouldn't...."

"I know you're frustrated."

"You aren't?"

"Baby, trust me, with a leg pushing your bladder, an arm pushing your stomach, and another extremity nudging your kidney for room...the last thing on your mind is adding yet another object to the mix." As it was a normal gesture, Alexis almost began rubbing Toussaint's thigh again. His legs were one of her favorite features. All three of them. But especially his thighs: thick and strong, yet soft to the touch. She and Toussaint were a very affectionate couple, very touchy-feely. She missed that.

Toussaint sat beside his wife, experiencing a rare moment of discomfort. The trip to Los Angeles hadn't helped—when it seemed like everybody and their mama threw themselves at him. He'd gotten sympathy from both Adam and Malcolm and having had their own battles with temptation, they'd both kept an eye on him the entire trip.

"Hey, baby."

"Hum."

"How is Candace handling all this?"

Toussaint understood Alexis's question. The family hadn't talked about it much, but Toussaint had confided in his wife about his mother's infidelity. He, too, wondered about his mother's thoughts. "She's been pretty quiet through it all, to tell you the truth. It's an understandably sticky subject. I know that everybody will be glad when this saga is over."

"It'll be all right, baby," Alexis said, wrapping Toussaint's arms around her stomach and cuddling against him. "The trial will get under way, Q will be convicted, and this whole ugly episode will be a thing of the past."

"Yeah, the mess with Quintin will hopefully be behind us," Toussaint replied. "But when it comes to his sister, Keisha, and the games she played with Jefferson, I think that is going to scar my cousin for a very long time."

★ ★ ★

Keisha made her way through the Hartsfield-Jackson Atlanta International Airport. Amazing what a difference an arrest could make. Just four months ago she'd come down this
very jetway with sons in tow, excited about her future in this
new city, envisioning herself as a stay-at-home wife. Now she
was back, alone and focused, determined to protect her future,
muting feelings for the man she so recently loved. Thinking
about Jefferson caused a bolt of pain to shoot through her
heart. How he'd cut her off so quickly and completely. As per
his e-mail, a woman representing Jefferson had contacted her.
At least, Keisha thought, that's what the skank had said. She'd
summoned Keisha down to her offices on Wilshire Boulevard,
where she'd given her a key to a storage space and her SUV.
Keisha had been instructed that she had six months to remove
the items from the storage before payments would be discon-
tinued, and that she could keep or sell the contents, Jefferson
hadn't cared which. Thankful to have her car back, Keisha had
raced over to the storage space, expecting to find the entire
household of furniture she'd purchased for her place in Atlanta. Instead, it was a small five-by-ten unit containing all of
her and her sons' clothes, their toys and electronic gadgets, and
Keisha's exercise bike. Conspicuously absent were the expensive furniture, flat screens, appliances, and—save for what she'd
taken to Jamaica—the jewelry Jefferson had purchased. Keisha
had been crushed, and couldn't understand how Jefferson
could have been so callous, how he could have thrown her
away so easily, like yesterday's trash. Amazingly, Keisha didn't
make the connection between the pain that she'd caused and
why she now suffered.

Because of her big brother, all was not lost for Keisha. He
had left instructions with Constance in case something ever
went down. The cryptic message delivered as he was hauled
away—*Get in touch with that crazy muthafucka*—was in reference
to his boy Rico. He had access to some of Q's money so for

now at least, Keisha was set and able to do her job: get her brother out of jail. For her, this trip was all about payback for how she and her brother—in their minds—had once again been wronged. Thirty minutes later, Keisha was in a rental car heading to a safe-deposit box in College Park, Georgia. Tomorrow she would meet with her brother and then with his attorney, Cooper Riley, Jr. *May I have your attention, please! Keisha's back in this, bitch. Now, let the games begin.*

58

Keisha hated prisons, everything about them: the barbed wire, the bars, armed guards undressing her with their eyes, other inmates doing the same. And every jail had a smell; an odor of defeat, anger, and restlessness. It mixed with the ammonia, pee, and underarm funk, and permeated the air along with the message felt when not heard: get me out of here!

Still, with all of that, Keisha felt better after having seen her brother. There was no glass thick enough to truly separate them. As always, he was the voice of reason, giving her strength even when he was in a position of weakness. He'd had nothing but time to think about their game plan. The instructions he'd delivered were specific and concise. Most of their talking had been in code, a throwback to the communication they'd developed as children to bypass the various "uncles" that often invaded their home. This morning, Keisha had felt anxious, nervous. Now she felt poised, relaxed. She'd been given a game plan and was ready to execute. *Showtime!*

Back at the hotel in College Park, where Operation Keisha was located, she quickly showered and changed. She was ready for her meeting with Cooper Riley, ready to push forward toward her brother's release. She unbound her freshly permed hair and brushed it until it hung straight and shiny down her back. She'd dressed carefully in a tan suit, the miniskirt and three-inch heels showing off shapely calves while a soft, off-white shell revealed just enough orb to be mouthwatering, Keisha applied her MAC makeup with care. Aside from her push-up bra, she wore no underwear.

At exactly one p.m., the time of her appointment, Keisha walked into Cooper Riley's law office. Q had warned her to steel herself against the opulence she might experience, to act like it was normal. But this office setting, with its plush carpeting, dark cherry wood, understated chandeliers, and large windows framing the Atlanta skyline, was hard to ignore.

The receptionist, an older African American woman with salt-and-pepper hair and a pleasant smile, greeted her warmly. "Ms. Miller?"

"Yes, ma'am."

"Please have a seat. I'll let Mr. Riley know you're here."

Ten minutes later, Keisha was being ushered into a large, corner office that, if not for the large windows, would have been stuffy. One wall was covered with law books, floor to ceiling. A massive antique-looking desk occupied one corner while a hutch containing a variety of trophies, plaques, and other memorabilia sat in the other. Keisha walked over with hand outstretched. "Mr. Riley, it's nice to meet you."

"Please, call me Cooper."

"And I'm Keisha."

Years of professionalism and stellar home training caused Cooper to greet Keisha Miller with that simple greeting and a smile. Inside, however, his heart was racing. He'd seen a picture of her, but it was clear immediately that the photo had not done her justice. He was used to being around attractive women, Shyla Martin among them. But quite simply, this woman-child, this vixen, was the most beautiful woman he'd ever seen, possibly the most beautiful woman in the world. "Why don't you join me in the sitting area?"

Instead of sitting across from him, Keisha chose to sit in the seat next to Cooper. She placed a hand on his forearm and smiled coyly. "Mr. Riley, Cooper, I want to thank you *so* much for representing my brother!"

Love and respect for his father aside, Cooper had never particularly cared for his name. But the way Keisha said it, the way her lips pouted while forming the *C* as she pushed the "*oo*" through lips lightly glossed with pink. Cooper almost became mesmerized as he looked at eyes framed by lashes so long they almost reached her thick, perfectly arched eyebrows. *You are not a teenager, man. Get ahold of your hormones and do your job!*

"Would you like something to drink, some water perhaps, or tea?"

"Actually, do you have some hot chocolate?" Keisha giggled. "I've been craving some all morning but didn't have time to stop at a coffee shop."

That he could provide this simple request almost had Cooper sticking out his chest and beating it like a victorious gorilla. It also gave him time to collect his thoughts so that he could be the excellent attorney Keisha and her brother deserved. While the receptionist brought in mugs of hot chocolate and mini-croissants, Cooper and Keisha shared small talk. Cooper had done his homework and probably knew more about Keisha than she would have liked, and he was impressed that, while she didn't highlight the hardships of her life, she did not try and hide them either. Within those first few moments, Keisha disclosed that she was the single mother of two boys by different fathers, and a fiercely independent soul shunned by a troubled mother, raised by a strict yet loving grandmother, and an ambitious spirit who fiercely desired a better life for her kids. Within moments, Cooper found himself wanting to be the man to give it to her. By the time the meeting was over, and Keisha had shared with Cooper the contents of the safe-deposit box, he would learn that Keisha and her brother could very well give him what he wanted as well.

59

"Cooper, it's Shyla."

"Hello, Shyla."

"I called to see what you were doing and what your plans are for the evening."

"I'm working, and tonight I am taking a client to dinner."

"Oh, really. I was hoping that you and I could have dinner tonight." For the past week, Shyla had been avoiding Cooper. She'd grown tired of his awkward advances and mediocre love-making, and had sought the refuge of an old-time flame. But she didn't want to stray too far from her goal: revenge against the Livingstons and a rich man in her future. She needed to keep the leash tightened with her beauty and charm.

"Another night, dear. This can't be helped." Cooper had noticed Shyla's absence, had intended to speak to her about it when he got home. *Now,* Cooper thought as he eyed a vulnerable-looking Keisha, *I might push her even farther away!*

Something about his tone didn't sound right to Shyla. He was a bit clipped, curt, not like Cooper at all. "Is everything all right, Cooper?"

"Yes, everything is fine. It's just been a busy day, and I'm trying to wrap up."

"Okay, I'll let you go. Why don't I meet you at your place later, give you a nice massage?"

"Thanks, Shyla, but I think I'll pass tonight. I think after dinner I'll go home, have a nightcap, and crash into bed. Let's talk tomorrow, okay?"

"Sure."

Shyla frowned as she hung up the phone. Something was niggling at her, something she couldn't quite put her finger on. *Maybe it's me,* she decided. It was that time of the month. After working a couple more hours, Shyla decided to call it a day as well. She went into the kitchen and decided to scrounge up something to eat. Belatedly she realized the pickings were slim. There was frozen hamburger and a package of wings in the freezer; in the fridge a head of cabbage and salad fixings; and in her pantry containers of dried beans, canned tuna, pasta, and rice. *Not too exciting, Shyla.* She grabbed an apple from a bowl on the table and picked up a handful of take-out menus. Nothing caught her eye in those as well. Then she got it. It wasn't the choices that were the problem, it was the fact that she didn't want to eat alone. That was probably what had given her pause earlier, too, she decided, when Cooper had plans for the evening. It had gone without saying that they spent most evenings together, unless she had other plans. Now that she thought about it, she couldn't remember a time when Cooper had something to do and she had to fend for herself. *Could it be that that fuddy-duddy is growing on me?* Shyla laughed at the thought, but grateful that she'd figured out the reason for her funk, she decided to do something about it. And since she was going out, she decided to do it big. She'd go to FGO.

For Gentlemen Only was a members-only club that catered to the city's movers and shakers. The only way to become a member was to be invited by another member in good standing. Until the mid-seventies, FGO was truly what its name implied: a men-only club. This all changed when a pillar of the community and one of Atlanta's most wealthiest families, black or white, willed his membership to his only child, a daughter. It was taken to a vote, and while a woman still could not become a charter member with the voting privileges and the power to implement rules, women could become "registered guests" of the community, afforded all of the other advantages of membership—namely, the invaluable networking and deal closing that often happened within the club's hallowed walls. Shyla certainly wasn't a charter member, or even a registered guest, but as the daughter of one of the members and a play niece to Harold, the longtime host, she occasionally got a pass and the chance to go inside. The last time had been when she met Cooper, almost five months ago. Shyla felt that enough time had passed for her to pay another visit. With any luck this would be the night where anyone with the last name Livingston had somewhere else they needed to be.

"Man, don't be so hard on yourself."

"It's hard not to, Cuz. How in the hell could I have not seen through her games? How could I have been so vulnerable?"

It was six thirty, relatively quiet at the Livingston Corporation for so early in the evening. But the executive offices were practically empty, with Adam and Ace having left to get in a golf game, the marketing department at a meeting off site, and both finance and operations all seeming to play hooky. This evening, Toussaint and Jefferson were two of the last men standing.

"Look," Toussaint continued. "A lot of times, we see what we want to see. Look at how long I messed around with Shyla, because she was beautiful, doting, and . . . okay . . . a pretty good roll in the sack."

Jefferson shook his head. "It's not the same. Shyla didn't steal from you."

She might as well have. Remember half of the severance money we paid her came from my personal account."

"Right . . . forgot about that major detail."

Toussaint's countenance grew stormy. "I'll never forget it."

"But that's what makes it so bad, Toussaint. I still miss her. Ain't that a bitch? With everything she did to me, everything she stole, I miss her. I want to hate her, but I don't."

"That's because you're a good man, Jeff. Better than she deserved. Come on. Let's get out of here."

"No, man. You go ahead. I'm not quite ready to go home yet."

"Who said anything about going home? I sure can't go there yet since I can't touch my wife. I thought we'd head down to the club . . . give old man Harold a hard time."

"I haven't been down there in forever."

"All the more reason to join me. Let's go."

Cooper waited until Keisha sat down in the booth and then walked over to the other side. "You look lovely," he said when he sat down. "Wait, did I say that already?"

"Yes," Keisha answered, accompanied by the coy smile Cooper had already come to love. "But I don't mind that you said it again." She took a sip of the lemon water the waiter had delivered. "Cooper, thanks again for agreeing to have dinner with me. I know I'm from LA, but honestly, I feel lonely being here all by myself."

Cooper reached over and patted her hand as he would a frightened child. Where both Bianca and Shyla were independent, confident, successful women who'd often made him feel inferior—because there was nothing he could give them that they didn't already have—this woman-child made him feel powerful, needed, and that felt good. "It's totally understandable, dear. I'm happy to be here with you."

"It's not only that," Keisha continued, her eyes wide, voice barely above a whisper.

"What is it, Keisha?" Cooper asked, his voice becoming lower as well.

Keisha looked around, scooted over to sit next to Cooper, and placed a hand on his leg. A nice, soft hand, Cooper noted. "You're my attorney, so what I share with you is in complete confidence, right?"

Cooper couldn't speak, simply swallowed and nodded.

"I used to live here."

Of course, Cooper knew this. Quintin had told him all about how he'd set up his sister with Jefferson to get back at the fact that Candace had dumped him, and Adam had subsequently run him out of business.

Cooper decided to disclose this fact. "Your brother told me," he said softly, squeezing the hand that rested on top of his thigh. "He told me everything, Keisha. And I promise... you have nothing to worry about."

Later, he'd be hard pressed to remember how it happened. But the next thing he knew, those soft, glistening, kissable lips that he'd admired all evening were pushed up against his thin, slightly dry ones, and her tongue was working better than any tube of Chapstick he'd ever owned. Never given to public displays of affection, no one was more surprised than Cooper when his arm came up around her shoulder and his other hand rested lightly on her leg. It wasn't a tongue-down-your-throat, go-get-a-room kiss. It was a sweet kiss, a bit tentative and unsure, that asked as much as it promised.

Shyla gave Harold an affectionate hug, and then stepped inside the cool confines of FGO. It was a light crowd, typical for a Thursday evening. From what she'd seen and heard, Mondays and Fridays were their busiest nights, plus Sundays during football season, or anytime when it was play-off this or championship that of any sport. Shyla imagined May was that hazy sports month when it wasn't quite time for any of the above, and men spent more time at home becoming reacquainted with their wives.

"What can I get for the lady?" the handsome, bald chocolate-drop of a bartender asked.

"Grey Goose martini, very dry." Shyla pulled out her phone and began checking her text messages. That's why she didn't see Toussaint and Jefferson come in. She didn't know of their presence until she heard a rare yet unmistakable commotion happening near the last booth.

"Keisha, you've got a lot of nerve, coming back here."

That's when Shyla's ears perked up. She'd heard something about a woman Jefferson was dating, someone who used to live in LA and had two kids. But that's all Bobby had told her.

The next voice was muffled, but there was something about its slightly nasally tone that caused the hair on the back of Shyla's neck to rise. She was walking toward the sound before even realizing she'd moved, her very dry martini having been very forgotten. The room was laid out in a bit of a semicircle, with the bar occupying the front part of the room. The voices were coming from around the corner. As soon as she'd rounded it, Shyla saw Toussaint. Their eyes met. Shyla's widened. Toussaint's rolled. "Come on, Jeff," he said. "Let's go." He grabbed his cousin's arm, directing him out of the establishment. They brushed past Shyla without a word. Fortunately for them, she had bigger fish to fry. She reached the booth to see a very attractive, seemingly distraught woman in Cooper's arms.

"Hello, Cooper," she said, her eyes pointedly not on Cooper but on the woman he placated. "Is this the client you had to take to dinner?"

In answer to her question, a waiter came around the corner pushing a tray of salad, sodas, jellies, and rolls. "Excuse me, ma'am," he said politely to Shyla, and then smiled before serving Cooper and Keisha.

Cooper was totally unversed in this type of drama. The closest he usually came to such madness was watching it on TV. He looked beyond the waiter at Shyla's miffed expression and tried to make the best of a bad situation. "Yes, this is my client. Shyla, this is Keisha Miller; Keisha, Shyla Martin."

Keisha showed her interest by turning her face farther into Cooper's chest, more to get her composure than anything else, and not from the confrontation she'd had with Jefferson. *Shyla is the one Q told me about, the bitch who bailed on him, the one he said not to trust as far as I could throw. Looks like there's something more that big brother didn't know about: a little fling between his attorney and his island cat. Well, well, well...* Keisha raised up to look at Shyla...and just missed being drenched by the glass of water Shyla tossed in Cooper's face. That was right after she'd told him to go to hell and just before turning, head held high, and marching out of the club.

60

It was time for damage control. Shyla had called Cooper all morning: his house, office, and cell phone. To get the silent treatment from him wasn't a total surprise. She could only imagine the mortification of this conservative son of a well-known judge, and knew that if the outburst had reached his mother Evelyn's ears that woman would need smelling salts.

Her reaction had surprised her. Shyla liked Cooper well enough, but she also liked pistachio mint ice cream. She wasn't in love with Cooper, as she had been with Toussaint. It had to be the she-devil in her, she decided, that self-preserving jealous streak that had caused her to see red when she'd spotted the attractive woman all cuddled up with her financially secure future, otherwise known as her man. Mildred, the law office receptionist, had obviously not been informed of the previous night's shenanigans, because when Shyla called, Mildred politely told her no, Cooper was not in court but was spending the day working out of his home office. *Perfect,* Shyla thought as she left the deli with a bag containing Cooper's favorite sandwich—roast beef on rye with pickle, mayo, and Dijon mustard—and a large container of potato salad. She figured that even a man hard at work needed to eat and hoped that this peace offering would set things right.

And then there was Keisha Miller, who she'd found out was Q's sister. *Pretty girl.* Quintin was very attractive and they were siblings so it stood to reason that she, too, would be pleasing to the eye. But where Quintin was a deep, creamy chocolate, Keisha was very fair. *Perhaps her father is a white man.* "Stunning" was the word that came to Shyla's reluctant mind, with a curvy body, large doe eyes, and what looked to be her own, real hair cascading halfway down her back. A slight curveball but a manageable one, Shyla concluded. After all, she and Q had a history; Shyla was on his side; Keisha was his young, uneducated, single mother sister who couldn't at all compete with the educated, well-bred, successful marketing guru, and successfully interacting with both Q and Keisha was the way Shyla would get back at the Livingston family for releasing her from the best job of her life. She'd be Keisha's friend, not her enemy. Perhaps after she left Cooper's house, she'd call Keisha, offer to buy her a drink, and apologize in person. *Yes, that's exactly what I'll do.* Shyla turned up the music as she drove the short distance to Cooper's house. Once again, the world was hers.

"Will you marry me?" Cooper tucked an errant lock of hair behind Keisha's ear.

Keisha giggled. "Yes, but not today!"

Cooper and Keisha sat curled up on the old, leather couch in Cooper's home study, happy as two clams in chowder. He'd insisted on bringing her back to his house last night, after the fiasco; did not want her to have to battle such unpleasant memories alone in a hotel room. She'd appeared angry and confused. *Is that your girlfriend, Cooper?* she'd asked. And then, *Why does she hate me? I don't even know her!* Cooper had admitted that yes, Shyla and he had dated, but that one, theirs was not an exclusive relationship, and two, there was absolutely no excuse for the way she had behaved! After he'd insisted that she accompany him home, Keisha had insisted that he get out of the wet, sticky shirt he wore. Cooper had been shocked but pleased when his shower door had opened and a naked Keisha had joined him under the nozzle. Cooper had never imagined himself a stud, but Keisha had cried out during their lovemaking, making him feel virile and important. Then she'd cried on his shoulder and asked him to help her, take care of her, keep her safe from those "rich, powerful people" who wanted to bring her and her family down. Cooper vowed that he would, and meant it.

Shyla walked up the sidewalk to Cooper's door, rang the bell, and then put her key in the lock. "Cooper, it's me!" she yelled out, removing her key and closing the door behind her. "Time for a break, Mr. Workaholic, I've got lunch!" She walked into the dining room, set down her keys and bag of food, and proceeded to the kitchen to get a couple bottles of the flavored water Cooper always kept in the fridge.

A chagrined-looking Cooper hurried around the corner, tightening the belt on his robe as he did so. "Shyla, what are you doing in my house?"

Shyla turned, her eyes widening in surprise. "Cooper, what are you doing in your robe at one o'clock in the afternoon?"

The answer came walking around the corner wearing nothing but one of Cooper's stark white shirts. Clearly, Shyla realized, she'd gotten to the house a few hours too late.

"Cooper, is this your secretary?" Keisha asked in an innocent voice. She took in Shyla's short dress and the food on the table. "Ooh, I'm starving. Did she bring lunch?"

Shyla knew that it wouldn't do to perform histrionics two days in a row, so she took a deep breath and spoke calmly. "Cooper, may I have a word with you? Alone?"

Cooper rose to his full height of five feet, ten inches and put a protective arm around Keisha's waist. "No, Shyla, you may not."

The errant thought that Cooper looked just like his father,

down to the balding hair and protruding gut, ran across Shyla's mind. Yet she didn't miss how Keisha huddled in his embrace and laid her head on his shoulder, undoubtedly making him feel capable and manly, something that Shyla had never done.

"Fine," Shyla finally said, forcing a smile to her face. "It's just as well since I owe you both an apology." Shyla looked from Cooper to Keisha. "I am truly sorry for my despicable behavior last evening. Although I'd love to blame it on being that time of month"—Shyla's attempt at levity failed miserably—"there is absolutely no excuse for my actions." She took a step toward Keisha. "I'm good friends with Q, and I'm just sick about what's happened. As soon as I saw it on television, I talked with Cooper and told him that he had to help, that Q was a good man. Didn't I, Cooper?"

"Yes, you did."

"I can understand your feeling upset and vulnerable, Keisha. It is rather how I felt last night, after seeing the man I've dated for months snuggled up next to his client. Like I said, my behavior last night was unacceptable, but now, I'm afraid I must say the same thing about what I'm seeing right now. Keisha, you're young and confused, and I know we all make mistakes. But this is crossing the line, and Cooper, quite frankly, I'm shocked by this unethical behavior. However, Cooper, because I know what a trying time it's been for you lately, and Keisha, out of respect for your brother, I'm willing to forget what I walked into just now." Shyla waved a dismissive hand in Keisha's direction. "Please, go get dressed while I call a taxi. I'll also call a nice male friend of mine who I'm sure would be delighted to keep you company during your stay here in Atlanta. His name is Jon Abernathy. He's a congressman, and quite attractive." Shyla stopped and silently commended herself on her performance. "Cooper"—she turned eyes of understanding in his direction—"we've had our moments lately, especially since I started back consulting. My schedule has been busy, and I've been neglectful. I forgive you for this." When neither Cooper nor Keisha responded to her heartfelt speech, Shyla clapped her hands together, signaling that the awkward moment was over and it was time to move on. She reached for her cell phone. "Keisha, where are you staying, so I can tell the taxi driver?"

Keisha looked up at Cooper, her eyes wide, pleading.

"There's no need for you to know that," he responded, fixing Shyla with a hard stare. "And the only one leaving my home right now . . . is you."

Shyla was stunned into silence. Where was the wimpy, henpecked guy named Cooper Riley, Jr., and who was this man with a backbone staring her down? Angry beyond words and embarrassed beyond all thought, Shyla snatched up her keys and marched toward the door.

"Shyla, wait!" Cooper scrambled behind her.

Shyla stopped suddenly without turning around. A smug look formed on her face. *He'd better have come to his senses before I leave.*

"Shyla?"

Shyla slowly turned around. "Yes, Cooper?"

He held out the bag from the deli. "You forgot your food."

61

It was a meeting of the Livingston men: Adam, Ace, Malcolm, Toussaint, and Jefferson. They, along with Sterling Ross, were sitting in the office of one of the country's most formidable prosecuting attorneys: Percillius Phelps. With a minimum rate of $1,000 per hour and a $100,000 retainer fee required up front, Mr. Phelps was definitely not the average person's attorney. His skills, knowledge, and expertise were reserved for those with deep societal connections... and deeper pockets. A slightly built man who stood just a little over five foot eight, Mr. Phelps had often been mistaken for a lightweight. But he'd proven time and again that when it came to the law, he stood among giants. In fact, the giants looked up to him.

"Gentlemen," he concluded, his soft, raspy voice commanding the room. "I believe we have a solid, airtight case. I meet with Mr. Riley tomorrow in judge's chambers, where both I and Mr. Bright's attorney will lay out our cases, present witnesses, submit evidence, and so on. Once that meeting is over, I'll know exactly what he's working with and therefore what we're up against."

"We appreciate your hard work," Adam said. "And I speak for the entire family when I tell you to spare no expense in bringing this man to justice." Adam had been livid after hearing about what had happened the previous evening at FGO. Cooper had every right to be angry at Bianca for breaking their engagement, but that he'd dine with Quintin's sister? When he knew Quintin was being tried for theft and attempted murder? It was all too much, *way* too much. The Livingston clan intended to come out with their proverbial guns blazing and, when the dust settled, to be the last men standing.

Across town, another decision: "Keisha, this is Chardonnay. I can tell by that lame-ass message you left on my phone that you've obviously got some shit twisted. I'm supposed to run shaking 'cause your ass is from LA? You ain't heard how we do it in the dirty South? Well, I tell you what, you run up on me with some bullshit, then you're about to find out. And when you come at me, have your story straight instead of accusing me of shit you don't know nothing about. I ain't scared of your high-yellow ass. You know where I work and you know where I live. Come get me."

Chardonnay hung up the phone and took a deep breath. She'd made her choice and she'd made the call. Now she only hoped that the decision to roll with the Livingstons was the right one.

62

The next morning a confident Cooper Riley walked into the judge's chambers. He was totally prepared for—even looked forward to—the meeting with America's hot-shot prosecutor, Percillius Phelps. The last time they'd stood toe to toe, Cooper had been the one who'd gone home in defeat. But not this time. Today, if Cooper Riley, Jr., was sure of nothing else, he was sure of victory for Quintin Bright.

"Hello, Judge," Cooper said upon entering the room. He'd been happy to hear that Judge Barr was hearing the case. He and Cooper's father, Judge Cooper Riley, Sr., had been friends for decades. The families had socialized for eons, attended each other's birthdays, graduations, anniversaries, and the like. Barr's presence in this matter only served to further solidify Cooper's confidence that before the week was over, his darling Keisha would be very proud of him.

"Hello, Cooper," Judge Barr replied. "How's the family?"

"Everyone's fine, sir. Dad sends his regards."

Judge Barr took off his glasses and cleaned them as he spoke. "You know that you're going to have to present a strong case to beat Percillius. That man's a beast when it comes to law. Outside, I'm your play uncle but in here"—Judge Barr replaced his horn-rimmed spectacles and fixed Cooper with a stern gaze—"I'm the judge."

Cooper smiled. Judge Barr had always been hard on him, and he appreciated this fact. It had made him a better attorney, which had been the judge's *modus operandi* all along. The two men shared small talk for several moments and then Percillius entered the room.

"Mr. Phelps," Judge Barr said in greeting.

"Gentlemen."

After another round of pleasantries, the men got down to business.

Percillius began the proceedings, laying out in clear and concise detail how the case against Quintin Bright would be handled. Regarding the felony theft charges, Percillius revealed several key pieces of evidence he intended to present, including bank and computer records, surveillance tapes, and men who would corroborate Percillius's claims of money laundering. As for the attempted-murder charge that he'd argue in tandem with the felony theft, Percillius listed less solid but powerful examples to back up his case and a list of witnesses, including Candace Livingston—to whom Quintin had made a direct threat against Adam—and the person to whom Quintin had confessed to the shooting, Chardonnay Wilson. "Your honor, for the last year this defendant, Quintin Bright, has had the audacity to travel the world at the expense of a man he tried to kill. All of what I've presented here today and plan to present before a jury will prove these findings decisively and conclusively, beyond the shadow of reasonable doubt. I ask that everything I've presented here be accepted and admissible in the upcoming trial."

Judge Barr, who'd been listening attentively as Percillius spoke, nodded his head. "Mr. Phelps, as always . . . very good work." He turned to Cooper. "The facts as they've been presented by counsel look pretty damaging for your client, Mr. Riley. What do you have to present?"

"Just this, your honor." Cooper then opened his laptop, inserted a DVD, and pressed PLAY.

A picture that told a very clear story began playing across the screen. Judge Barr frowned, even as he scrunched his eyes while leaning forward to see more clearly. Percillius's countenance was stoic, even as his stomach knotted up. Cooper sat with tilted chin and steepled fingers, saying nothing.

The DVD's contents lasted approximately ten minutes. For a minute or so after it ended, no one spoke. Finally Percillius looked at Cooper. "What in the hell is this?" he quietly asked.

Cooper sat back, wiping off *his* glasses. "A game changer," he replied.

Percillius Phelps prided himself on being a fastidious man, a meticulous attorney who not only paid attention to detail but had a near-photographic memory. Where the Livingstons were concerned he'd done his homework, researched the options, asked the right questions. All except one.

As soon as he reached his car, he punched in Adam Livingston's number on speakerphone. "Adam, Percillius."

"Mr. Phelps," Adam said, getting up to close his office door as he did so. "What can I do for you?"

"I was wondering if you have a few minutes. I need to see you in person, and I can be by your office in about ten minutes."

"Sure, that's no problem. I assume this is about the case."

"Yes."

"Good, I'll round up Ace and the boys and we'll be waiting for you."

"No, Adam. For this meeting, I need to see you alone."

Exactly ten minutes later, Adam's assistant directed Percillius into Adam's office. Adam took in Percillius's demeanor and immediately knew that something was wrong. "What is it?" he said as soon as Percillius had joined him in the sitting area farthest away from the door.

Percillius replied, "I can show you better than I can tell you." With that, he pulled a portable DVD player from his briefcase, flipped it open, pressed PLAY, and handed it to Adam. Then he got up and went to look out the window, sparing his client what was sure to be a moment of profound embarrassment.

Adam watched Percillius walk to the window, then his attention was pulled back to the DVD when a picture came on the screen. He frowned when he noticed what was clearly a man's naked back hunched over a bench or something and performing some sort of exercise? Adam found the volume button and turned it up slightly.

"Uh-huh, you love this big dick, don't cha? Don't cha?"

Adam's eyes watched almost incomprehensively as the man he detested placed his hand under his wife's knee and lifted her leg. They were positioned on a long, backless chaise in what Adam assumed was Q's private office at his old gym. Candace had one foot on the floor and one on the chaise while Q—with one knee on the chaise as well—seemed to effortlessly support her weight.

"Ain't nobody ever gonna be able to hit these buttons that I do, baby," Q murmured, as he gripped Candace's butt with one hand and cupped her breast with the other. *"That's why you're gonna keep coming back to me."*

Adam continued to watch as Q motioned for Candace to lay on the chaise. He felt his stomach begin to churn as Q positioned himself on top of her, pummeling her with one of the biggest dicks Adam had ever seen. He closed his eyes at the sound of Candace moaning louder and louder with each pelvic thrust.

"I know you wanna scream, baby, but you gotta squash that shit." In this moment, Adam knew that Q was well aware of the camera. He'd spoken this directly into its lens.

"I'm trying to, but, but . . ." Candace couldn't finish the sentence, but simply panted between each thrust.

"This dick is finger-lickin' good, ain't it?" Adam's jaw tightened and his hands clenched into fists as once again Q looked at the camera, this time with a big smile on his face.

"Uh-huh. Feels . . . so . . . good . . ."

"Does it?" Q's *motion went from in and out to side to side.*

"Ooh . . ."

"This feels good?" Q's *hard, round ass bounced as he pumped* more *rapidly.*

"Yes."

"What about this?" He *slowed down, pulled out to the tip,* plunged *in, and repeated.*

"Oh, baby . . ."

"Uh-huh. I thought so."

Adam's eyes misted over and a lone tear fell as he watched the hard, cold evidence of his wife's betrayal. *So this is where it happened, how it happened.* . . . Ever since the affair came to light, he and Candace had worked hard on their marriage, had struggled to put her infidelity behind them. Adam thought they'd been successful. He'd even prided himself on coming out of his conservative shell, had found a small degree of enjoyment in the occasional dirty movie or using one of the toys that Candace kept in her "goody box." Adam didn't realize he'd zoned out until Q's voice jolted him back to the present, and to the horror he was watching on-screen. How long had they been fucking, Adam found himself wondering. *Ten minutes? Twenty? Thirty?*

"You want me to come for you, baby?"

"Yes, oh yes!"

"You want me to come inside you?"

Neither Adam nor Percillius heard the answer to Q's question. The DVD player shattered into several pieces after Adam hurled it forcefully across the room.

"I'm sorry," Percillius said after several long, painful moments had gone by. Adam said nothing. Percillius rejoined Adam in the sitting area, gave his shoulder a squeeze, and allowed several more moments to pass so that Adam could gain some semblance of emotional control. Married to his college sweetheart for almost twenty-five years, Percillius couldn't begin to imagine what his client was feeling, would rather die than have someone watch his wife in the throes of passionate sex. And this kind of ammunition in the hands of the enemy? This thought reminded Percillius of the seriousness of the moment, and of what he had to do. It was hard, it was right, and it was also a damn shame.

"They want to cut a deal," he said, trying to belie the harshness of his message with the softness of his voice.

Adam shook his head. "That low-down, lowlife mutha-fucka."

"Dropping the charges in exchange for their destroying the tape."

"That no-good . . . worthless son of a bitch!"

"This is deplorable, Adam," Percillius agreed. "But we've got to call a meeting and talk about this now. The defense wants an answer back within twenty-four hours."

The next day an emotionally drained and exhausted Per-cillius returned to Judge Barr's chambers. He'd always admired the Livingstons, but after last night his respect for this close-knit clan had gone to a whole 'nother level. The Livingston family's portfolio was valued in the tens of millions. Percillius now knew firsthand that they were worth every dime.

Judge Barr's countenance was as serious as Cooper's was smug, as the men gathered around the table. "Well, Mr. Phelps," Judge Barr began after a brief recount of the previous day. "What is your client's response?"

In answer, Percillius opened his briefcase, pulled out a recorder, and pushed PLAY. Cooper immediately recognized the voice.

"Q! What's up, big brother?"

"What's up, sis?"

"I was just thinking about you!"

"Yeah, right."

"Wait a minute," Cooper demanded. "Stop the tape." After Percillius complied, he continued. "Keisha and Quintin are siblings, everyone knows that. We also know that Keisha and Jefferson were lovers, and we'll even go so far as to concede that this relationship was set up by Quintin Bright and that Keisha knowingly went along with it in an attempt to get back at the Livingstons for what she perceived as wrongdoings done to her brother—so what? It may be in very bad taste to use an individual, but the last time I checked, counselor, questionable morals is not a crime."

"No, being an asshole is perfectly legal," Percillius agreed. "But aiding and abetting a felon is against the law." He clicked the recorder back on, forwarded the tape a bit, and pressed PLAY.

"Keisha!"

"I'm sorry, brother, what did you say?"

"I asked when you were going to LA."

"Hey, you know what? Maybe I'll come see you instead!"

"Girl, you really tripping now."

"No, I'm serious, Q. I need to get away for a minute. You were right; this family is a trip, a bunch of stuck-up bougies who think their shit don't stink. I can book a flight to see you and then meet them in LA for the opening."

"What about the boys?"

"They'll come with me. Dorian asks about you all the time. It will be good for you to see them."

Cooper again objected to what he felt was meaningless chatter between relatives, but Percillius silenced him by raising his hand.

"Fine, but before you come over, I need you to do something."

"What?"

"Make one more transfer from your boy."

"Q, no. I told you before that last time was the last time! We took almost two hundred thousand from his account. That should be enough!"

"I'm not thinking about me now, Keisha. I'm thinking about you. If anything ever happens to me, I want you to be okay."

"Jefferson will take care of me."

"Jefferson is a Livingston. Nuckas like that only care for themselves."

Percillius shut off the recorder but remained quiet, letting what had been said on the recorder sink into Cooper's astute mind. Then he began to speak—quietly, firmly, like a man who knew that the game had changed again.

63

"I'll never forgive myself." Candace and Diane were trying to relax in Candace's beautiful sunroom. At least they were trying to. Even after a pitcher of frozen margaritas, Candace was still on edge.

"You can't keep beating yourself up, Can," Diane offered. "You didn't know."

It had been two weeks since the world as Mr. and Mrs. Adam Livingston knew it had come crumbling down . . . again. And again, a man named Quintin Bright dealt the crushing blow. The sex tape had changed everything. Its existence brought back all of the horrible memories of the previous year and threatened to undo all of the progress that had been made in repairing Adam and Candace's marriage.

Candace angrily brushed away a tear. There had been too many shed already. "Because of me, the man who shot my husband will get off scot-free."

That was true, pretty much. Cooper Riley and the defense, on behalf of Quintin Bright, agreed to not release the sex tape in exchange for the Livingstons dropping the more serious attempted murder charge. Percillius Phelps and the prosecution, on behalf of the Livingstons, agreed to not file felony theft charges against Keisha Bright. If the sex tape ever became public—by anyone for any reason—Keisha Bright's children would be taken away, and she would be prosecuted to the fullest extent of the law.

The felony theft charge against Quintin was another matter, one which the Livingstons could do nothing about. Q's scheme involved international money laundering and falsified bank documents filed in several states. Quintin Bright would see jail time, but instead of looking at twenty-five to life, he'd more than likely be out within three to five years.

"Are y'all talking at least?" Diane gently asked.

Candace shook her head. "Not about that. I've asked him to share his thoughts, to tell me how he was feeling so that we could work through it. I've even suggested counseling. But he hasn't mentioned another word about the tape since that night. . . ."

"Hey, baby," Candace said, wiping her hands on a dish towel as she rounded the corner and entered the living room. "I didn't hear you come in." She walked over to kiss her husband. He flinched. She pulled back. "Adam? Adam, what's wrong?" Adam fixed her with a look that almost broke Candace's heart, a look that balled pain and grief and anger together and threw it in her face. *Has he been crying?* "Baby, you're scaring me. What is it? Did something happen at the job? Is it one of our sons?"

Adam looked at her another long moment, then walked toward the window. "I saw it, Candace," he said, his back to her, his voice strained. "Something I never thought I'd see, never wanted to see."

Candace walked over to the window. "What did you see, baby?" She reached for him and again he jerked away from her grasp. *What could he have seen that has him upset with me?* Right now, Candace's mind was drawing a blank.

Adam walked from the living room to the den. He went to the bar, poured two fingers of premium cognac, drained the glass, and poured two more. Candace, who'd followed him into the room, stood in the middle of the floor confused, waiting.

"He taped y'all, Candace."

Adam was talking so low, Candace could barely hear him. "Huh? What did you say?"

He turned to face her and this time it was unmistakable. There were tears. "When y'all were . . . when you cheated on me with that . . . that lowlife. . . ."

Candace gasped as realization dawned. *Q?*

"It's all on tape," Adam said, once again walking to the window and talking to himself, almost as if in a trance. "Lawyer came by the office today with a deal from the defense. Said that they wanted us to drop the charges. Of course I thought it was bullshit, told him there was no way we weren't going to do everything in our power to put that asshole behind bars. And then he showed me why they'd had the audacity to make such a request. Phelps showed me their ammunition." Adam turned to look at Candace, and this time, along with the pain, grief, and anger, Candace saw something else: disgust. "You and he, on a bench in the office, going at it like rabbits. I had to sit there, while another man who'd also seen it stood in my office, and watch my wife"—Adam's voice broke—"watch . . . my wife!" Adam hurled the tumbler across the room. Even though he'd thrown it in the opposite direction from where she stood Candace jumped as the glass hit the wall and shattered into a thousand pieces.

Candace went numb with grief, became paralyzed with fear. "Oh, Adam." Now she, too, was crying. "Baby, I'm so sorry. I had no idea."

"Just when I thought I'd gotten over it, when I thought I could put it behind me . . . here it is right back up in my face, live and in living color. . . ." He began walking out of the room.

"Adam, wait!"

He stopped, but did not turn around.

"What are we going to do?"

"What can we do, Candace? We give them what they've asked for. Otherwise they've threatened to splash the ass of my wife, and the mother of my children, all over the Internet." Adam turned around, his body a study in weariness. "I don't think we can afford to have that happen, Candace . . . do you?"

Diane walked over to Candace, laid a comforting hand on her arm. "Give it time, Can. He'll come around."

Candace shook her head.

"Adam loves you, Candace. Time heals all wounds. And love conquers all."

"No, it doesn't!" Candace shouted, months of frustration and weeks of fear bringing her close to hysteria. "Sometimes love is not enough, and now might be one of those times. I thought like you did, that time had changed things. But look! It just took one moment, one DVD stuck in somebody's player, to snatch off the scab and start our marriage bleeding all over again.

"This situation is hopeless, Diane. My life is all messed up. I gave up everything for my marriage, including the best sex I ever had." When Diane started to protest, Candace stopped her. "Yes, dammit, I'll say it. What has it gotten me to deny how I feel? I loved Quintin, Diane! There were moments I thought of giving up everything for him! But I didn't. I stayed in my marriage! I did the right thing. And look what it's gotten me. Nothing!" Candace stood panting, out of breath from screaming. Tears streamed down her face, her sobs were wrenching, coming from deep down in her soul. "I lost Quintin, and now I'm going to lose everything."

"Shh, it's going to be okay."

"How?" Candace cried. "How do you think this can ever be made right? How?"

A ringing phone interrupted Diane's answer. When Candace didn't move to answer her phone, Diane reached over and grabbed it instead. "Hello?"

"Aunt Diane?"

"Hey, Toussaint."

"Sorry, I thought I called Mama's house."

"You did, I'm over here. Is everything okay?"

"Everything is fine, but y'all better get over to the hospital."

Diane's eyes widened. She motioned to Candace to listen in as she put the call on speaker. "Why, is Alexis in labor?"

There was laughter in Toussaint's voice as he answered. "She was only in labor for forty-five minutes. I'm the proud papa of a healthy baby girl."

Shyla logged out of her computer and closed the laptop. She hadn't been able to concentrate all morning, and even though she was scheduled to give a presentation later in the week, her mind had been consumed with one thing and one thing only: getting Keisha Miller out of Cooper's life. She was still reeling from how everything had happened so quickly. One minute she was designing Cooper's townhome and wriggling out of constant invitations to move in, and the next she was putting a key that no longer worked into a changed lock and hearing a disconnected number recording on his home and cell phones. Shyla could not for the life of her figure out how the heifah had done it—how had Keisha Miller wormed her way into Cooper's heart and home in just two weeks?

"There's only one thing left to do, sistah," Shyla said to herself as she went to the phone. She scrolled through her address book and was soon punching in a rarely used number. "Mrs. Riley? Hello, it's Shyla." Pause. "Shyla Martin." Shyla paced her living room as she and Evelyn exchanged pleasantries. "That is kind of you to ask, Mrs. Riley. I'll be sure and tell my parents you said hello. Listen, I may be way out of line with what I'm about to share with you, so please accept my apologies in advance if you find this to be the case."

Evelyn, who'd been watching the housekeeper polish silver, walked into another room and shut the door. "Go right ahead, dear, but I can probably guess why you're calling."

"Oh, so you already know about Keisha Miller?"

"Keisha? Who's that?"

"Mrs. Riley, she's bad news: the sister of the client Cooper is representing and, as of a week ago that I know of, an occupant in his home."

There was silence on the other end of the phone as Evelyn absorbed this news. "I thought you and Cooper were dating?" Evelyn said.

"I thought so, too," Shyla replied. She then shared what she'd seen at FGO, conveniently leaving out her water-throwing part of the drama. "I was ready to forgive him considering the circumstances," Shyla concluded. "But he won't even talk to me."

"Shyla, I appreciate your thinking enough of my son and this family to bring this to my attention. Cooper has been hard to reach as of late, and now I know why. Thank you."

"You're welcome, Mrs. Riley. I'm glad to know this wasn't a bother. But please, since you didn't know about Keisha, why did you think I was calling?"

"I thought you were calling to talk about how Toussaint Livingston almost ended up delivering his own child." Evelyn's tinkling laughter accompanied this news.

"What?" Shyla had almost forgotten about Alexis being pregnant.

"Yes, this just happened earlier today. His wife went into labor, and it happened so quickly that their precious baby girl almost made her intro to the world at a traffic light!"

Bianca's hands gripped the sheets as Xavier went lower, his tongue drawing a wet line from her navel to the valley below.

He placed feathery kisses on the insides of her thighs, before parting her folds with his fingers and slowing sucking her nub into his mouth.

"Ah!" Bianca cried.

"Umm," Xavier replied. His cell phone rang. He ignored it.

Xavier placed his hands on Bianca's squirming thighs. He liked the fact that he could do this to her, make her out of her mind with want of him. They'd been like this together from the beginning—hot, explosive, magical. He spread her legs farther until she was open and vulnerable before him. He blew air on the soft, sensitive exposed flesh, then once again buried his mouth in her juices. Over and over he lapped, like a kitty with his first saucer of milk, and Bianca mewled as her kitty was satisfied. Her legs began to shake as he deepened the exchange, allowing a finger to venture inside as his tongue continued to flick and lick, and his mouth continued to nibble. Soon, he felt Bianca's legs tremble, heard her breath become ragged as the oncoming orgasm built in intensity. Just as she was about to go over the edge, Xavier rose up and sank eight-and-a-half, hard thick inches into her warm heat. Bianca cried out in ecstasy. Xavier placed his hands under her buttocks and drove himself inside her, pulled out to the tip, and plunged in again. His favorite place in the world to be was inside this woman. Every time he swore that it couldn't get any better...and every time it did.

Xavier pulled out and once again lavished oral attention on his beloved. He turned her over, giving her a tongue bath over every inch of her body. Bianca joined him, lavishing love on his firm, tanned chest, buttocks, and thighs. She swirled her tongue around his mushroom tip, and when he hissed loudly, she laughed out loud.

Her cell phone rang. She ignored it.

"Come here," Xavier growled lowly, directing Bianca to her knees. She laughed, tossed her head back, grabbed the headboard, and hung on for the ride. The springs creaked and bed shook from the force of his pounding, but the lovers were too caught up in their pleasure to take notice. For the next hour they performed the dance of love—on the bed, on the floor, in the bathroom, in the kitchen. Finally, after Bianca had cried out from the force of her fifth orgasm, Xavier joined her, his climax cataclysmic as he, too, went over the edge.

Later, they lay in each other's arms, relaxed and satiated. They had spent a glorious day at Malibu, Bianca's first day off since coming to California.

"Baby," Bianca said lazily. "Didn't I hear your phone ring?"

"Yes," Xavier answered. "I thought I heard yours, too."

"Yeah, but I don't want to check mine. It might be work, and I'm not going in."

"I'm not so excited to check mine either."

"Your father?"

"Of course." Xavier's father had been relentless since Xavier's arrival in America, leaving caustic, threatening messages about Xavier absconding responsibility and being cut out of his father's will. "I need to check them, though," Xavier said, reaching for his phone. "Prince Harry may have responded to my TOSTS invite."

"I always thought he was the cute one."

"Hey, careful. He can't be too cute to you . . . otherwise I won't bring him over."

Xavier listened to his messages, his mood quickly changing as he did so.

"What is it?" Bianca asked as soon as he'd ended the call.

Xavier sighed. "It's my grandfather," he said. "He's in the hospital. My family wants me to come home."

"You've got to go, Xavier."

"But I don't want to leave you. Will you come with me?"

"Xavier, your family hates me."

"They don't hate you. They don't even know you."

"They wanted you to marry somebody else."

"They need to meet the woman whom I chose as my wife."

"Baby, I have a business to run." Xavier frowned, obviously upset with that answer. "You fly over, assess the situation, and gauge how long you'll be there. If it's more than a week or so I promise to join you. Deal?"

"Deal."

Bianca reached for the cell phone resting on the nightstand. "I'd better check my messages, too. Crystal is probably about ready to whip my butt." Bianca listened to the message and shrieked.

"What?" Xavier asked.

"Toussaint and Alexis had their baby. I'm Aunt Bianca! They had a baby girl!"

Jefferson sat on Divine's couch, blissfully buzzed. She'd sold three expensive pieces to a Dutch art collector, and had popped a bottle of premium bubbly to celebrate, and then another. It had taken all of her persuasive skills to talk him into coming over but now, Jefferson was glad he'd accepted the invite. This is the best he'd felt since pulling the knife Keisha had stabbed him with out of his back.

"Come here, you," he said, lazily reaching for Divine who sat a couple feet away from him. "What are you stiffening up for ... come here!"

"Jeff, you're drunk, and you're on the rebound. Let's not do anything tonight that we'll regret later."

Jeff pulled Divine into his arms, looked into her eyes. "We've been friends a long time, right?"

"Right."

"But we've never even kissed. Why is that?"

Divine hoped the bottomless love she had for this man didn't show in her eyes, and lowered her lashes before responding. "I've wondered that, too. Timing, I guess. Our being in relationships at different times."

"Neither one of us is in a relationship now."

"And then there is the fact that," Divine did look at him now, "that I'd rather be your friend forever than your lover for a little while."

Jefferson licked his lips, the bubbly having loosened his inhibitions and tightened his groin. "I want to kiss you."

"No, Jeff..."

"Just one..."

Before Divine could respond, she was being crushed against a wide, hard chest, her lips were being devoured and a stiff tongue was searching for her equally excited one. She knew she should stop this, but was hopeless against her own desire. She'd dreamed of this moment since the day Jefferson had walked into her gallery. The reality was far better than the dream.

Jeff deepened the kiss, ran a finger up and down Divine's bare arm, and noted the goose bumps that followed in its wake. His hand continued to the silky top that Divine wore, and dropped to the soft cotton jeans that covered what he was after.

"Jeff, wait," Divine whispered against his mouth. Her hand stayed his. And then Jeff took her hand and placed it on the evidence of his desire. Instinct took over as Divine lost all rational thought. She ran her hand along his arm, his thigh, then placed it back on his exclamation.

This feels good, Jeff thought, as he eased a hand underneath Divine's blouse and tweaked a nipple. His hand ran down her toned, flat stomach. *This feels like silk too,* he thought as his hand continued to rub her baby soft skin, going down, down, even farther... *This feels like... this feels like... a dick?*

"Oh!" Jefferson exclaimed as he jumped off the couch. "What the hell is that in your pants?" In this moment, Jefferson knew he'd consumed more champagne than he realized. *That's got to be it. I'm drunk and she's, she's...* Jefferson couldn't even finish the thought.

Then he noticed how Divine hadn't moved, or answered his question. "What did I feel just now?" he asked, his voice pitched high with shock.

Finally, Divine stood. "Jeff, please, let me explain."

"That's *exactly* what I want you to do. Tell me what I felt just now."

"Despite how I was born, I've always been female."

"How you were..." Jeff stumbled back as if struck. "You're a man?"

"Jefferson, I..."

"Answer my question, dammit!" Jefferson's voice had gone from high and shocked to low and lethal.

Tears formed in Divine's eyes. "I'm transgender," she admitted. "It's one of the reasons I didn't want us to..."

Jefferson reached for his keys and strode toward the door.

Divine chased after him. "Jeff, please. You're my best friend. I'm still Divine. What you felt back there is just a formality."

"A formality, huh?" Jefferson said as he spun around. "Well, so is this."

For the first time in his adult life, Jeff hit a man and laid him out cold. His cell phone vibrated, but he didn't feel it as he left the gallery and walked blindly to his car. It buzzed again, but Jefferson was oblivious. It would be the following day before he found out that Toussaint was now a dad.

Chardonnay bobbed to her car, happy to be off work and heading for drinks with Zoe. She was feeling better than she'd felt in days, especially upon hearing the news that Quintin had accepted a plea bargain and was getting shipped upstate. Chardonnay knew that it was just a matter of time before she got her money. With plans for a car, new hair, and clothes, half of her reward cash was already spent.

As she started the car and fastened her seat belt, her phone vibrated, indicating an e-mail. Belatedly, she remembered that she'd been too busy to check them for the past couple of days.

She saw that one was from Toussaint. *Oh, ain't this nice. He's probably e-mailing everybody about his baby.* When she opened the mail, she realized that the e-mail that had come from Toussaint's e-mail address was a forward from an attorney's office. *Now, this is what I'm talking about! This is better than baby news right here. This is about show me the mo-nay!* Smiling, she clicked on the link. As she read, the smile quickly faded.

Mrs. Chardonnay Wilson: Please be advised that the Livingston family has decided not to pursue attempted murder charges against Quintin Bright. Therefore the reward money offered for the arrest and conviction of above-mentioned defendant in this case is hereby nullified. However, for your willingness to cooperate in this matter, the family has graciously awarded you ten thousand dollars. A check in said amount may be picked up at our law offices . . .

Chardonnay threw down the phone without reading the rest of the e-mail. She snatched her car into gear, and peeled out of the parking lot. "Uh-huh," she grumbled, as she weaved in and out of traffic. "Those mutha nuckas think they're slick, think a sistah was born yesterday. Quintin's ass is in jail!" She yelled and pounded her hand on the steering wheel. *Those scheming mutha nuckas done got what they want and now they damn sure bettah give me what's mine!*

64

The minister dipped his fingers in the antique crystal bowl that Marietta Livingston had provided, the bowl that had belonged to her grandmother. He made the sign of the cross on the newborn's forehead, blessing her in the name of the Father, Son, and Holy Spirit. He held her up before the beaming crowd. The baby, dressed in a frilly white concoction of satin and lace, was a gorgeous combination of the best of her parents: silky caramel skin and a head full of curly black hair, dimples, seven pounds and twenty inches of perfection. "And now, everyone, it is my pleasure to present to you, Miss Skylar Tiara Livingston!"

A garden full of Livingstons and other immediate family, in-laws, and friends clapped politely, with a few yells and whistles thrown in for good measure. The minister handed off Skylar to her obviously proud father, Toussaint, who then leaned over and kissed Alexis tenderly on the cheek. Both of the new parents wiped tears from their eyes. It was a poignant moment that reminded everyone present just how precious and miraculous life really was.

After the brief ceremony, guests mingled as they enjoyed free-flowing champagne and gourmet hors d'oeuvres. Two photographers mingled with the crowd, capturing every moment.

"She's absolutely gorgeous," Victoria said as she and Malcolm came up to once again congratulate the couple. "Now Victory has a little cousin, isn't that special?"

"Little troublemaker most likely," Malcolm added.

"If she's anything like her father and uncle," Alexis chimed in. "Right, Malcolm. Malcolm?"

"Oh, sorry y'all. I just saw Jefferson walk up. He's been on my mind lately. I think I'll go holler at him for a minute."

Victoria turned to Alexis. "So Bianca couldn't make it?"

Alexis shook her head. "She wanted to be here, but Xavier's grandfather passed. I told her that the place for her to be was in Paris, by her husband's side. I understand that Xavier and his grandfather were extremely close, plus there was some big deal about the reading of the will." It would only be later that Bianca would learn just how big of a deal it was. Xavier, who'd been cut out of his father's inheritance, was given a gift from his grandfather: three hundred million dollars.

"This turned out beautiful, Candace." Diane looked around the crowded patio, noting the people laughing, hugging, and having a good time. "Even Adam seems to be enjoying himself."

The two women watched as Adam, Ace, Malcolm, Toussaint, Jefferson, and a few other men shared conversation. There was absolutely no doubt about it: the Livingstons produced good stock.

"Is it getting any better?"

Candace knew exactly of what Diane was speaking.

"You said to give it time, so that's what I'm doing."

Later, as the photographer came over to take a picture of the baby with its grandparents, Candace boldly put her arm around her husband and reveled in the feel of him, in his nearness and his embrace, if only for the camera. In that moment, Candace knew that she'd wait as long as he needed to come back to her, a lifetime if she had to. Through all of the heartache, she and her husband had done a few things right. Skylar Tiara was living proof of it!

"Baby," Candace said, turning to Adam with love brimming in her eyes. "I think she has your nose."

Adam knew how hard his wife was trying to reconnect, to win back his love. "Toussaint has my nose, Candace," he finally replied.

"Same difference," she said with a laugh.

"Yeah, I guess so." They stood and watched Toussaint take the baby around and show her off like his latest trophy. "But you'd better not hear Toussaint say he has my anything. I've never seen a father so proud."

"I have," Candace said, smiling at her husband. "And I'm looking at him now."

Adam simply nodded. But his hand reached over and lightly squeezed the arm of the woman he loved.

On the outside, Candace remained casual when her husband touched her. But inside, she jumped with happiness. *Maybe everything is possible given time. Maybe we can put Quintin Bright behind us once and for all.*

Keisha watched her brother come through the door on the other side of the glass in the jail's visitor area. She took in his appearance as he walked to the chair. He looked good, strong, better than she'd hoped. But she could still see the anger and sense the sadness behind his smile.

They picked up the phones.

"Hey, little sis," Quintin said.

"Hey, big bro. How you doing?"

Quintin shrugged. "As well as can be expected."

"I'm sorry, Q. I wish we could have gotten all of the charges dropped."

"Don't worry about it, Keisha. You did what you could. And got a little something in the bargain."

Keisha smiled.

"I'm right then, huh. You still hanging with Mr. Cooper."

"Ha! Yes."

Q nodded. "Cool. You need to hang on to him. We can use a lawyer in the family."

"I think I will."

They talked about a few other things, mostly family. Then Q changed the subject. "You seen any of them?"

"The Livingstons?"

Q nodded.

"No. And I don't want to."

Q laughed. "Not even your boy Jefferson?"

"Especially not him. Honestly, Q, I feel bad about what happened. I know you don't like them, but he's good people, and he was good to me. I'm just glad that we got you the lightest possible sentence. In twelve to eighteen months you'll be out. This whole saga will be over and we can put this behind us."

"You think I'm going to let them put me in here and it's a rap, it's an okey-dokey?"

"You pled guilty, Q. It could be worse . . . for both of us. Let's just move on and be glad this shit is over."

Q's face hardened. He leaned into the glass. "That's where you're wrong, baby girl. Just wait and see."

In the tony suburb of Buckhead, Chardonnay sat in the Taste Of Soul parking lot thinking the exact same thing. Her calls to Toussaint had gone unanswered. Same thing with her texts—no reply. *Maybe I should leave well enough alone.* But as she ground out ther Newport and headed into work, Chardonnay knew there was no use accepting "well enough" when "better" was just around the corner.

MIND YOUR OWN BUSINESS

Lutishia Lovely

ABOUT THIS GUIDE

The suggested questions that follow
are included to enhance your group's
reading of this book.

Discussion Questions

1. In the Livingston clan, competition is a way of life. How do you feel about this? Is it healthy for family members to compete against each other in the workplace?

2. Bianca knew when she returned from Paris that she wasn't in love with Cooper. Should she have broken their engagement earlier? Why or why not?

3. What are your thoughts on the relationship between Xavier Marquis and Bianca? Did she make the right choice?

4. Xavier's surprise Las Vegas engagement/wedding for Bianca is one of the most romantic scenes I've ever witnessed. What is the most romantic thing your significant other has done for you, or that you have heard about?

5. How do you feel about the fact that Jefferson hid his relationship with Keisha? How big of a role should your family play in whom you choose to marry?

6. Toussaint has come a long way from his player days. What are your thoughts on his marriage to Alexis?

7. Do you think Keisha ever really loved Jefferson, or was it always about the money?

8. How do you feel Keisha's nonrelationship with her mother affected her life?

9. Because of Keisha's sons, Jefferson talked his family out of prosecuting her. Do you agree, or should she have gone to jail?

10. Keisha quickly jumped from Jefferson to Cooper. What do you think the odds are for this relationship lasting?

11. Instead of Keisha, Shyla Martin could have been the woman in Cooper's life. Would she have been a better choice? Why or why not?

12. Chardonnay...money hungry or business savvy?

13. Bobby Wilson...wimp or real man?

14. Jefferson and Divine...did you see that coming?

15. Quintin Bright shot Candace's husband, yet she still found herself attracted to him. Have you ever experienced an illicit attraction...one you knew you shouldn't have yet couldn't resist?

16. Undoubtedly, Quintin Bright did some bad things. But do you think he was a bad man? Why or why not?

17. Sterling Ross seemed like not only a top-notch investigator, but a top-notch man. What are your thoughts about him? Would you like to see a storyline revolving around his life?

18. Ace and Diane Livingston have enjoyed a loving marriage for thirty-plus years. Have you witnessed a love like this? Are you experiencing one? Do you think such a love is possible in today's social climate?

19. Unlike his twin, Adam Livingston's marriage has been a challenge. Do you think he and Candace will survive her scandal of being caught on tape? Should it last? Why or why not?

20. Which character did you most enjoy in this novel? Which did you like the least? Which one could you most relate to? Which one's story would you like to know more about?

Stay tuned for another helping of
Lutishia Lovely's new series following the
hot tempers and tantalizing temptations of a family
whose restaurant is *the* place for a tasty meal. . . .

Taking Care of Business

Coming in April 2012 from Dafina Books

Here's an excerpt from *Taking Care of Business . . .*

All was quiet on the West Coast front. And all was cozy in Bianca Livingston's world as she lay cuddled up next to Xavier Marquis, her husband and the love of her life. Had it only been seventy-two hours ago when she thought she'd go crazy?

Just three short days before this moment, Bianca had stood in the center of TOSTS—her pride and joy—ready to pull out the hair she'd decided to grow long again. The chic, quaint eatery on Los Angeles's west side, formally named Taste of Soul Tapas Style, was two days away from its one-year anniversary celebration. The place had been in chaos. The truffle, caviar, and special champagne shipments had all been back-ordered, the cleaners had destroyed the new wait staff uniforms, and the chef had been called away due to a death in his immediate family. The stress had brought on the unexpected arrival of Miss Flo, Bianca's monthly, complete with bloating, cramps, and a pounding headache. What was a sistah to do?

Put on her big-girl panties and make it happen, that's what. What other choice was there? Forty-eight hours ago, Bianca had huddled with her assistant and the sous chef, who'd then called all over America until they found last-minute supplies of truffles, caviar, and bubbly. After ripping the cleaners a new a-hole, Xavier had called in a favor from a designer friend and had ten new uniforms whipped up posthaste. Finding a selfless bone in her weary body, Bianca had flowers delivered to the funeral home that housed her chef's brother and Miss Flo, who'd shown up two weeks early due to stress, had vanished just as quickly as she'd arrived.

Twenty-four hours ago, Bianca had finished her day at the second LA Livingston Corporation establishment, the increasingly popular soul food restaurant, Taste of Soul. She'd spent two hours on a conference call with her brother, Jefferson, and the finance department at corporate headquarters; overseen a fiftieth birthday luncheon for a party of twenty-five; and soothed the soul of a hapless vegetarian, who was losing her mind because she'd eaten the cabbage and *then* realized that this particular selection was seasoned with smoked turkey legs. Bianca had found it ironic that sistah-girl had eaten the entire plate before making this observation, demanding her money back and threatening lawsuits. Not to mention that she'd somehow missed reading the ingredients to the Chaka Khan Cabbage side dish clearly listed on the menu. Bianca was furious, but had too much work and too little time to argue. She'd given the emoting customer a gift certificate for two free dinners and a menu to take home so that she could study it before placing her next order. With a bright smile to hide her frustration, Bianca had asked Ms. I-Haven't-Eaten-Meat-In-Twenty-Years to pay particular attention to the items with a small *V* beside the name, identifying them as vegetarian dishes.

Eight hours ago, Bianca had linked arms with her husband and officially welcomed the guests to TOSTS' one-year anniversary. Tickets for the evening's event had been steep, six hundred and fifty dollars, but the price included an all-you-can-eat buffet, a champagne fountain (filled with the double-priced bubbly that had to be rush-ordered and Fed Ex'd to the event), and an intimate evening with the night's entertainment, John Legend. As if pleasing the palate and the auditory senses weren't enough, the tickets were also tax deductible, with part of the proceeds benefiting a soup kitchen. Following in the footsteps that the Taste of Soul founders, Marcus and Marietta Livingston, had set, the establishments Bianca managed did their part in making the communities around them a better place.

An hour ago, Bianca had kicked four-inch-high stilettos off her aching feet, slid a Mychael Knight designer original off her shoulders, separated herself from a Victoria's Secret thong, and eased into the master suite's dual-marble shower. Seconds later, Xavier joined her.

"*Mon bien-aimé de chocolat*," Xavier murmured as he eased up behind Bianca and wrapped her in his arms. "You are the chocolate on the menu for which my heart beat all night long." He took the sponge from her hand and began soaping Bianca's body from head to toe.

"Umm, that feels good," Bianca said. She leaned back against her husband's wide, firm chest. Moments before, she'd been dog tired, but now her husband's ministrations were filling her with new, lusty energy. She wriggled her soapy body against his, and was immediately rewarded with a long, thick soldier coming quickly to attention. They made quick work of the cleaning process before Xavier lifted Bianca against the cool marble wall and joined them together in the age-old dance of love. The contrast of the cool marble, hot water, and even hotter desire swirled into a symphony with a melody known by Xavier and Bianca alone. This was their first time together in almost seventy-two hours. Ecstasy came quickly, and then they climbed into bed for an encore.

Five minutes ago, Bianca shouted out her second hallelujah, or more like an "uh uh uh oh oh oh yes yes yes...ahhh." Xavier, the quieter of the two lovers, had shifted rhythms from second to third gear, before picking up speed and heading for his own orgasmic home. He hissed, moaned, squeezed Bianca tightly, and went over the edge. Too spent to move, Bianca had kissed Xavier on the nose, turned herself to spoon up against him, and vowed to take a shower first thing in the morning. She smiled as Xavier kissed her on the neck. *That man knows how to rock my world,* she thought as she looked at the clock. It was 4:45.

At 4:50, a shadowy figure crouched along the buildings on Los Angeles's west side. He stopped, looked both ways, and walked purposefully toward a door on the other side of the alley. It was the back door to TOSTS. In less than one hour, Bianca Livingston's world would get rocked again.